Addicted

Addicted

LYDIA PARKS

APHRODISIA

KENSINGTON BOOKS
http://www.kensingtonbooks.com

APHRODISIA BOOKS are published by

Kensington Publishing Corp.
850 Third Avenue
New York, NY 10022

All Kensington titles, imprints, and distributed lines are available at special quantity discounts for bulk purchases for sales promotions, premiums, fund-raising, and educational or institutional use.

Special book excerpts or customized printings can also be created to fit specific needs. For details, write or phone the office of the Kensington Special Sales Manager: Kensington Publishing Corp., 850 Third Avenue, New York, NY 10022. Attn: Special Sales Department. Phone: 1-800-221-2647.

ISBN-13: 978-0-7582-2845-1
ISBN-10: 0-7582-2845-7

First Trade Paperback Printing: September 2008

10 9 8 7 6 5 4 3 2 1

Printed in the United States of America

Contents

Once Bitten

1

Jake Brand tipped his chair back on two legs, wrapped his hand around a glass of whiskey, and took in the sights as if he had all the time in the world. In a way, he did. At least, in the foreseeable future, he had a decent shot at eternity.

The young blonde leaning over a table, shaking her backside in his direction, was another matter. In a few short years, her firm breasts would start to sag and her tight ass would droop. If she were lucky, some lonely trucker would offer her his life savings and a ranch-style home in the outskirts of Albuquerque before that happened.

But tonight, Jake planned to entertain the sweet young thing in exchange for dinner.

"You sure are taking your time with that drink," the blonde said, frowning at the five-dollar bill on his table.

Jake plucked a folded fifty from his shirt pocket and dropped it on top of the five. "I've got nothing but time, darlin'."

The young woman's eyes widened and her red, full lips stretched into a greedy smile. She snatched the bill from the table and stuffed it into the back pocket of her denim mini-skirt.

She winked at him. "I'll be back for you in just a minute."

"I'll be right here," he said, grinning. He watched her hurry to the bar, toss her towel under it, and whisper something to the bartender.

The burly redheaded bartender glanced over at Jake and nodded, and the blonde started back for Jake's table, swinging her hips as she tapped out the background song's rhythm with her high heels. He liked the way the shoes made her legs look a mile long. The thought of those legs wrapped around him caused a pleasant reaction, and he moved to adjust his tightening jeans.

She didn't stop at his table, but continued forward until she stood straddling his thighs, her hands locked behind his neck as she swayed back and forth in time with the music. "My name's Candy," she said, her voice soft in his ear. "You like candy, don't you?"

"Hmm," he said, inhaling her scent, weeding out vanilla shampoo, cheap perfume, stale cigarettes, whiskey fumes, and sweat. Yes, he definitely had the right dinner partner. "I can eat candy all night long."

"Oh, baby," she whispered, "you make me hot."

He chuckled at the insincerity of her words. Undoubtedly, few of her many customers cared if she meant them or not, and he didn't, either. Before the night was over, he'd get the truth from her, and she'd be more than just *hot*.

Jake ran the tips of his fingers up the backs of her exposed thighs.

She stepped back to frown down at him. "No touching. That's house rules."

He grinned again, enjoying the way her simple emotions played across her face.

He lowered his voice a notch. "I could bring you to a quivering climax without touching you, but it wouldn't be nearly as much fun."

One corner of her mouth curled up in cynical amusement. "You think so?"

"I know so." Jake used the Touch to retrace the paths of his fingers with his thoughts, remembering the warmth, the smoothness, the soft hairs on her upper thighs.

"*Hey.*" She took another step back and stared into his eyes.

Jake pushed a simple concept into her simple mind. *Pleasure like you've never known.*

She swallowed hard, hesitated, and then moved forward to straddle his thighs again. He could smell her excitement as she sat on his legs and wrapped her arms around his shoulders. "I don't know how you did that," she said softly. "And I don't really care. You wanna go in the back room?"

"I think we should go up to my room."

She nodded, then turned her head to kiss him. Her warm breath caressed his skin before her lips met his, and he closed his eyes to enjoy the heated tenderness of her mouth. Her tongue slid across his lips, moving precariously close to the razor-sharp points of his teeth. Jake let a groan escape as he enjoyed the way her heat enveloped his growing erection, in spite of the clothes between them.

Candy ended the kiss and stood, drawing Jake after her with her small hand in his, leading him upstairs. The noise of the saloon-turned-strip joint faded below them as they climbed, leaving only a bass vibration in its wake.

"Which room?"

He nodded toward the door at the end of the small hallway. "Six."

"The best." She raised one eyebrow. "You rich or something?"

"Something."

"Oh, I see." She tossed her head, sending her blond waves into a dance around her shoulders. Candy knew exactly how attractive she was. "So, you're a man of mystery. Your name isn't *John*, is it?"

"No, it's Jake." He withdrew the key from his pocket, unlocked the door and pushed it open, then stepped aside as his young visitor entered. She didn't look around; she'd seen the room before.

"Jake." She turned in the middle of the room and smiled as she surveyed him from head to toe. "You know your fifty bucks don't buy you much. You want a blow job, or straight sex?"

Jake laughed then. "How do you know I'm not a peace officer?"

"A cop?" Candy grinned. "I know cops. Half the force comes in here after their shift. You're different, but you ain't no cop."

He nodded as he crossed the room and sat on the foot of the bed. "You're right about that. I'm different."

Candy tugged at the hem of her shirt, her head cocked seductively. "For twenty more, I take off my clothes just for you, baby."

Jake pulled off his boots and dropped them onto the floor. "I've got a better idea. How about a wager?"

The young woman straightened and narrowed her eyes. "You tryin' to tell me you ain't got no more money?"

He withdrew a hundred from his pocket and dropped it onto the bed. When she reached for it, he covered her hand with his own. "Not so fast there, sweet thing. Don't you want to hear my proposal?"

"*Proposal?*"

"For a wager."

Candy withdrew her hand slowly, then folded her arms across her chest. "I'm listening."

Jake stretched out on his side, studying the girl. "How long have you been at this?"

"At what?"

"Hooking."

Candy frowned. "You ain't some kind of preacher or something, are you? If you think you're gonna convert me—"

Jake silenced her by raising one hand. "You've got me all wrong, sweetheart. I'm definitely not a preacher."

She waited, her hands now on her hips.

"I'm willing to bet you one hundred dollars that I can bring you to a screaming climax in the next half hour."

Her eyebrows shot up and then she burst out laughing.

Jake watched her, enjoying her amusement.

"Right," she said between guffaws. "A *screaming* climax?"

He nodded.

When she managed to regain control of herself, she dropped down onto the edge of the bed, extending her hand. "You're on, Jake."

He took her hand in his, enjoying the warmth. Then he sat up and raised her hand to his lips.

"But you gotta wear a rubber."

Jake looked into her blue eyes. "Do I?"

Candy nodded. "Safe sex or no sex, that's how I stay alive."

"I promise we will run no risk of infecting you with anything."

Jake rose and drew Candy up to stand in front of him. Watching her face, he ran his palms slowly up her sides, peeling her shirt off over her head.

She stared at him with calm resolve, but goose bumps rose

on her skin where he'd touched her. "Your hands are cold," she said.

"You'll just have to warm them up for me, darlin'."

He unsnapped her skirt and pushed it off in the same manner, sliding his palms over her rounded buttocks and down the backs of her thighs. As she stood before him in her high heels, he stepped back to drink in the sight of her.

Her breasts were full and firm, with large, dark areolae. As he studied them, her nipples puckered, and he knew she liked to be watched.

Her waist, narrow with youth, led his gaze down to her partially shaved pubic mound, the line of dark brown hair giving away her true color.

Then there were those legs. Damn, they were long.

"Oh, yeah," he said, aloud but to himself. "This will be fun."

Jake stepped closer and eased his hands down from her shoulders to her breasts, memorizing the shape and warmth of them, twisting the nipples playfully before moving on to her waist and then her ass. *Nice*. He nuzzled her neck to get more of her scent, then pressed his lips to the top of her shoulder. The sound of her heart beating drowned out the hum of the room's air conditioner, and he let himself enjoy it for a few moments before turning back to the task at hand.

He moved his mouth to hers, covering her lips with his own as he eased one hand into her soft blond hair. His other hand he slid down her back to the smallest point and pulled her gently to him.

Her hands rose to his chest for balance.

He opened her mouth then, and ran his tongue around hers, catching the taste of whiskey and tobacco, as he moved his hand around her hip and eased it between her legs. Her swollen vulva parted for his fingers as he slid them back and forth, hinting at entering her, stirring her juices.

Her hands flattened against his chest.

Jake eased one finger deeper, stroking her clit, and her fingers curled. She drew on his tongue, and he continued to stroke, enjoying the way her hot little bud swelled.

Candy tore her mouth from his. "You said . . . a *screaming* climax."

"Yes, I did," he said, his mouth near her ear.

Her hips began to rock to the rhythm of his hand, and she gripped the front of his shirt in her fists. "Damn, you're good," she said, "but I don't scream for no man."

Jake chuckled as he slid his hand out from between her thighs. "Good, darlin', 'cause I don't want this to be too easy."

Candy rubbed against the front of his bulging pants. "Even if I ain't screaming, you don't have to stop."

"Don't worry, sweet thing, I'm not about to stop." He reached down with both hands, cradled her ass, and lifted her from the floor.

She wrapped her legs around his hips and her arms around his neck.

Jake carried her to the bed and eased her down as he kissed her. The girl knew how to kiss, and he felt his erection hardening to the point of discomfort. He unbuttoned his pants to relieve some of the pressure, then he withdrew from her.

Her eyes blazed as she looked up at him, partly with passion and partly from whiskey, no doubt.

Jake parted her legs, knelt at the edge of the bed, and kissed the insides of her thighs as he drew her to his mouth.

Her cunt was hot, salty, and wet, and he slowly licked the length of her, savoring the taste. Her legs opened more in response, and her ass tightened. He continued with long, slow laps as he listened to her suck air between her teeth, and he enjoyed her quickening heartbeat. Not long now, and he'd have her ready, sweetened, primed for him.

Jake pushed his tongue between her cunt lips and lashed at her clit, then drew it carefully between his teeth and sucked.

Candy's back arched, and she moaned as she neared an orgasm.

He moved away, nibbling at her thighs.

She grunted in frustration and he smiled.

Closing his eyes, Jake pushed his thoughts out then, moving the Touch up the length of her body like a hundred butterfly wings, caressing every part of her at once, flitting across her nipples and stomach, as he slid his fingers into her cunt.

Her hips rose up off the bed and she cried out in joy. "Oh . . . God . . . that's good," she said between panted breaths.

She clamped down on his fingers and flooded them with her juices as he moved in and out of her, traveling across her damp skin with his thoughts, feeling the conditioned air blow across her breasts, finding her pulse in a hundred spots at once.

His burgeoning cock emerged from the front of his pants as he enjoyed Candy, pulling her to the edge of her resistance, then pushing her away.

She cooed, and then groaned, and then growled with disappointment.

Continuing the Touch, Jake rose and removed his clothes. He loved the feel of heated flesh against his own when he drank. Letting the Touch drift lower now, he stretched out on top of Candy and kissed her neck, her jaw, and her shoulders.

She wriggled under him as the treatment intensified. His thoughts rolled over her cunt, then dipped in and out.

"Fuck me," she said, digging her fingers into his back. "Please. I'm on fire."

"Yes," he whispered, easing his cock between her legs.

She thrust up into him, taking him into her all at once, and he almost lost her.

"Oh, no, you don't," he said, drawing back.

She locked her legs around him before he could withdraw.

"Good Lord, get on with it."

Jake glanced over his shoulder, surprised to find Thomas Skidmore standing beside the bed, pale hands fisted on his narrow hips.

"Go away," Jake said.

"Why do you insist on doing it this way?" Skidmore waved dramatically with one arm, his style mimicking the British theater of years gone by. "I've never known anyone who felt they had to get permission. You are strange, dear boy."

Jake returned his attention to Candy, rocking against her in time with her growing need. She hadn't noticed the intrusion.

"Just hurry. We have places to go." Skidmore closed the door behind him as he left.

"Oh, God," she said, louder now. "Don't stop. Fuck me. Harder."

Jake turned his head to speak softly into her ear. "I need more than your cunt, sweet thing. I need your blood."

He felt her tense as fear crept into her fevered excitement.

"I won't hurt you," he said. "We'll come together."

After a moment of hesitation, she turned her head, offering her neck to him as she writhed in anticipation, her hands fisted against his back.

Jake pressed his lips to her neck, thrilling to the pulse rising and falling beneath the surface. He let loose of the reins then, thrusting into her sizzling cunt as his cock hardened to steel, pushing deeper, needing release nearly as much as he needed to feed.

His fangs lengthened, and he opened his mouth. Trying to

hold back, savoring the anticipation, he smelled her approaching climax. Yes, she was ready.

Jake pressed his fangs into her neck and she screamed. He closed his eyes as her orgasm flooded him, first biting down on his pulsing cock, then flowing through his veins and exploding in his brain. He drew hard as he pumped his seed into her, letting her fill him with need, fulfillment, dreams, wants, desires.

He knew her arousal as she danced for hungry eyes, her smug disgust as sweaty men humped her for money, her euphoria as she lay alone at night with a vibrating orgasm rolling through her narcotic haze. And he felt her ecstasy as his own. She came again as he thrust harder, longer, until he'd taken all he could, and given all he had.

Jake held his mouth to her neck for a moment to stop the flow, then moved it away and slowed his thrusts to nice, easy strokes.

Her grip changed to a shaky hold on his shoulders, and her cries softened to weak groans.

He stilled, then withdrew and rolled onto his back to enjoy the sensations of nerves popping and firing through his entire system, waking from a long sleep. After more than a century and a half, he still loved the vibration, especially when sweetened with orgasms.

"You win."

Jake turned his head to find Candy lying with her eyes closed and her arms at her sides, her body glistening with a fine sheen of sweat. Already, the small wounds on her neck were nearly healed, and her heart rate had begun to slow.

He grinned.

If not for Skidmore waiting impatiently outside somewhere, Jake might have spent a few more hours with his little morsel. But the old man was right; they had places to go.

After getting dressed, he dropped the bill onto Candy's bare stomach, then leaned over and kissed her soundly.

She hadn't moved much, and smiled up at him. "You come back anytime, Jake."

He winked at her, then tossed the room key onto the bed beside her before leaving his dinner guest and the air conditioner's buzz behind.

Downstairs, he found the tall, thin vampire in an out-of-place purple velvet suit, standing in the shadows near the door, and Jake made his way through the maze of tables, young strippers, and horny old men.

"It's about time," Skidmore said, wrinkling his nose with disapproval.

"Some things shouldn't be rushed." Jake picked up his black felt Stetson from a hook by the door and slipped it on as he stepped into the New Mexico night. Warm, clean air swept over him as if he were no more than another jackrabbit making his way across the desert, and a star-filled sky opened above as Jake strolled across the parking lot to the convertible parked near the exit.

"Will you please get a move on?" Skidmore hurried ahead, hopping effortlessly into the passenger's seat. "I refuse to spend another day trapped in the boot of this wretched beast. It'll take at least four hours to get to the mine, and that's thirty minutes more than we have."

"Don't sweat it," Jake said, trying not to get annoyed with his fellow traveler. Skidmore tended to get on his nerves after a month or two of whining. "We'll be there in three."

Jake started the Impala and pulled out onto the narrow highway, turning north. With no one else around, he easily pushed the car to ninety and they roared through the darkness.

"Oh, I nearly forgot to tell you what I heard," Skidmore said.

It was a lie; the older vampire never forgot anything. Jake waited, but Skidmore just smiled.

"What?"

"A very special friend of yours will be at the meeting. If we get there early enough, perhaps you'll have time to get reacquainted."

"Katie?" Jake glanced over at his companion, whose face seemed to glow in the starlight.

Skidmore grinned and ignored his question.

2

Jake felt her presence long before they arrived. Excited by the prospect of seeing Katie again, in spite of his best efforts not to be, he'd left the abandoned mine shaft where he and Skidmore had spent the day, early enough to give off smoke.

Holding a blanket over his head like some kind of television criminal, Skidmore had trotted along behind him, muttering, "Bloody hell, I don't know why I travel with such a fucking lunatic."

They'd driven with the top up until well after dark.

Now, a mere fifty miles from their destination, he felt her. After decades of sharing blood, they were one in many ways. Not spouses in the human sense, but much more, although they'd only lived together for fifteen years. Even that was unusual in vampire circles with the exception of a few rare couples, most of which had come to the Night together. As a rule, vampires tended to be loners—partly by necessity, and partly because eternity made it hard to put up with others for too long.

Jake slowed the car as they wound into the Sangre de Cristo

mountains, and enjoyed the scent of evergreens in the cool night air. An owl screeched overhead, soaring above ponderosa pines, and he suddenly recalled a night long ago he'd spent chasing Lucky Bill Wainright across the state. He'd lost a damn good buckskin gelding to a prairie dog hole on that ride, and he'd taken his wrath out on the outlaw when he'd caught him. Lucky Bill hadn't looked so lucky riding back into Lubbock with two black eyes, lips so swollen he couldn't speak, and a nasty gash across his cheek. But it had been a fair fight—Jake wouldn't have given the man such a beating otherwise.

He shivered at the vibration running down his spine. Even thinking about the past didn't help as he closed the distance between himself and Katie. How long had it been? Ten years? No, more like twelve. Maybe more.

Jake swerved off the road at a wide spot, cut the engine, and jumped out, grabbing his hat from the backseat. He started across a field, headed for the trees, forgetting about his travel partner.

"Dammit, man, slow down," Skidmore said.

Jake glanced back. "I thought you were in a hurry."

"Not quite so much as you." Skidmore waved him off, obviously annoyed. "Go on, then. We'll rendezvous at the cabin."

In the cover of trees, he moved faster, picking up scents and noises of night creatures, soundlessly passing coyotes, rodents, bats, and owls.

Halfway to the cabin, he stopped.

For a split second, he could have sworn he'd heard a human heart. Turning a slow circle, he listened and searched the darkness, but detected nothing resembling a man.

Shaking his head at his folly, Jake continued on, but at a fast walk just in case. Who would be out alone in the mountains at such an hour? In the old days, it might have been a shepherd—a young son proving his worth by watching over the flock for a long, sleepless night—but those days were gone. Jake sometimes wandered upon campers now, but they were rarely quiet enough to go undetected.

No, he must have been imagining things.

As he approached the site, he heard conversations and recognized some of the voices of the two dozen vampires in and around an old log cabin.

"I thought that might be you."

Jake spun around at the voice to find Katie standing close, her eyes glistening and her wild auburn hair brassy in the moonlight. He smiled.

She slid her hands across his chest, cooing softly. "It's been too long, Jake." Leaning forward, she ran her tongue slowly up the side of his neck, tracing the line of his jugular.

Jake shuddered at the pleasure and grabbed her waist. "Oh, yeah," he whispered. "Way too long."

He wanted to fold her in his arms and drink from her until he'd had his fill of the bliss she would offer, but he knew Katie McMillan as few others ever could. Katie would never be dominated by a male of any species, now that she had a say in the matter. With Katie, it was better to wait, and he knew she'd make the wait worth his while.

She pressed the points of her fangs against the skin of his neck as she reached down to rub the front of his pants.

Jake's knees shook. "Damn, woman, you're making it hard—"

"Umm," she purred.

"—for me to stand up."

Katie straightened, knocked his hat off his head, wrapped her arms around his shoulders, and kissed him. Her full, sweet lips met his squarely, and she worked his mouth open with her own as she gripped a handful of his hair.

Jake steadied himself by widening his stance as he kissed her back and drew her close. They fit together just as they always had, like two halves of a whole. Katie's tongue circled his, then slid along the sides of his growing fangs. The sensations running through him were like electrical currents zapping his limbs, and his cock also grew in response. Katie slid her knee between his thighs, pushing just enough to make him groan again.

She tore her mouth from his and stared at him with her golden glowing eyes. "Spend the day with me, my love."

"As you wish," he said, grinning again. "I can't think of anything I'd rather do."

Katie raked her fingers through his hair, then drew him to her for another kiss.

"Oh, please." Skidmore leaned close to their faces. "Must you do this in public? It smacks of romanticism so unbecoming of our kind."

Katie smiled against Jake's lips, then glanced over at Skidmore. "Don't worry, Thomas. I promise you'll get the spanking you deserve."

Skidmore grinned, his own eyes twinkling with a bit of gold. "Then I shall not complain. Come, the meeting's about to start."

He led the way into the cabin.

Jake snatched his hat from the ground. He held Katie's hand until they reached the door, then he released her, stepped inside, and found a place against the back wall.

As members of the enforcement committee, Katie and Skidmore wound their way to the front, and André, the elected leader, moved forward.

Jake preferred to stay out of the politics of the group, although he'd often been called on to lend expertise from his human life in law enforcement over the past century or so. In spite of the group's mission to protect its members, anarchy tended to reign when there was no outside threat. Several times, Jake had helped track down one of their own.

But tonight, excitement filled the room like the scent of frying bacon.

André silenced the group with a look. His age alone would have commanded respect—Jake estimated him to be about fifteen hundred years old—but the ancient vampire also possessed wisdom nearly everyone appreciated. He'd held the top position for over a hundred years.

"My brothers and sisters," André said, his voice just above a whisper, "I'm happy to see so many here. We've suffered several recent losses, and I will sorely miss Shadow and William Sears."

Jake glanced around the room, lit by a half dozen oil lamps. He hadn't yet noticed the absence of the two mentioned, perhaps because he was having a difficult time taking his eyes off Katie. Her invitation had left him way beyond horny. His hands shook with anticipation, so he tucked them into the pockets of his pants.

André had his attention now.

"Society changes. The reason we are here, when so many before us have perished, is that we have learned to change with it. Many times, I've seen scourges that have threatened to wipe us out—periods in history where belief has made us visible to our mortal prey. One such scourge is upon us again."

Whispers rose as vampires discussed this news.

André raised one hand, and the cabin fell silent again.

"This threat has come," he continued, "in the form of vampire hunters, produced by the recent popularity of *Van Helsing*."

Ah, the old moving pictures. Jake had realized they'd be a hit the first time he'd seen one, and he certainly hadn't been wrong.

"When the *myth* of vampires—"

Chuckles filled the cabin.

"—was rekindled in recent times, we were endangered by those who wished to emulate us. They were able to see us for what we were. But this is much worse. The vampire hunters know our weaknesses. They are effectively armed and determined to wipe us from the face of the earth."

A fair fight. Jake grinned. How long had it been since he'd stared a worthy opponent in the eye, when he'd stood an equal chance of living or dying? The thought caused his heart to quickly beat several times in a row.

One thing he'd missed since coming into the Night was standing on even ground, testing his nerve against that of another man, feeling the weight of his revolver on his hip. He'd nearly given up early on when he'd realized there was no challenge.

And then he'd spent several decades playing with fire, running the risk of exposure just to test his courage. Skidmore had actually saved him once when he'd decided to see how long he could face the sun. He'd purposely driven to a spot in the high New Mexico desert where he had no shelter, then waited. The sun had not just burned his skin as he'd expected, but had sucked out his strength so that he collapsed, unable to move. As he cried out in excruciating pain, he'd suddenly been whisked into darkness, and discovered caves he hadn't known existed. Skidmore had laughed at his folly, then nursed him back to health.

That was when he'd met Katie.

"I think we should round them all up and drain them," Katie said. "We'll show them who they're messing with."

Cheers of support rose, but André raised both hands. "One moment, please."

Katie folded her arms across her chest and frowned.

The ancient vampire spoke again. "We cannot simply have a portion of the population disappear without lending credence to their claims of dangerous monsters. I propose that we first study the group—find out exactly who they are."

"Know your enemy," Jake muttered.

"Once we understand them, we will find a way to discredit them."

"I prefer Katie's method," Skidmore said. Several others in the room agreed with him.

"I understand the desire for action," André said. "That desire is in our makeup. And it is what will be our undoing if we are not careful. We don't want to create more vampire hunters than already exist, do we?"

Jake sighed, impressed once again with the ancient's wisdom.

"I suggest we allow our enforcement committee to do its duty, and perhaps reconvene in two weeks. During that time, we can all keep our ears open for information. Sound reasonable?"

Nearly everyone nodded.

"Fine. Is there other business?"

Any minor squabbles that had existed prior to the meeting had vanished.

André nodded dismissal, then turned to talk to his enforcers.

Jake greeted several vampires he knew as he made his way toward Katie.

She watched him approach, her eyes glowing and a smile threatening at the corners of her luscious lips.

André gripped Jake's shoulder in a friendly greeting. "Perhaps we can persuade you to assist us, dear friend."

"Perhaps," Jake said, focused on the object of his intense and growing desire.

"You have contacts in Santa Fe, do you not?"

Jake nodded.

"Good. Let me know what you learn."

"Will do." Jake held out his hand to Katie. "It's getting late."

"Very," she answered, flashing a quick smile at André as she entwined her fingers with Jake's.

Ignoring the attempt by others to engage them in conversation, the two left the cabin and hurried into the woods where they could find some privacy.

If Skidmore didn't hurry, Jake would leave for Katie's place without him. The old vampire would have to fend for himself.

Katie's body vibrated. The energy of desire flowed from her fingers like waves of electricity as she ran her hands over her own skin.

Jake watched, his eyes glowing, his erection large enough to make her drool. His body was long and lean, but his limbs were powerful, and his stomach and chest rippled with muscles. She'd always loved his physique. And she loved to make him tremble with wanting her.

Flickering candlelight sent shadows dancing around Jake as Katie moved in time with the music playing on her Victrola. Blues. She loved blues. She loved to dance naked to blues.

"Damn, woman," Jake muttered, "you're driving me nuts."

"Good." She moved closer, her arms folded behind her head. "Anticipation raises the heat."

"Gets much higher, I'll burst into flames." He stroked his cock with one hand as he watched her and gripped the seat of the chair with the other. His fangs dented his bottom lip, and his blue eyes sparkled with golden streaks.

Katie danced around to the back of the chair. She ran her fingertips up the outsides of Jake's bare arms, across his shoulders, and slowly up the sides of his neck. He made a noise that was something between a groan and a growl, and it vibrated through the entire room.

She shuddered in response. Her own fangs dropped to their full length and began to throb with pleasant longing.

Moving to face him, Katie dropped slowly to her knees. She shoved his hand away and he didn't protest. His erect cock stood straight now, and his eyes held no hint of blue. Yes, he wanted her as much as he ever had.

And she wanted him, too. There had never been another like Jake Brand, once a hardened lawman, now a tough old vampire. Even though he was nearly a century older than she, Katie knew exactly how to handle him.

Holding his thighs, she teased the head of his cock with her tongue.

His head went back, leaving his mouth open to reveal glistening fangs.

She licked him in long, slow strokes.

He groaned quietly.

Then she took his cock in her mouth and sucked, and his entire body jerked.

"Damn you, Katie," he breathed.

As she drew away, she ran her teeth up the sides of his prick, careful not to damage the silky skin.

Jake whimpered softly.

Heated passion ran through her veins as she straddled him, leaving his erection unsheathed, to his obvious dismay, but he knew better than to complain. With her hands on his wide shoulders, she kissed him, drawing hard on his tongue, moving up and down against his stiff rod until she couldn't stand the building need for another moment.

She rose up higher until the head of his cock nudged against her cunt, and she smiled as she eased her way down, watching the effect on his face and in his eyes. Without regard to what he wanted, she rubbed and pushed, using his cock to stroke her swelling clit.

Had she been human, she would have come.

Jake's lips curled back in a snarl as his gaze moved down from her eyes to her neck.

Katie grabbed his hair, jerked his head back, and bit into the side of his neck.

She exploded with the taste of him, her body slamming against his in horrific need, her head swimming with sweet release. Ecstasy pulsed through her cunt, and she drew harder.

He cried out, wrapped his arms around her, and pulled her down onto him, trembling with desire now, ready. She could taste his need and his pleasure, and knew how much he'd missed her and how desperately he wanted her, how he'd spent long days dreaming of fucking her.

Releasing his head, she offered him her shoulder, and he took it with greedy abandon. The sharp piercing of her skin only increased her orgasm, and he drew from her as he released his seed into her with brutal thrusts, holding her down.

Then the purest bliss flooded her as she tasted her own joy in his blood, and knew he did the same, and they met again in another climax that rose above mere physical joining. The circle closed, fusing them into one writhing beast of rapture, and she clung to his body and his thoughts, relishing the strength in both, feeding from him.

With practiced precision, they withdrew their fangs simultaneously, and rode out the last of the orgasms until all was quiet.

Katie rested her head on Jake's shoulder and he held her, stroking her back and kissing her neck.

"I've missed you," he whispered.

Katie smiled and raised her head. "Shall we try the bed now?"

Jake leaned back and frowned at her. "Are you trying to drain me?"

She grinned. "Perhaps."

Jake suddenly jumped up, scooping her into his arms, and carried her across the room.

There weren't many men she'd allow to carry her in this manner. In fact, Jake was probably the only one, and he knew it. He knew everything about her. At least, everything she'd allowed him to know. Katie had learned how to lock thoughts away back when she was still mortal, and had carried that ability with her into Darkness.

Jake tossed her onto the bed and flung himself down beside her. "It's not bad," he said. "Pretty good bed. Glad we tried it."

"That's not what I meant." Katie crawled over on all fours and straddled him.

Jake smiled up at her, his arms out to his sides, his gray and brown hair spread around his head in nearly a perfect circle. She liked the way his hair rested on his shoulders when he stood, and the gentle wave that made it always look a little wild. He was forever thirty-five, just as she was forever twenty-three, but his thirty-five mortal years had been tough ones. He still sported a variety of scars, including two from bullets, one from a knife fight, and two that he said came from barbed wire, but had never really explained.

"Tell me again why I only see you every decade or so," he said, his voice deep, softened now with satisfaction.

"Because we drive each other crazy."

"Do we?"

"Yes. Don't you remember?"

"Not at the moment."

She smiled. "Good."

They both looked over as the bedroom door opened and Skidmore stepped in. "Am I not invited to this little soiree?"

Katie laughed. She'd always had a soft spot for Thomas Skidmore, in spite of his annoying personality. If nothing else, he excelled at following directions—at least, in the bedroom.

"Take off your clothes," she said, "and sit over there until I tell you otherwise."

He did as instructed, settling into the leather chair closest to the bed.

Katie returned her attention to Jake. She lowered her hips and stroked his somewhat flaccid cock with her pussy lips, moving slowly up and down, kissing his nose and cheeks and lips as she reached them.

Jake closed his eyes, and she felt his cock quickly respond to her caresses. "Oh, yeah," he whispered. "That's nice."

"Just nice?" She sat up, pressing his erection against his abdomen, and drew her fingernails down the front of his body, leaving red welts in their wake.

He writhed a bit, frowning now.

Katie moved down, started at his belly, and licked long, slow lines back up the welts, stopping to circle his nipples. His body quivered under her mouth as he groaned.

She sat up and glanced at Thomas, who squirmed in his chair. Motioning with her head, she said, "Come here. Suck my tits."

The older vampire jumped from his chair and slid into bed beside them. He leaned around Katie and suckled, his tongue circling her nipples at dizzying speeds. Pleasure fluttered through her torso and down to a point on her lower back. The sensation also drew wetness from her cunt that drenched Jake's cock. Jake's hands ran up and down the fronts of Katie's thighs.

She rose up, positioned herself, and took Jake's swollen rod in an inch at a time as she held Thomas by a handful of his blond hair.

With Jake's cock sheathed, she stopped a moment to enjoy the fullness inside her, then began to ride back and forth, thrilling to the way his erection continued to grow.

She moved Thomas's mouth down the front of her body, and he kissed, and licked, and nipped at her skin, and her senses seemed to take off on their own.

"Oh, yes," she breathed. "Lower."

Then she released Thomas and leaned back, exposing her filled cunt. Thomas's tongue flicked back and forth against her swollen clit and Jake's cock, and Katie held perfectly still to enjoy the blissful attention.

"Damn," Jake said, his voice deep with desire. He gripped Katie's thighs.

Katie ran her tongue along her fangs, massaging the aching need until she couldn't stand it anymore. She grabbed Thomas by the hair, raised him up, and bit into his pale shoulder. He whimpered as she drew hard.

Her world exploded once again, with an orgasm racking her body as Thomas's desire racked her brain. Need swam through her, tearing at her veins, tugging at her cunt as she ground down on Jake's cock.

And then she felt Jake's strength, bursting with desire, flowing into her, filtered through Thomas's fulfillment. She opened her eyes and found Thomas's mouth on Jake's wrist, the older vampire stroking his own spewing cock.

Jake's eyes were closed and his mouth open, and his body moved against her thrusts. His need made her cry out as she released Thomas and pushed him away. Thomas rolled to his back to enjoy the last of his orgasm alone.

Katie leaned down and pressed her shoulder to Jake's mouth. He didn't hesitate, but penetrated her skin quickly and wrapped his arms around her as his cock erupted inside her. She sank her fangs into his neck and took back the pleasure, letting it roll violently over her, clinging to him as she rode the waves.

For the second time, their bliss entwined into one, terrifyingly perfect joy, and Katie held on longer than she should. Jake released her, but she continued to feed, her cunt contracting almost painfully.

"Katie," Jake whispered, pleading.

She broke the bond then, sat up, and let contentment flow across her skin and through every nerve.

She met Jake's heavy-lidded gaze. "Are you all right?"

He grinned. "You bet."

"Good." She rolled off him and stretched out between the two men, a hand on each of them. Thomas had already succumbed to sleep, and Jake yawned. Dawn, well under way, burned in her bones.

"Will you help with the hunters?" she asked Jake.

"I guess so." He yawned again.

"I still think we should drain them all and get it over with."

"Hmm."

"Are you listening to me?"

He didn't answer.

Katie rolled over, moved his arm so that it encircled her, and rested her head on his shoulder. She ran her hand over his cool skin and her fingers through the hair on his chest.

"Just watch your back, Jake Brand. I'd hate to lose you."

3

Jake settled onto a stool. "Beer," he said, nodding at the young man behind the bar who wore a straw cowboy hat with an overly curled brim, a T-shirt with rolled-up sleeves, and low-riding jeans. Colorful tattoos covered his arms and several earrings glistened in each ear. Not quite the cowboy of old.

"What kind?"

"Surprise me." Jake turned to check out the crowd. The patrons were typical of Santa Fe—a variety of wild haircuts and clothes on semi-drunk twenty-year-olds, older hippies-turned-artists, California film critics, a few local descendants of conquistadors, and some he just couldn't identify. Still, out of all the places he'd visited in the three days since leaving Katie, Cowgirl's felt the most comfortable.

He listened to conversations, searching for anything hinting at vampire hunters. This wasn't really a place he expected to find such conversations, but he wasn't leaving any stone unturned. Besides, he liked the smell of cooking ribs, even if he'd pretty much forgotten how they tasted. And it was still too early to find anyone at the Tunnel.

"Beer's getting warm."

Jake swung around to the voice and found a young woman sitting on the stool next to his. She wore her reddish brown hair in a braid that fell halfway down her back, and her green eyes sparkled with unusual clarity. Her skin looked as smooth as silk under a sprinkling of freckles.

"I like it warm," he said.

"Do you?"

He smiled, listening to her heart rate increase.

She wore clothes similar to those of the other patrons—jeans low on her hips, a short, sleeveless shirt that showed off the gold ring in her navel, tight-fitting high-heeled boots, and a black overshirt, long and unbuttoned. But there was something different about her. She didn't quite fit in, although she seemed to be trying to do so. As he leaned closer, he got a whiff of her scent, and gulped.

She smelled way beyond good. It wasn't the perfume she wore that hinted at night-blooming flowers, but something about her natural scent that had him practically drooling.

Damnation, she reminded him of Iris.

Jake sat back, working to erase Iris from his thoughts. "You come here often?"

"I think that's the oldest line in the book." She leaned forward, trying to get the bartender's attention.

Jake couldn't imagine how the young man managed not to notice her.

"I'm older than I look," he said. "I wrote the book."

"Oh? And you can't come up with something more original?" She straightened as the bartender approached. "White wine, please."

Jake turned to face her squarely, leaned close, and lowered his voice. "You must be the most gorgeous creature that has walked this earth in a hundred years. Your eyes hold the depths of the oceans, and your scent leaves me weak and wanting more."

She stared at him, then blinked twice. "Wow. That was pretty good. A little over the top, maybe, but still not bad."

"I meant every word of it, darlin'."

The young woman narrowed her eyes. "I'm not your *darlin'*."

He extended his hand. "Jake."

She studied his hand for a moment, then took it. "Athena."

Holding her hand in his, Jake laughed. "Of course, a goddess."

She blushed, which only enhanced her beauty.

"I meant that as a compliment." Jake raised her hand to his lips.

Her heart pounded now—he could hear nothing else. She was attracted to him, and knowing that made her all the more enticing.

Jake released her hand as the image of Iris rose in his thoughts again. Not the young, beautiful Iris, standing gloriously naked before him, offering him everything, but the cold, dead, Iris, lying on his bed, beyond his reach. He remembered the pain and sorrow that had overwhelmed him as he lay beside her body for days.

His hands began to shake with a fear he hadn't felt in decades. It wasn't the fear of another being or of a beast bent on destruction, but the fear of his own uncontrollable desires.

He stood quickly, pulled a twenty from his pocket and dropped it on the bar, then nodded to Athena. "Have a wonderful life, my dear."

She watched him leave the bar; he felt her eyes on him as he grabbed his hat, yanked open the door, and hurried out into the courtyard.

Jake pulled on his hat as he marched past tables of partiers, raising glasses and laughing. He suddenly didn't care what the hell they were saying. He didn't care if every one of them was hunting him—let them come. He needed a good fight more than he needed to feed.

Past the archway, he turned right, walked quickly down the sidewalk to the Santa Fe River, and ducked into the shadows of giant cottonwoods. He stopped, leaned against the coarse bark of one, and tried to calm his racing thoughts.

The sounds of the city whispered around him. He heard music from all directions, some accompanied by words in Spanish. The river gurgled past on his left, and cars rushed by on his right. Two homeless men, sitting on the bank of the river, argued over a bottle of wine.

In an alley across Alameda, a young man leaned against a wall with one hand, holding a younger woman around the waist and fucking her from behind. Jake focused his attention on the couple, who were trying to keep their activity a secret from tourists walking past but not completely succeeding. The man grunted as he peaked, and the woman whimpered, then both quieted. He withdrew quickly, and she straightened her short skirt as he zipped his pants.

"Good shit, baby," the man whispered.

Jake huffed a laugh. So much for romance.

But the distraction had calmed him, and he felt control returning. He filled his lungs with cool air and looked up into the darkened sky. A slice of moon shone between branches, and a dozen stars twinkled through the lights of town.

He allowed himself to think about the young woman in the bar now that he could do so rationally. What was it about Athena that reminded him of Iris? It wasn't her looks. Iris had been dark where Athena was light, and slender where Athena was sturdy. Certainly Iris's body hadn't been pierced, and she hadn't shown so much of it in public. Jake smiled at the thought. In 1880 when he met Iris, she'd been covered from head to toe.

But Iris's scent had been magical, too, just as Athena's was. He'd fallen for her instantly, and decided at once to take her as his mate—his wife.

He wouldn't make that mistake twice.

Better to walk through eternity alone than suffer such pain.

Determined to enjoy the pleasant evening, Jake pushed off from the tree and strolled through the park. He turned up Galisteo and slowed his pace as he wound through packs of tourists. At the plaza, crowds grew and gathered around a local mariachi band. Some of the tourists clapped in time with the music, and others tried to sing. Jake winced at the unwelcome level of noise and hurried past.

The crowds thinned out as he made his way down narrow back streets until he found the doorway he wanted—nondescript, wooden, decorated with wrought iron, it opened to a staircase leading down. At the bottom of the stairs, Jake knocked twice on the interior door, waited, knocked once, and then twice again.

The door opened to a room painted black, already filled with the usual Tunnel patrons. These were not the same people who hung out in Cowgirl's, or Maria's, or any of the local bars. Those in the Tunnel were vampires, wannabe vampires, and soon-to-be victims of vampires. The latter two categories were often the same.

Jake tossed his hat onto a hook as he approached a familiar face at the bar. Antonio, who had worked at the Tunnel for at least thirty years, was tall and pale with shoulder-length black hair and black eyes. His father had been Apache, and his mother a beautiful flamenco dancer, according to him.

"House special?" Antonio asked.

Jake nodded and leaned against the bar. "How's it going?"

The bartender shrugged. "Same as always." He placed a chilled glass in front of Jake.

The house special resembled wine, but was, in fact, mostly Type O. The donated vintage had none of the pleasant effects of the embodied variety, but it took the edge off. Jake swigged it down.

Antonio waited on several more patrons, then returned to lean on the bar near Jake. They watched inebriated men and women dancing with vampire partners, and young people dressed in black fondling each other on the dance floor.

"Did you make the meeting?" Antonio asked.

"Yep. That's why I'm here."

"Oh? And I thought it was for the classy company."

Jake chuckled. "What do you know about vampire hunters?"

Antonio turned his head to frown at Jake. "I don't understand. Vampire hunters have been around . . . well, forever, I guess."

"The council's concerned about the new craze stirred up by the movie *Van Helsing*."

"Oh. Yes, I guess there is more activity than usual. Did you hear about Shadow?"

Jake nodded. "And they got Billy Sears, too."

Antonio shook his head. "I hadn't heard about Billy. Too bad. He was a nice old guy."

Jake shot him a glare. "He wasn't that old."

"Getting touchy, huh?" Antonio grinned.

"Go to hell," Jake muttered, returning his attention to the dance floor.

"I'm sure I will."

"Yeah."

Music stopped and some couples walked to tables. Others waited for the next song to start.

"Well, I don't think you'll find hunters in here," Antonio said.

"Why not? This is exactly where I'd expect to find them. A smart hunter knows where the prey hide."

Antonio snorted. "Who said anything about these guys being smart?"

Jake found himself hoping there were at least a few smart hunters out there. How could he fight a good battle without a worthy opponent?

"Sweet Billy and Shadow weren't exactly the brightest of the bunch," Antonio continued. "It wouldn't have taken much to catch them off guard."

"I guess not." Jake's spirits began to droop. "Still, I suppose I better mix in, see what I can pick up."

"Help yourself."

"Keep your ears open, will you?"

"Certainly." Antonio moved away, wiping the bar as he went.

Jake skirted the dance floor, looking more closely at couples. A few were same-sex; most weren't. Several were vampire couples looking for the wild ride and checking out possible victims to share. Some were vampires trying to win the trust of their soon-to-be victims.

A redhead he'd seen before ran her long fingernails down the outside of her mortal date's muscular arms. "I'll make you come 'til it hurts," she whispered. The young man grinned.

"Hi."

Jake turned to the voice, surprised to find Athena standing beside him, black outer shirt draped over one arm. Her bare shoulders drew his attention because of their rounded firmness and the freckles splashed over them. The sleeveless shirt she wore hugged her breasts just enough to make his mouth water, and her belly ring glistened in the blue lights.

He frowned. "What are you doing here?"

She nodded toward the back of a young blond man walking

toward the bathrooms. "Chris says this is a great place." She glanced around. "Looks a little creepy to me."

"It is creepy. Take my word for it and leave."

She looked up at him, her green eyes capturing whatever pieces of shattered soul he had left. "You're here."

He grinned and leaned close to her, unable to resist inhaling her scent once more. "True, but I know what I'm getting into."

Her face reddened a little. "I'm not an idiot. I know what goes on in these places."

Jake felt his cock harden just from standing near her. He leaned closer, focused on her now, unable to turn away. Her very presence held a promise of strength and pleasure he found irresistible. "I don't think you do."

She shrugged and turned her gaze to the dance floor. "Drugs, sex. I know."

He held his mouth an inch from her ear. "And so much more, sweet thing."

A shiver ran through her—so slight, a mortal wouldn't have noticed it. Jake's fangs dropped almost instantly in response.

"Like . . . what?" she whispered.

He stepped around to stand behind her, touching her silky hair with his fingertips. "Games of pain and joy, life and death. And ecstasy like you can't begin to imagine."

She gulped.

"Hey, what the hell—"

Jake glanced up at the male standing in front of Athena. Her date's eyes widened when they met his, and Jake guessed that his own irises had turned golden already. He couldn't seem to control his reaction to the young woman standing before him.

He placed a hand on one of Athena's bare shoulders and glared. "She's with me now. You can go."

"But—"

Jake slung a thought of painful challenge and defeat into the blond man's head, and the mortal staggered backward in response. Then the young man turned and hurried toward the door, glancing back once before disappearing.

"I can't believe you did that," she said.

He breathed in the smell of her hair, imagining it loose and draped across her bare breasts. "He shouldn't have brought you here."

"Great, but now I don't have a ride home."

Jake bit back the desire that threatened to overpower him. He couldn't allow himself to indulge—not with this one. He closed his eyes for a moment to regain control, then straightened and stepped to her side. "Don't worry, I'll take you home."

She looked up at him, studying his face intently. "How do I know I can trust you?"

He smiled. "You don't, and you can't."

She turned away. "Maybe we should stay here awhile."

He glanced around and found several of the locals watching Athena, sizing her up for a meal. "Only if you stay with me. I know some of these *people*. You really don't want to get cornered by them."

She shrugged, feigning indifference that her racing heartbeat exposed as a lie. "Whatever."

Trying to refocus on his task, Jake listened to a few more conversations, then realized he needed to get into the thick of things, but he couldn't run the risk of leaving Athena alone for even a moment. He leaned toward her. "You want to dance?"

"I suppose."

He offered his hand and she took it. Jake led her onto the dance floor and pulled her into his arms. She fit too well.

Now, he'd had every intention of leading her around to where he could do a little eavesdropping. It wouldn't have taken more than a dance or two, and then he could have persuaded her to leave. The last thing he wanted was to keep Athena exposed to the vampire community any longer than he had to. Some of the younger ones in the Tunnel had no code of ethics. They'd think nothing of draining her for a night's entertainment.

But something about the woman made it impossible for him to concentrate on anything else when she stood in his arms, her hands on his shoulders and her hot breath caressing his neck. Her scent had a stronger effect on him than any opiate could have when he was human. He seemed to lose all sense of reason.

"What is it about you that's so different?" he whispered, sliding his hand down to the narrowest part of her back where it met bare flesh. His body responded by shuddering.

"Different from you?"

"No," he said, "different from any other woman."

She huffed softly. "Look, you got me with the line about my eyes holding the depths of the ocean and my scent leaving you wanting more. You don't have to keep trying."

Jake lowered his mouth to her ear. "I can't seem to help it, sweet thing. I want you like I've never wanted another."

She made a soft noise of surrender, and he tightened his grip on her, pulling her to his body. He pushed his thigh between hers as they stepped, and she slid her crotch against it. Her heat nearly seared his skin through the clothing.

Jake leaned down and captured her mouth, tasting her, savoring her. As she welcomed him and drew his tongue in, he slid a hand down to touch the outline of her breast. He rubbed her hardening nipple through the soft fabric, and a growl of need escaped his throat.

When she pressed her abdomen against his hard-on, Jake tore his mouth from hers and rested his chin on the top of her head. He wasn't ready for her to see the vampire yet. She drew him to the edge of control, even in front of this crowd. He'd never felt so helpless.

"Maybe you should show me where all this, um, other stuff happens," she said.

"You mean the sex or the drugs?"

"I'm not really into drugs."

Jake grinned. Why was he so intent on keeping the vampire chained? All he needed was a taste of sweet Athena and he'd feel differently, wouldn't he? In 120 years, he'd learned self-control. He wouldn't make the same mistake he'd made with Iris. "Maybe I should."

Her heated palm sliding up his side burned away any doubts.

Jake released her by all but her hand and led her through the crowd until he reached the back hallway, a tunnel-like passage for which the place was named. He listened as they passed closed doors, searching for a room where they could have privacy. Cries of ecstasy and growls of vampires feeding provided unnecessary fuel for his desires.

"Jesus, it's dark in here," Athena said.

He opened the door to an empty room, pulled her in, and closed it. Leaning against the wall, he gave her a chance to look around.

The soft glow of blue lights, hidden at the top of the walls, lit the room. In the center was a large round bed, and near it a Victorian-style chaise longue, both covered in black velvet.

"A little tacky, isn't it? All it needs is a velvet Elvis painting." She ran her fingers across the back of the chaise longue.

"It's not the room I'm interested in, darlin'."

She glanced at him and he wondered if she could see his transformation in the weak light. If so, she didn't react.

Jake crossed the room to stand behind her. To her credit, Athena didn't move, but her entire body shook. He ran his palms over her shoulders, barely touching the skin. "You really think you're ready for this? For me?"

She nodded, gripping the back of the chaise longue.

Unable to stop even if he'd wanted to, Jake ran his hands down her sides until he reached her bare midriff, then slid them back up the front of her, under the fabric. Her skin was warm and smooth, covered in places with small bumps from his touch. Her quickened breathing and pulse urged him on. He skimmed the mounds of her breasts and felt the taut nipples, then moved down to her flat stomach, tracing the belly ring.

He stepped closer until his erection rested against her ass, the clothes a frustrating barrier that he decided to leave in place for the moment. Nuzzling the back of her head and her neck, he unsnapped her jeans and slid one hand inside her panties as he wrapped the other arm around her waist.

Athena sucked in a surprised breath. "What are you—"

Jake pressed his mouth to the top of her shoulder as he slid his fingers slowly across her cunt, feeling the fleshy indentations and rises.

Her head went back to his shoulder and a shudder ran through her.

Beneath his lips, her pulse raced through her veins, calling to him as clearly as music, and her scent filled his head with sweet fog. He kissed her shoulder and eased two fingers into her warm, wet cunt.

She gasped, her body quivering in response.

Jake held her tighter and slid his fingers across her swelling clit, spreading her juices, inhaling her wondrous scent of desire.

Athena's hips moved in time with his fingers as her breathing grew ragged. She approached the precipice, ready for him, groaning for him.

He pressed the tips of his fangs to her tender skin, anticipating the incredible joy that would soon flood his senses, and his cock ached to plunge into her slick cunt.

How a picture of Iris could invade at that moment, he had no idea. He heard her cries of joy and pain, and then her weakened moans as he drank from her, and finally her pathetic whimper of despair as the last of her life slipped away.

Jake turned his head to the side as he drew Athena into an orgasm. She cried out and tightened around his fingers, her body undulating against his. She reached back and gripped his ass to hold him close, as the spasms shot through her cunt, grabbing at him, inviting him deeper.

Damn, he'd never had to work so hard to restrain himself as he thought about how amazing it would be to fuck her and taste her climax.

Holding her close, he let her ride his hand to the end, until she collapsed against him.

"Oh, my God," she whispered.

After a long moment, she reached back and ran her hand down the front of his pants, stroking his cock through the denim.

He grabbed her wrist to stop her and pulled her hand away. "Not now," he said, his voice barely recognizable even to himself.

"Why not?"

"Because you wouldn't survive it." He turned his head and kissed her neck.

"I don't understand." She moved her head sideways to give him access.

"Good." Jake swallowed hard as he lifted his mouth away from temptation. "It's time to take you home."

"But don't you want to . . . you know, continue?"

Jake ran his hands up her sides again to her breasts, enjoying one last touch. "Later, sweet thing."

She pushed back into him and he growled accidentally.

4

A shot of "house special" Jake grabbed on the way out combined with cool night air managed to douse the flames running just under his skin. Or, at least, bring them down to a manageable level. He steered the Impala through the narrow, crowded streets until they'd left the Plaza behind and entered what passed in Santa Fe for suburbs.

"Turn right here," Athena said, pointing at the next corner.

Jake followed her instructions and pulled into an empty driveway in front of a small stucco house that looked very much like every other house on the block. A dog next door barked at the intrusion.

Athena glanced at him, her hand on the car door latch. "Aren't you coming in?"

He smiled and shook his head, regretting the words even as he spoke them. "I don't think so."

She looked at the house, and then back at him, her heart suddenly thundering in the night. "But, what if Chris is waiting in there for me?"

"Chris?"

Athena nodded. "You know, the one you told to get lost. He's probably really pissed off."

Jake frowned at the house. "Would he hurt you?"

She shrugged. "He might."

Rage swelled unexpectedly in his chest as he thought of someone hurting Athena, and he cut off the car's engine. He followed her to the front door.

"Does he have a key?"

She nodded as she unlocked the dead bolt. "We've been dating for a few months."

When she opened the door, Jake stopped her with a hand on her arm and stepped inside. "Don't turn on the lights," he whispered.

"But, how will you see?"

Ignoring her question, he walked silently through the small house, checking for any hint of a heartbeat. Discovering nothing, he relaxed and returned to the front door.

He found Athena standing where he'd left her, but now she stood before him naked, leaning coyly against the wall in the living room, smiling. A single lamp cast a soft yellow light on her body, and Jake stopped.

He hadn't correctly guessed just how gorgeous her body was—firm in all the right places, with naturally full breasts and small pink areolae. Her waist, not too narrow, but not overly large, gave way to wide hips marked by reddish pubic hair, growing in a full bush. And her legs aroused him even more as she drew one foot up, sliding it along the front of her shin. She held her braid against the front of her body between her breasts, twirling the end in one finger.

"I think we should finish what we started, Jake. Don't you?"

He clenched his jaw at the wave of undeniable hunger washing through his body as he strode to her and held her bare waist. Then he took her mouth, unable to make himself stop, needing to taste her, needing all of her. He sensed her fear—this wasn't usual for her, he could tell—but the thirst swelled faster than his cock, and all rational thought disappeared. Only senses remained, open and receiving everything she offered: her beauty, her scent, her warmth, her touch.

She pulled his shirttail up and her fingers singed lines into his skin.

He pinned her to the wall and caressed her breasts, enjoying the way they filled and heated his hands. He rolled the hard nipples between his thumbs and forefingers; she groaned into his mouth.

Athena unbuttoned his pants and reached in to stroke his cock, and Jake's knees nearly buckled. Her touch was magnificent, intense, nearly unbearable.

"Damn," he muttered against her lips. "I want to be inside you when you come."

"Yes," she whispered back.

"But there's more," he said, reaching between her legs, finding her pussy dripping for him.

"What?" she said, then gasped as he stroked her clit.

"I need more than your gorgeous cunt, sweet thing."

She pulled his rock-hard cock forward, raising herself until she gripped it between her thighs. "What do you need, Jake?"

He groaned and eased forward and back, letting her stroke him and coat him with her juices. "I need to taste you, Athena. I need—"

The world crashed to a halt as white-hot fire exploded through his chest. Jake yelled and straightened, then spun around.

The man from the Tunnel—what the hell was his name? Chris?—stood with his hands in front of him, his feet spread, and his eyes wide.

Behind Jake, Athena screamed and slid along the wall.

The pain continued, burning through him like molten lava.

Jake looked down to find a bloody point protruding from his chest. His knees gave out and he dropped to the floor.

"Are you okay?" his attacker asked.

Jake followed Chris's gaze and found Athena shivering in a corner, her arms wrapped protectively across her chest. For a moment, he regretted that he couldn't come to her rescue, until he saw her nod.

Jake steeled himself against the pain. "Why?" he managed to get out.

"We search out creatures like you," the man said, sneering. "We must protect the mortal world, even if they don't believe."

Hunters. They were both goddamn hunters.

So much for a fair fight.

Jake reached back and yanked the stake from his back, crying out at the unbelievable pain as he did. Resting on all fours, he worked to steady himself as blood dripped to the floor beneath him. He looked up at his assailant, smelling the young man's fear.

"You shouldn't . . . have done that," he said. Then he struggled to his feet.

Faster than the mortals could see, Jake charged across the room, grabbed Chris's shoulder and his hair, and pushed his head to the side. Showing no mercy, he bit into the boy's neck and drank, letting the healing liquid fill him with strength and warmth and pleasure.

Athena screamed and charged forward, pounding against Jake's back with her fists.

He held her off as he took another long draw from Chris, then he released the young man, who crumpled to the floor in a heap.

Jake drew Athena close and stared into her beautiful green eyes. "I had no intention of hurting you, sweet thing."

She pulled away and collapsed against the wall when he released her arm.

He hurried out the front door, straightening his clothes and buttoning his pants as he staggered to the car. The hole in his back bled profusely, draining his strength almost as fast as he'd drained his attacker.

Driving like a maniac, Jake managed to get to an abandoned field, where he drove his car across the dirt and parked under an elm tree. He stumbled out, unlocked the trunk, rolled in, and pulled it shut. Just as he heard the lock click, he passed out.

Athena huddled in the corner, shaking uncontrollably, trying to get her mind around what had just happened. One moment she'd been in the arms of the most attractive man she'd ever met, and the next she'd been standing in front of a monster with glowing gold eyes and fangs, blood smeared across his mouth and dripping from his chin.

The memory played over and over, coalescing into three words.

Vampires are real.

How could this possibly be?

She remembered the first night Chris had told her about his mission.

"People are in denial. It's easier to pretend they don't exist than it is to face the truth."

She studied his face, his youthful skin lined with worry and determination, his blue eyes glistening.

"What truth?"

He glanced around as if he expected to find people crouching behind him, then leaned across the table and whispered one word. "Vampires."

Athena bit back a laugh, immediately understanding how important this absurd idea was to him. "Vampires?"

He nodded, watching her face for a reaction.

She swallowed hard, trying not to compare her would-be boyfriend to her alcoholic father swearing his bed was filled with spiders and scorpions. They'd been every bit as real to him as the whiskey he craved.

"Chris—"

"They're real. I've seen them."

The red-checkered table, mugs of coffee, crowds of fellow diners, and sound of Metallica grinding from oversized speakers faded.

Soft moans drew Athena from the memory. She pushed herself up on shaky arms and crawled across the floor. "Chris?"

Blood pooled around his head and shoulders, oozing from the gash on the side of his neck. But for all the blood, the wound wasn't bleeding as much as she would have expected, as if it were closing on its own. Or maybe he didn't have much blood left.

"Chris?"

He groaned in response and reached toward her with one bloodstained hand.

She grabbed his hand and held it tightly. "I'm so sorry I didn't believe you."

His breath came in shallow gasps.

With her heart pounding in her ears, Athena brushed matted blond hair from his face. "Hang on. I'll call an ambulance."

Four days and three nights passed in a painful blur as Jake worked his way west. He lost the car somewhere, and vaguely remembered cornering a coyote in order to feed. Finally, he found himself crawling up the red rock trail that led to Skidmore's castle. Unfortunately, weak and helpless, he collapsed before he reached the doorway. Giving up, he turned onto his back to face the morning sun.

The morning sun, however, did not rise onto his lifeless body to finish him off. Instead, he woke in a small, dark room that it took him a while to recognize.

Careful not to move, he tried to clear his thoughts, but the fog seemed to thicken. He turned his head to look. Beneath a half dozen paintings, the wall appeared to be smoothed red rock. It must be one of the numerous rooms Skidmore had carved out to create his elaborate underground mansion. Relieved, Jake closed his eyes again.

"Dear boy, are you still with us?"

Thomas Skidmore's voice.

Jake nodded.

"Well, I'm delighted. I have a drink for you. Not exactly herbal tea, but I do believe it will help what ails you."

The scent of red blood cells snapped Jake's eyes open. He sat up, grabbed the glass from Skidmore, and gulped down the nourishment.

Almost instantly, warmth spread through his limbs and torso, and the healing power fired him from the inside out. Unlike the drink at the Tunnel, this was fresh, warm, and full of vibrant emotions.

"What . . . who . . ." He stared at the glass.

Skidmore took the glass from his hand and smiled. "Oh, we have quite a few donors at the moment. When you feel more like your old self, I'll show you around." He rose and stood beside the bed. "Take your time. I've left clothes for you in the bath. Make yourself at home."

And then he left.

Jake rolled off of the satin-covered bed and stood on shaky legs. His face seemed to be covered with mud and no telling what else, and he wore ragged, filthy clothes. The hunger still nagged at him, but seemed to be manageable. He pulled open his shirt and looked at the nearly healed hole in his chest.

No dusty street, no *mano a mano*, no matching wits, no fair fight, just a stake driven through his back while he was distracted.

"Bastard," he whispered.

After a long, hot shower, Jake wandered through the maze

of hallways, following hints of voices until he found Skidmore talking to several of his lackey vampires. The conversation skidded to a halt when Jake walked into the sitting room.

"Dear boy, you look immensely better. Here, have another drink." Skidmore filled a glass from a dark pitcher and handed it to him.

Unable to stop, Jake drained the glass, then frowned at it. "What did you mean by 'quite a few donors at the moment'?"

Skidmore waved off the question. "There's plenty of time for that. Tell me, what happened?"

Jake shrugged. "I found some of the hunters."

"I could have guessed that much." Skidmore motioned to the others and they hurried from the room. Then he settled into an oversized chair near an empty fireplace. "You must have uncovered quite a large group."

Jake huffed. "Yeah, two."

"Two? *Two* mortals did this to you?"

Jake upended the glass to get the last drop, then placed it on the serving table and sat in the chair opposite Skidmore's. "Unfortunately, one of them was a very tempting redhead." He ran his fingers through his wet hair.

"Ah." Skidmore steepled his fingers under his chin. "So they found your weakness. That seems to be the modus operandi for this bunch."

"What do you mean?"

"Modus operandi is the term—"

"I know what an MO is." Jake frowned at his host. "What the hell are you talking about?"

Skidmore sighed as he rose. "Unfortunately, this group is more of a threat than we knew. André's remains were found at the cabin in the mountains. In several pieces."

"What?" Jake's chest tightened with instant sorrow at the news. "But, how?"

"One can only guess. He'd sworn off human blood centuries ago, so it is unlikely he was in search of a meal. The signs suggest he stopped to help someone and was attacked by a group of at least four hunters armed with stakes and swords. He fled back to the cabin, where they caught up with him and . . . beheaded him."

Jake stared at the Navajo rug under his feet. André's wisdom had been a guiding light for so many for so long. The world became a darker place without him.

"Son of a bitch."

Skidmore sighed again. "Crudely put, but a true sentiment indeed. And there are others unaccounted for."

Jake's gaze snapped up to Skidmore as his sorrow turned to fear. "Katie?"

Skidmore shrugged. "She's not due in for another night or two. I wouldn't worry too much, however. She's armed with the knowledge of their methods, and, as we both know, she's a formidable foe."

Jake knew well just how formidable Katie could be, but that wouldn't stop him from worrying about her. After all, *he'd* been caught off guard.

"No, I'm not overly concerned about Katie, but I fear the worst for Michael Ponce and his friends."

Jake knew Ponce, but not well. He moved more in Skidmore's circle than Jake's. Still, the idea that some of the older vampires had been hunted down had his attention. "What are we going to do?"

Skidmore, with another of his dramatic waves, motioned toward the door. "Come, dear boy, let me show you what we're already doing."

Jake followed Skidmore down several long, winding hallways, which seemed to take them well below ground level. The last hallway opened into a tremendous room filled with people, vampires, and a variety of mechanical devices. Rings protruding from rock walls held chains attached to the wrists and ankles of men and women, many lacking clothing. Even the vampires wore little more than loincloths.

"Welcome to my dungeon," Skidmore said.

Bile rose in Jake's throat. "What the hell are you doing, torturing them?"

"Torture?" Skidmore laughed. "No, dear boy, I would never do that. Here, let me start at the beginning." He led the way to a heavy wooden door and pulled it open to reveal a room full of mortals lounging in chairs and on sofas, most watching television or playing video games. "See? These mortals are my guests."

One of the nearby men sneered at the two of them. "You motherfuckers are doomed to walk through eternal hell."

"Ah, yes." Skidmore grinned at Jake. "Such a pleasant lot." He led the way back out and closed the door.

"As we find hunters," he explained, "we give them two days to decide if they wish to continue to hunt us, or join us. If they make the choice not to join us, they're moved into the donors' room." He walked to the next door and slid back a small window.

Inside, a dozen or more mortals lay on tables, hooked to IVs. A young female vampire worked at switching out full bags for empty ones.

"They're all drugged," Skidmore said. "As far as they're concerned, they're simply sleeping. After a week or so, we'll finish them off, and they'll move into death. All in all, not a bad way to go."

Jake shook his head. "I don't know. This doesn't bother you, huh?"

Skidmore stiffened. "Dear boy, I watched my family, friends, and most of the village I grew up in die slow, agonizing deaths at the hand of the Black Death. *That* bothered me. This is a pleasant way to dispose of a very unpleasant part of the population." He sighed. "And don't forget what you are, after all. Their blood sustains us. You made the choice to live this way."

Jake decided not to argue the point. He hadn't actually made an educated choice when he was brought into the Night, but he hadn't fought it, either.

"So, what about the others?"

Skidmore relaxed again. "Those who choose to join us will either be allowed to remain mortal, or offered eternity. We must first decide their worth. And that is the group you see here." He motioned toward the vast main room. Lowering his voice, he leaned close to Jake. "This is my favorite part."

Skidmore led the way around the room. "Only a few will be given eternity. The rest will be allowed to go, once we're assured of their allegiances. But first, we must be sure that the ones we choose are truly sensuous creatures." He stroked the side of a young woman's face as she looked up at him with wide eyes. "This is Ruby."

Ruby had lips as red as her namesake stone, and coal-black eyes. Long, dark hair hung in front of her shoulders, partially covering her bare breasts, but not enough to hide their fullness. She wore jeans cut off into shorts, and as Jake studied her, her hands slid between her thighs and her legs opened just enough to suggest interest. Above her bare feet, fur-lined cuffs encircled her ankles, attaching her to the wall.

In spite of his weakened state, Jake felt his body react, and a mild ache started behind his fangs. And then he heard all the heartbeats in the room, as soft and sweet as songbirds on a cool, fall morning.

"Ah, dear boy," Skidmore said, his hand falling on Jake's shoulder. "I see you haven't lost your interest. Good. You may help me *weed* through them. What do you say?"

Jake remembered Athena, standing before him gloriously naked, using her beauty to lure him into a trap. And he had been terrified of hurting her. The betrayal still stung when he thought about it. "What the hell?"

Skidmore beamed. "Wonderful. I have a perfectly marvelous idea or two. I'm quite sure you'll enjoy assisting me."

Jake watched the tip of Ruby's tongue run slowly over her top lip.

"But first we take care of your more immediate needs." Skidmore took Jake's arm and turned him toward the main door. "We want you in prime condition, my boy."

"What exactly do you want me to do?"

Skidmore's smile grew into a wicked grin. "You'll see."

5

The next evening, Jake rose feeling far better than he had the night before. He climbed out of bed, showered, and slipped on jeans and a T-shirt. Hunger gnawing at his insides led him toward the main part of the underground castle.

The grand salon, as Skidmore called it, was deserted, as were the kitchen and master bedrooms. Jake poured himself a chilled drink and downed it, then wandered back toward the dungeon.

Skidmore still hadn't explained his ideas for sorting out the human contestants, and Jake found himself less interested in helping than he had been earlier. As the sting of betrayal focused down onto an individual, his desire for one-sided revenge on the misguided humans waned. His true interest lay in looking for Athena. Her scent still haunted him. *She* needed to be taught a lesson.

"Skidmore?" Jake wound through passageways, trying to recall his route from the night before. He stopped at a door and listened.

Noises from inside suggested several people whispering, and

then he heard Skidmore say, "Yes, I think this will be quite interesting."

Jake eased the door open, leaned in, and found a room lit by candlelight with a large bed in the middle holding four or five entangled humans kissing and touching each other.

Skidmore looked up and smiled. "Come in, dear boy. We started without you."

Jake had never quite understood his friend's taste for groups, and started to back out. "That's okay. You go right ahead."

Skidmore, dressed in a red silk robe, rose from the bed and crossed the room in the blink of an eye. "Nonsense," he said, taking Jake's arm and pulling him forward. "I told you I needed your help. Do you plan to deny me?"

Jake sighed, letting himself be led into the room.

"Here," Skidmore said, releasing him into a strangely shaped round chair covered in dark cloth. "You can simply watch if you wish."

He had no great desire to watch, but he knew it would be useless to try to explain that to Skidmore. The older vampire often related stories of orgies with humans and vampires, and couldn't seem to understand why they didn't interest Jake. As a lawman, spending days alone in the high desert and on the range, he'd often thought about female company, and he'd had two women at once several times, when he could afford it. But old ways die hard, and he'd barely adjusted to having Skidmore in his bed when he shared it with Katie.

Still, he couldn't go back on his word. And he had, after all, shed his mortality a long time ago. Hell, maybe it was time to shed some of his Victorian morals, too.

Jake relaxed and studied the pile of writhing bodies, sorting out torsos in the flickering light. There seemed to be two men and three women, all young. Most sported tattoos—the latest rage—and one of the women was a blonde from a bottle. One woman was dark, as was one of the men, and she seemed to have the largest breasts, which drew the attention of both men. Not too surprising.

Skidmore stretched out on the far side of the bed where he could observe the action closely, occasionally stroking one or more of the participants and purring like an overgrown house-cat.

"See how nicely this one moves," Skidmore said, in a voice Jake doubted the humans could hear as he touched the muscular back of the darkest young man.

The subject of his attention had just pulled the blonde up to her hands and knees and was entering her with urgent thrusts, to which the blonde grunted as her head went down. She pushed against each thrust and Jake suddenly caught a whiff of her scent.

The second man, who had a tattoo of a dragon on his right shoulder, slid underneath the blonde, catching one of her swaying breasts in his mouth and sucking, as his swollen cock disappeared into the mouth of the third female, whose hair, a mousy brown, fell across her face. She brushed it back with one slender hand while she held the base of Dragonboy's cock with the other.

Jake watched the young woman work, her mouth sliding up and down the slick cock, her eyes closed. She withdrew completely, then circled the head with her pink tongue as she moved her hand up and down the shaft. The young man's body jerked, and his hips rose and fell in time with her movements. She sucked the head back in and slid halfway down the shaft again.

A growl vibrated through the room. Jake frowned when he realized the noise had risen from his own throat, and that he was rubbing the front of his jeans where his erection grew. He dropped his hand to his side and swallowed hard.

The mousy girl rose onto her knees and straddled Dragonboy, aiming his swollen cock between her legs. Jake watched the impressive organ disappear, then studied the girl's face as she rose up and down, fondling her own small breasts as she moved. Her eyes closed and her mouth opened as she worked to satisfy her needs.

Jake's gaze slid down her thin body with slow, deliberate pleasure. Her up-and-down movements changed to a grinding ride as she neared her peak. He could smell her now, taste her need in the air.

Dragonboy's hands grabbed her ass then, and his fingers dug into her flesh as his hips rose completely from the bed. He grunted in time with his release, then collapsed back.

The mousy girl frowned down at her partner, her desires unfulfilled, and looked across at the dark-haired man who drove his seed violently into the blonde as she screamed her orgasmic joy.

Ignoring the smaller girl, both men panted and eyed the enormous breasts waiting on the dark-haired woman, then fell on her as if to devour her.

The little mouse looked around, her eyes glistening with unshed tears, and her gaze stopped on Jake.

Somehow, he lost his clothes as he moved from the chair to the bed, and he sat in front of the abandoned girl, stroking her soft cheek with his fingertips. Damn if she wasn't pretty in a subtle kind of way. He wondered how she'd ended up with the vampire hunters.

Her gaze slid down to his already stiff cock, and Jake grinned as he lay back and drew her to him. Tentatively, her warm hands on his chest, she mounted him.

Jake closed his eyes to enjoy the feeling of her wet, velvety warmth swallowing his prick, then opened them again to study her face. Dark eyes, an uncertain color, lost focus as she began to move, and candlelight danced on her pale skin.

Her already swollen clit rubbed against his cock like a small stone as she slid back and forth. He stroked her thighs and then her breasts, enjoying the way her juices flowed and her need grew.

She clenched her jaw as the climax approached and grabbed his shoulders, then she cried out, ground her biting cunt onto him, and rode him without mercy. Her small body quivered with release.

"Nice," he heard Skidmore whisper.

Just to his left, one of the men grunted again as he fucked the dark-haired woman with abandon.

Jake looked up to find Skidmore standing at the edge of the bed behind the mousy girl, who now smiled.

"What's your name, my dear?" Skidmore traced the lines of her shoulders with his fingers.

"Beatrice," she said.

"Beatrice. Isn't that lovely?"

Jake slid his palms slowly up and down her sides, enjoying her heated skin.

"Have you ever had two men at once, Beatrice?" Skidmore raised one eyebrow at Jake as he spoke.

The girl shook her head.

"Would you like to try it?"

She swallowed hard, then nodded.

Skidmore grinned as he stepped closer. "Good." He glanced at the others. "And you, my dear," he said to the blonde. "Join us."

Jake could tell without looking that the second young man was finishing his turn humping the large-breasted, dark-haired beauty, which would probably leave the two human male participants without much initiative to continue.

The blonde crawled across the bed and kissed Skidmore, then leaned over and kissed Jake. Her mouth, hot and wide, promised wild, erotic joy, and he responded by pulling her in for another taste.

When she straightened, she looked at Skidmore.

"Sit here," he said, patting the bed beside Jake.

As she did, Skidmore stroked her bronze thighs, then slid his hand between them. "Beatrice has beautiful little breasts, don't you think?"

Taking the cue, the blonde leaned forward and attended to Beatrice's breasts with her tongue, circling them, then sucking.

Beatrice responded by flooding Jake's cock as her excitement grew, releasing her wonderful scent again.

Jake's fangs dropped and his cock swelled.

"Yes," Skidmore said softly. "Lean forward just a little."

Jake watched the girl's face as Skidmore kissed her shoulders. He could tell by the frown that furrowed her brow that Skidmore worked on entering her, easing his way into her tightest opening.

And then Jake felt the intrusion of slow, easy strokes, and sweat popped out on Beatrice's face.

"Oh," she said, her voice soft and deep, "so full, so . . ."

"Yes," Skidmore whispered. "Now move up slowly, feel Jake inside you."

Beatrice did as instructed, and Jake felt spasms starting in her tight cunt. As she slid back down, her body shook and her hand curled into a fist against his skin. Her mouth opened and her head went back.

Skidmore pressed his fangs into her shoulder then, and Beatrice cried out. Her wonderful cunt clamped down hard, squeezing and releasing as her orgasm pulsed through her. And pushing against Jake's own erection, Skidmore's rock-hard cock pumped in slow, easy thrusts.

Jake ached for release, needing to taste her climax, every nerve screaming for more. He reached up, pulled the girl from Skidmore's grasp, and pierced her neck.

Achingly exquisite joy flowed through him like molten lava

as he knew the extent of the orgasm burning through her torso and down to her toes. Erotic fulfillment edged out sorrow, fear, wounded pride, years of hiding in the shadows. Pulling her closer, Jake pushed Skidmore away, rolled over on top of Beatrice and filled her with deep, hard thrusts, unable to stop, unwilling to slow. Her heartbeat thundered in his head. Fingers dug into the muscles of his back and she cried out near his ear. "Oh, God, yes!" Her climax continued drawing him deeper.

Approaching the edge of reason, Jake withdrew his mouth from the fountain of sweet nectar, but continued to ride the waves of release with his mousy mate. She thrust up against him again and again, gasping now, cooing as she slowed.

Jake opened his eyes to enjoy the way her face relaxed as the last of the need left her.

He glanced over to find Skidmore between the blonde's thighs, fucking her as he drank from her tattooed breast. The girl arched up into him as she came.

A whimper drew his gaze to where the dark-haired woman watched them, her hand sliding ineffectively across her cunt. "What about me?"

Skidmore raised his head, smiling as he licked the last drop from his lips. "Don't worry, my dear," he said. "You're next."

The old vampire had stamina—Jake had to give him that. His own fires had been quenched to little more than smoking coals, and he returned his gaze to Beatrice as she caressed his face with her fingertips. He kissed her again, then rolled over to his side to watch the rest of the show. He heard a strange tinkle like pieces of glass colliding, and decided it must be his shattered Victorian morals raining down on the stone floor.

Skidmore nipped at the blonde's stomach as he moved off her, then he sat up, cocked his head to one side and studied Jake. "What's wrong, dear boy?"

"Nothing's wrong."

Skidmore nodded toward the dark-haired woman. "Would you like to do the honors?"

Jake shook his head. "No, thanks."

The older vampire sighed as if in sympathy. "I believe your metabolism is just too slow for this lifestyle."

"Probably." Pulling Beatrice into the curve of his body, Jake lounged and watched Skidmore work on the dark-haired woman's incredible breasts with his hand between her legs. He brought her to two rather rapid climaxes, leaving red love bites on her skin.

Something about the moans of pleasure, the scent of female cum, and the way Beatrice began to push back against him soon had Jake aroused again, much to his surprise.

"Take me," she whispered, turning her head to see him over her shoulder.

Jake lifted her hips into him and entered her quickly, nearly desperate to sheath himself in her hot cunt.

With one hand on her abdomen, he fucked her with slow, deep thrusts, pushing against his own palm. Beatrice reached back and grabbed his ass, holding him close, and he pressed his lips to the top of her shoulder.

She moved his hand down and he fingered her hard little clit as she writhed and groaned, and then she came, slamming back against him as she flooded his cock once again. He slid his fingers around the union of his cock and her pulsing cunt until they were drenched.

Beatrice brought his hand up to her lips and drew his fingers into her mouth one at a time.

Jake shuddered at the erotic motion of her hot tongue caressing and sucking his fingers. He turned her head and kissed her, circling her wondrous little mouth with his tongue.

Turning, he drew her up under him as his need became more urgent and his cock ached for the deepest part of her.

She raised her head beside his, panting her own need, arching against him.

"I need to drink," he whispered.

"Yes," she breathed.

When he drank from her again, all else around him disappeared as they rose together into a cloud of bliss. He knew her now—knew her need and her joy at finding him, knowing him, fucking him. Her life of pain revealed itself slowly as it fell away from her, and he filled her and took from her until he found nothing left to take.

Jake raised his head as he pumped the last, and he felt Beatrice collapse under him.

The cloud cleared, and he realized he'd taken too much from the mousy little girl. Growling, he rose from her and gathered her into his arms. Her small, thin body seemed to be losing heat at an alarming rate.

"Don't worry," Skidmore said. "I'd already planned to welcome her into the fold. Of all here tonight, she's the only one."

Jake glanced around at the four remaining mortals who lay sprawled on the bed, recovering from their wild activities. "What about them?"

"They weren't made for eternity, dear boy. Our Beatrice is another matter. Why don't you carry her to my bedchamber? I'll take care of the rest of it."

Skidmore knew of Jake's mistake early in his Dark life, and understood his reluctance to try again.

Jake followed Skidmore down the series of hallways, deposited Beatrice in the middle of the lavish bed, then kissed her cool lips before retreating.

He stood in the hall, listening, but heard nothing. Had he just killed his little mouse? He sincerely hoped not.

Returning for his clothes, he found the group asleep on the bed. He knew Skidmore was right—they weren't made for eternity. They were just a bunch of misguided children in adults' skins.

He went back to his own room then and found his boots and hat. The only thing he really had a stomach for was wandering the desert, remembering the old days.

And perhaps he'd run across his backstabbing little vixen somewhere out there.

6

Athena checked the dark sidewalk behind her as she hurried toward her apartment, grocery bags clutched in her hands. Soup cans clanged together as she broke into a trot.

For days she'd felt as though someone were following her, but she hadn't seen anyone when she'd ducked into doorways. After the bizarre events of two weeks ago, however, she knew monsters lurked in the shadows.

The whole thing had started out as a lark—a stupid game to keep Chris from dumping her. Who in their right mind believed in vampires? If only she had someone to run to now—someone to keep her safe. With both parents long gone and no siblings, or even friends, Athena felt more alone than she had since her father's death.

Fumbling with the keys, she glanced around as she worked to unlock the door. A soft evening breeze danced through leaves on small trees and made flowers sway, but she heard no footsteps over the music coming from a dozen apartments. When she finally got the door open, she hurried inside, closed and locked the door, and leaned against it for a moment to catch her breath.

As soon as she shut her eyes, she saw the vampire's face as plainly as she did every night. His dark blue eyes, his lean, chiseled, weathered features, his waves of long brown hair streaked with gray—they combined to enhance his sexy, crooked smile. The man had been downright gorgeous. And he'd caused reactions in her body unlike anything she'd ever known before.

But he hadn't been a man, had he? In her vision, his blue eyes began to glisten gold, glowing with a light of their own just as they had when he'd turned to look up at her after Chris's attack. Had he really been concerned for her welfare at first? She could have sworn she'd seen something in his expression, something overriding the pain. Something quickly replaced by fury.

The worst part was the guilt. She hadn't worried for her safety the way Chris had insisted she should. She'd been certain, somehow, that Jake wouldn't hurt her as soon as he'd smiled at her. And somewhere along the way, she'd forgotten her mission to lure him into a trap. After the encounter in the back room of the Tunnel, all she'd been able to think about was how wonderful it would feel to have him inside her. When he'd searched the house without finding Chris, she'd assumed something had gone wrong and had secretly rejoiced at the prospect of an entire night alone with him. At that moment, she'd have done anything he asked without giving Chris a thought. *Anything*. How could anyone, or anything, have that kind of power over her?

She wouldn't make that mistake again.

Athena opened her eyes, trying to push back confusion and fear and guilt, and walked quietly to the kitchen. Tuned in to every noise around her, she unloaded grocery bags and placed canned goods in a cabinet. Next door, two small children yelled at each other in Spanish, and their father bellowed for them to shut up. Or maybe he wasn't their father. Who knew, these days?

She placed a bag of spaghetti noodles next to the soup cans, then removed a jar of grapefruit juice. After stuffing the plastic bags under the sink, she turned to put the juice in the refrigerator and screamed as she dropped the jar.

He stood before her, looming over her, glaring.

Athena staggered back until she hit the counter.

He stepped forward, stopping less than an arm's length away.

"What . . ." she stammered, "how . . . the door . . ."

His lips curled into something resembling a grin as he held up her jar of juice, effortlessly snatched from the air as it fell. "I believe you dropped this."

Athena stared at the bottle, and then at the monster, her body shaking uncontrollably. She reached back to steady herself with the counter.

He turned and, as if he were simply a welcomed guest, opened her refrigerator, placed the juice inside, and closed it.

Her brain refused to move beyond panic as she watched him.

He turned to face her again, this time leaning against the opposite counter and folding his arms across his chest. He wore jeans, cowboy boots, and a dark blue shirt that would have made him even more attractive if she hadn't known what he was.

Dear God, she was about to die.

She had to get away.

Unable to do anything else, Athena turned and bolted for the door.

She stopped with a jerk like a dog at the end of a leash as he caught her by the arm.

"Oh, no, you don't."

He pulled her up to him, backed her to the wall, and leaned close, moving around her head as if he were sniffing her.

A deep, terrifying growl vibrated through the room.

"It took me a week to find you, *sweet thing*. You don't want to leave just yet."

His throaty voice, dripping with poisonous danger, made her shiver as she closed her eyes. Her heart pounded, her stomach knotted, and her knees buckled.

"Yeah," he whispered, nuzzling her hair, "that's better."

Still gripping her arm, he stroked her shoulder with his free hand, and she suddenly realized he might have something else in mind besides killing her.

"Please," she managed to croak, "don't."

"Don't what?" His voice vibrated directly in her ear.

"Don't . . . hurt me."

She opened her eyes as he pulled away and found him staring at her.

And then he laughed.

Athena's mouth went dry and she worked to swallow.

Cruel amusement sparkled in his eyes as he touched her face, following the line of her jaw with a deceivingly tender touch.

"Tell me, darlin', just what do you think would be a fair trade for attempting to end my existence? Your life? Your *virtue*?"

She tried to swallow again, but without success.

He suddenly spun her around to face the wall and held her, his arms around her waist, as he moved his mouth over the top of her shoulder.

In spite of her fear, the memory of Jake holding her in the back room of the Tunnel, bringing her to a wondrous climax with his expert touch, flooded her senses with a strange excitement. Athena reached out and pressed both hands against the wall. She tried to speak—to ask him again to stop—but nothing came out.

"Last time we did this," he whispered, "you came all over

my fingers. Remember?" His hand slid down the front of her shorts, covering her crotch as he nipped the skin on the side of her neck. "This time, we'll try something a little different."

Her body reacted to him as it had before by tightening and tingling from her neck to her knees. Her nipples puckered almost painfully, aching to be touched.

He dragged one strap of her sleeveless shirt from her shoulder with his teeth, then kissed the exposed skin with cool lips, tasting, licking.

Her body shook again, but this time not from fear. God, how could she crave the touch of this monster? She wanted his fingers against her skin, stroking her clit, teasing her cunt, not outside her jean shorts.

And then a strange tingle, almost a touch but not, started up the backs of her thighs, as if a dozen feathers moved across her skin.

A soft noise rose from Athena's throat and she fell forward against the wall.

"Yes," he said, his voice deeper, gravelly, "this time I won't ask."

As he kissed her shoulder, sucking on one spot, a wave of desire washed through her, leaving an aching emptiness between her legs. She wanted to beg him to fill her need. She remembered his hard penis in her hand, between her thighs. She knew the size of him and craved it; she pushed back into him.

His lips curved into a smile against her skin, but she didn't care.

Her body vibrated, needing more. The feathers moved up to her torso, teasing her skin, her tits. She groaned.

And then unexpected pain hit as he bit into her shoulder, and she cried out.

He growled, holding her close.

In a flash, the pain transformed into the strangest pleasure she'd ever known, and her body seemed to ignite—to burst into flames. An orgasm spread through her, starting deep in her womb with pounding spasms, but ending in waves of unimaginable bliss as they passed through every muscle and nerve. The world spun out of control, and the flames continued to consume her, to burn off existence, to erase her memory and her life.

On and on it went until she no longer felt tied to her body, but took up space without form, pulsing with joy and fulfillment.

Then the darkness came like an inky lake, starting at her toes and rising, swallowing her legs, and then her body, and then her head. Satisfied, she slipped into nothingness as vast as the universe.

Athena opened her eyes, but didn't move. She wasn't sure if she could. Her arms and legs felt like jelly.

Where the hell was she? The floor in front of the mat on which she lay, in a dimly lit room, was stone.

Not finding any points of actual pain, she eased up until she sat against a wall. When she drew her feet under her, something dragged along behind them.

Athena frowned at the leather cuffs around her ankles.

"What the—?"

The cuffs led to chains attached to a ring in a wall.

She pulled and pushed on the fleece-lined cuffs, but found them immovable with no sign of a buckle or knot, and puzzled over how they were attached. At least they were soft. She grabbed the chains and tugged on the ring, but it gave no hint of yielding.

Abandoning the effort for the moment, she looked around the empty room, slightly bigger than a jail cell, which seemed to be carved out of rock. A cot stood nearby, and five feet away was a toilet hidden behind an Oriental screen.

"All the comforts of home," she whispered.

Continuing her examination, she found a wooden chair clearly out of her range, and, just past it, a dark window.

No, a mirror.

Or maybe it was a one-way mirror, and someone stood on the other side watching her.

"Hey," she said, "who's there?"

Her voice echoed back.

"Where am I?"

Nothing.

"Hey!"

Still nothing.

Athena rested her head back against the wall and tried to remember anything about how she'd ended up in this prison.

The first thing she recalled was the vampire's sudden appearance, and then she remembered him holding her, and touching her, and then biting her. Her hand rose to the spot where his teeth had penetrated her skin and she touched two small bumps. They were tender, but didn't actually hurt. And then she fingered the small bruise on the inside of her right arm, in the center of which was a small red mark. A needle mark.

She swallowed hard.

As far as she could tell, he'd taken her blood, doped her up, and then kidnapped her. That must be what had happened. The vampire had imprisoned her.

Why hadn't he killed her?

And how could he have made her feel so incredible? The memory of the pleasure sent a wave of heat through her, and she shuddered. Certainly what he'd done to her was something no human could ever do. Or had it just been drugs playing tricks with her memory?

A knot of self-loathing burned in her stomach. Now she'd pay for not trying harder to escape when she had a chance.

* * *

Jake stood perfectly still, watching.

Athena's auburn braid lay across her shoulder and hung down in front of her right breast. He remembered the silky feel of her hair against his cheek and closed his eyes for a moment to enjoy it. He could still smell her scent on his skin.

After a week of tracking her, he'd meant to have his revenge. And he had, in a way—he'd felt her fear and tasted its citric flavor in her blood.

He'd meant to drain her, and he'd nearly done it, but at the last crucial moment he'd stopped.

Why?

He studied her. What was it about this one?

She sat still now, her head resting against the wall, her arms propped on her knees. The sleeveless top left her lovely shoulders bare and hugged her full breasts, and the neckline revealed a hint of cleavage. He knew the feel of her breasts in his hands, but wondered at the taste of them. Would they be as special as her scent? The jean shorts she wore were so short, they barely covered her sweet pubic mound, and Jake found himself staring. His body reacted to the memory of his fingers inside her.

He sighed, and walked from the small room, closing the door quietly behind him.

Now he had to decide what to do with her. Skidmore had called him a raving idiot when he'd carried Athena in and asked for her to be given a transfusion.

"We don't give them blood, dear boy. We take it. Remember?"

But he'd agreed, and Athena's life force had slowly returned. After three days, she'd finally regained consciousness.

Now what?

The fact that he couldn't decide angered him, and he felt his fangs lengthen in response.

"Jake?"

He spun around at the voice and smiled when he found Katie walking toward him. She wore a dusty khaki outfit suited for a safari and held a bullwhip coiled in her hand. He'd taught her how to use that bullwhip and sometimes wondered if that had been a wise move.

"Katie. I'm sure glad to see you."

She wrapped her arms around his shoulders and kissed him soundly, then slapped his chest. "Why? Were you worried about me?"

"Yeah." He grinned as he held her close.

She pushed out of his grip and frowned at him. "Sounds like I'm the one who had reason to worry."

Skidmore must have told her about his encounter with the wooden stake.

Jake shrugged.

Katie shook her head as she looped her arm through his. "Come, let's find our host. He said he had business down here somewhere. Then maybe we can *share* a snack."

They followed voices to the main part of the dungeon where they found Skidmore sitting in a wooden chair, involved with several of his contestants. Jake stopped just inside the door, unwilling to interrupt or get involved, and Katie released him to continue forward in order to stand beside Skidmore, her hand on his shoulder. But Jake found himself watching with interest.

A young woman, shapely and naked, sat on a low wooden stool with her legs spread wide for a fair-haired man on all fours in front of her, his face buried between her thighs. A fine sheen of sweat covered her body and her back arched as she grabbed a handful of her partner's hair.

Before she reached a climax, another man, darker, a little older and covered with tattoos, knelt behind the first male, grabbed his waist, and entered him with steady, hard strokes. Dark green drawings covered a torso of roping muscles, and his buttocks tightened into rocks with each stroke. The blond man grunted in response, his head up, his body tightened and shaking.

Once he adjusted, the blond returned his attention to the woman's needs, licking and sucking loudly, and the dark-haired man leaned forward to kiss her, his tongue visibly thrusting into her mouth as he held the back of her neck.

Jake felt his cock swell as he watched, wondering how long they could sustain the activities. He remembered the feel of restraint he'd tried to practice as a mortal, and the way it felt to roll over the precipice, unable to stop the flood.

The tattooed man's thrusts quickened and grew more brutal, and the woman began to grunt as she neared release. She suddenly fell back to the wall, her back arched in sweet agony, and the dark-haired man pumped his seed into the blond as the room filled with the noise and scent of sex.

Jake bit back a groan. Maybe he'd been at Skidmore's a little too long.

"Ah, bravo," Skidmore said, clapping his hands as he stood. "What a lovely way to start the night's activities." He motioned to one of his vampire underlings. "A new batch, please. I think I'd like to be more directly involved this time. Katie? I see you're prepared." He grinned as he eyed her whip.

Katie laughed. "This one would leave marks."

Skidmore's grin widened as he untied his robe and let it drop from his pale shoulders. "Might be fun."

"Next time, Thomas," Katie said, slapping the whip against her thigh. "I've got other plans right now." She motioned toward Jake.

Skidmore shrugged as he sat in one of the round upholstered chairs Jake had seen earlier. The blond man who'd just participated in the show knelt beside him, waiting for a command, and the other two were escorted back to the holding room.

The whole thing reminded Jake a little too much of slavery, although the mortals certainly seemed to be willing enough.

Katie winked at Jake as she passed him, headed for the door. "You want to stick around and watch?"

He shook his head. "No, I think I've seen enough for now."

She laughed. "You haven't seen anything yet. Come."

Jake followed her through passageways to a guest bedroom where Katie held the door. "I need to get freshened up, first, so please make yourself at home." She raised one eyebrow suggestively. "You can scrub my back if you want to."

He returned her smile. "You know I do."

Katie shed her dusty clothes without thought and led the way to a white-tiled bathroom with an oversized shower on one side and Jacuzzi tub on the other. Skidmore had certainly spared no expense when furnishing his palace. Of course, over the centuries he'd probably amassed quite a fortune. It wasn't that hard to do when you could influence the stock market with a thought.

"You probably want to get out of those," Katie said over her shoulder as she turned on the water. Steam billowed from the glass stall when she opened the door to step in.

Jake followed her, enjoying the heated water on his cool skin, and delighting at the sight of Katie under the shower's spray. Her body was as beautiful as ever—he'd long ago memorized every curve and dip. He stood, waiting for her to initiate contact.

And she did with her hand wrapped around his stiffening cock, nipping his chest. As she cupped his balls and squeezed, he sucked air between clenched teeth.

Katie laughed and released him. "I want you on your knees, Jake."

He knelt and she draped one leg over his shoulder. With warm water running over her breasts, down her belly, and around his mouth, Jake nipped at her thighs, and then licked long, slow laps across her cunt.

Katie moaned softly at his attention, cradling his head in her hand. "Nice," she whispered.

He focused his attention on her clit, circling the hardening nub with his tongue, and her leg tightened around his shoulders.

"Oh, yes."

Feeling his prick swell with desire, he continued to suck and lick her until Katie pulled his head away. She drew him up in front of her and kissed him, biting his bottom lip and demanding his tongue as she caressed his cock with strong fingers. He jerked in response to her movements, wishing she'd offer him more but knowing not to push.

After a few delightful moments, Katie shoved him away with a laugh. "Enough for now. I need to wash, and then we'll continue."

Jake soaped her back and front, then waited while she rinsed. They emerged from the shower holding hands, and Katie draped a towel across his shoulders. He wondered at her sly smile as they dried off.

"And now for the snack," she said, returning to her room.

Jake followed, surprised to find her soiled clothes removed from the floor and a dozen candles burning on the dresser, desk, and bookshelves.

In the middle of the large bed lay the dark-haired tattooed man who'd been center stage in the dungeon a little earlier. His wrists and ankles were tethered to the bedposts, which clearly made him uncomfortable, although Jake wasn't sure if it was the binding or the fact that he was naked and exposed that bothered him. The young man frowned at the two of them.

"This is Raul," Katie said. "Before becoming a hunter, he spent time in jail for rape."

Jake glanced at her and noted the fire in her eye, a dangerous sign.

"Katie—"

"Now, Jake, we're just going to have a little fun. You don't mind, do you, Raul?"

"Look, I don't—" Raul started to protest.

But Katie paid no attention. She crawled across the bed and gently gripped his flaccid prick in one hand, then licked big, wide circles on his muscular stomach, flicking her tongue across his dark tits. His cock responded in her hand, widening and hardening until it pointed to the ceiling.

"No," Raul whispered, "I don't mind at all."

Katie smiled at Jake.

He started to sit in a chair near the foot of the bed, but she shook her head. "No, over here."

Reluctantly, he walked to the other side of the bed and stretched out beside Raul, propped on one elbow. If nothing else, Katie's little game would probably take his mind off Athena.

7

Raul glanced at Jake, then focused his attention on Katie as she ran her fingernails up and down his torso, leaving red welts in their wake. The young man squirmed as she crossed his ribs and other sensitive spots, and his breath became more audible.

Then she reached into a bedside table drawer and withdrew a pink plastic phallus, which she held up. "This is one of the best inventions of the last century," she told Jake. She twisted the base, and the plastic prick began to hum and vibrate.

Jake watched her move the vibrating toy over her body, circling her breasts, pushing it against her nipples, then sliding it down her belly. She spread her thighs and ran the toy in circles around her cunt, and her eyes closed with pleasure. As she dipped the tip between her folds, Jake slid his hand down to his own swelling cock.

After a few deeper plunges into her cunt, Katie withdrew the glistening toy and moved it to Raul's body. She slid it up and down his torso, circled the base of his cock, and slipped around his balls. Raul groaned as his hips rose from the bed.

Katie then looped a leather thong around the young man's cock, and Raul raised his head. "What the hell's that?"

She grinned. "Oh, just something to increase our fun. Wouldn't you like to stay hard for hours?" And then she rolled the vibrating toy up the length of his cock.

"Oh, yeah," Raul said as his rod hardened to an impressive size, the skin sleek and taut as though it were about to burst. At that point, Katie tightened the thong.

Raul groan and strained against his tethers. "Oh, shit," he whispered. "That feels good."

Katie continued with the vibrator for awhile, alternating between her own body and Raul's. Jake felt the hunger begin, urging him closer. He listened to the human's heartbeat and watched the veins in his neck pulse softly under his dark, illustrated skin.

Katie stood over Raul then, the toy cast aside. She spread her legs, stroking herself with her fingers, and looked down at him. "Do you want this?"

Raul jerked at the restraints. "Untie me, lady, and I'll fuck your brains out."

Katie smiled as she crouched, her cunt just inches above Raul's straining cock. He raised up as far as he could, unable to reach, and grunted. "Prick-teasing bitch. Untie me and I'll show you how it's done. I'll fuck you until you beg me to stop."

Katie's smile grew into a satisfied grin. "The leopard's spots never change," she said.

Raul ignored her comment, intent on reaching her.

Katie held herself up with her hands on the man's chest, then lowered her wet cunt slowly down the length of his shaft.

Jake watched the cock disappear into Katie, knowing the wet, cool feel of her, stroking his own prick in time with his growing need.

Raul shook, his eyes closed, his mouth open, as she took him in.

Once sheathed, Katie rode back and forth greedily, rubbing her clit and rolling her hips.

Raul's hands reached for her breasts, straining to break the ropes that held him.

He grunted louder and louder, then began to groan. "Oh, fuck, my balls are going to explode. Get that fucking strap off."

Katie slapped his face then, hard enough to leave a red print on his cheek, and Raul glared up at her. "What the fuck—"

She slapped him again. "You don't talk until I tell you."

Muscles in Raul's body roped in anger then as he glared hatred at Katie. Digging her fingers into his massive pecs, she continued to ride.

Jake watched Raul, torn between anger, pleasure, and pain, and sympathized with the young man. He sat up and was about to leave the room when the door opened and Beatrice tiptoed in, as naked as she had been the last time Jake had seen her. Katie didn't seem to notice.

Beatrice walked over to where Jake sat and kissed him, leaving him momentarily surprised by the coolness of her lips. Then he realized how she'd survived. "Hey there, little mouse," he whispered.

She smiled at him and knelt on the floor, leaning across the bed, and turned her attention to Katie and Raul. Something akin to joy lit her eyes. Her small hand slid into Jake's crotch, and he moved his own to enjoy her attention. When she replaced her hand with her mouth, he groaned.

Beatrice's lively pink tongue ran circles around Jake's cock until he didn't think he could take another minute of the pleasure, and then she took him into her mouth all at once.

His hands curled into fists on the bed as his fangs pricked his lower lip. The hunger flared with renewed vigor.

He opened his eyes when she withdrew and found her looking at him, waiting. He knelt behind her and entered her tight cunt with careful thrusts as he dropped his forehead onto her back between her shoulder blades.

Beatrice seemed to purr as he fucked her, riding slow and easy, enjoying the feel and scent of her, his arms around her small waist.

"Are you ready?"

He looked up at Katie's question to find her sitting behind Raul's glistening, swollen cock, releasing the leather thong. The young man cried out as his seed erupted, spewing into the air a good two feet.

Katie capped off the eruption with her cunt and leaned forward, her fangs bared.

Unwilling to stop the chain of events, unable to stop the wave of pleasure as he rode his little mousy mate, Jake closed his eyes and was surprised when Beatrice suddenly tightened around him and came.

He pierced her flesh, enjoying his own release, tasting her pleasure and joy as it flooded his brain. He drew hard, knowing her thrill of revenge as she bit into Raul's arm, feeling her terror and pain wash away with Raul's blood, and he understood what another man had done to her long ago in a dark alley with a brutal assault. In ten minutes of eternal nightmare, the beast—not unlike Raul—had destroyed her life and soul.

And then he lost the thread as he withdrew from her flesh, and simply held her, his stilling cock sheathed. Her pleasure continued to pulse much longer than it should have, and Jake opened his eyes. Through his haze of pleasure, he saw the dark-haired tattooed felon's life draining away and felt no remorse.

The room finally quieted and Jake relished the remnant pleasure. He withdrew from Beatrice, who then crawled up to where Katie beckoned. With Raul a forgotten distraction, Katie stretched out on the bed, kissed Beatrice's forehead, and held her.

Jake struggled to his feet, fighting fatigue, pulled on his pants and shirt, and left the two women alone. He understood something about them that he hadn't necessarily wanted to know, but it strengthened his belief in fair play. Raul had experienced some of the horror he'd inflicted, but he'd probably enjoyed it a lot more than his victims had.

Although his hunger was sated, Jake couldn't stop his thoughts from turning to Athena. He didn't just want to take her, he wanted to hold her, sleep with her in his arms, bare his soul to her. He wanted to offer all of himself to her.

Those desires terrified him.

He slipped into the small viewing room and gazed through the one-way glass. She paced the length of her restraints, swinging her arms and lifting her feet high.

Then she stopped and stared at the mirror, and Jake wondered for a moment if she saw him.

"Is anyone in there?"

He balled his hands into fists at his sides to keep from answering.

"Look, just tell me what you want. You can't keep me like this forever." Her voice faltered on the last word, then she turned and faced the wall. Pressing her palms against the rock, she stretched as if she were trying to move the world.

Athena sat cross-legged on the mat, wishing for something to do. A pale woman had brought her food that hadn't been half-bad. Or maybe she'd been too hungry to judge fairly. She'd tried to get the woman to talk to her, to tell her where she was, but she hadn't said a word. An hour later, the woman had returned in silence to retrieve the tray.

That left Athena wondering if there were more vampires around. She didn't know for sure about this woman, one way or the other. How did one tell from a distance? She hadn't believed Chris when he'd told her about Jake, but, amazingly, he'd been right.

How could she have been stupid enough to let her guard down?

How long had she been in this place? A day? Two? Surely someone would be looking for her by now. She should have been at work. Her boss must have called the police.

Athena sighed. Who was she kidding? Her weasel of a boss would be thrilled that she didn't show up and simply hire one of his bimbos to fill in behind her, someone he could screw in the storeroom at night. It didn't take a master's degree to deliver hamburgers and French fries.

Who else would miss her? Chris should be worried. He'd gotten out of the hospital two days before she'd been abducted, and she'd spent most of those two days at his place cooking and cleaning. He hadn't asked her to spend the night, but she'd guessed he was still recovering. Actually, though, he'd acted almost mad at her. Had he realized how ready she'd been to give herself to Jake? Was he pissed at her because she hadn't been able to stop the attack?

If Chris abandoned her, she had no one else to count on.

The realization brought tears of self-pity to her eyes, and she let them roll unchecked down her cheeks.

The door to her cell suddenly screeched on its hinges, and Athena straightened and wiped her face, hoping for more food. In spite of the generous portions she'd consumed, hunger still knotted her insides.

When Jake stepped in, her heart jumped into her throat.

He stared at her for a few long moments, his expression

dark, then he crossed to the chair and sat. Leaning forward, he rested his elbows on his knees and clasped his hands together.

She waited, barely able to breathe, until it was obvious he didn't plan to start a conversation.

"Now what?" She flinched when her voice squeaked.

He shrugged. "I don't know. Why were you hunting me?"

"I wasn't. My—"

She started to say *boyfriend,* but realized the inaccuracy of the word.

"—friend was."

"Why?"

She shook her head, dropping her gaze momentarily to the floor. "I don't know. Maybe because you're a bloodsucking monster? Because you kill people?"

He straightened and frowned at her. "I don't go around killing people."

"You tried to murder Chris."

"*Tried* to?"

Athena clamped her mouth shut when she realized he thought he had succeeded in killing Chris.

Jake raked his fingers through his hair and glanced around the small room. "Well, I'm glad he didn't die. Maybe next time we'll have a chance at a fair fight."

"*Fair?* How could a fight with you be fair?"

He ignored her question, rose, and paced back and forth across the room. He may be a monster, but he moved like a human. If she hadn't seen his transformation with her own eyes, she still wouldn't believe he was a vampire. He seemed to be trying to make some kind of decision.

"What now?"

"I don't know," he muttered. "I can't just let you go."

"Why not?"

"You know about us now." He shot a glare her way, but continued to pace. "Besides, I don't want to."

He practically whispered the last sentence, and Athena wondered if she'd heard correctly. "You don't *want* to? And that gives you the right to hold me prisoner?"

He stopped and looked at her, a strange smile suddenly playing at the corners of his mouth. "As you've so correctly pointed out, sweet thing, I'm not part of your world. I can do whatever I want with you. And to you."

Athena swallowed hard and scrambled to her feet. If he planned to attack her, she wouldn't take it sitting down. Of course, she already knew his strength. She didn't have a prayer.

"What do you want from me?"

He shook his head and laughed, and turned toward the door. "You wouldn't believe me if I told you."

"Try me."

Jake stopped at the door and looked back at her. "I want you to want me."

Athena sucked in a breath of surprise and watched him leave the room.

"What?" she whispered.

Trying to avoid the torture, Jake decided not to visit Athena again that night, or the next. He wandered in the desert around Skidmore's instead, watching stars twinkle as they traversed the sky, listening to the howl of coyotes. He thought back to the old days when he'd lived in a saddle with only his wits and a six-shooter, and longed for the challenge.

Sitting on a boulder in the narrowest part of the canyon with a night wind caressing his skin and soft sounds echoing off rock walls, he returned to his mortal days. He remembered a night outside Abilene, on the way to deliver cattle to the rail yard. One of the boys showed up at camp with whiskey and women, and he'd spent a wild night screwing a large, rounded blond woman, Millie. They'd shared a pint of cheap whiskey, then she'd stretched out on the ground on her belly, using his bedroll to prop up her creamy white ass, and he'd fucked her without restraint. Millie had been an enthusiastic partner, letting out a whoop and holler when she came the first time that started a stampede, but he hadn't cared. They'd both come at least three times that night before collapsing onto the west Texas ground. The next day, he'd ended up raw where his saddle rubbed sand into his legs as he rounded up scattered cattle. The younger boys had teased him for days.

He smiled at the memory.

But even escaping to the past didn't work. He couldn't stop thinking about Athena. She'd gotten under his skin, and he craved her scent and taste in a way that nearly drove him mad. When he came in just before sunrise the second day, Katie waited at his bedroom door with a fist on her hip, wearing a dark red silk robe.

"I was starting to wonder if you'd decided to end it all," she said.

Jake huffed a laugh. He couldn't even consider that option at the moment; Athena had instilled in him a desire to survive. Ironic indeed, as Skidmore would say, since he wanted nothing more than to drain away her life.

"Come, Jake, darling," Katie said, snaking her arm through his. "I have a treat for you."

Jake pulled his arm away. "No thanks. I'm not up to it."

Her eyes flashed gold streaks of anger and she frowned. "No *thanks*?" Her upper lip curled. "It wasn't a request."

Sighing, Jake gave in. It wasn't that he feared Katie, but he knew that crossing her could mean a decade or two without her. And for whatever reason, he enjoyed seeing her regularly. The sex was always great, but he enjoyed the companionship most.

When he offered his hand, Katie took it, her eyes returning

to their natural color. She led him down the hall to her own room.

He wasn't surprised to find a new victim tied to Katie's bed, but as soon as he stepped close enough to see who the victim was, he froze.

Athena lay sprawled across the bed, naked, her wrists and ankles bound.

Jake turned to Katie, gripping her hand tightly. "What the hell's going on here?"

"Just a little late-night snack. Thomas says she's up for grabs, since you seem to have abandoned her. I thought you might want to—"

"No!" Rage swelled in Jake's chest, and he pushed Katie toward the wall, then rushed to the bed.

Athena looked up at him, her green eyes filled with fear and tears. She shivered and bit back sobs.

He pressed his hand to her cheek. "It's okay," he whispered. "You're safe now."

Jake suddenly flew backward as Katie grabbed the back of his collar and flung him to the floor. "How dare you push me?"

He jumped to his feet, but stopped when he found Katie sitting beside Athena, her hand on the woman's throat. With just a squeeze, she could kill the mortal in a flash, and he wouldn't be able to stop her.

The vampire rose in Jake now, ready to fight to the death, ready to kill, but he struggled to hold it back. He knew his eyes flashed gold, and his lip curled up to reveal his fangs.

Athena stared with wide eyes, tears still streaking her precious cheeks.

Katie glared. Anger flashed in her eyes for a long, terrifying moment, then subsided. "Well, now, Jake, I don't know that I've ever seen you like this before. It's not a side of you I much care for." Her fingers flattened and her hand moved down the middle of Athena's chest, as if she were comforting a small child. "I'll probably regret this, but if you want her so much, she's yours." Katie smiled down at Athena. "Beware, my dear. Men can break your heart. Even immortal men. Don't ever give them the upper hand."

Katie rose and walked to the bedroom door.

Jake took her place, quickly untying Athena's wrists and ankles. He gathered her into his arms and she clung to his neck as he carried her from the room.

In the dark hallway, her soft sobs echoed off the walls and broke Jake's cold, dead heart. He nuzzled the top of her head and tried his best to comfort her.

With great tenderness, he placed her in his bed, pulled the cover over her, and sat beside her, stroking her hair back from her forehead. "I'm sorry, sweet thing," he whispered. "I shouldn't have brought you here."

Athena studied his eyes as he looked down at her, and her sobs stopped. She swiped at the tears with the back of one hand.

He leaned forward and kissed her forehead, trying not to inhale her scent too deeply. It didn't matter; just touching her aroused him.

Then he rose. "You'll be safe in my room. I promise, no one will touch you."

Athena grabbed his hand. "Don't leave me here."

He covered her hand with his, sliding his fingers over hers.

Wondering if he could control himself near her, Jake sighed, pushed off his boots, and crawled into bed beside her, stifling a yawn brought on by the rising sun.

Athena turned on her side, and Jake wrapped his arm around her, drawing her head to his shoulder. Her sweet, warm breath caressed his neck, sending a shiver down his spine. "I just hope you're safe from me," he whispered.

After a long time, she quit shivering and cautiously draped her arm across his chest.

Trying not to think of Iris, Jake closed his eyes and gave in to sleep, wondering if he'd dream of Athena with her so close.

He also wondered if she'd still be in his arms when he woke.

8

Athena opened her eyes and waited for them to adjust to the near darkness, then struggled to roll over under the weight of Jake's arm. She stared at his face, so lifeless that he could be dead, and then realized that technically he was. Wasn't he?

One blue eye snapped open and he stared at her. "Why are you awake?"

"I'm hungry."

Both eyes opened and he smiled. "So am I, sweet thing."

She gulped at the implication of his words. "Yeah, but I don't want to *be* breakfast."

"Dinner," he corrected.

Athena glanced around, looking for anything resembling a clock. "How do you know?"

He smiled again and shrugged with one shoulder. "I just do. I can feel it."

His hand slid down her body, and she enjoyed his touch in spite of herself, even through the satin sheet.

"You saved me last night," she said.

Jake propped himself up on one elbow. "I can't imagine

Katie hurting you. She generally likes women." He drew his hand up to brush the backs of his fingers across her cheek. "And you wouldn't have been in danger if I hadn't brought you here."

"Why did you?"

Jake stared at her for a moment, then sat up, turning his back to her.

Athena wanted to reach out and touch his broad shoulders, run her fingers through his hair. She wanted to tell him what effect his actions had had on her the night before, when he'd rescued her. No one had ever done anything like that for her before. And she knew he'd snatched her from the edge of death, no matter what he said.

But she couldn't tell him. He was a *vampire*. How could she care about a vampire? And how could a vampire care about her? It didn't make sense.

Jake rose, pulling on his boots. "I'll see what I can find. Skidmore usually keeps food around for his guests."

Athena watched him cross the room in long, easy strides. He glanced back from the door with an unreadable expression, flipped a light switch, and then ducked out, closing the door behind him. The room took on a soft purplish glow with light emanating from hidden bulbs near the ceiling.

She sat up in bed, studying Jake's room. Did he live here? It didn't sound like he did. Interesting paintings covered the walls, and a nearby bookshelf held volumes that drew her attention. She crawled out of bed and tiptoed across the cool floor to get a better look.

Athena ran her fingers over the books' spines, surprised to find leather and other unidentifiable materials. They were old, maybe first editions, probably valuable. She pulled several partway out to see the front covers. Most had nothing written on them, but those that did had titles in gold.

She glanced around. What other treasures did this place hold?

Before she could snoop enough to answer her question, she heard footsteps approaching the door and dove back into the bed, covering herself.

Jake walked in with a tray, placed it on the bed beside her, and removed a tall, dark glass that he obviously meant for himself. She tried not to think about what the glass must hold.

Letting the sheet fall to her waist, she pulled the tray close and examined its contents, surprised to find slices of beef, cheese, and bread, surrounded by fresh strawberries and cherries. There was even a glass of cold milk. "Wow. This looks good."

Jake nodded as he watched her, studying her hands and face, and then every inch of her exposed flesh. It didn't take long for his gaze to unnerve her.

Athena swallowed. "You're staring."

He chuckled quietly. "I'm afraid you're just a little too tempting." Sipping from his glass, he turned so that he faced the wall to her left.

Athena wolfed down the food. Why was she so hungry? She still felt like she hadn't eaten in a week.

By the time she reached the bottom of the plate, however, her hunger had subsided. Draining the glass of milk, she studied her captor's profile.

He really was good-looking, in a rugged sort of way. She'd expect him to be pale, since he was a vampire, but he wasn't pale.

"How old are you?" She wiped her mouth with the cloth napkin and dropped it onto the tray.

Jake turned to study her, his blue eyes darkened by a frown. "Why do you want to know?"

She shrugged. "Just curious."

Her heart skipped a beat when he suddenly appeared right

in front of her, his face inches from her own. "Curiosity isn't necessarily a good thing," he said, his voice a dangerous whisper.

Athena leaned back and hit the rock wall with her head, unable to escape. "Fine." She gulped. "I get the message."

For a long moment he stayed perfectly still, staring into her eyes, then he backed off, returning to where he'd previously sat.

What had she been thinking? Did she really think she could strike up a friendship with this monster? This inhuman *thing*? He wasn't like her, and she had to remember that she couldn't trust him, no matter what he'd done the night before. He was, after all, the one who had imprisoned her.

"May I at least have some clothes?" The steadiness of her own voice surprised her, under the circumstances.

Jake motioned toward a door with a nod. "There's a robe in the bathroom. You can wear it while I look around for something else."

Athena crawled across the bed and hurried toward the indicated door, closing it behind her and collapsing against it. What the hell was she going to do now?

Her entire body jumped at the loud crash from the next room. She waited, holding her breath, but heard no other sound. After a few minutes, she pulled the silk robe from a hook on the wall, slipped it on and tied it around her waist, then opened the door enough to peek out.

The room seemed to be empty.

On tiptoes, she ventured out and looked around, discovering the source of the noise. The glass from which Jake had been drinking lay in pieces, shattered against a wall now marred by a dark red stain.

Jake stood just outside the cavern opening, staring up at the brightest stars, waiting for his senses to clear. A cool night breeze blew across his face and through his hair, and he filled his lungs, instinctively sorting out the scents. Sagebrush, dust, rabbit, coyote, distant car exhaust, campfire smoke.

But no matter how many scents he inhaled, he couldn't get rid of hers. It wrapped around him like a mummy's bandages, choking off his will and self-control. If he'd stayed in the same room with her another minute, he would have drained her.

And she had no idea.

"Damn you, Athena."

Which was exactly what he wanted to do. But how could he?

Mostly, he tried not to think about what might happen when he left the face of the earth. As a lawman, he hadn't thought much about God, or the Devil, or questioned what was out there, if anything. He'd assumed that his short life was it.

Unfortunately, he didn't completely believe that anymore. He'd seen things and felt things when he died that just about convinced him there was more. He'd probably pay for his mistakes some day.

And he'd made a lot of mistakes over the course of a century and a half.

"Damn."

Footsteps on rock and gravel drew his attention from the heavens and he watched Katie approach. She wore pants and a high-collared cream-colored blouse that made her look even more enchanting than usual. Her eyes glistened in the starlight as she smiled.

"I've decided to forgive you." She circled him, trailing one hand up his arm and across his shoulders.

"Thank you."

"Did you have fun with your little morsel?"

Anger flared in him unexpectedly, but he fought it back.

When he didn't answer, Katie moved around to stand in front of him, studying his eyes. He knew he couldn't hide the truth from her.

"*Jake*. You haven't gone soft on her, have you?"

In spite of her annoying attitude, Katie's concern for him was real and Jake smiled. "Probably."

She ran her hands up his chest until she gripped his shoulders. "My poor dear," she whispered, standing on her toes to kiss his cheek and then his mouth.

He welcomed her kiss, enjoyed it, and drew her into his arms, but he thought about Athena.

Katie withdrew from him and stepped back, her palms spread on his chest. "Your heart just isn't in this, is it?"

Jake frowned, wishing for once that she didn't know him so well.

"Do you plan to introduce her to the Night?"

He raised his gaze back to the night sky. "I can't."

"*Can't?*"

"I tried once before and it didn't work. I won't risk it again."

Katie took another step away from him. "I won't help you."

"I wouldn't ask you to." He considered what it would be like to have Athena linked to Katie by blood. Definitely not a good idea.

She started back toward the underground castle, but stopped just before she stepped through the dark entrance. "You could ask Thomas to help. He's had a lot of practice."

Jake nodded, and Katie disappeared.

True, he could ask Skidmore for help. He'd brought many people into the Darkness, and they didn't seem to have trouble breaking the bond.

But could he doom Athena to walk the night as he did, especially if it meant spending eternity in hell, or something like it?

Furthermore, would he still love her without her spark of life? Maybe that's what drew him to her in the first place.

"Ask her, Jake." Katie's voice floated over the evening breeze like a thought.

Maybe Katie was right; maybe the time had arrived for a little honesty.

Jake filled his lungs one more time, and then strode back through the front door.

He made his way deliberately down the main passageway to his room, walked in, and closed the door firmly behind him.

Startled, Athena huddled back against the pillows, staring at him. She wore the green silk robe and held a book she'd taken from the shelf. He couldn't see the title as she placed it at her side.

The green robe looked fantastic on her, and he realized she'd showered and rebraided her hair. Her scent, sweetened with herbal soap and shampoo, permeated the room, causing him to lose track of his mission for the moment.

Athena glanced around and zeroed in on his face with her gorgeous green eyes. "How long are you going to keep me here?"

Jake took a deep breath and shrugged. "That's what I want to talk to you about."

The fear faded from her eyes, and he regretted his earlier behavior. Raking his fingers through his hair, Jake walked to the bed and sat, studying the floor.

"Athena, I want to offer you a gift, but one I'm not sure you want. Not sure you should want it, even."

"What kind of gift?"

He looked at her, waiting to gauge her reaction. "I want to offer you eternal life. Or something close to it."

Her eyes widened again, but not with fear this time.

"You asked me earlier how old I am. How old do I look?"

She swallowed hard and shrugged. "I don't know, somewhere between thirty and forty?"

"I was thirty-five when I came into the Darkness. I was born in 1845."

Her eyes widened even more. "*1845?*"

He nodded.

Athena closed her eyes and shook her head as if to clear her thoughts. She crawled across the bed and stood, then walked a circle in the room, rubbing her forehead. "You were born a hundred and sixty years ago?"

"More or less."

"Holy shit." She stopped and frowned at him. "And you want to make me a *vampire*?"

He winced at the way she said the word. "I want to make you my mate."

"Your *mate*?" She started in a circle again. "What? Like, 'til death do us part? But that wouldn't work. You're already dead, right?"

Jake crossed the room to block her path, and held her arms.

She looked up at him.

"Listen to me, Athena. Your scent intoxicates me. It's as if you were made just for me. I want you with me always, by my side, in my bed. I'm not talking marriage here, but something far beyond it. I'll protect you forever, give you whatever you want.

"But there is a price. You have to abandon your life and everyone you know and love. And you risk damnation, if there is such a thing. You also give up the sunlight, and that's much harder than you can imagine. Believe me."

Releasing her, he sighed and moved across the room to put some distance between them.

"I won't force this on you. You have to make the decision. If you ask me to make you what I am, I will. If you don't, I'll take you home and you'll never see me again."

He raked his hair back one more time, trying to decide if he'd made his offer sound tempting or like a nightmare.

"You have three nights to decide."

Then he walked back to her and touched her warm cheek. "One thing I will promise you is sex like you can't even imagine."

The blood rose in her cheeks then, and Jake felt his fangs drop.

He leaned forward and kissed her forehead. Then he hurried from the room before he changed his mind about letting her choose.

Athena spent three of the strangest days she could ever have imagined.

No, that's not true. A mere month ago, she could never have even imagined such a situation.

All the things that had seemed important to her—paying bills, getting a better job, finding the right guy, buying a car, wondering if she'd ever have kids—faded away like pages of an old newspaper, no longer important enough to read. Now she considered whether or not she wanted to live forever.

The crazy part was the idea of making such a decision. If she were watching this happen to someone else, she'd think, who wouldn't want to live forever? But faced with the reality, it was much more than that.

First, there was the question of how long forever would be. Jake had mentioned damnation. She'd never really had strong religious beliefs, but if there was something else, what then? Of all the things she'd ever done, none of them had been *that* bad, certainly not bad enough for eternal punishment. This, however, might be.

And then there was Jake. She hadn't figured him out. Of course, she had no frame of reference. He was a vampire—one who fed off human blood, was capable of unbelievable feats of strength and speed—yet he'd held her with tenderness the night she'd slept in his bed. He wanted her as his mate.

A quiver slipped up her spine at the memory of his promise of unimaginable pleasure. Was it true? Would sex with him be unlike anything she'd experienced before? The times he'd touched her had certainly been unbelievable. But sex had never really held all that much interest for her.

Was she ready to give up her mortal world? What exactly would she be leaving behind besides a crappy job and a tiny apartment? There was Chris; he'd miss her, wouldn't he? What would he do when he got out of the hospital and found her gone?

Athena straightened at sounds issuing from the hallway. In two nights, she hadn't wandered far from Jake's room, and he hadn't returned. Trays of food had been left for her and removed, and she had managed to locate a kitchen and an empty sitting room. Always, she felt as if someone were watching her, but she never saw signs of anyone.

"Come, my dear. We'll hunt together tonight."

The woman's voice sounded familiar, but Athena couldn't be sure. She pulled the door open just enough to peek out and saw the backs of two women disappearing around a corner. Closing the door quietly, she followed.

At the entrance to the sitting room, she stopped, caught in the gaze of the two women. One was the woman Jake had fought with—Katie?—and the other was much smaller and looked to be about her own age.

Katie glared at her for a moment, and then motioned her forward. "Don't worry, we won't touch a hair on your precious head." This statement held more than a hint of bitterness, but Athena bit back her fear and stepped forward.

"I . . . was just looking for Jake."

"Were you now?" The larger vampire grinned, revealing a set of fangs that caused Athena's heart to thump, and stroked the smaller woman's hair. "I'm sure he's around here somewhere, although he has kept to himself the past few nights. I believe that's your fault."

In a move similar to one Jake had made several nights earlier, Katie suddenly appeared in front of her with her face inches from Athena's. "Beware what you wish for. Once you're brought into the Darkness, there's no going back. And then you're fair game."

Athena gulped, but stood her ground, fairly sure she was truly safe from attack. She wanted to ask what was meant by *fair game*, but couldn't find her voice.

After a long moment, Katie strolled back to her companion and draped an arm across the woman's shoulders, and the two of them left.

Athena pushed her hair back from her face as she hurried to the kitchen where she filled a glass with water and drank it. Wondering how much longer she had to make up her mind, she returned to the sitting room, sank into a plush sofa with a sigh, glanced up, and jumped.

"She's right, you know. There's no going back."

Jake sat in a chair facing the cold, dark fireplace, his long legs stretched out in front of him and his fingers steepled under his chin.

"Where . . . how long have you been sitting there?"

"I came in while you were talking to Katie." He gathered his legs under him, rose, and stood by the fireplace.

Studying him in profile, she was struck again by his good looks. The strength of his features hinted at something from a distant past—something masculine and wild. And the way he stood perfectly still made her think of a wildcat stalking its prey.

She gulped as she realized she was that prey.

"What she said about being fair game . . . what did she mean?"

He turned to face her then, taking her in with a slow, steady gaze. "Once you're one of us, you'll be fair game for the hunters." He strolled across the room and sat beside her, turning to face her. He eased a strand of hair behind her ear and stroked the side of her face with a soft, tender touch. "But you, sweet thing, won't have to worry. I'll be at your side."

Athena met his gaze and her body shook. Sitting beside Jake was a little like sticking her head in a lion's mouth, yet she wasn't as afraid as she was sure she should have been. What if he changed his mind about letting her choose?

He sat back, letting his hand fall to his thigh, and frowned at her as if she'd just insulted him. Could he read her mind? That possibility hadn't occurred to her.

He rose and returned to the fireplace. "I feel your doubts," he said, answering her unspoken question. "You have to be certain about this, my dear. I won't ask twice."

Jake glanced at her. "You have one more hour."

And then he was gone, as if into thin air.

Jake stood in the darkness, letting calm wash over him. Athena's effect seemed to get stronger the longer he waited. If he'd sat beside her for one more minute, she would have lost her chance to choose, and her life, most likely.

"Jake."

The purr of his name accompanied the low, pleasant vibration that usually accompanied Katie's appearance. He stood with his eyes closed, enjoying the feel of her fingers sliding across his shoulders.

"Don't you think you're carrying this just a little too far? If you want her, take her."

Her words stirred the beast, and his fangs ached in response. He needed to taste Athena, to make her his own, to feel his joy filtered through hers, to draw her life from her precious neck. A shiver ran through him.

But not without permission.

"No," he whispered, opening his eyes. "I can't—"

Katie was gone.

He inhaled, but found only a lingering hint of her scent.

A mere hour—nothing in the expanse of his existence—and he'd have his answer, one way or the other. And if she said yes?

Jake hurried back through the entry into Skidmore's castle. He had one more thing to do in order to prepare.

9

Jake stood before the doorway to his room, his hands flattened against the cool wood, his eyes closed. He listened to her strong, steady heartbeat through the door. Would she say yes or no?

If she said no, would he be able to keep his promise? He honestly didn't know.

With his resolve as firmly in place as it could be, and the beast reined in, he opened the door and stepped inside.

Athena sat on the edge of the bed, gripping her jean-clad thighs, her green eyes wide as she studied him.

Jake crossed the room to stand in front of her and extended his hand, palm up. "This is it, my dear. Take my hand and join me in eternal life."

She stared at his hand, looked up into his eyes, then stared at his hand again. Just as he was about to abandon all hope, she reached up and slipped her hand into his.

Smiling at the overwhelming sense of joy, Jake drew her into his arms and took her sweet mouth, opening it with his own, tasting her fear and excitement, enveloping her shaking body. Her magic scent floated into his head, promising secrets and wonders, and he dove deeper into kissing her as she surrendered to him.

His own excitement grew by leaps and bounds, but he wrestled it back in order to maintain the control he'd need tonight. Tearing his mouth from hers, he kissed the side of her neck, tasting her smooth, silky skin. He wanted her like he'd wanted no other. Not even Iris could have quelled his pleasure or his hunger this time.

"Will it hurt?" she asked, her voice a husky whisper.

"Yes." He slid one hand down her back as he dragged his lips across her skin.

She whimpered.

He released her, drew her shirt off over her head, and tossed it to the floor. She didn't resist.

Lowering his mouth to her luscious breasts, he licked and teased her tender, hardening nipples as he unbuttoned her pants and pushed them and her panties to her knees and she stepped out of the last of her clothes. Anxious to feel her flesh against his, Jake took no longer than necessary to peel away his own clothing. Then he wrapped his arms around Athena and lifted her from the ground, suckling her full breasts. She kneaded his shoulders as she wrapped her legs around his waist.

Her heat seared his skin. Jake growled at the sudden intense longing clawing at his flesh. Desperate for her mouth, he lowered her down the front of his body until her hot cunt rested precariously close to his cock, and he kissed her again and ran his hands over her warm flesh. Then he eased her down onto the bed and rested between her creamy thighs, glowing in the white-hot desire to mount her.

He kissed her face and neck, drawn to the gentle pulse of blood pumping just below her pale skin.

Athena rolled her head to the side, baring herself to him, surrendering.

Jake growled, fighting temptation, and raised himself up to

his elbows. He turned her head until her green-eyed gaze met his.

"Not yet, sweet thing."

Her eyes widened as she stared first into his eyes, undoubtedly golden by now, and then at his fangs.

"You see only the outward signs of the vampire. There is much more. There is strength, unmatched by any other creature, and abilities you can't imagine. But for everything good, there is a price."

"What . . . price?"

"The vampire's hunger is one. You'll learn to control it, but it takes time. And tonight," he said, nuzzling her neck again, "will be my test."

She shuddered under him as he kissed her shoulder.

Focusing on her outward taste in order to resist the final bite, Jake moved his mouth down the front of Athena's body, one nip at a time. She squirmed under him and groaned softly as he licked circles around the sensitive spots—her breasts, the base of her ribs, her navel. He flipped the little belly-button ring with his tongue. Continuing down, he brushed his face across the soft hair of her pubic mound, and licked a line down the front of one trembling thigh. In spite of her willingness to offer her neck, she pressed her legs together as much as possible with him between them.

"Spread those thighs for me, sweet thing."

He felt the tension against his ribs ease.

"Yes, that's it. A little more."

She opened herself to him, spreading her legs, and he followed the inside of her thigh slowly, savoring her scent, the hunger grabbing him by the balls and throat.

He gave her a long, soft, slow lick, running his tongue from bottom to top of her cunt, and she sucked in a stuttered breath as her hips rose to follow him. He licked her again, and again. And then he narrowed his attention to the little nub reaching out for him, and pushed it in circles with the tip of his tongue, then flicked it back and forth.

"Oh, God . . . what . . . yes."

Her juices flowed and he drank, needing every bit of her as if he were dying of thirst. Then he sucked on her swelling clit.

"Oh . . . oh!"

She neared the precipice—he smelled her excitement as her buttocks quivered in his palms. He turned his head and pricked the tender flesh of her inner thigh with one fang.

She jumped.

He nearly swooned when he smelled her blood. Perfection . . . yes, and promise. He pressed his tongue to the tiny wound and groaned as the small drop of her essence floated through him like a dream, caught in an eternal ocean of longing.

Knowing the extent of her arousal nearly drove him to spill his seed, but he needed more than just a drop. Denying himself another appetizer, he turned his attention back to her mortal needs and drew her into an excruciatingly slow, powerful orgasm. She cried out as she came, her cunt pulsing around his tongue and filling his mouth. He held her tightly to him to enjoy every last wonderful spasm.

When she relaxed, he released her to crawl back up the length of her body, licking and nipping again as he enjoyed her heated flesh seasoned with a hint of salt and sex. Lying on top of her and resting on his elbows, he kissed her lips and brushed her hair back from her face. Her eyes glistened with fresh satisfaction.

"That was—"

"A warm-up," he said. "A taste."

"But I've never—"

He stopped her with a kiss to her lips. "That was nothing, my sweet, compared to what this night holds. And many more after."

Flirting with disaster, he pressed the head of his cock to her heated folds.

Her fingers ran up and down his back, causing him to shudder, and she locked her feet around his legs, drawing him in.

Kissing her, he eased into her wet cunt, just enough to know what awaited him. Hot, tight, welcoming. Jake dropped his forehead to hers.

"Made for me," he whispered.

She raised her hips and he pushed, sheathing himself, unable to stop. Her gasped breath felt like feathers against his skin, and he closed his eyes to concentrate, starting the Touch at her ankles and drawing it up slowly, savoring each sensation, then adding more from her shoulders, moving between their pressed flesh, covering every bit of her.

She panted and let out small cries of pleasure, and her body writhed beneath him.

Someone entered the room—Skidmore, no doubt—but Jake tuned him out and continued, intensifying the Touch as it consumed her, circling her cunt, dipping and sliding.

"Oh, my God, it's too much. Oh."

He held his mouth near her ear. "Come for me, my love. Surrender yourself."

Her fingers dug into his back as she began to thrust up with release, and he pushed deeper, savoring each biting ripple of her cunt. His fangs ached as the hunger grew, tearing at him, twisting his limbs. He let the Touch fade.

"Yes, dear boy, she's ready. Shall I—"

"No!" Jake glared at Skidmore.

The older vampire raised both hands and backed away. "Fine, fine. I'm here if you need me."

No longer able to consider letting Skidmore taste Athena's blood, he hoped like hell he could figure out how to stop at the right point. He had to bring her to the point of dying without losing the spark of life, then offer himself to carry her back.

With his swollen cock still buried inside her, he wrapped his arms around her and pressed his face into the crook of her neck, tasting her skin, listening to the beat of her heart—still strong, still singing to him.

"Give yourself to me, Athena. Surrender your life," he growled.

She trembled under him and clutched his shoulders as she turned her head.

Desire hummed through him, washing away all thought until nothing remained but animal need.

He sank his fangs into her neck.

She screamed and struggled to push him away.

Her nectar filled his mouth, and then exploded in his brain like a charge of TNT. He took her as man and beast, excruciating pleasure coursing through every fiber of his body, every nerve firing at once.

Suddenly, he knew her, all of her, every emotion. Her life sliced through him, shredding his senses, splaying open his heart to her pains and pleasures, joys and fears, dreams and dashed hopes, everything. Her innocence, her wonder, her unfulfilled needs, her hopeless search for love, embarrassed by desire, by lust. Wanting pleasure, afraid to ask. Memories, terror, bliss.

Too much, too fast, too deep, yet he needed more. He needed to be deeper, filled with her, a part of her. Sweet Athena.

"Now. Stop!"

He struggled against the hands that pulled him from her until a hint of sense returned. Gasping, he raised his mouth from her neck and struggled to focus on the face to his right.

Skidmore frowned. "You must stop, or you will take too much." His pale blue eyes moved from Jake to Athena. "Release her now, or you will simply pull her into hell, dear boy."

Whimpering at the physical and mental pain, Jake backed

off from Athena, terrified by her pale, lifeless appearance. "I killed her."

Skidmore leaned close, stroking her hair. "No, not quite." Then he rose. "If you are to finish it, it must be now." He turned to Jake. "Remember what I told you. You are there to bring her back. If you lose track of what you're doing, you will both die." His hand rested on Jake's bare shoulder. "No matter what you believe, dear boy, if you don't come back, you won't be going with her anywhere. Do you understand?"

Jake nodded.

"Good." Skidmore straightened, produced a jeweled, gold knife, and handed it to Jake.

He pushed the point of the blade into the flesh of his chest and pulled it downward an inch, then handed it back to the older vampire. As he stretched out beside Athena and drew her mouth to the wound, he heard Skidmore withdraw and wondered if he'd left the room completely.

But the question didn't last long.

Following instructions Skidmore had given him just an hour earlier, he released his hold on the present and Earth itself. Fighting powerful fear churning deep in his gut, he closed his eyes and drifted into emptiness, sliding closer to death than he had in more than a century.

Athena stretched her arms over her head and smiled, enjoying cool grass against her heated skin. Above her, the sun shone without even a whisper of a cloud to dim its warmth. She turned her head to find a clear-water creek gurgling its way over rocks just an arm's length away.

She sat up, a little surprised at being naked, and quickly glanced around, but saw no one. Where was she? And how had she gotten here? It looked like paradise, with endless rolling green hills.

A strange drowsiness kept her from scrambling to her feet, even when she heard a man's voice calling her name. She twisted around to find Jake strolling toward her in his long, easy gait, dressed in jeans, a black shirt, black boots, and a black corduroy jacket.

"Athena?" He crouched beside her and studied her face. "Can you hear me?"

She nodded, as she looked around again. "Where are we?"

"I don't know, exactly." He shrugged off his jacket and wrapped it around her shoulders. "Do you remember what I offered you?"

She drew his jacket around her and frowned at him as memories slammed into her, turning her stomach: Jake's face as he looked down at her with golden eyes, a growl vibrating between them, the pain of his teeth sinking into her flesh. She shivered.

But the nausea subsided as she studied him. He looked different, less harsh somehow. His blue eyes seemed lighter, as did his hair, and then she realized why.

"The sun," she said. "I thought you couldn't handle sunlight."

"I can't," he said, his crooked smile softening his features. He glanced over his shoulder. "Except here." His smile widened. "I'd forgotten what it was like." He reached out, but stopped just short of stroking her hair. "You're beautiful in sunshine, Athena."

"Jake, my boy, you must hurry."

Athena jumped and searched for the source of the voice, but found none. "Who was that?"

Jake rose quickly and stood over her. "I offered you eternity, Athena. Now you must decide. You can stay here, or come back with me." Slowly, deliberately, he extended his hand, palm up, just as he had before.

"What happens if I stay here?"

"I don't know."

She stared at his strong, steady hand. "And if I go back, I'm a vampire."

"Yes."

Her gaze followed his arm up to his face where she saw a momentary look of fear in his eyes that took her by surprise.

"I'll take care of you," he said softly. "Please."

A strange tingle danced across her skin as she took his hand and he drew her to her feet, then wrapped his arms around her. She hugged his waist and pressed her face to his chest.

"Thank you," he whispered.

After a moment, he stepped back, turned, and started walking, drawing her after him. She trotted through the grass to keep up.

"Where are we going?"

"Back," he said.

"How?"

He didn't answer, but continued on, moving faster now. She stumbled along behind him.

And then they suddenly stopped and she peered around him and gasped. Before them, a cliff dropped off into a black void. Somehow, they had reached the edge of the world.

She gulped. "What . . . ?"

Sunlight faded like a lamp dimming, and she looked up into a dark purple sky, unlike anything she'd ever seen before.

"Athena, listen to me." Jake took her face in his hands and stared into her eyes. "You have to trust me. Can you do that?"

Oddly enough, her fear crumbled as she stood trapped in his gaze. "Yes, Jake."

He smiled then and kissed her gently on her lips. "Good."

As he pulled her to him, the jacket fell from her shoulders.

"Close your eyes and hold onto me, sweetheart."

She did as instructed, and he encircled her with his arms.

Her feet left the ground.

She wondered why she felt no fear as wind whipped her hair against her shoulders. Perhaps it was because of his strength, or that she knew how much he cared. No one had ever cared for her like this, never loved her.

Did he love her?

And then the wind stopped, and lights glittered behind her eyes like Fourth of July sparklers she couldn't quite see. A band of pain tightened around her head. Horrendous pain. She groaned.

"Drink now," he whispered.

His command made no sense. She had nothing to drink, and she wanted to ask what he meant, but the pain intensified and she felt as if her head were about to explode.

Instead, something *inside* her head suddenly exploded, something in her brain, and then the pain disappeared as memories flooded her senses, memories of hot, dry days, burning sun, and scents of leather and horses and sweat. Cool water, a lake, diving in and swimming in the dark, water splashing around her, slippery rocks beneath her bare feet.

A woman with long dark hair, dark eyes, smiling as she unbuttoned her dress. A strange dress, long and full and heavy.

A deafening *pop* and the smell of gunpowder, and then the scent of warm blood as she looked down with satisfaction at a blossoming red hole in a man's chest. Her own side burning now, and blood oozing from between her fingers.

No, not her fingers, his.

His memories, his emotions.

And then darkness and hunger, and she shook with fear.

A cool hand stroked her hair. "You're all right now, sweetheart. Just relax." Deep and sexy, near her ear. "Sleep."

And she slept, but not as she ever had before. Her body didn't relax slowly, letting her thoughts drift into quiet dreams. Instead, she stepped into a hole of nothingness. No sound, no thoughts, no dreams.

Had she died?

Even as she asked, something inside her stirred, a feeling deep in her intestines, an awareness.

And then the hunger hit. Not a usual hunger, but something brutal, primal, severe, taking over her entire body. She needed . . . what?

Struggling to consciousness, she opened her eyes and found Jake lying beside her, watching her, his hand sliding across her bare stomach. He smiled as he met her gaze and rose up over her.

When he kissed her, the hunger grew. His mouth covered hers and urged hers open, and his tongue slid across her lips as if tasting her for the first time. When the tip of his tongue touched her teeth, she jumped as a strange jolt of pleasure shot through her body.

He groaned in response and wrapped his arms around her, and she reciprocated, thrilling to the smooth coolness of his skin. His chest hair brushed against her breasts, and the muscles in his arms bunched over hers. His fingers felt rough where they touched her back. How was it she'd never noticed these sensations before?

He deepened the kiss, groaning softly when she welcomed him, caressing his tongue with her own. She wrapped her legs around his and opened herself to him, needing more.

His rock-hard erection pressed against her thigh and she reached down to touch it, enjoying the way he jumped. The cool skin felt silky and tight, and when she wrapped her fingers around his prick, she was amazed at how large it was. He hadn't been nearly so large before.

Her pussy twitched in response, anticipating his entry, wanting him. In fact, her whole body wanted him, hungered for him, ached with wanton lust.

She scratched her fingers up his back and lifted herself into him.

Jake tore his mouth from hers. She tried to reclaim it, but he held her down by a handful of hair at the back of her head.

"Hold on, sweet thing. This first time will be intense. Let me lead. Okay?"

She nodded, licking her lips in anticipation.

He closed his eyes as he eased his cock into her, filling her completely.

Yes, sweet, wonderful sensations. She moved to the rhythm starting inside her, rubbing her swollen clit against him.

Then he drew a line up the side of her neck with his tongue and lips and everything jumped into a higher gear. Her body quivered and she cried out. Her mouth ached to bite something. Anything. Desperate, she would have bitten her own hand if Jake hadn't had her arms pinned.

"Please," she whimpered.

He matched her rhythm then, thrusting into her as he opened his mouth on her shoulder. Cold, sharp points of teeth punctured her skin slowly, deliciously, and she trembled in response. Her body tightened with the need of release as she spread her legs wider, raising her hips higher, craving more.

And then he drew her head forward until her mouth found his shoulder and she bit down hard, feeling his flesh give way. Salty coolness flooded her mouth and her world turned inside out.

She felt his orgasm from inside him as her own ripped through her, lifting her into a swirling bliss of mind-numbing fulfillment unlike anything she'd ever imagined. On and on, spasms of delight racked her body and she felt—no, tasted her own joy and his melting together, blended forever into one blissful wave of perfect pleasure.

Unending, unearthly ecstasy.

He yanked her head away.

"Enough," he growled.

Athena lay back and enjoyed sizzling pleasure pumping through her with the last spasms of climax as he thrust once more and then withdrew. Although she felt abandoned by the loss of him, she'd never known such intense satisfaction could exist. And more than anything, she savored his pleasure as it coursed through her veins. "Jake," she whispered.

When he didn't answer, Athena opened her eyes and looked around.

The room glowed, but without any source of light. And every color seemed intensified until she felt it, rather than just seeing it. Sitting up, she studied the room. "Jake?"

"Right here, sweet thing." He strolled into the room, holding a towel to his shoulder, smiling at her. His gorgeous body shimmered as he sat on the bed beside her.

Athena drew his hand and the towel away and stared with horror at the gash in his shoulder, then wiped her mouth and found blood smeared across the back of her hand. "Oh, God, what did I—"

"Shh, it's all right." He stroked her cheek with the tips of his fingers. "Don't worry."

"Don't *worry*? I just bit a chunk out of your shoulder." The weird thing was that the thought of drinking blood from Jake didn't turn her stomach in the least. In fact, it excited her, in spite of her horror.

"Hey." He raised her face with a finger under her chin. "It'll heal. And we'll soon have this perfected, darlin'."

She looked at his shoulder again and found a puckered, healing wound. As she watched, the skin drew together and the gash shrunk. "Wow."

He grinned. “We have a few things to discuss.” He tossed the towel aside and crawled up over her as she lay back. “Later.”

Squirming with excitement, Athena gazed up into Jake’s golden eyes. “We can do it again? Now?”

He nodded, his grin growing wicked. Fangs dented his lower lip.

10

"Well, dear boy, you look a bit pale, but quite pleased with yourself."

Jake stretched his legs out in front of him and raised his glass in salute. "I appreciate the help."

Skidmore acknowledged the thanks with a mock bow.

Jake drank deeply, taking in much-needed sustenance, feeling strength return to his limbs, and remnants of love bites smooth out and fade.

"Now for the real test."

Jake frowned up at the older vampire, who stood with one arm resting on the cold fireplace mantel.

"The first fresh meal," Skidmore said. "You do remember, don't you?"

Jake thought back to his second night in the Darkness, to the thrill of tasting a strong, young life force, full of emotion and sexuality. He'd taken that life, the first of many, and regretted it later. After a few years, he'd perfected the art of drinking without killing, but many lives had been wasted in the process.

"You can teach her," Skidmore said. "If I may suggest . . ."

"Of course."

"Filter her first few tastes through your system and let her adjust to the ambrosia before sipping from the source."

Jake sighed at the thought of ending the honeymoon. His obsession with his lovely Athena had not waned after five nights of nearly constant attention, and he felt so much more for her now than he had before. He knew her more intimately than he'd ever known anyone; she hadn't even tried to hold back the details of her life. And he'd shared more of his past and himself than he had before. He truly felt as though he'd found a half of himself he hadn't known was missing.

"And I'm always happy to help."

Jake shot Skidmore a warning glare that only made the older vampire laugh.

"Relax, dear boy. I'll wait for an invitation."

"Jake?" Athena's sweet voice echoed down the hallway tunnel.

Jake smiled and then rose, finishing off his drink.

"Your bride awakes," Skidmore said. "Shall I send a suitable donor?"

"Yes, please."

"Male or female?"

"Female." No way he was bringing another man into his bed. Not yet, anyway. Besides, Athena should understand and more easily assimilate a woman's emotions.

He knew he'd someday have to release his sweet Athena to the world, but he wasn't ready to do so just yet.

She stood in the middle of their room wearing a thin white robe, her red hair loose around her shoulders. Her green eyes glistened as she smiled at him.

"Hey there, gorgeous. 'Bout time you woke up." He snagged her around the waist with one arm and drew her close, nipping at the side of her neck.

She purred in response and kneaded his shoulders.

Before he could get too far off track, he eased her away and she frowned in response, her irises already glittering. "Aren't we going to . . . ?"

"Fuck?"

She cocked one eyebrow. "I hadn't planned to be so crude."

He grinned as he leaned close. "I like crude."

"I noticed," she said playfully, moving to the bed and sitting on the edge. "Well?"

Jake sat beside her, but not too close. "I have other plans for tonight."

"Like?"

"Like helping you understand what you've become."

"You mean, what you've *made* me."

He flinched, surprised by her statement, and noticing the hint of reprimand. "Are you sorry?"

She shrugged. "I don't really know. The hunger is still difficult to handle, and I'm still having problems with my vision." She glanced around the room, which he'd purposely left almost dark for her sake.

"There's more," he said softly, drawing her attention back to him. "So far, you've only taken blood from me. Drinking from a mortal is different."

"In what way?"

"I can't describe it, exactly. More intense."

"*More* intense?" Her eyes glowed and her tongue darted across her lips.

He moved closer and held her shoulders. "Listen to me, Athena. The hunger can be a beast, ruling your existence if you let it. You don't want to let it take control, no matter how tempting."

"You have."

He sighed. "Yes, and I regret all the lives I took before I figured it out. Someday, I may have to pay for those lives. Of course, I already have a lifetime's payment on my head. But I can't bear the thought of you owing the same price. Do you understand?"

She nodded.

"Good." He brushed her hair back and kissed her forehead. Then he smiled at her. "The lessons start tonight. And they can be fun, if you listen."

She nodded again, then jumped at the tap on the door.

Jake turned on a bedside lamp, harsh light compared to the darkness, then strode across the room and opened the door. A young blond woman stood in the hallway dressed in shorts and a T-shirt.

"Hey, there," Jake said, holding out his hand. "What's your name?"

The woman slipped her warm hand into his. "Elaine."

He urged her into the room, admiring her full figure and deep tan. "Don't worry, Elaine, we won't hurt you."

"I hear her heartbeat," Athena whispered from beside him, grabbing his arm.

He glanced down at her, then returned his attention to the visitor. "Yes, and a lovely, strong heartbeat it is."

As he spoke, Elaine's heart rate shot up.

Jake turned his best smile on the girl, hoping to calm her fears without invading her thoughts just yet, but it didn't help much. He wanted to keep his thoughts tuned to Athena instead, who clung to him as he led the young woman across the room.

"Do you know what we want?" he asked.

Elaine shrugged, licking her lips and swallowing hard, glancing from him to Athena and back, trying to look calm and seductive, but not quite pulling it off. "You're vampires, right?"

"Yes, we are." He leaned close to her, taking in her scent and finding a pleasant aroma that aroused him. "We need your blood, sweet thing, but I promise you'll enjoy it."

She gulped, then nodded just slightly.

"Do I have your permission?"

She nodded again, this time with more certainty as he ran his fingers up the side of her arm, and then her neck.

"Good. Get comfortable."

Elaine walked to the edge of the bed and undressed quickly.

"Jake," Athena said, her confusion etching a frown on her beautiful face.

He drew her to him and held her as he whispered in her ear. "My sweet, you know now how I feel about you, don't you?"

She nodded against him.

"And I've tasted your feelings for me growing since the first night."

She nodded again.

"We're vampires. We take blood to survive, but it doesn't have to be unpleasant for them. Tonight, I'll show you how it's done. Trust me."

"Yes, Jake."

"But you must do exactly as I tell you."

He took her mouth then, savoring her sweet taste, thrilled to find her even more perfect as a vampire than she had been as a mortal. Athena molded her body to his, and he groaned at the pleasure the feel of her promised.

Then he eased her away. "Now, come to bed with me, and stay close. All right?"

She nodded, her eyes starting to glow again.

"When the hunger hits, you take me, not her. Do you understand?"

"Yes."

He untied the belt at her waist and pushed her robe to the floor, then quickly added his own clothes to the pile. Hand in hand, they moved to the bed where Elaine waited, watching them.

Knowing how delicate the situation could become, Jake positioned himself between the two women. His sweet Athena had no idea how strong the hunger would get, but he did. He'd do his very best to help her tame the beast.

Keeping himself tuned to the soft vibration emanating from his mate, he turned his attention to the mortal woman who lay as if posing, but with her legs and arms pressed to her body. The bronze color of her skin faded to milk at her breasts and between her legs. She jumped at first as he stroked her cheek with the back of his fingers, but didn't move to block his touch.

"Hmm," he said, "nice." He explored her soft, warm flesh gently, letting his hand drift across her breasts and belly and down her thighs. Then he leaned over and kissed her full, moist lips and listened to the steady thud of her heart.

Athena's vibration increased in intensity, and he glanced at her and winked. She smiled weakly, but nodded to reassure him.

Jake drew the mortal closer and kissed her heated mouth again, this time opening it with his own, tasting her, stroking her tongue with his. She responded with experience that he enjoyed, running her hand up his arm to his shoulder.

Cooler fingers chased a tingle up his spine, settling at the center of his back, and he groaned at the pleasure of Athena's touch as he drew Elaine's leg toward him and pinned it with his own. Then he studied the shape of her breasts, teasing the nipples to hard buds before moving his mouth down to replace his hands. Suckling, he dipped a finger into her hot cunt, pleased to find moisture. She gasped and arched her back.

Athena's touch intensified with her growing excitement.

Unable to take the time he usually would have, Jake moved over the mortal woman, settling between her warm, soft thighs, easing the head of his swelling cock against her cunt. She cooed, opening her legs wider, inviting him in.

Taking her mouth again, careful not to cut her with his

fangs, he entered her carefully, easily, enjoying her tight warmth. Soft, sensual noises rose from her throat as he began slow, easy strokes.

His own hunger rose, urging him on as he moved his mouth to her neck, tracing the pumping pulse with the tip of his tongue.

She tightened around him, matching his thrusts, approaching release.

Athena growled, filling the room with a low, guttural noise as she moved closer. Jake reached over and took her hand in his. Her cool lips touched his shoulder, and his strokes quickened in response to his growing desire.

With the first spasm of her cunt and cry of her release, Jake sank his fangs into Elaine's neck, nearly overwhelmed by her exploding pleasure. Joyous ecstasy flowed like molten lava through his veins, scorching away all earthly connections, drawing a volcanic eruption of cum. Athena's nails dug into the flesh of his buttocks, and her fangs scraped furrows across his back, sending his senses reeling. He drew harder on Elaine's neck and her second orgasm started. Thrusting fiercely, he pumped until he had nothing left and felt her sweating body collapse under him.

His connection to Athena quivered as she growled in his ear, a beast now, and reached for the pulsing vein in Elaine's neck with her mouth as soon as he raised his head.

"No!" He grabbed her by the back of the neck, drew her with him, and rolled her over until he had her pinned. Her fangs had extended to their full length, and her feral gold eyes no longer looked at him with love. "Drink," he whispered, exposing his neck.

She bit into him with animal need and he grunted at the attack. The desperation with which she fed sent him over the edge and he plunged his suddenly exploding cock into her greedy cunt, lost. All sense of time and place dissolved as she took from him, and he found her flesh, drinking his own pleasure, feeling the renewed eruption of mortal emotions, closing the loop. Entwined, they drank, sharing fading passion, merging into one.

He returned to his senses on his back, Athena straddling him, impaled, her head back and her fingers curled around his shoulders. Acute satisfaction flowed from her trembling body to cover him, too, and he smiled as he ran his hands up and down her sides.

"Oh, yes," she breathed, falling forward onto his chest.

He wrapped his arms around her, buried his face in her hair, and held her until she stopped shaking.

"Jake," she whispered.

"Yes, sweetheart."

"How do you handle it?"

"Practice."

She shuddered, then relaxed against him.

Athena stretched as she woke. She'd been a vampire for ten days now. Or maybe ten nights was more accurate.

Jake groaned and rolled to his back.

She still wasn't completely sure this wasn't all a dream. Only a few short weeks ago, she'd been sure vampires weren't real. She'd also believed she'd never find a man who loved her, and now she had the ultimate mate. And he was a vampire. How bizarre her life had turned out.

Although technically, this wasn't her life anymore. This was her death.

She shivered instinctively.

Her initial change had been immediate when Jake drained her and then brought her back. Her heartbeat slowed to once every few minutes or less, depending on what she was doing, and her skin felt cold. And *felt* had become a relative term. She sensed many things, most better than she ever had before, but she didn't feel pain in the way she had when she was alive.

However, change had continued over the past ten nights, some of it more obvious that the rest. Her skin had paled from its state when she lived, and she didn't crave food or drink, only blood. The less outward change was in her feelings for Jake. She knew him now in a way mortals could never know each other. He'd shared what he felt the first time he shot a man, and when he lost his virginity in the neighbor's hayloft, and every other important moment in his life. She knew he shared them on purpose, yet she hadn't figured out how to choose what he saw. When he was in her head, she saw what he saw as if watching a movie, reliving the moments. Very odd.

"Evening, darlin'," he drawled softly.

Athena smiled and turned her head to meet his gaze.

"Hungry?"

She nodded.

"Me, too." He stretched his arms over his head and his whole body quivered like a taut rubber band. Then he flipped over and crawled toward her on all fours, grinning wickedly.

His physique still excited her. His strength was that of at least twenty men, yet he held her carefully when he drank from her. He'd been right, they'd perfected the sharing of blood. Most times, he offered himself to her first. The pleasure, the hunger, the satisfaction were indescribable, and the sex was unlike anything she'd expected. Jake knew every move she wanted before she wanted it, and he'd shown her how to reach the most amazing climaxes, much more than mere mortal orgasms. They would withdraw their fangs simultaneously and hold each other as the bliss softened and faded.

When he'd shared mortal blood with her the first time, she'd been terrified by the loss of herself to the hunger. But he'd been right about that, too. With practice, she'd felt some measure of restraint. He hadn't allowed her to actually drink from a live human yet, but she'd learned to respect the limits he placed on her. Someday, she'd be the one to feel that first emotional charge and share it with him.

So, what was this restlessness invading her joy?

Jake nipped at the flesh around her belly button and flicked her gold ring and she buried her fingers in his thick hair.

"Jake."

"Hmm?" His hand slid up the inside of her thigh.

"Can we go out tonight?"

He raised his head and looked at her. "Out?"

She nodded. "I'm feeling a little like a prisoner in here."

"Are you now?"

She smiled. "In a good way, of course."

"But still a prisoner," he said.

"Yes."

He crawled up her body to stare into her eyes. "Give me what I want first, and then I'll take you out."

She grinned. "You're telling me you wanna fuck?"

He returned her grin. "Damn right, darlin'."

Jake held Athena's hand as they stepped from the mouth of Skidmore's cave. Although happy to inhale the night air and see stars again, he felt as if he were losing something precious. He led her down the main trail until they reached the bottom of a canyon and he stopped.

Standing perfectly still, he turned back and studied her face, soaked in moonlight, radiant.

"What do you hear?"

She cocked her head. "Water, the wind, insects, a car somewhere."

"Listen closer."

Her brow furrowed for a moment, then she smiled. "Footsteps, soft."

"Coyote. Do you smell it?"

She raised her nose into the air and inhaled. "Yes."

"Follow it." He released her hand and watched her start forward, one hesitant step at a time, and he dropped back to give her space.

She picked up speed until they ran through the sage, startling a sleeping rabbit, passing a nesting hawk. When she caught up to it, she stopped, facing the coyote, and they all stared for several long moments. The coyote turned and dashed away, glancing over his shoulder.

Athena turned to Jake, laughed, and threw her arms around his neck. He hugged her, appreciating her joy as if it were his own.

"This is wonderful," she said, stepping back from him, but holding his arms.

He nodded.

"What else? Show me."

He took her hand again. "Come on."

They strolled back to the bottom of the canyon and he led her to a large flat rock beside the creek. He sat, drawing one leg up to rest his arm, and she settled beside him. He pulled her around so that he sat behind her and leaned close, his mouth near her ear.

"Close your eyes, sweet thing. Your mind is only as limited as you make it. Release your hold."

He felt her tense, and he laid his hand over hers. "It's all right, I'll keep you safe. There's an owl twenty paces in front of you. Can you feel him?"

She shook her head.

"Let go. You can follow the owl, be the owl, see what he sees. He's lifting off now. Follow him, just as you followed the coyote, but with your mind. He's passing overhead. Feel his wings stir the air."

Her body stilled, and he waited, listening to the owl's screech echo off canyon walls. He knew she floated above shrubs, reaching the cliffs, and looked back at where they sat together. She saw the glow of far-off cities and headlights on the highway.

"Now, come back, sweetheart. Come back to me." He waited a moment. "Athena, come back."

She jerked and straightened. "Wow," she whispered.

Jake smiled.

"Is there more?"

He laughed and hopped to his feet, offering her a hand, which she accepted. "Isn't that enough for your first outing?"

"I suppose."

They strolled alongside the creek for a half mile or so like kids on a date. Jake couldn't stop smiling as he shared the night with the woman of his dreams.

As they crossed a rocky ledge, she tugged on his hand and he stopped. "What's wrong?"

She grinned. "Nothing." Then she drew her blouse off over her head.

Her breasts stood out full and firm in the night, and her skin shimmered. Jake stepped closer to watch, but didn't touch. Her scent filled the night air and wrapped around him, seductive and sweet.

She unsnapped her jeans and stepped out of them.

"Damn," he whispered. "You look too good to resist."

"Then why are you resisting, Jake?"

He glanced around, checking the horizon for any hint of a threat. When he lost himself to her, they were both vulnerable, and he wouldn't risk her safety.

But he sensed nothing else to hold his attention, so he returned it to his lovely Athena, his sweet midnight goddess.

She stepped closer, unbuttoned his jeans, and reached inside. His cock needed little stimulation; his hunger for her tended to stay constantly just below the surface, waiting for any chance.

Jake wrapped his arms around her marvelous body and

lifted her until she hooked her legs around his waist. Then he kissed her, nipping her lips and licking at her growing fangs as he eased her down onto his waiting shaft.

Sucking in air through her teeth, she turned her head, offering him the first bite, and he took it, penetrating her flesh slowly, gently. Sheathed in her perfect cunt, he tasted true love for the first time and groaned as he held her tighter.

11

"We need your help."

Jake frowned at Katie, then filled a glass from a decanter and sipped. He sank into one of the armchairs, holding the glass close to his chest as he let the nectar work its magic.

He looked up at her. "What kind of help?"

"Professional help, of course." She settled onto the love seat beside Beatrice, who had matured since coming into the Darkness but still sat quietly, watching them. "After all our efforts, we still have one active group of hunters out there causing a great deal of irritation."

Skidmore filled his own glass. "I'm the eldest member of the council now."

"What about Ponce? And Liam?"

"Ponce never returned to his den, and Liam has simply vanished. Their remains have not been discovered, if they still exist."

"Shit." Jake deposited his glass on a side table and rubbed his forehead with his fingers. He hadn't had a headache in nearly a century and a half, but he could have sworn he felt one coming on.

The air buzzed as Athena entered the living room, and he raised his gaze to her.

Glancing around at the group, she skirted the room in silence to stand behind him, resting a hand on his shoulder. He reached up and briefly touched her fingers, then sighed as he returned his attention to Katie and Skidmore.

"Can't you get any information from your prisoners?"

"We have only a few left, and things have changed since our raids. A bit of reorganization, perhaps a power struggle or two."

"What do you expect me to do?"

"We expect you, dear boy, to help us locate the head of this gang of thugs." Skidmore draped one arm across the mantel. "They seem to be centered somewhere in your old stomping grounds."

"Santa Fe?"

"In the general vicinity."

Jake glanced at Katie to find her glaring at Athena. "Perhaps your dear friend can help us. She should know exactly where they live."

Athena's hand slid off his shoulder.

Jake felt anger rising and shot a warning look at Katie, which definitely wasn't appreciated. "I'll check around."

She snarled quietly, then purposely ignored him, fondling Beatrice's small hand.

"I'll snoop around in Albuquerque," Skidmore said, ignoring the exchange. "I still have a few friends there. Shall we rendezvous here in a night or two and compare notes?"

"Sounds like a plan." Jake drew his legs under him and rose, glancing back to see if Athena would follow. Dawn approached, and his bones ached with weariness.

"One thing," Skidmore said.

Jake turned back to him.

"Don't be too late returning, dear boy. I'll assume the worst."

"Don't worry, I'll be back." Jake headed down the hallway with Athena close behind.

"Sweet dreams," Skidmore called after them.

Jake closed the bedroom door and pulled off his shirt and stepped out of his pants as he headed for the bed, fighting the urge to drop into unconsciousness as he went. "I'll be back in a few days."

"What?"

He dropped onto the bed and rolled to his back. "I'll be back—"

"You're not going anywhere without me."

With one eye open, he turned his head to find Athena sitting cross-legged on the bed beside him. Using his last bit of strength, he dropped his hand onto her leg. "Sweetheart, you're not ready."

Her eyes widened. "Jake, you're not leaving me here alone."

"Look, darlin'—"

"You have no choice in this. I'm going with you."

"Dammit, Athena, let's talk about this later." He yawned. "Come here, sweet thing."

"Jake, I'm serious."

He groaned and drew her to him, ignoring her struggles as he dropped off.

"What the hell do you think you're doing?" Jake glowered at her.

Athena fought the urge to cower and purposely went about making herself comfortable in the front seat of the car. The vehicle, something roomy with a leather interior, must be quite a bit older than she was.

"I told you to stay here," he said, his voice approaching a growl.

She turned her toughest glare on him, her eyes narrowed. "And I told you I'm going with you."

One eyebrow crooked up as he continued to glare for a long moment, and then he sighed. "Damn, you're a pigheaded female."

She smiled to herself as she glanced out the passenger-side window.

Jake started the car's monstrous engine, but they didn't move.

"Listen to me, Athena."

Hearing the solemn note in his voice, she turned to him.

"You better do exactly what I tell you to do. You don't know these people."

"I know them better than you do."

"No, you don't. You knew them when you were mortal, and you thought it was all some kind of crazy game. But I've tasted their hatred. And now that you're one of us, you're just another monster to be exterminated. You'll get no sympathy from this lot." He sighed again. "I've been around for a hell of a long time, sweet thing, and been through a lot, both good and bad. But I swear, if something happens to you, I won't survive."

Athena gulped at the emotion knotting in her throat. Without any effort, she suddenly appeared in Jake's arms, and he grunted.

"Nice move, sweetheart," he whispered. "You remember that one."

She nodded against his shoulder.

He held onto her for a long time, then eased her away. "All right, enough sentimentality. If we're going, let's go." With a wink, he shifted the car into gear and dirt flew up behind them as they took off.

Had it really been less than three weeks since she'd been captured by Jake? The whole thing seemed like a lifetime ago.

In a way, it was.

It hadn't even occurred to her to wonder where they were, but now she watched the passing mountains for something familiar. After miles and miles of winding dirt roads, they broke through to pavement, and then to interstate, and she realized they were in southern New Mexico, somewhere around Hatch, and headed north at outrageous speeds. With the roads fairly empty because of the hour, they blew through Albuquerque, only slowing as they started into downtown Santa Fe.

Jake drove slowly through clumps of traffic, mostly near the bars, scanning crowds. She did the same, surprised by a strange sensation that hit just below the center of her ribs as they passed one tall, dark man who spun around and stared at them.

"Is he . . . ?"

Jake nodded. "Yep. He's one of us."

It startled her to realize she could have walked past this man, or rather, vampire dozens of times before without realizing what he was.

Had she walked past Jake the same way?

Glancing at his profile, glowing in soft light from the dashboard, she decided she would have noticed him even if she hadn't known what he was.

As if sensing her thoughts, he reached out and gave her hand a quick squeeze, then he pulled into a parking lot. He grabbed his cowboy hat from the backseat and put it on, then rose from the driver's seat.

Athena got out and shut the car door, looking around. "Isn't that place around here, the one . . . ?"

"Where we had our first *introduction*?" He grinned at her over the top of the car.

She nodded.

"Yep, just around the corner."

Hurrying to where he waited on the sidewalk, she looped her arm through his. She took a deep breath, enjoying the scents of the city, most of which she'd never noticed before.

They all seemed jumbled together, and she worked on sorting them out as they strolled.

A strange noise drew her attention away from the smells and she searched for the source. It was a soft thumping sound, very regular, and then was joined by another, and another. Mixed in were several voices, male and female, and laughter, and the whole thing grew louder until she felt as though people were yelling directly in her ear. She tightened her grip on Jake's arm.

"You okay?"

"It's so loud," she said. "And I hear . . . what is that?"

"Their heartbeats, darlin'. That's what you're hearing. You have to learn to tune them out." His voice seemed so soft, she wasn't sure he actually spoke out loud for a moment, and looked up at him.

He smiled. "We can talk under their hearing. Just move your voice down deep in your lungs."

She focused on his words, and lowered her voice. "Like this?"

"Deeper."

"This?"

He nodded.

They continued on, winding around though an alley and then stepping through a doorway. As they descended the stairs, she remembered being worried she'd fall in the dark last time. The stairwell didn't seem so dark now.

At the interior door, Jake knocked twice, once, and twice again, and the door opened.

The biggest difference in the place, aside from a major decrease in the number of patrons, was that she could tell which customers were vampires. They all seemed to give off a strange vibration she hadn't noticed so much at Skidmore's. The combination of sensations made her dizzy.

"Jake, I feel strange."

He wrapped his arm around her shoulders, drew her close, and led her across the room to the bar where a familiar dark-haired man—no, vampire—waited.

"Antonio, this is Athena. Athena, Antonio."

The tall man with shoulder-length black hair studied her intently. "Haven't we met before?"

She shrugged. "Sort of."

The bartender glanced at Jake and then nodded slowly, as if understanding a secret. "I see. Last time you were here, you were mortal," he said softly.

"Yes."

"Crowds are a little thin," Jake said.

Antonio leaned forward with his elbows on the bar. "I'm afraid they are."

"Problems?"

"A few patrons have met untimely demises after leaving the premises."

Jake settled onto a bar stool and drew Athena to the one beside him. As she sat listening to the exchange, the dizziness lessened, and she guessed she was getting used to the strange vibrations.

"Hunters?"

"Looks that way."

Jake nodded. "That's why we're here."

"I was hoping you'd say that." Antonio placed two glasses on the bar and filled them from an unmarked bottle. "I'm growing tired of looking over my shoulder every time I go out."

Athena sipped from the drink, closing her eyes as the first wave of warmth hit her system, awakening her hunger. She took a greedy gulp, then looked up to find Jake and Antonio watching.

"Sorry." She wiped her mouth with the back of her hand and continued to sip.

"What's the plan?" Antonio asked.

Jake turned to look out over the small crowd. "I don't know yet. Just trying to figure out where to start looking."

Athena followed Jake's gaze to where several dozen people danced and gathered in small clusters to talk. She watched one young man walk across the far side of the room. He was alone, not too tall, fairly thin with short brown hair. He looked familiar somehow.

When he turned, she gasped, sucking in too much of her drink and choking momentarily. The young man frowned at her, then took off at a brisk walk toward the door.

"Athena?" Jake frowned at her.

She pointed. "I know him, Gary, one of Chris's friends. Computer geek."

Jake squeezed her arm. "Stay here."

He moved so fast through the crowds, she barely saw him.

"Wait for me." As she rose, Antonio grabbed the back of her blouse, and she spun around to glare at him.

"You better stay here. Jake knows what he's doing."

Where the hell had he gone? Jake stopped at the entrance to a dark alley and listened. After weeding out noises from the street, he heard nothing.

Wait, there it was, a human heartbeat all the way at the end of the alley.

With preternatural speed, he whipped to the end of the alley, only to find it empty. Stopping again, he cocked his head and heard no unusual noises. He should either hear the man moving, or hear his heartbeat, or something.

Wait, there was a sound around the corner. Leaning out, he caught sight of the man disappearing around the next corner.

Unable to move quite so quickly down a populated street without attracting attention, he ran, only to find the next street empty.

Excitement prickled his skin as he walked, listening and looking, feeling like the lawman of old searching for a wanted criminal who might hop out at any moment with a loaded pistol pointed at his heart. Now, of course, it would take more than a pistol.

A sign ahead drew him on, and Jake continued the cat and mouse game for nearly an hour, winding through miles of roadway of downtown Santa Fe. When he finally caught sight of his prey walking along the Santa Fe River, he raced across the street, grabbed his shoulder, and spun him around only to find someone else.

"Hey, man, watch it."

Jake frowned at the whiskered face. He'd assumed this was the young man he'd been chasing because of the clothes. "Where did you get that jacket?"

"It's mine." The homeless man wrapped the jacket tightly around him and glared a challenge.

"I don't want it," Jake said. "I just want to know where you got it."

The dark-haired man relaxed a little and shrugged. "Some kid ran by and gave it to me."

"How long ago?"

He shrugged again. "I don't know, twenty minutes?"

That didn't make sense. Twenty minutes ago, he'd been chasing Gary down a street at least ten blocks away.

Excitement suddenly faded to something completely different—confusion, laced with a touch of dread. Had he been the mouse in this game instead of the cat?

Abandoning the chase, he headed for the Tunnel at a trot, scanning crowds he passed, but with no luck. The closer he got, the worse he felt.

Running now, he descended the stairs in a blur, stopped at the open door, and walked in with all senses alert.

People and vampires milled around in a group at the side of

the bar, all talking in hushed voices that wove into something foreign in Jake's head. He shoved his way through to find Antonio on the floor.

Or what was left of Antonio.

A wooden arrow protruded from his chest. As Jake knelt at the vampire's side, he watched Antonio's skin shrink to thin, gray paper and crack, puffs of dust rising into the air. His long, black hair curled and crumbled, falling from the skeletal face.

"Son of a bitch," Jake muttered. He turned to the onlookers. "What happened?"

He zeroed in on the closest young man, who shrugged. "It all happened so fast. These four guys suddenly ran up to the bar, shot the bartender with a crossbow, and took off with the girl."

"What girl?" Jake rose.

"Some redhead who was hanging out at the bar. They put a sack or something over her head and one of them carried her out."

Terror gripped him as he checked the crowd. Athena wasn't there. Still, it could have been someone else.

"This girl, what was she wearing?"

The man shrugged.

"Jeans and a white cotton top, tight. She had a ring in her belly button. Great figure."

He spun to face the young vampire giving him the description that might have raised his hackles on any other occasion. "One of us?"

The vampire nodded.

"Shit." Jake glanced back down at the disappearing Antonio. "Anyone see which way they went?"

"Out the door," the first man said.

Approaching sirens drew everyone's attention. Jake grabbed

the young vampire by the sleeve. "Get rid of him," he said, nodding toward the body.

The vampire nodded.

"Okay, folks," Jake said, hands raised. "We need to vacate the building right now." Sending out vibes of danger and urgency, he herded the group to the door. The wave of terrorized people slowed approaching police long enough to clean up the mess before questions were asked.

Cops grabbed a few escapees, but their stories only created confusion.

Jake bolted to the bar, where his assistant raised a garbage bag over his shoulder. "He was falling apart," he said, nodding toward his load with a sick look.

"Thanks," Jake said. "Name's Jake."

"Colin," the young vampire answered.

Jake nodded. "Follow me."

He led the way through the hallway to the end and pressed the panel just to the left of the corner to activate the secret doorway, held it open for Colin, then followed him up the dark stone steps. At the top, Jake slipped to the front, eased the door open, and peered out.

No one in sight.

"Clear," he whispered, then held the door again.

The two stopped at the corner, standing in shadows of an adobe wall.

"You know what to do with him?" Jake asked.

"Yeah."

Jake patted his shoulder. "Thanks for your help."

After watching Colin make the corner, Jake eased around to the front of the building where he could see the Tunnel's entrance. Cops and spectators crowded the street. He caught pieces of a conversation from two of the senior law enforcement representatives.

"No sign of a body, no blood, no nothing."

The silver-haired captain rubbed the back of his neck and glanced around. "Must be a false alarm. No one's going to clean up a murder scene that fast. Maybe someone's idea of a practical joke."

The first cop nodded. "Could be. The place is weird enough."

"Yeah. Wonder how long it's been here. Sure as hell doesn't have a liquor license."

Assured that the cops were busy, Jake turned his attention to locating Athena. He closed his eyes a moment and recalled her memory of her former boyfriend, Chris. He'd lived in an old house just off St. Francis last time she'd visited. Snarling, he recalled her memory of sex with Chris, an event she hadn't enjoyed. He'd been clumsy, selfish, and rough on sweet Athena. "Bastard."

Once he had the place fixed in his mind, Jake opened his eyes and ran to the house, dodging through traffic, moving too fast for drivers to even see him.

But the house was empty.

Forcing the back door open, he walked through vacant rooms, checking closets and cabinets. No one lived in this house now. He couldn't even smell the man's scent.

Jake slammed an interior door, shattering the frame. With his frustration intact, he marched out to the front porch and stopped, hands on his hips.

"Dammit, girl, where are you?"

Somehow, in spite of what had happened to Antonio, he knew Athena was still among the undead. He felt a hint of something, as faint as a spiderweb strand, attached to his heart. When they were together, she produced a wonderful vibration that ran the length of his body. God, he missed that vibration already.

With dawn only a few hours away, he had no time to waste.

There were still many memories to search and addresses to look up. Nothing like good old-fashioned police work to keep him focused.

He *would* find her, and her captors *would* pay.

Fighting a pounding headache, Athena forced her eyes open. Where the hell was she? Normally, she could see in darkness these days. Now all she saw was more darkness. Reaching out with one hand, she found nothing but empty air and a cold, metal floor.

Metal?

On her hands and knees, she followed the cool metal to a corner, where she found more metal. She pounded with her fist, but produced only a dull thud.

"Hello?"

Her voice echoed back at a painful volume and she winced. Whispering, she tried again. "Hello? Is anyone there? Hello?"

Nothing.

Fright took hold, and she hit the wall harder, but left nothing in the way of a dent. Two more whacks, and still nothing.

Athena turned and wilted down the wall to sit with her knees pulled up in front of her.

The last thing she remembered was sitting in the Tunnel, facing Antonio, worried about Jake. Antonio had glanced over her shoulder, his eyes had widened, and then a wooden arrow had suddenly appeared in the left side of his chest. He'd frowned down at the arrow's shaft, looked at her, and dropped to the floor.

Before she could even react, there'd been hands on her arms, a sharp sting in the side of her neck, and then nothing.

Athena reached up and found a tender spot on her neck. Someone had injected something there, but what? What would knock out a vampire? She'd never thought to ask Jake that question.

There were many questions she hadn't asked Jake about being a vampire.

Sighing, she dropped her arm to her knee. What now? Was this it? Had her eternity with Jake Brand been cut short to a few weeks?

When a bright light suddenly blinded her she screeched and turned to cover her eyes with her arm.

After a moment, she lowered her arm and squinted up at the single spotlight shining from ten feet above her.

She sat in a ten-foot-square metal box with one door on the right wall. No handle, but still a door.

Hopping to her feet, Athena pushed on the door, then threw herself against it without result.

"Hey! Who's out there?"

"Where are the others?"

Athena backed up, searching the top of the wall from which the sound had come. She found something she could just barely see next to the light—a camera lens, or speaker. Maybe both.

"What others?" she asked.

"The others like you. The vampires."

The voice seemed familiar even through electronics, and she cocked her head. "Chris? Is that you?"

The lack of answer verified her guess.

"Chris, it's me. I haven't changed. Not really. You were wrong about them . . . us. We don't want to hurt anyone."

"You're all bloodsucking monsters who deserve to die! Tell me where the others hide when the sun's out."

She thought the whole vampire-hunter thing had been just a game to him. But something in his voice made her realize he truly hated vampires. Had Jake's attack been the seed for his loathing? Or had it been there all along?

Athena slid down the wall, returning to her seat. "I don't know where they are."

"You're lying!"

She leaned her head back against the metal wall and closed her eyes. "I'm not lying. I don't know where they are."

To some extent, her statement was true. She had no doubt that Jake would be searching for her. She hoped he didn't walk into a trap.

12

With smoke rising from his shoulders, Jake staggered into Skidmore's cave, stumbled into the main room, and fell to his hands and knees.

"My dear boy," Skidmore said, appearing at his side. "Whatever happened to you?"

"They took her."

"What?"

"The bastards took her. They staked Antonio."

Skidmore rested his hand on Jake's back. "The hunters?"

He nodded as he worked his way to his feet, scorching pain in his shoulders fading. "They're in Santa Fe somewhere."

Katie handed him a glass, which he chugged. Thankful for the rejuvenating warmth shooting through his veins, he wiped the back of his hand across his mouth and handed back the glass.

"Thanks."

Katie stroked his cheek. "Poor Jake."

He made his way to a chair and eased into it. "I searched until the sun started up. No luck."

"Are you sure she's—?"

"Yes," he snapped at Skidmore.

Biting back his anger, he touched the middle of his chest with his fingertips. "I feel her here."

Skidmore nodded. "And you tried to contact her?"

Jake frowned his confusion.

The older vampire raised his eyebrows as he settled onto the sofa. "Weren't you taught anything by your master?"

"No. I only saw her that first night, and then she left."

"Greedy little bitch," Skidmore said. "One should never shirk one's duties to the fledglings." He clucked quiet reprimand as he shook his head. "You have a special connection with your little morsel, since you're the one who made her. You can use it to locate her. Unless, for some reason, she doesn't wish to be located."

"What do you mean?"

Skidmore just shrugged in response and continued. "If you haven't worked to develop that connection, it may take some doing, but it's there nonetheless."

"What do I do?"

"I know you've learned how to set your thoughts free."

"Yeah, but if I don't know where to send them—"

"Use that feeling you mentioned, the one tied to your heart. Think of it as a string and follow it. Picture her at the other end of that string."

Jake closed his eyes to summon up the image of his sweet Athena attached to the string, but found himself too tired to concentrate.

"Not now, dear boy. You must be refreshed first. You'll need your strength. And then, the closer you are to her, the thicker the string will be, and the easier to follow."

Jake dragged himself to his feet.

"I'll send Elaine to you this evening," Skidmore said.

"No, thanks." He couldn't imagine wanting another woman, and would settle for bottled O-positive.

"You'll need her," the older vampire said. "No one has touched her since the night you rather *overdid* it."

Jake winced, remembering how he'd lost control with Elaine under him and Athena at his side.

"Don't worry, she has quite recovered. I'm sure she's more than willing to help."

Yawning against the sunrise, Jake staggered down the hallway and into his room, where he collapsed without removing his boots.

He woke in what seemed like moments, but he felt the sun setting. Shedding his clothes, he hurried to the shower, cleaned off the road dirt, and stepped out.

"Hi."

Jake turned to find Elaine standing in the bathroom doorway in jean shorts and a T-shirt. Her heartbeat sang with amazing volume.

"Hey there."

"Thomas said you need me."

Jake grabbed a towel from the rack, dried off, and wrapped it around his waist. He ran a comb through his hair, then walked to the bedroom.

Elaine followed him. "Jake?"

As he withdrew clothes from the dresser, he spoke over his shoulder. "I'm sorry, but I'm in a hurry."

"Thomas said you might not survive without me. Without my blood."

Sighing, he dropped the folded pants and shirt on the bed. "Listen, sweet thing, I'd love to spend time with you, but—"

"You don't have to have sex with me, Jake."

He turned to find her standing right behind him.

She raised her head to one side, baring her neck.

Dear God, but her heartbeat was strong. He watched the

blood vessel at the side of her throat rise and fall, and his fangs dropped in response. He couldn't have resisted her if he'd wanted to.

Wrapping one arm around her waist, he drew her to him, nuzzling her soft hair, inhaling the artificial fragrance of flowers. The scent of her heated skin worked its way through the smell of shampoo, and his prick lengthened, too. Yes, he should just take a quick drink. He needed the strength.

Moving his mouth to her neck, he licked her salty skin, then rested his lips above the pounding artery. Closing his eyes, he remembered Athena's touch to his back the last time he'd tasted Elaine.

A soft moan vibrated through her skin, and her warm hands ran up his bare sides.

The hunger took over then with startling speed, releasing the beast, and he ripped off her shorts and walked her backward.

She gasped as she hit the wall.

"Now you're mine," he growled.

Tearing away his towel, he lifted her, held her legs on each side of him, and entered her with a greedy thrust.

She cried out.

He sank his fangs into her neck then, and she cried out again, this time at the brutal pleasure as her body jerked with ecstatic spasms and her cunt gripped his cock in a rapid-fire orgasm.

And he pumped his seed into her as he drank the wondrous nectar she offered, drinking deeply. Amazing strength shot through his body, firing muscles, sparking nerve endings. He took more until he felt her flow waning.

Pulling his mouth away, he kept her pinned to the wall as he thrust one last time and then held her.

"Dammit," he whispered, withdrawing and lifting her into his arms.

He stretched her out on the bed and listened to the slow but steady beat of her heart. He stroked the side of her face with his fingertips.

"Can you hear me? I'm truly sorry, sweet girl."

After a moment, she groaned softly as her head moved.

Jake sighed with relief. How long had it been since the beast had taken over like that? God, he'd seen too many women hurt both before and after his death. He sure as hell didn't want to be one of the perpetrators of that violence.

"I'm sorry," he repeated.

Her eyelids fluttered and she groaned again.

Behind him, the door opened. "My dear boy, she'll be fine, don't worry."

He glanced up at Skidmore. "I didn't mean to—"

"I know, you're a little preoccupied. Come, we should hurry."

"We?"

"I'm going with you. I found no signs in Albuquerque, so they must be headquartered in your town."

Jake shook his head as he rose. "No, I'm going alone."

"And why on earth would you think that's acceptable?"

He snatched the pants and pulled them on. "This is my fight."

"*Your* fight? Don't be absurd."

Pushing his arms into the shirt, he crossed the room to his dresser where he yanked open the top drawer and picked out the old leather holster. Inside the coiled belt lay his six-shooter, the pearl-handled .45 Colt, a sweet revolver. He'd carried it for the last two years of his law enforcement career.

"What exactly do you intend to do? Call them out with the sun at your back at high noon? 'This town ain't big enough for the two of us, pard-ner.'"

Jake growled in frustration, dropped the holstered revolver back into the drawer, and slammed the drawer shut. This wouldn't be a fair fight. If he got close enough, he'd rip them all apart with his bare hands.

He turned to face Skidmore as he buttoned his shirt. "I don't want you there when I find them."

"And why is that?"

"If she doesn't make it, I'm taking as many of those bastards with me as I can." He crossed the room, stopped in front of Skidmore, grabbed his shoulder, and looked him square in his pale blue eyes. "You've been a good friend, Thomas. I don't want you there."

Skidmore took a deep breath and sighed it out. "I'm not used to such theatrics from you. Now I'm truly concerned."

Jake stepped into his boots, then grabbed his hat and coat. He paused at the door. "If I don't come back, take care of Katie."

"Of course." Skidmore followed him from the room. "And you know to return if you can, I assume."

Jake grinned at the old vampire, then pulled on his hat and hurried out the front door and past the cavern opening, squinting against an orange-tinted horizon.

One thing he knew for sure: Athena needed him. And, damn, but he needed her, too.

"Jake?" Athena opened her eyes and frowned at the strange surroundings.

For a moment, she could have sworn she'd heard Jake calling her name, but it wasn't him standing in front of her. It was . . . Chris?

He glared at her with unbelievable hatred as he stood clad in khaki pants and a brown pullover with his hands on his hips, his feet apart, wearing some kind of strange holster, looking like a yuppie pirate.

When she tried to get up, she realized she was bound, and turned her attention to the ropes holding her feet together, her arms at her sides, and, presumably, her hands behind her back. She should be able to snap the flimsy ropes, but couldn't.

"They're soaked in garlic," Chris said, his lips curling into a victorious snarl. Behind him, two more men stood just inside the closed door, one holding a crossbow and the other holding a sword.

"Chris, it's me, Athena."

"No! You used to be Athena. Now you're a freak just like the rest of them. A bloodsucking freak."

"But I'm not. I don't—"

"Shut up!" He glanced back at the others as if to say, *See? I'm in control.*

Athena decided to wait him out, figure out what he had planned. Not that she had any real options. The garlic-soaked ropes seemed to have drained her strength, and the stench wound its way into her sinuses as a throbbing pain. She'd never loved garlic; now, she despised it.

Chris stepped closer, more sure of himself. "Tell me where the rest of them are."

"I don't know."

"Yeah, right." He snorted a laugh. "Poor little innocent Athena. You never did know anything, did you?"

Her gut clenched as she realized he'd never cared about her. And she thought she'd loved him. How could she have been so gullible?

Closing her eyes, she thought about Jake and her skin tingled in response. How crazy was it that she'd found the love of her life after death?

"I'm talking to you!"

Her eyes snapped open and she found Chris leaning over her.

"You have two choices," he said. "If you tell me where the others are, I'll make sure you're killed quickly."

She frowned at him, hoping the second choice was better.

"Otherwise, you'll lie here until you starve. Have you ever seen a vampire starve?" He straightened and sneered again. "It isn't pretty."

He paced back and forth in front of her like a schoolteacher on a roll. "First, you'll thrash around until you work the ropes loose, leaving raw cuts that don't heal. Of course, you won't be able to escape." He motioned with one hand. "This room is welded steel all the way around.

"You'll pound on the wall until you break all the bones in your hands." He stopped. "That'll only take a few days. Then it gets worse. You'll bite your own arms in desperation. And after a few weeks, you'll stop moving. But you won't be dead. You know how I'll know you're dead?"

She stared.

"You'll turn to bones, and then to dust. And the best part is that no one will miss you."

Sorrow took over then. Tears burned behind her eyes, but she refused to give him the satisfaction of letting them flow.

"Think about that for awhile." He spun and marched out with his mini-army at his heels.

The door slammed and the noise echoed in the tiny room for several long seconds. And then the light disappeared.

If only Jake were with her, everything would be all right.

A strange little pinch started somewhere inside her chest as she thought about Jake, a gentle tug, like a doctor pulling stitches through numbed skin. She suddenly remembered getting a cut on her leg sewn up when she was a kid. How odd; she'd forgotten about that.

Jake. God, she wanted to touch him. She wanted him to—

Athena squirmed around and sat up.

Could she use the skills he'd taught her to find him? To let him know where she was? If she released her hold, could she set her mind free and have it escape this steel box?

If Jake showed up, they'd kill him.

Whenever she thought of Jake, she reacted physically. There must be some kind of connection. What if she accidentally drew him to her?

"No."

She *wouldn't* think about him.

Jake stood beside the river and closed his eyes. He pictured Athena attached to him, her heart tied to his heart, her beautiful body naked and smooth.

For a moment, he thought he felt something, like a magnetic force turning him to his right.

And then it was gone.

"Dammit."

Taking a deep breath and blowing it out, he tried again.

Footsteps padded on the sidewalk—someone in soft-soled shoes. A cat screeched in surprise. Television voices rose from the next block. Traffic flowed past in waves.

Nothing.

His hands curled into fists, he turned to face the street. What now?

He'd tried all the places Athena knew about, and he'd sat in front of the now-closed Tunnel for an hour.

Where would he go if he were hunting vampires? How much did the hunters really know about the Community?

With his senses tuned for any unusual movement, voice, smell, or sight, he walked up Galisteo to San Francisco. Narrow streets funneled sounds, and buildings smelled of dusty stucco and old wood. People passed, paying little or no attention to him. Tourists mostly. A local drove by with music blaring, and he winced.

Before him, the cathedral's unfinished spires rose against a dark sky like beacons calling to a lost ship and he picked up his pace.

He dashed up the stone stairs and marched around to the side of the massive building, his boots thudding on rock. At a heavy black door, he stopped and listened.

Although he heard noise on the other side, it was subdued,

distant. Carefully, he pushed the door open, slipped inside, and closed it behind him.

Jake walked quietly down the narrow hallway, checking each room he passed. Scents of candles and incense washed over him, mixed with many others—flowers, dust, sweat, beans simmering. Although it had been at least fifty years since he'd traveled this hallway, he remembered which door to turn into, but when he found the office empty and dark, his hopes dimmed.

It hadn't changed much. Books still lined the walls, standing and stacked on shelves, and papers covered an ancient wooden desk. He pulled a chain to flick on a desk lamp, bathing the room in yellow light, and checked more closely.

The room had been used recently; smoke hung in the air. He smiled when he recognized the sent of cheap cigars.

"What the hell are you doing here?"

Jake spun around to find the priest filling the doorway. Although at six-one he was Jake's own height, his flowing black robe always made him appear bigger.

"Father Daniel."

"I asked you all to leave me alone."

Jake took two steps and sat in the metal armchair beside the desk. "We did as you asked."

After a long moment, Daniel walked to his desk and sat, his back stiff. "Until now."

"Yes, until now."

Jake stared at the vampire, sizing him up. He had to be the strangest case around, the only priest-turned-vampire known to the community. He'd taken his vows shortly before being brought to the Night eighty years ago, supposedly seduced with wine and beauty. Some even suggested that Katie had brought him across, but Jake knew better. Whoever it was had left behind a reluctant child intent on making up for all his sins, both in life and death, before meeting his maker.

"How's the parish?"

"Fine. Why are you here?"

So much for niceties. "I need your help."

"My help?"

"I'm looking for a group of hunters."

"Vampire hunters?"

"Yes. I need to know where they're holed up."

Daniel glanced around the room. "I heard someone was doing God's work in this town. What makes you think I would tell you if I knew?"

Jake bit back the urge to close the distance between them and rip the vampire's throat open. "God's work?" He sat forward. "An innocent woman is at risk. She's being held—"

"A vampire, I assume."

"Yes, a vampire, but an innocent."

"That's a contradiction in terms. There's no such thing as an innocent vampire."

Jake rose and stalked slowly, deliberately, toward the desk. "This one is. She hasn't killed anyone, and she won't." He towered over the priest, glaring down at him.

Daniel looked up with wide eyes. "Why do you care?"

Jake leaned closer. "Let's just say she's special."

The priest dropped his gaze. He knew something.

"Tell me where they are."

Pushing his chair back, he rose and moved out of Jake's immediate reach, fingering a row of books as if looking for something. "I don't know where they are."

"But?"

"One's a member of the church."

"What's his name?"

"Gary."

"Skinny kid, short brown hair?"

Daniel nodded.

"Gary what?"

He hesitated, then sighed. "Rosier."

Jake turned and perched on the edge of Daniel's desk. "Now, that wasn't so hard, was it?"

Daniel responded with furrowed brows.

"Got any of those cigars left?"

Sighing as if resigned to the visit, the priest motioned toward the desk with his chin. "Top drawer."

Jake opened the drawer and plucked a cigar from a box. He hadn't had a good smoke in years, and, judging by the scent as he drew it under his nose, this didn't promise to be one. But, it might help to spend a little quality time with Father Daniel, make him comfortable while assuring that he didn't contact Mr. Rosier.

"Read any good books lately?" Jake scraped a match across the box and lit the cigar, puffing to get it started.

"Several."

"Here." Jake handed Daniel a cigar and held out the match.

Daniel puffed without making eye contact. Not a good sign.

"Like what?" Jake returned to his chair, took a long draw on the cigar, and blew out a sweet stream of satisfying smoke. It took every bit of restraint he had not to dash out to look for Athena, but he wouldn't be able to rescue her if he walked into an ambush.

"I've been rereading some of the classics." The priest also blew out a long stream and settled back into his chair. "I just finished *Moby-Dick*."

Jake nodded slowly. "I never cared much for all the whaling details, but it sure was one hell of a good fight."

"Yes." Daniel puffed. "I didn't know you were a reader."

"Oh, yeah. Used to carry books around in my saddlebags. Not much else to do out there on the trail all alone for months at a time. My favorites were Mr. Clemens's books. The man had a way with words. A bit irreverent at times, but he sure could make me laugh."

Daniel studied him now, his expression guarded.

"Did I ever tell you about the time I met him?"

That perked him up. "You met Samuel Clemens?" A hint of gold glittered in his eyes.

"Yep." Jake grinned. "We met on a train. I was just a kid, but I'll never forget it."

Hang in there, sweet Athena. It won't be long now.

13

Jake stood outside the small one-story stucco house, listening. He heard sounds inside, but had trouble identifying them. Someone pounded on something and wood splintered.

Growling with frustration, he crept to a side window, but couldn't see through thick curtains, and he found the same situation at the next window, and the next. Then, as he approached the backyard, a gargantuan black dog charged the fence, barking loud enough to wake the dead.

"Shit." Jake crouched and held out a hand. "Hey, boy, it's okay. I won't hurt you."

The dog continued to bark, slobber flying from snapping jaws, blinded by canine rage.

So much for surprise.

Jake raced back to the front of the house, kicked open the door, and charged inside.

He stopped momentarily in a dark front room, completely devoid of furnishings or decorations, and followed a shaft of light into the next room where an overturned stool lay on a carpeted floor, still settling into place. He listened, but heard nothing other than continuous barking from the backyard.

As quietly and quickly as possible, he checked the house, stepping into each room and listening, but found no one. The place had to be empty, or he would have detected a heartbeat at the very least. Gary must have fled when he heard the commotion.

"Damn dog," he muttered, returning to the formerly occupied room. He snatched the stool from the floor and righted it in front of a table cluttered with tools and pieces of wood.

No, not just pieces of wood. Stakes.

The bastard had been sharpening the ends of stakes with a hatchet. The table also held a number of wooden crossbow bolts, and a container of what smelled like garlic juice.

Something clicked.

Jake whirled around.

The bolt sliced through his bicep and lodged in his side, pinning his arm to his body.

Gary Rosier stood ten feet from him holding a crossbow, trying to reload. The young man fumbled the new bolt, which fell to the floor.

Jake grabbed the shaft protruding from his arm, gritted his teeth, and yanked, yelling at the scorching pain ripping through his body. The shaft must have been coated with garlic juice, or something equally hideous. He staggered, but kept his footing.

Snarling, he looked up to find the crossbow now on the floor and Gary Rosier gone.

The boy couldn't have gotten far. Ignoring the pain, Jake dashed out through the front door.

At the sidewalk, he stopped, surprised to find empty space in both directions. How was it this skinny prick seemed to always disappear into thin air?

Jake marched around to the fence, glared at the snapping

dog, and shoved forward an angry thought. The dog dropped to the ground, suddenly quiet, panting, waiting for a command.

"Thank you."

Jake returned to the house for a closer look.

One thing for sure, Gary Rosier didn't spend much time in this house. The place held nothing but the basics: a table, stool, and two chairs, two single beds, one in each bedroom, a few clothes, and minimal toiletries. It looked more like a hideout than a home. Perhaps that's what it was.

As he searched the second room, Jake realized the scent hanging in the air didn't belong to Gary. More than one person hid out here.

What bothered him was the strange assortment of things in the closets. No footballs, photographs, or girls' underwear. Instead, he found crossbow strings, quivers with arrows, wooden crosses, and lots of batteries. What was wrong with these strange kids? No one had taken vampire hunting so seriously in centuries.

And what the hell were the batteries for?

He found no answers in the two hours it took him to search every square inch of the place. In fact, he noticed a very deliberate lack of connection to the rest of the world: no phone numbers scribbled on scraps of paper, no answering machine, no address book, no computer. Not even a television.

Not a damn thing.

Furious and frustrated, he marched outside, stood in the middle of the street, and turned a slow circle. People slept and traffic had dropped to a minimum.

He tried the connection thing again, picturing Athena looking up at him with lust and hunger, attached by a heartstring.

Nothing.

He'd told Skidmore he planned to take as many of the

hunters with him as he could if he couldn't get her back. He hadn't considered what he'd do if he couldn't find any of them.

Approaching dawn planted weariness deep in his bones. Without time to get back to Skidmore's, he had only one alternative and started back for the Plaza at a trot. Father Daniel wouldn't refuse him a bed, now that they'd established a friendship of sorts.

Jake returned to Gary Rosier's hideout shortly after sunset the next night. He found no occupants inside and a hungry canine whining at the fence.

"So they just left you, huh?"

The dog wagged its tail at the question and looked up at Jake with big sad eyes. Quite a change from the night before.

"Okay, let me see what I can do."

He slipped inside the house and located a bag of dog food he'd noticed during his initial search. The dog bolted down two bowlfuls, then licked the back of Jake's hand.

"So, boy, I don't suppose you know where to find your master, do you?"

The dog whined.

Jake tried offering a mental picture of Gary Rosier, but the dog simply sat in response and cocked its head to one side.

Jake patted its shoulder. "Okay, don't worry."

When he left, the dog followed him out.

"Not much of a bloodhound, are you?"

The canine glanced up as he matched Jake's pace.

The two of them spent the next two nights searching Santa Fe, sleeping in the basement of the church, where Father Daniel's welcome grew thin. Several times, as he walked narrow streets, Jake thought he felt someone following him, but even when he slid behind walls and waited, no one ever appeared. He looked for anyone familiar and any hint of Athena in ever widening circles until he'd reached the outskirts on the south end of town. The dog limped with weariness, and Jake sagged with disappointment and unspent fury as he started back up Cerrillos Road to where he'd left the car, a blue '57 Chevy. Could the hunters have left town with Athena? Was he wasting his time on a cold trail?

When he opened the driver's door, Dog jumped in, stretched across the rest of the front seat, and began snoring within seconds. Jake pointed the car out of town, pushing his speed to beat the dawn.

Skidding to a stop in the old barn used to hide cars these days, Jake jumped out and dashed into the cavern and through the front door, where he found Skidmore and Katie lounging in the front room with *nightcaps*, as Skidmore called them.

"Jake, my boy, wonderful to see you in one piece." Skidmore rose from his chair and started for the service tray, but stopped.

A low growl rose from Dog, who stood at Jake's right, leaning against his leg.

"What's this? A pet? I thought you only took up with horses."

Jake patted Dog's head. "It's okay, boy. They're friends."

The growling stopped, and Dog slinked across the room to lay on a rug in front of the cold fireplace, keeping a wary eye on the group.

"Drink?" Skidmore asked, continuing his interrupted path.

"Yes, thanks." Jake dropped his hat on the table, accepted a glass, and eased onto the sofa next to Katie.

She stroked the back of his head, then fingered the hole in the arm of his jacket created by Gary Rosier's bolt. "Poor Jake. I take it you didn't find her."

"No."

"Did you try the technique we discussed?" Skidmore asked.

"Yeah. I thought I felt something right at first, but then it disappeared."

"Very strange. Even at fairly great distances, you should be able to pick up something. A hint, at least."

Jake drained his glass and then sighed as he rose. "I'll try again tomorrow."

"You want company today?"

He glanced back at Katie, surprised by her offer.

She laughed. "Not me, Jake. I don't ask so nicely."

He shook his head and turned toward the hallway. "No, thanks."

Dog followed him to his room, settling at the foot of his bed, and Jake stripped off his ruined jacket and shirt, then pulled off his boots and stretched out.

The truth was, though, that he did want company. He ached to hold Athena next to him, and as bone-tired as he was, he couldn't sleep, even when he knew the sun had completely risen.

When his door opened, he folded one arm behind his head and smiled at Elaine. She tiptoed in, closed the door, and drew off her nightshirt in one movement that left her naked.

She wasn't Athena, but she sure as hell was pretty.

Grinning seductively, she crawled up from the foot of his bed, her blond hair shrouding her breasts like a dancer's veil.

Jake's body reacted to the sight of her as any man's would have, and her grin grew wicked as she eyed the growing bulge in his pants. Her hair tickled his belly as she leaned over him and kissed him, one hand sliding up the center of his crotch. She straddled him and flicked her hot little tongue across his nipples as she released the button on his jeans.

"Damn, girl, you're too good at this."

She glanced up and smiled, then returned her attention to his chest, licking and biting, as she drew his zipper down the front of his hardening erection.

He jumped when her warm fingers slid down the front of his cock and curled around it, stroking slowly down the shaft.

"Hmm, nice." He closed his eyes.

She kissed him then, pressing her heated lips to his, opening her mouth to invite him in, and he took the invitation, exploring, tasting, enjoying her warmth. He ran his hands up her sides to her breasts and fondled them both, so full and soft.

She stroked harder, drawing a groan from him in the process.

Jake wrapped an arm around the girl's waist and rolled over, pulling her under him, and buried his fingers in her soft hair. His fangs ached for her flesh, but he refused to rush this time. He still had some rotten behavior to make up for.

He started the Touch at her face and moved it down her body an inch at a time as he kissed her deeper, stroking her tongue with his. She clutched at his sides in response, and spread her legs under him. He pressed his denim-clad thigh into her crotch and she raised her hips in jerky motions.

Enjoying the feel of her more than he'd expected to, Jake wrapped himself around Elaine and let the Touch roam her whole body at once. She moaned into his mouth and quivered all over, and her undulations became more pronounced. Her heartbeat thundered in his head, singing to him, beckoning. The beast whispered to answer its call.

But he ignored the whisper and ran his fingers over the soft, warm skin of her back and buttocks and thighs.

She murmured a protest when he released her long enough to strip off his pants.

"Don't worry, sweet thing. I'm not done with you."

Her blue eyes glistened as she watched him, but when he tried to return to where he'd left off, she pushed him away, raised up to her hands and knees, and straddled his chest with her back to him.

He splayed his hands over her tender skin as he watched the muscles in her back react to her movements. She grasped his cock and stroked it, fondling his balls with wonderfully experienced fingers, then leaned over and took him into her fiery mouth.

Jake groaned and closed his eyes.

The motion of her mouth taking him in, her lips slipping up and down the length of him, drew him as close to release as possible, and summoned forth the monster within. She moved faster, lifting him off the bed with each stroke.

Using every bit of restraint he could muster, he grabbed her arms and drew her back until she'd stretched out on top of him. With his mouth on her shoulder and his hands cupping a breast and her cunt, he rolled them over and pressed her to the bed with his weight.

She raised her sweet ass and he entered her with slow, tender thrusts, burying his cock in her hot, wet cunt. She gasped when he reached her depth, and he made sure not to push too far. As he traced the top of her shoulder with his tongue, he traced the swollen nub of her clit with his finger. She jerked in response and sucked quick breaths.

Jake growled with pleasure as she lifted her ass higher and tilted her head to the side. He hungered for the taste of her blood, for the joy of release, for the rush.

Not yet.

With a steady, easy rhythm, he drew her to a long, leisurely orgasm, thrilling to the way her heart raced and she cried out in pleasure, savoring the way her cunt clamped down, anticipating the flood of emotion she would share.

Her pulses slowed.

He opened his mouth, pressed the sharp points of his teeth to the salty skin of her shoulder, and pierced her flesh gently, slowly.

She gasped.

Her life force filled his mouth and hit his brain with amazing strength, her orgasm still sweetening her taste.

She cried out as the second orgasm started, and Jake drank

deeper, giving in to his own release, holding her tighter. He felt her excitement, her pleasure, the touch of fear, her needs and desires washing over him like warm honey.

And he thought of Athena. Sweet Athena.

"Jesus!"

Dog growled from the foot of the bed.

Jake's eyes snapped open and he realized someone stood behind him in the doorway. Withdrawing from Elaine, he jumped up, landing on his feet beside the bed to face a young man he'd never seen, apparently human, armed with a crossbow, and wearing a sword at his side. He also wore a strange, thick black vest. Kevlar? One thing Jake couldn't understand was why he couldn't hear the man's heartbeat, or maybe it was there, but faint, barely audible. He definitely wasn't a vampire.

In the time it took him to think these thoughts, the crossbow fired, sending a bolt through his chest. He tumbled backward, again assaulted by horrendous searing pain. This time, however, he realized just how serious the situation was when he looked down at the wood protruding from the left side of his chest.

This kid was a better shot. Had he pierced the heart?

Jake watched blood ooze from the wound into a rivulet down the front of his chest, and waited for the lights to fade.

Dog's growl changed to an angry snarl as he stalked toward the intruder who drew his sword and sliced at the charging canine.

Dog yelped and staggered sideways, then dropped.

Elaine scrambled across the bed to his side, and he pushed her behind him as well as he could. "Don't hurt her. She's mortal."

In an amazingly short time, the assailant sheathed his sword, reloaded his crossbow, aimed, and shot again.

Another molten blast sliced through his chest, and Jake yelled through gritted teeth.

He glared up at his killer.

Holding the wall behind him and Elaine's arm, he struggled to stand. He couldn't just lie there and let the kid shoot him until he managed to get it right. Since the lights hadn't faded, he could only assume both bolts had missed their mark.

Elaine broke loose of his grip and charged the young man as he worked to reload.

The bastard drew his sword and ran her through, and she screamed as the bloodstained sword emerged from her back.

"No!" Jake staggered forward.

But he was too late. The blond woman crumpled to the floor in a heap, her blood pooling around her. Enraged but weak, Jake fell to his knees beside her, trying to pull her into his lap.

The young man in the strange jacket loaded another bolt and raised the crossbow, aiming again at Jake's chest.

"Son of a bitch," Jake hissed, fighting excruciating pain to stay upright. "Do it right this time."

The kid grinned a nasty grin, exposing a large gap between crooked front teeth. Jake ached to jam his fist into that stupid grin.

Elaine gasped a final convulsive breath and went limp.

Time slowed as the kid took more careful aim, his finger pulling back on the trigger.

Jake's ears buzzed from the pain, but he still heard the wicked scream of a banshee as the bolt slipped through the air and passed well over his head.

The assassin stumbled forward, releasing both crossbow and sword and fell onto his face with Beatrice clinging to his back, her once mousy appearance now feral with fangs bared, her face streaked with blood like war paint. She opened her mouth, ready to rip the assassin's throat open.

"No!" Jake clawed his way forward, intent on stopping her. "Beatrice, don't."

She looked up, eyes blazing blood red, fangs glistening in the dim light.

"I need him," Jake said. "He can help me find Athena."

Her gaze moved from Jake to her victim and back, and she closed her mouth.

The young man started to squirm.

"Boy, I sure as hell wouldn't move, if I were you," Jake said.

Movement stopped.

Jake looked around to where Elaine and Dog lay dead, then crawled over to the edge of the bed, which he propped himself against. Steeled against what he knew was coming, he grabbed the small amount of shaft showing from the first bolt, closed his eyes, and pulled with every bit of strength he could muster.

The damn thing hurt worse coming out than it did going in, and Jake groaned in spite of himself. After a moment's rest, he did the same with the second.

He sat still until the worst of the pain had passed, then glanced over at Beatrice, who watched with sympathetic wide eyes, her captive firmly pinned. The smell of blood permeated the room.

The young man's heartbeat thundered now, and Jake clawed his way toward it, the beast fighting to take charge. But he had work to do, and couldn't allow himself to get lost in the moment.

He grabbed his would-be assassin, yanked him forward, and flipped him over.

The young man's grin had disappeared, replaced by pale-faced fear. And rightfully so. For what he'd done to Elaine, Jake would gladly hand him over to Beatrice as soon as he'd finished with him.

"Where are you keeping Athena?"

The prick gulped, but remained silent.

Jake smiled, lifted him to a sitting position, and knelt behind him. Fading quickly, he had little time to consider anything but the nourishment pumping through the young man's veins, and only briefly wondered at the vest before pushing the kid's head sideways, ripping down the collar of his shirt, and sinking his fangs into warm flesh. The boy's struggles did little but increase his already racing heart rate.

Jake had forgotten how intoxicating fear tasted, and almost lost track of his mission.

Shoving back all other thoughts, he concentrated on two: Athena's location, and healing the two gaping holes in his chest. It took only a moment to extract the first, and another drink or two for the second, and he released his victim with a satisfied growl.

Wiping the back of his hand across his mouth, he yanked the young man around to where he could now investigate his odd piece of clothing. It was a Kevlar vest, but more. Inside the front, he found a switch, and when he toggled it up, the vest emitted a strange, bland noise that masked the young man's heartbeat. Jake flipped it on and off several times, then opened it farther to find several rows of batteries taped inside.

"I'll be damned," he muttered.

No wonder he'd had such a hard time tracking Gary Rosier. The boy must have been wearing one of these vests, which was also why he'd been able to hide in the house.

It suddenly hit Jake that all the commotion in his room should have attracted the attention of at least Skidmore and Katie, and he raised his gaze to Beatrice.

"Where are the others?"

His question drew tears to her eyes that tightened a noose around his heart.

He tossed the boy aside, grabbed his jeans and tugged them on, then dashed from his room and ran down the hall. He stopped at the door to Katie's room and grabbed the frame to steady himself.

Katie's beautiful body had already transformed into a skeleton with auburn waves falling from her cruelly grinning skull.

He fell to his knees. "No, Katie, not you."

His insides burned with heartache he couldn't begin to express, and he took one long look before turning away.

Just inside the door lay the body of an attacker, clad in the same electronic vest, his neck torn open. Jake only wished he could have been the one to end the sorry bastard's life.

Pushing himself to his feet, he turned back down the hallway and trotted to Skidmore's door, which he pushed open without stopping.

Thomas Skidmore lay sprawled on the floor, three wooden bolts protruding from the back of his red silk dressing gown.

But he wasn't dust.

Jake hurried to his side. "Thomas? Can you hear me?"

The ancient vampire groaned.

Allowing himself a sigh of relief, Jake gently lifted his friend and carried him to the bed, placing him on his side. The crossbow bolts had gone more than halfway through his body, two very close to his heart. One might have even nicked the precious organ, but he hung on.

Suffering almost as much pain as he'd felt when he worked on his own injuries, Jake broke off the tail ends of the bolts and drew them through Skidmore's body, eliciting only whimpers. Once that was done, he rolled the vampire onto his back and offered him a wrist.

Skidmore responded, latching onto Jake's arm and drinking greedily, until Jake felt his own strength waning.

"Okay, Thomas, that's enough." Wrenching his arm free, he stumbled backward on wobbly legs, glad to see Skidmore moving now, his head lolling from side to side as he smacked his lips.

A hand on Jake's back caused him to jump, and he spun

around to find Beatrice holding out a glass. He downed the contents in two gulps.

With a bit of his strength restored, he returned the glass. "Thank you."

She nodded and moved toward Skidmore.

Jake touched her arm, momentarily stopping her progress. "And thank you for saving my butt, sweet thing."

She smiled and then continued to the ancient vampire's side.

Leaving her to her work, Jake walked the length of the cave, searching every room. He found three slain vampires in their beds and one more dead hunter in the living room and deduced that Beatrice had chased him down. His little mouse had proved to be a ferocious cat when provoked. He understood her actions; they'd both miss Katie terribly.

The front door lay open. Jake closed it and slipped the bolt into place, then stood, one palm pressed to the door as the horror of truth washed over him.

These vampire hunters had followed him to Skidmore's. He was the one responsible for the slaughter.

He straightened. This was a guilt he'd carry for a long time to come.

But for now he had work to do and went about removing corpses. He tossed the assassins' bodies in a heap in the empty dungeon, then carefully placed Elaine's body on a table in the donors' room. Pushing her blond hair back from her face, he studied her pretty features.

"I'm truly sorry about this, dear girl. You sure as hell didn't deserve to die." He kissed her forehead, still warm with life, and then covered her with a sheet.

He carried Dog to another table and was about to cover him when he heard a small thump, and then another. Jake pressed his ear to the beast's chest and listened to the struggling heartbeat.

He dashed back to his room for needle and thread, then returned to the dog's side.

"I'm not a veterinarian, but I've worked on a horse or two over the years," he said to his unconscious patient by way of apology up front. "I'm guessing we're all alike in some respects."

Threading the needle, he went to work, sewing up the long gash across the dog's chest. When he was done, he carried the canine to the front room, where he made a bed for him in front of the fireplace. Dog made a soft, encouraging noise when Jake laid him down.

Weary to the point of dropping, Jake returned to his room long enough to dress, then stretched out on the sofa in the living room, his revolver on the floor beside him. He still had time to sleep before sunset, and now he knew for sure that Athena had still been a prisoner two days ago. He could only hope that he wasn't too late. One thing he'd learned from the young man's blood was that the hunters didn't intend to keep her prisoner for long.

14

Jake stood at the doorway, squinting against a deep red sky. "Come on, dammit, set."

As he stood watching, he realized he'd been cleansed of the desire for a fair fight. In fact, the more one-sided, the better. And if they'd hurt Athena, he'd rip their beating hearts out.

He waited as long as he could, then dashed out, jacket pulled over his head, heat blistering his shoulders and back. When he stumbled into the barn, a cloud of smoke followed him. He tossed the holstered six-shooter onto the front seat of the old Chevy, cranked the engine, and backed out with tires squealing, not bothering to close the barn door.

By the time he reached the outskirts of Santa Fe, the sky had darkened to a rich, royal blue, and stars twinkled overhead.

It took little time to find the house, built off a narrow road behind the racetrack, little more than a door in a mound of dirt. After screeching to a halt in a cloud of dust and jumping from the car, Jake stopped at the edge of the road and studied the camera eye above the door for several moments.

If he dashed forward and flattened himself to the door, it

didn't look like the camera would be able to see him, and he'd be nothing more than a blur as he passed by. Someone would have to be watching very closely to detect his presence.

Jake strapped on his holster, pulled his hat down hard, and took off at preternatural speed. He stopped with his back pressed to the steel door and listened. No noise at all came from the other side.

He tried the handle and found the door locked. Gripping the doorknob, he pressed with his shoulder and a latch inside gave way. The door swung open into darkness. Jake stepped in and eased the door shut. One lesson he'd learned as a gunfighter was never to stand with the light behind him, unless it was the setting sun.

As soon as his eyes adjusted, he studied the strange entry. The room had been painted black, and crosses and crucifixes covered the walls. Some of them could be antiques and were quite attractive.

Jake grinned. He'd found a weakness; the hunters didn't know the difference between the myths and the truths about vampires. He might be able to use that to his advantage.

Only one door led out of the entry, and Jake hurried through it. He knew from the boy's fading memories that there were other cameras around the place, but he couldn't place them. He also *remembered* the general location of the room where they'd held his mate two days earlier. He could only hope to find her still there.

The hallway led past four doorways, two of which were open. Jake stopped beside the first open one and listened. As he leaned forward to look in, the appearance of a face looking back made him jump.

A young woman stood on the other side of the doorway, apparently as startled by him as he was by her. Before she could react, he whipped around the door frame and grabbed her, one hand over her mouth.

She stared up at him with wide terror-filled brown eyes and trembled. Her body heat radiated through her strange army attire, and she smelled warm and soft.

Was she one of them, or another hapless victim like Athena had been?

"Where is she?"

The woman continued to stare.

Jake raised one eyebrow and leaned forward, his face less than three inches from hers. He felt her quick breath on his hand. "Where is she, sweet thing? You really don't want to die for this, do you?"

She swallowed hard, then motioned with her eyes, indicating the path he'd started on.

"Good."

Closing his eyes for a moment, Jake pushed forward a single word. *Sleep*.

He caught the young woman as she collapsed, gathered her up, and carried her to a small bed. Placing her on her back, he straightened her arms and legs, then hurried back to the hallway and continued.

No one else appeared. No alarms sounded.

He made his way down a staircase at the end of the hall that doubled back on itself. At the landing, he drew his revolver. If another one of these pricks decided to put a piece of wood in him, he would return the favor with a bullet.

Halfway down the second flight, something hit him with the force of a headlong gallop into a brick wall, and he stumbled sideways, catching the handrail.

It wasn't anything physical, but something more. He sat down hard.

A pinch in the middle of his chest doubled him over for a moment, and then he straightened. The strange sensation tripped up and down his spine.

"Athena," he whispered.

After all this time, he finally felt her, but the feeling wasn't good. Desperation stung the back of his throat.

Pushing himself back to his feet, he picked up the pace.

The room at the bottom of the stairs looked like any basement, lined with crude shelves filled with junk. But the door he was looking for lay hidden behind a bookshelf at the back.

Jake felt around the bottom of a shelf until he located the button, pushed it, and stepped back, ready to shoot as the shelf swung open.

But no one waited on the other side. The hair on the back of his neck stood on end as he traversed a narrow passageway. He heard no heartbeats, although he now knew that meant nothing. And the closer he got to the prison cell, the sicker he felt.

He stopped at a large, steel door with a small peephole at eye level. After glancing around, he leaned forward and looked inside.

His gut clenched at the sight. "Damn."

He wrenched open the door and hurried across the metal room to where Athena lay curled in a corner, facing the wall, shaking.

"Sweetheart, can you hear me?" He pulled her gently around.

She looked up through golden eyes and hissed.

"It's okay. You'll be all right as soon as we get out of here."

"It's about time you showed up, you son of a bitch."

Jake glanced toward the door.

Chris stood just inside with a crossbow in one hand and a large silver crucifix in the other, sneering triumphantly. "You can put the pistol down now and push it over here."

Jake stood, holding his revolver at his side. He had no doubt he was faster than the bastard, but he couldn't take the chance of a bolt hitting Athena in her weakened state. She wouldn't survive. And the punk wore one of the Kevlar vests. Jake had never been that great at head shots.

He took a step to his right.

"I said, drop it." Chris aimed the crossbow.

"Okay, whoa." Jake raised his empty hand in surrender as he placed the revolver on the floor and pushed it forward. He took another step to his right.

Chris held up the crucifix, hooked the crossbow on his belt, and leaned down to pick up the pistol and jam it into his belt.

Under normal circumstances, Jake would have taken advantage of this moment of weakness to attack, but strange sensations assaulted his senses, momentarily immobilizing him. By the time he shook them off, Chris had his crossbow leveled at Jake's chest again.

Anger threatened to make him careless. "Why the hell have you treated her like this? She thinks you loved her once."

The boy huffed. "She's a vampire."

"She's still Athena."

"No, she isn't." He tossed a disgusted glance at the corner where Athena lay curled and shaking. "She's one of you now."

"Why are you hunting us like this? Don't you have better things to do with your life?"

"Shut up!" Chris held out the crucifix as if brandishing a weapon.

Jake flinched and stepped back, deciding it best to let his opponent think himself more armed than he was.

Chris followed him a step, closing the distance between them by a foot or two. "Now I decide what to do with you. Maybe I should lock you both in here and let you starve together. It could be an interesting documentary for the army."

"The army?"

"Of vampire hunters."

Jake raised his eyebrows in surprise. "I didn't know there was such a thing."

Chris grinned. "There seems to be a lot you don't know."

"Like what?"

Jake took another step back, and Chris took two forward.

"Like the fact that we've been watching you for days. Like the fact that we've figured out how to hide from you. Like the fact that we're going to wipe you all off the face of the earth."

"Son, you sure seem to be taking this personally."

"Yeah?" Chris stepped closer and narrowed his eyes. "One of you fuckers took my mother."

"*Took?*"

"Yes, took. He broke into our house and kidnapped her when I was four. Her body was never even found."

"You sure she didn't just leave?"

"Shut up!"

"Women leave their families sometimes. Maybe the vampire story was a kid's way of dealing with his mother leaving."

"Oh yeah?" Using the hand holding the crucifix, he yanked down the collar of his shirt to reveal angry red scars left by Jake's fangs. "Did I *imagine* this?" He pointed with the cross, stepping closer. "You tried to kill me."

"If I remember correctly, it was self-defense."

"Shut up!"

The young man stood less than six feet from him now, and Jake knew he could easily disarm the punk, in spite of the mental disruptions from Athena.

But he didn't get the chance.

In a flash of color accompanying a surreal screech, Athena flew to Chris's throat, one hand on his forehead, the other clenched on his shoulder, and sank her fangs in faster than even Jake could see. He dashed forward, wrenched the crossbow and crucifix from the punk's hands, and hurried to the door to make sure no one waited on the other side to lock them in.

Surprisingly, they seemed to be alone. Hopefully, the rest of Chris's army had died at Skidmore's.

Tossing the weapons aside, Jake returned to where Athena drank greedily from the mortal, who sank to his knees, pale and wide-eyed.

"Athena, stop. You're taking too much." He grabbed her arm.

Her golden eyes snapped open and zeroed in on him with animal distrust as she growled a warning.

"Athena, it's me, Jake. Come on, sweetheart." He knelt and grasped her shoulders as the predator and prey fell to the floor. "Athena."

She turned on him and sank her fangs into his arm, not to drink but to bite.

Jake winced.

She tore herself from his grasp and backed away until she hit the wall and crouched, looking around like a cornered wild beast, shaking and growling.

He knelt to meet her at eye level. "Athena, listen to me. The vampire has taken over. You have to fight it. I know you're in there, sweetheart. Please come back to me. I need you."

He reached out and she flew at him, clawing at his arms as she bit into his shoulder.

Jake stood and held her to him in spite of the pain of her attack. He closed his eyes, pushing forward thoughts of love and peace. "It's okay. I'm here."

In spite of the violence, his body reacted to the sensual element of her bite.

After a few moments, she stilled in his arms, drinking from him, and the growling stopped.

He stroked her hair with one hand as he held her, and kissed the side of her head. "I love you, Athena."

Her hands flattened and then slid around his shoulders as she withdrew her teeth from his flesh. She pressed her face into his neck.

The noose around his heart finally loosened as he held her, and she quit shaking. He inhaled her special scent and smiled as it wound its magic through him.

"Jake," she said, her voice rusty.

"Yes, darlin'. It's me. You're okay now."

She nodded.

Holding her, he pushed Chris with the toe of his boot and saw no reaction, and he heard no hint of a heartbeat. He leaned down and took his revolver from the boy's belt, shoved it into his holster, and carried Athena from her cell.

He stopped outside the steel door and released her. "Sweetheart, you wait right here for just a minute."

She slid slowly down the front of his body until her feet touched the floor, then stood looking up at him with blood smeared across her face.

"I'll be right back," he said.

He wound his way to the observation booth and eased the door open on an unoccupied room. Stepping in, he glanced around, impressed with the amount of surveillance equipment. Chris and his buddies had spent a pretty penny on this place. They must have some wealthy backer somewhere, or Chris had a fortune stashed when he lived in the run-down house in south Santa Fe with the other hunters. He'd have to look into that.

Later. Now he needed to get rid of a few things.

He pressed buttons until tape machines popped open, and he rifled through cabinets. Grabbing a metal trash can, he tossed in every videotape, photograph, and note he could find. Then he pulled a book of matches from his pocket and lit several pieces of paper. Fairly sure the can's contents would catch, he hurried back to Athena and scooped her into his arms.

"Okay, sweet thing, let's get you out of here."

She wrapped her arms around his neck and rested her head on his chest as he hurried back out. Flinging mental curses over his shoulder, he slid Athena into the passenger's side of the Chevy. After kissing her head and closing her door, he strolled around to the driver's side and climbed in.

Athena studied him for a moment without speaking, then stretched out on her side with her head on his thigh. He stroked her hair as he drove, and she clung to his leg and slept.

Athena awoke standing in a warm spray of water.

She jumped, terrified that her captors had found some new way to torture her, waited, then looked over to find Jake standing beside her, holding her upright in the shower.

"It's all right, sweet thing." His deep drawl flowed over her with the water, warming more than her skin.

As she stood, watching, he washed her gently from head to toe, soaping her skin and rinsing it in the shower's spray. Then he dropped the soap, leaned forward, and kissed her.

His mouth covered hers with tenderness, offering comfort and stimulation, and she accepted both.

They stood together for a long time, Jake with one hand pressed against the shower wall behind her and the other holding her waist, kissing. She clung to his wide shoulders, opening her mouth to him and taking him in. When she found the sides of his fangs with the tip of her tongue, he groaned softly. That one sound sparked instant hunger deep in her belly.

She ran her hands over his chest and down the length of his lean stomach, finding each scar and indentation, enjoying the way his muscles quivered beneath her fingers. His hand slid up and down her back and over her buttocks.

She reached down and touched his swelling erection, and he groaned again, this time his own hunger resonating in the sound.

He raised his head and frowned down at her. "Are you up to some lovemaking, darlin'?"

"Are you?"

He chuckled and glanced down. "I thought that was obvious."

She also looked down to where her fingers curled around the shaft of his cock. "Yes, I guess it is." Then she raised her face back to his.

He took her mouth, more ardently this time, and she felt his hunger as her own. She slipped her arms around his neck and surrendered.

With his strong hands spread on her butt, he whispered, "Wrap those incredible legs around me, sweet thing," and lifted, and she did, locking her feet behind him.

He held his mouth near her ear, whispering as he eased into her. "Sweetheart, I need to be inside you, to taste your joy, to feel you. Hmm, so good, so damned perfect."

She enveloped his growing erection completely, gasping at the way he filled her.

"Oh, yeah," he said, his voice deeper. "Perfect."

To have him as part of her again promised more joy than she ever remembered feeling. The shower took on a strange gold and blue glow as her lust grew and her eyes changed. She opened her mouth to let her fangs press against her bottom lip, and they throbbed with pleasant longing.

He turned to press her against the shower wall, sliding his cool lips over the side of her neck, sending a shiver up her spine. She raised her head, exposing her most vulnerable spots to him. He eased in and out of her in a wonderfully luxurient rhythm, warm water flowing over, around, and between them. His mouth came to rest on her shoulder, and she felt the tips of his fangs against her skin.

His rhythm sparked her own, curling her body to his, heightening her longing to something more. She needed more of him, all of him.

"Now, Jake. Take me now."

He clamped down on her shoulder and thrust harder, filling her, his chest vibrating with low, contented growls.

She bit into his neck and an exquisite orgasm rolled through her body, pure ecstasy, bliss, expanding her being to take up all space, then squeezing her back into her skin.

And then she tasted her own orgasm pulsing back through her and knew Jake's joy as they both came again, crashing together in perfect harmony, clinging to each other as if they would do so forever.

"Yes, sweet thing," he whispered in her ear.

She raised her mouth from his neck and dropped her head back to the wall, smiling as she licked her lips.

Jake held her pinned to the wall and ran his hands over her tingling wet skin. "Now, that was worth waiting for, darlin'."

"Yeah, it was."

He kissed her lips.

Jake left Athena stretched out on his bed, pulled on his jeans, and wandered down the hall in search of drinks. They both needed nourishment before sunrise. He stopped at Skidmore's room and knocked on the door.

"Come in, dear boy."

Jake grinned and eased the door open.

Skidmore lay propped on a pile of pillows, wearing a black silk dressing gown, and holding a blue glass.

"You're lookin' a little better than you were last time I saw you." Jake crossed the room and winked at Beatrice as he sat on the edge of the bed.

She'd returned to her mousy state, but the lioness's fire still glowed through her eyes from somewhere down deep. She sat on the floor beside the bed, petting Dog, who lay with his head in her lap. Skidmore twirled a strand of her hair in his long fingers.

Dog, apparently on the road to recovery, opened one eye and whined softly.

"Don't tell me you're surprised that I've survived," Skidmore said, scolding.

Jake shook his head. "No, not really."

"Of course, I still have a strange taste in my mouth." He cringed. "I believe it is . . . cowboy, *pard-ner.*"

Jake laughed, then they sat quietly as the specter of Katie rose around them.

"We'll all miss her, dear boy. She was a force."

"Yep, she sure as hell was."

"So," Skidmore said, adjusting himself on the pillows, "what will you do now?"

"I think we'll head up to my place."

"You don't plan to live in that infernal rat's nest, do you?"

Jake frowned. "It's not that bad. All it needs is a woman's touch."

Skidmore sighed. "Don't forget to write."

"How about I just drop by now and then?" He rose. "Will you take care of Dog for me?"

"His name is Sir William. We refuse to have a beast named *Dog* living with us, don't we, my dear?"

"Yes, Thomas," Beatrice said, her voice soft and sweet.

Jake stopped at the door to glance back at the strange new family, then continued to the kitchen. He poured two glasses and carried them to his room.

Athena lay sprawled on his bed, her gorgeous body milk white in the dim light. With one arm over her head and her legs partially open, she looked relaxed and a little too tempting. Jake grinned as he settled onto the bed beside her and handed her a glass.

She sat up and scooted back to the headboard, took a long sip, then stared at the glass she held in both hands. Her beautiful brow furrowed. "Jake."

"Yes, sweet thing."

"Do you think there are more of them?"

"The hunters?"

She nodded.

"I don't know." He sighed. "Did you find out anything from Chris?"

Her gaze rose to his. "You mean, when I attacked him?"

Noting guilt in her eyes, he rested a hand on her thigh. "That wasn't your fault. You can't blame yourself."

She looked down at her glass again and shook her head slowly. "I don't even remember it, Jake. Not really. I mean, I know I did it, but it was like I was watching someone else. You know?"

"I know exactly. That's what it's like when the vampire rules. Some aren't strong enough to keep the monster on a leash. You're doing just fine, darlin'."

"The only reason I came back at all was because of you."

He winked and raised his glass. "I'm yours, sweetheart."

She met his toast and sipped, then returned her glass to her lap. "For how long?"

"For as long as you want me."

A smile slowly brightened her gorgeous face, and they finished their drinks without further conversation.

"I see what you mean about feeling the sunrise," she said, pulling covers over her bare legs. She yawned and turned to her side.

Jake stripped off his pants, stretched out behind her, and drew her into him, nuzzling her hair. She smelled of lilac blossoms on a summer breeze and sweet sex. God, he wanted her again.

She yawned, then relaxed against him.

Jake closed his eyes, but couldn't imagine sleeping. If anyone walked through his door this day, he'd be there in a flash. He wasn't letting anything happen to Athena now that he had her back where she belonged.

Damn, he wished she'd remembered Chris's thoughts. He'd like to know how many more fanatics were out there.

15

"This Is it?"

Jake lit a lantern, lowered the glass, and turned to study Athena. She stood a few feet away, hands in the back pockets of her jeans, cringing as she looked around at the sandstone walls of the mine's entrance.

"Well, it gets a little better. Come on, I'll show you around."

They walked the length of the opening and stopped in front of the end wall. Jake glanced back at her and grinned. Her green eyes glistened in the lamplight.

He reached out and pressed the small switch disguised as rock, and a hatch at their feet rose. Holding the lantern out just above the opening, he nodded. "After you, sweet thing."

Athena sighed heavily and started down the timber ladder. Jake followed.

At the end of the small gallery, he opened a second hidden door and led the way into the larger gallery he'd spent ten years carving out.

She stepped around him and strolled to the end of the shadow-marred room, pressed on the bed as if to test the mattress, then turned in a slow circle. "*Jake.*"

"Hang on. Maybe a little light will help." He flipped on the first row of blue lights, illuminating bookshelves, the stereo and television, and a red velvet sofa he took a liking to the moment he saw it in a store in Colorado. The delivery truck driver hadn't really wanted to place it in the back of the old pickup truck, but had agreed after seeing the hundred-dollar tip.

Athena stepped forward, her face transformed with a tentative smile.

"Better?"

She shrugged. "A little."

He hit the second row of switches and twin alcoves appeared in the sidewall, holding the fireplace and reading chair in one and the refrigerator and cabinets in the other. And with the final panel of lights, the gold-fixture bathroom appeared, complete with glass-enclosed shower and deep, wide tub.

"Oh, Jake, this is nice." She dashed across to the tub and ran her fingers along the edge.

"The best part isn't in here."

"No?"

He shook his head, grinning at the thought of sharing the night with her, then motioned with his head. "Come on."

She followed him back the way they'd come, taking his hand as they emerged from the adit opening. "What is it—?"

They stopped at the *pop*. A small rockslide dribbled down the hillside behind them.

"Gunshot," Jake said, pulling Athena to his side.

Another *pop*.

They dashed to the closest clump of trees.

Athena gripped his arm. "What happens if we get shot?"

"Well, it most likely won't kill you, but trust me, you won't feel real good."

A shot sent bark into the air just above their heads.

Athena jumped. "Who's shooting?"

Jake peered around the tree. "I don't know. But it sounds like a handgun." He wished he had his Colt.

Although he couldn't see too many details without moonlight, he could definitely see a car parked at the base of the hill, and there seemed to be someone crouched behind it. He could just make out a head poking up above the hood and starlight glistening off the barrel of a revolver.

"You get him talking, and I'll get behind him."

Jake tried to start forward, but Athena grabbed his arm. He turned back.

"Be careful, Jake. I don't want to lose you."

He leaned down and kissed her wonderful mouth, smiling against her lips. "Don't worry, sweet thing, you're not getting rid of me that easily."

Pop.

Athena drew in at the zing of a bullet whizzing past, then leaned back around the tree. She'd lost track of Jake, but guessed he must be halfway down the hillside to the road.

"Who are you? Why are you shooting at us?"

Instead of an answer, she heard muttering, then another shot that thudded into the ground at least ten feet in front of her. Whoever was shooting wasn't very good at it.

She cocked her head to listen to a second round of muttering—the shooter seemed to be having trouble with the weapon—and decided their attacker was female.

"Who's there?"

In a flurry of movement, the muttering rose to muffled screams and something clanged to the ground, then a shadowy figure rose beside the car. As the figure moved forward, she realized it was Jake holding their attacker in front of him, his hand over her mouth. Athena walked out to meet them.

"Do you know her?"

She studied the dark-haired woman, dressed in khaki, glaring at her with brown eyes. She couldn't be much more than twenty, and was about Athena's own size, maybe a little smaller.

"No. I've never seen her before."

"I have," Jake said. "We ran into each other when I was looking for you."

Athena leaned closer as Jake removed his hand from the woman's mouth, but still didn't recognize her face. "You're a hunter?"

"You bitch! You killed him!"

Athena flinched.

"He loved me," she continued. "How could you do it?"

Athena studied the woman's eyes, which were filled with hatred, terror, and loss.

"How do you know he loved you?"

She hesitated a moment. "He told me so."

Athena glanced up at Jake, who stood behind the woman holding her arms, then returned her attention to their attacker. "He told me the same thing. Now I know it wasn't true."

"Liar!"

She shook her head slowly, sympathy growing in her chest for Chris's latest victim. "I'm not lying. He told me I was the only person who ever understood him and knew how to make him happy, that I knew how he felt because I didn't have anyone else in the world, either."

The woman's eyes widened at her words, most likely words she'd heard, too.

"What's your name?"

"Sally," she answered in little more than a whisper.

"Sally, Chris used me, and he was using you. If he hadn't already asked you to be the bait in his hunt, he would have."

Sally stiffened. "He never would have risked my safety. He loved me."

Athena shook her head. "No, he was too obsessed. He couldn't love anyone."

"That's not true."

She sighed and glanced up at Jake again. "What now?"

"How many more hunters are there?" Jake asked his prisoner.

Sally clenched her jaw. "Hundreds."

Jake raised one eyebrow in a gesture of disbelief, then he spoke softly to Athena. "There's only one way to find out."

She nodded, and answered just as quietly. "We don't have to kill her, do we?"

"No."

"Good."

Jake wrapped his arm around Sally's waist, and she started to struggle. "What are you doing?"

He used his free hand to pull her dark hair back, exposing the side of her neck, and spoke within her hearing range. "I promise, this won't hurt much. In fact, sweet Sally, I promise you'll enjoy it if you relax."

Watching Jake nuzzle the woman's neck stirred a strange excitement in Athena's belly, reminding her of the first time he'd shared mortal blood with her. She felt her fangs grow, and the air seemed to crackle with electricity.

"That's better," Jake said as he ran his lips along Sally's exposed shoulder.

Sally's eyes fluttered and she leaned her head to the side as she released a soft groan.

Athena stepped closer, hearing the woman's heartbeat now, calling to her as if by name.

Jake's gaze rose to meet hers, and she saw gold glistening in his eyes as he drew his lips back to bare his fangs.

She reached out and stroked Sally's arm, then touched Jake's shoulder.

Jake growled softly and pierced Sally's flesh.

The memory of ecstasy closed Athena's eyes for a second. She opened them and watched Jake drink.

Sally cried out, then whimpered as her body jerked against Jake's hold with orgasmic movements, and he slid one hand to her crotch.

When he lifted his mouth away, his eyes remained closed for a long moment, and his tongue slid over his lips. Then he leaned over Sally's shoulder and met Athena's demanding kiss with his own. She tasted the hint of Sally's essence and saw strange flashes in her mind, faded photographs someone flipped through like flashcards.

When he ended the kiss, he smiled down at Athena. "She's the last."

Athena nodded, relieved by the news. "Now what?"

"Now we clear her memories."

"How?"

Jake scooped the nearly unconscious Sally into his arms and carried her down to her car.

Athena followed. Standing a few feet away, she watched.

Leaning back against the car, Jake held Sally in his arms like a lover, although her arms hung limp at her sides. He closed his eyes and nuzzled her neck and hair again, but this time Athena felt strange vibrations coming from him. They rippled through her and over her skin until she had to sit down.

He continued, kissing the side of Sally's neck and then holding her close, her face against his chest. She stirred a little, raising one hand to his shoulder. And the vibration continued to strengthen for at least another ten minutes.

Finally, the sensations stopped abruptly, and Jake sagged against the car, Sally still in his arms.

Athena jumped up and ran to him, propping him up with an arm around his waist.

He smiled down at her weakly. "Can you drive us out of here?"

"Sure."

Athena helped him get Sally into the backseat where she slept, and then held the door open for Jake to flop into the passenger side of the Ford. She glanced over at him as she started the car and found his eyes closed.

"Are you okay?"

"Yep. Just a little tired at the moment, sweet thing. Let's get Sally back to Santa Fe before she wakes up."

Jake sank to his neck in steaming water, sighing as warmth enveloped him. He leaned back on smooth rock and relaxed, feeling the strength ooze back into his body. Small waves lapped against his chin as Athena settled in beside him.

"This is wonderful," she said.

"Yep." He reached out and took her hand. "The best part of the place."

Opening his eyes, he looked up at the star-filled sky and smiled. As beautiful as it was, though, the view improved when Athena leaned over to fill it with her gorgeous face.

She straddled him, holding his shoulders, and studied his face. "You look a little better."

"I'm glad. You look fantastic."

She smiled. "So, what did you do to her?"

He shrugged and ran his hands up her bare thighs to her waist. Heated water pressed against his skin as it flowed past, suggesting a liquid blanket of pleasure.

"I gave her memories to replace the ones she had of her time with the hunters."

"What kind of memories?"

"Pleasant ones. Moonlight walks on the beach with a handsome stranger, that sort of thing."

"A tall stranger with blue eyes and a seductive drawl?"

He smiled at her mischievous grin. "You guessed it, darlin'."

She kissed him and wrapped her legs around him, and they bobbed together in the water. Then she rested her head against his and he held her close.

"Will you teach me how to do that?" she asked.

"Of course."

"Good."

As they sat together quietly, an owl screeched nearby, and the night wind whistled through the tops of ponderosa pines. Peace floated down around them like fall leaves.

"It's getting late," she whispered.

"Uh-huh." He ran his fingers down her back and back up, enjoying the feel of her submerged skin.

She pressed her mouth to his ear. "Wanna fuck?"

He laughed. "I do believe you've become a crude woman, Athena."

"It's your fault."

He turned his head and took her waiting mouth, groaning softly as his fangs lengthened. Smiling against her lips, he said, "I like crude."

Reaching between them, she guided his cock to her. "I know."

Bite Me Again

Prologue

"Lookin' for some fun?"

Daniel Ward glanced down into the bloodshot eyes of the young woman who had weaved into his path.

After a month of fasting, he was indeed searching, but not for what this one offered. He needed strength, not addiction.

"No, thank you."

As he started around her, she maneuvered to remain in front of him.

"Name's Elena. What's yours?" She moved closer and reached for the front of his pants.

He grabbed her wrist and glared down at her dirty face, assaulted by the smell of stale sex, sour booze, and sweat. His initial irritation with her insistence, however, dissolved into pity as he saw through her alcoholic haze to the desperation barely hidden below.

In a delayed reaction to his annoyance, she drew back.

For a moment, sympathy and need battled within him as he listened to the steady, thundering beat of her heart and felt her quickening pulse against the palm of his hand. Just a small taste and the moon beast inside his chest would retract its ripping claws.

"Maybe, uh, I should go," Elena said, trying to pry his fingers from her wrist, fear causing her heart to race.

And he recalled his own fear as if he'd felt it only yesterday: the fear of pain, hunger, cold, and eternal loneliness.

Stepping back, he bowed, raised her hand to his lips, and pressed bills into her palm. He straightened. "Indeed, you should."

She stared at the money in her hand, and then up at him.

Daniel smiled and winked. "Farewell, Elena. Perhaps we shall meet another time."

Still trying to emerge from the residue of his wretched past, he hurried on.

Across Paseo de Peralta, he spotted a familiar figure approaching and felt his spirits lift. The voluptuous brunette grinned and waved.

Hunger hacked at his soul as he followed her into a darkened alley, his entire body aching now with need.

"You been away awhile," Tina said.

"Yes." He wrapped an arm around her waist.

"Why?" She pressed her hands to his sides.

No longer interested in self-examination, he drew back the collar of her blouse, exposing her tender flesh as he fell backward against the wall.

"Still turning tricks?" he asked.

"Yep." She made quick work of his shirt buttons. "Gotta pay the rent, sugar." With experienced ease, she opened the front of his pants and extracted his hardening phallus.

Daniel closed his eyes and dropped his head back to the stucco wall to enjoy the feel of Tina's hot mouth on his cock. She took him in with big, slurping gulps, sucking and sliding along the length of him.

Pleasure crept up his spine and along his limbs, chasing out the darkness. If he wasn't careful, that darkness would someday take over his existence, extinguishing the last of his light, and he'd disappear.

But not tonight.

The beast rose within him, awakening to the promise of bliss, growling with delight.

He lifted Tina by the arms, turned around, and pinned her to the wall.

She wrapped her legs around his hips, laughing. "In a hurry, huh?"

"Yes." He entered her as quickly as he dared, burying his cock in her wet heat.

With his lips pressed to her neck, he started the slow, steady rhythm he knew she liked, and her laughter lowered to low, guttural noises of pleasure. He enjoyed the hard nubs of her nipples against his chest as her breathing grew shallow and fast.

Yes, this was exactly what he needed, to feel life and joy and pleasure, to experience it all.

Her pulse quickened as she approached the precipice, and he matched it with his thrusts. Opening his mouth, he held his fangs poised over her flesh, waiting for just the right moment.

"Oh, yeah," she breathed. "That's it." Her body tightened and her fingers curled into fists against his shoulders, then she bucked under him in uncontrolled spasms.

He pierced her neck.

She cried out, her voice muffled in his shirt.

Her orgasm ripped through him, spurring his body to respond, and he savored the light of her ecstasy as he filled her. Emotions and strength snapped and fired in his brain, and he shook with delight.

The monster drank, elated, enraptured, greedy.

Her sweet nectar inundated the voids, and he groaned as he withdrew, knowing just how much could be extracted without notice. He covered the wounds with his mouth until they healed.

Her warm breath heated his neck as the two stood joined together.

Why did he torture himself with questions? The past was irrelevant, and certainly unalterable. Perhaps this was the truth he sought.

Tina had wanted physical pleasure. No more. She harbored no lofty goals or secrets. He'd provided the pleasure and shared in her joy.

Now he was happy.

Could it be that simple?

Carefully, he straightened, lowering Tina to her feet. She smoothed her skirt and blouse, and buttoned his shirt as he closed his breeches.

She smiled up at him. "You're the only one who knows how to make me come. I sure wish you'd stop by more often."

He stroked her warm cheek. "You know what they say about too much of a good thing."

"Yeah, but they're full of shit," she said.

Daniel laughed and kissed the side of her head as he tucked bills into her blouse pocket. "Perhaps they are."

As he emerged from the alley, he inhaled cool night air, sipping at the scents of Santa Fe as if they were wine, and he vowed to keep the past where it belonged.

1

"Come on, Carrie. Don't be a pussy."

"I'm not. I just feel . . . *sick*."

Daniel crouched on a roof's edge, listening to the exchange on the sidewalk below between a young redhead and a blonde, the aforementioned Carrie. The two women appeared to be in their middle twenties, but he knew enough to have no faith in his estimate.

"Well, I'm not sitting around here all night watching you puke your guts out," the redhead said.

Carrie lowered herself somewhat less than gracefully to the curb and waved her friend away with one hand. "Go on. I'll wait here."

"You can't just sit here on the street."

The young blonde dropped her head into her hands and groaned.

"Great." The redhead stood with her fists on her practically bare and quite lovely hips, searching for an answer to her dilemma. Faithful friendship or the call of the wild? "All right, fine. I'll go see if I can find us a ride back to the hotel, okay?"

Carrie nodded without raising her head.

"So much for a night out on the town. Here we are in Santa Fe, New Mexico, and you can't even handle—"

The redhead disappeared into the building on which Daniel perched.

In the weeks since emerging from his last bout of self-denial, he'd decided his initial impression was correct. His greatest source of pleasure lay in discovering what mortals truly wanted and trying his best to provide it. Certainly the young Carrie needed assistance locating her road to happiness.

At first he thought she might be starting to lose the contents of her ailing stomach, but then he realized she was crying, sobbing softly into her hands.

He leapt to the ground, landing silently on the sidewalk behind the young woman, and then sat beside her. "Poor dear," he said.

Startled, Carrie jumped and scooted away from him. Her eyes, red and swollen, glistened with tears in the streetlights.

Several drunken individuals stumbled from the bar behind them and started down the sidewalk, singing an unidentifiable tune, but Daniel ignored them. He focused all his attention on the young woman sitting an arm's length away, her misery plain to see, and more than just physical in nature.

"You aren't having much fun, are you?"

Carrie glanced around, her eyes wide. "Where . . . who . . . who are you?"

He smiled his best to put her at ease. "Daniel Ward, at your service."

Her brown-eyed gaze settled on his face, then slid down to his boots and back up. "Are you an actor or something?"

He shook his head. "Although I have participated in the profession in the past, I no longer take to the stage. I prefer a more personal touch."

"You're from England, aren't you?"

"Originally, yes."

"I thought so."

Judging by her scent and the movement of her eyes, her nervousness lessened as they spoke.

"And you're not from this area, either. Let me guess." He squinted his eyes and tapped one finger to his lips, as if identifying the origins of her speech patterns were a difficult task. "The upper Mississippi valley, perhaps in the St. Louis area, but not the city itself. Something smaller, more quaint. Am I right?"

Her eyes widened again, but this time suggesting surprise more than fright. "Union, Missouri. How'd you know?"

"I make it my business to know such things. I've studied linguistics, somewhat informally, for many more years than you'd guess."

"Wow." Carrie brushed her hair back from her face with both hands. "Do you live here?"

"At the moment. I like to move around, keep things interesting." He could smell her fear subsiding, and enjoyed her soft lilac fragrance rising above the street stench. Leaning a little closer, he ascertained that the scent originated in her yellow-white hair and wondered if it was as soft as it appeared to be. "Are you feeling better?"

She shrugged with one pretty shoulder. "I guess. I'm just not a drinker."

"I understand. It takes some conditioning."

"Do you drink a lot?"

"Only when necessary." He eyed the gentle rise and fall of the vein in her neck that whispered to him in a steady, soft drumbeat of hidden pleasures.

She swallowed hard. "You're not, like, some kook or something, are you?"

"I don't believe that to be the case. Do you know many kooks?"

She shook her head. "Everyone I know in Union is normal, and boring, just like my soon-to-be ex. The only thing he ever did that wasn't boring was sleep with my ex–best friend."

"Ah." He rose. "A scorned woman, out to mend a broken heart. It's excitement you're after." He extended his hand.

Carrie glanced back at the door of the bar, then up at him. "My friend Amber is coming back out any second now."

"Yes, I heard her say that. Should we check on her situation?"

After several moments of hesitation, Carrie placed her hand in his and Daniel drew her to her feet. Offering his arm, he led her into the drinking establishment.

The bar, somewhat off the beaten path, was overly dark and full of people, but Daniel had no trouble locating the woman in question amid a group of older men searching for lost youth and young men sporting drinks, gangly limbs, and, no doubt, falsified identification. "I believe your friend is over there," he said to the woman beside him, indicating with a nod.

Carrie stiffened beside him. "She was just going to leave me out there. What a bitch."

It took little time to sort out the true state of affairs in this minor theatrical performance.

Daniel leaned close to the young woman. "Do you wish to make your friend jealous? And, perhaps, find a little of the excitement you crave in the process?"

She glanced up at him, her eyes reflecting blue and red lights from over the bar, and she nodded as a smile tugged at the corners of her luscious mouth.

"Then let us proceed." Drawing himself up to his full height, he caressed Carrie's arm with his fingertips and focused on her his most enraptured smile. "Tell me, dear Carrie, do you like to dance?"

"Dance?" She glanced around. "I guess, but I'm not real good at it."

"A simple waltz, perhaps?"

"A *waltz*? You're kidding, right?"

"Not at all. Here, trust yourself to my care." He took her hand, drew her into his arms, and led her to the small impromptu dance floor where he adapted his steps to match the modern beat. Their waltz wouldn't have met with Fred Astaire's approval, but Daniel enjoyed holding Carrie close.

He liked the latest fashions, which allowed for so much bare skin to peruse. He studied the indentations and freckles on her shoulders as he nuzzled her soft yellow hair. She smelled of more than just lilac. He picked out soap, cigarette smoke, tequila, sweet human sweat, Egyptian incense, and a touch of sexual stimulation.

Carrie's feet collided with his when they started out, but he found her a quick study. Before the end of their second circle, she'd caught on.

"Wow. This is cool," she said.

"I am pleased you find it so," he whispered into her ear.

"You must dance a lot."

"I have not danced in far too long."

When the music stopped, he stepped back and bowed, and Carrie giggled. Then he led her to the bar, an arm's reach from her friend. Carrie raised her nose and cast a disdainful glance at the redhead.

"It was great finding you here, Daniel," she said, loud enough for her friend to hear. She pressed her palm to his chest.

"Indeed it was my good fortune, dear Carrie," he replied, leaning close to her shoulder.

The vein in her neck pulsed gently, temptingly. Daniel watched it for a few long moments, and then pressed his lips against her hair.

"You smell wonderful," he whispered.

Her breath caught in her throat, and he turned her face toward him. No longer aware of others in the room, he kissed her lovely, warm lips.

Her mouth resisted his at first, her lips hard with surprise, but he lingered as he stroked the side of her jaw with one finger.

When he opened his mouth to hers, she responded, inviting him to explore, and he accepted her invitation with enthusiasm. Wrapping one arm around her waist, he eased her up against him, thrilling to her soft, heated flesh under his palm, and her full breasts pressed to his chest.

She slid her arms around his neck.

"A-hem."

Sensing a presence to his left, Daniel withdrew his attention from Carrie, but encircled her shoulders with one arm.

Her redheaded friend stood before them, arms crossed, glowering. "What the hell are you doing?"

Carrie didn't answer right away.

"How do you do? I'm Daniel, and I understand you are a friend of my dear Carrie's?"

"Uh, yeah." The redhead's forehead wrinkled with confusion.

"This is Amber," Carrie finally said.

"Ah, Amber, what a lovely name. Perhaps you'd care to join us?"

"*Join* you?"

"In a drink." He waved to the bartender. "A bottle of your best champagne, please."

When neither young woman responded, Daniel motioned to the closest empty table, and Amber led the way.

He leaned close to Carrie as they walked. "You needn't actually drink, if you don't wish to. Simply pretend to. That's what I often do."

She smiled and nodded.

Daniel seated himself between the two young women and draped his arm across the back of Carrie's chair. Just under the din, he heard her heartbeat quicken and knew she enjoyed their little charade.

Not one to miss an opportunity, the bartender quickly appeared with a '96 Dom Perignon, filled three glasses, and then unceremoniously deposited the bottle on the table with a warning glance.

Daniel knew the look well. It said, "Don't even consider leaving before your bill is paid." He nodded his reassurance to the man, unsure of its effectiveness.

Daniel raised his glass. "To new friends in old places."

"Yeah," Carrie said, raising hers.

Amber joined in the toast, but with obvious reservations.

They sipped, or pretended to in some cases, and Amber's reservations appeared to slip a notch. "Damn, that's really good," she said, studying her glass.

"It should be." Daniel winked conspiratorially at Carrie.

"I've heard of this stuff," she continued, checking the bottle, "but I've never tasted it. Is it really like a hundred bucks a bottle?"

"Something in that vicinity," he said.

Even Carrie's eyes widened.

Amber seemed to suddenly remember herself. "It's not bad."

"Cost, however, is irrelevant. The best drinks, money cannot buy. What's important is the company one keeps. Don't you think, Carrie?"

She nodded and sipped her champagne.

"Hey, man, what are you doin'?" A large man wearing jeans, a too-tight shirt, and a poorly fitting jacket placed his pawlike hands on Amber's shoulders and leaned against the back of her chair. "You can't hog all the pretty girls at one table."

If there had been a candle burning on the table, the intruder's breath would have likely started a conflagration.

Daniel rose quickly, donning his most dangerous sneer. "I suggest you find your entertainment elsewhere, *friend*."

The drunkard stared him in the eye for a moment, but finally stumbled back a step, then turned and made his way to the bar. His surrender did not prevent him from grumbling loudly his complaint about the clientele allowed to drink in this establishment.

Daniel gave the man a moment to quiet down. When he didn't, Daniel excused himself and strolled to the dolt's side at the bar.

"Sir," he said to the bartender. "We'd like some light fare, nachos perhaps, at our table. Can you provide something?"

The bartender nodded, but kept an eye on the two men.

Being under such close scrutiny when he worked would have been a problem eons ago. Now it was merely a challenge Daniel couldn't resist.

With a gentle nudge, he distracted his mark long enough to slip the man's wallet into his own pocket. "Perhaps," he said, "we can settle this bit of unpleasantness in another manner. Do you know this game?" Daniel drew forward a leather cup from the counter and shook the die inside.

"Sure," his opponent answered.

"I'll make you a wager, then. Say, fifty dollars from you if I win, against an invitation from me to join us if you win. Sound fair?"

The man stiffened his back and grinned as he reached for the cup. "Why not?"

Daniel stayed his hand. "Your money first, sir."

He laughed, but the laughter froze in his throat as his hand slid into an empty pocket. "What—"

The drunkard suddenly sobered as he checked other possible locations in his clothing, then spun in a circle, examining the bar and floor. "Where the hell's my wallet?"

At this, the bartender took an interest. "You owe me for that drink," he said, pointing to a drained glass of ice and skewered olives.

"Perhaps you should retrace your steps from earlier in the evening," Daniel suggested. He drew a bill from his own pocket. "And allow me to cover your tab."

"Yeah, thanks," the man said as he continued to search the dark floor on his way to the door.

Daniel watched him stop at a table of associates, explain his situation, and then leave, and smiled to himself at this simple success. He was about to turn back to his female companions when his gaze stopped on a woman across the room who stared at him through wide eyes.

At first he thought he knew her, that recognition was the reason he noticed her. She stood slightly taller than average, had light brown hair, wore denim pants and a denim jacket over a white blouse, and had a rather plain, boyish figure. Nothing about her really stood out, except perhaps the hint of secret knowledge glistening in her green eyes.

The hair on the back of his neck rose.

No, he had not seen this woman before. What was it about her that demanded his attention?

He purposely broke eye contact and returned to his seat as he worked to ignore the strange woman's existence. He'd already found his entertainment for the night, and it held a great deal of promise.

As he took his seat, he returned his arm to the back of Carrie's chair, lightly caressed her bare shoulder with a fingertip, and met her questioning gaze with a smile. "I've ordered a snack over which we can discuss plans for the rest of the evening. Do you have anyplace in mind? Or would you prefer a tour of the town? If you promise not to tell, I can offer a midnight romp through any place that interests you. The Santa Fe Opera perhaps? Or La Posada's haunted hallways?"

"You mean, like, we could go into the old cathedral and look around?"

Daniel winced before he thought not to. "If you wish." He always felt a little ill in holy places. "I assure you, however, the views are much more spectacular from the opera house."

"Okay." Carrie sipped more champagne.

"Uh, I think we should go to the little girls' room."

Carrie glanced across the table to where Amber raised her eyebrows in a meaningful gesture, and she shrugged. "Whatever."

As she rose, she smiled at Daniel and rested her hand for a moment on his shoulder. He savored the warmth of her touch and watched her walk away. She would, no doubt, prove to be a tasty companion.

"You're good."

Surprised that he'd been so distracted as to allow someone close without realizing it, Daniel turned to find the woman who had attracted his attention earlier standing less than an arm's length behind him. "I beg your pardon?"

"I know you picked his pocket."

He rose to face her. "I'm sure I don't know what you mean."

"Look, bud, I'm not saying I actually saw the wallet come out of his pocket, but I know you did it."

He started to protest, but she raised her hand to stop him. "Don't insult me. I know a pickpocket when I see one, classy or not."

"Are you a peace officer of some kind, then?"

She grinned. "Yeah, something like that." Her gaze darted across the room to where two men rose from a table, left cash, and started toward the door. One man stuck a toothpick in his mouth as he looked around, spotted Daniel's accuser, and slowed.

The woman suddenly stepped forward and raised her hands to Daniel's chest. "Darling," she said, "I forgive you."

As he watched, astonished, she stood on her toes, grabbed the back of his head, and planted a big, wet kiss on his lips.

Her actions stunned Daniel for a moment, but then he understood. He was being employed as a shield.

And something about her touch, her taste, sent his senses into a tailspin. His heart would have stopped, if it had needed to beat in the first place.

Without conscious thought, he drew her up close and kissed her back. Her warmth spread through him like molten lava, promising an eruption of emotion.

"Whoa." She pushed back from his embrace, staring up into his face with her emerald eyes, her lips parted. Then she gulped. "You, uh, really get into your role, don't you?"

She glanced around. "Look, I appreciate your help, Mr.—"

"Daniel," he said. "And you are?"

"Meg."

Struggling to contain his reactions to this stranger, Daniel stepped back and bowed. "Meg. My pleasure. My greatest hope is that I'm able to *assist* you again in the future."

A flash of color rose in her cheeks as she smiled. Then she spun around and hurried from the bar.

Daniel inhaled a faint trace of her unusual scent before it, too, disappeared.

Shaking his head to clear the momentary fog, he returned to his seat, pretended to drink, and focused his preternatural hearing on the ladies' restroom.

"What the hell are you doing?" Amber asked.

Water ran as one of the women washed her hands.

Carrie's voice provided the other half of the conversation. "What do you mean?"

"This guy, Daniel. Where did you meet him?"

"Outside."

"You mean, just now?"

No verbal response, most likely a gesture.

Amber spoke again. "I swear, you're as dense as concrete. What if he's a psycho killer?"

Carrie guffawed. "Don't be stupid. I'm not going home with him. I'm just, you know, letting him show me around. No harm in that."

"I saw you kissing him."

"Yeah. So?"

"In front of everyone."

"Hey, you're the one who said we were here to have fun, shake off the farm dust. I can't help it if I find a gorgeous guy while you're wasting your time with geeks. Besides, I'm supposed to be here to get Buddy out of my system, remember?"

Amber didn't respond, and Daniel grinned. Carrie had had her revenge; her friend was jealous.

Someone ripped a paper towel from the dispenser.

"Maybe he has a friend he can introduce you to," Carrie said.

"Oh, *right*."

"Come on, don't be a . . . what was it you called me? A pussy?"

A moment of silence ensued.

"I'm not," Amber said, her voice a little whiny. "I just don't want to get split up. Remember, we made a pact to stick together."

Another moment of silence. He wondered if Carrie would point out that she was the one who had been abandoned, but she must have decided against that option.

"Fine. I'll tell him we already have plans."

2

Daniel studied the two women as they emerged from the water closet. Carrie had been forced into a situation that left her less than pleased, giving Amber the upper hand once again.

He was about to be abandoned.

Glancing around the bar, he decided he didn't wish to start the evening over. He'd just have to change the direction things were headed.

"Ah, there you are." He rose. "I was beginning to worry."

"Look, Daniel, I'm afraid we can't go with you to the opera."

"I understand your reluctance to travel with a stranger. Wise." He left payment on the table. "I know of a wonderful club within walking distance, just around the corner, an unusual spot most tourists never find. Perhaps, if it is excitement you seek, the three of us should visit. Interested?"

The women exchanged looks, Carrie's hopeful and Amber's guarded, then Carrie grinned at Daniel, raising her chin in a worldly gesture. "Sure."

Outside, he offered arms to both women, and the three of

them squeezed onto a narrow sidewalk, falling into periodic shadows as they followed a side street.

Sounds of the city rose around them in the form of automobile stereos, engines, cantina music, and laughing crowds, and a soft breeze carried hints of exotic flowers blooming in front of extravagant hotels. He also detected the acrid smell of roasting chili signifying the coming of fall to northern New Mexico. Nights continued to lengthen, bringing out moon-worshipping creatures like himself.

Below city noises, he heard the steady heartbeats of his two companions, and allowed himself a moment to study their sweet scents. Floral additives, alcohol, and female excitement. *Lovely.*

"What do you do, Daniel?" Amber asked.

"In what way?"

"For a living."

"Ah." He grinned down at her. "I have no need to earn money."

"You mean you're, like, a millionaire or something?"

"Yes."

"Wow."

Her brown eyes glistened and he knew he'd won her over with that simple declaration. In some strange way, he was disappointed. He enjoyed a challenge now and then.

He guided them away from the busiest parts of the Plaza, and the noise level dropped.

"There's a club back here somewhere?" Carrie looked around.

"Yes." Daniel smiled at her. "As I said, it's unusual. Very few locals even know about it."

"I can see why."

"It's quite a place." He released the women, pulled open an ancient wooden door, and motioned toward the darkened stairway leading down.

"I'm not going first," Amber said.

"Please, allow me." Daniel led the way, moving slowly to let his guests catch up.

Amber nearly tripped, and Carrie giggled.

At the bottom of the stairs, Daniel knocked twice on the door, then once, then twice again.

The door screeched open. Artificially cooled air, blue lights, and heavy, dark music poured out.

Daniel stepped into the doorway and motioned his guests inside. "Welcome to the Tunnel."

Amber held Carrie's arm as they walked in together, looking around like waifs entering some magnificent castle.

"Wow," Carrie whispered. "I've never seen a bar like this."

Although it was too early to be crowded, the Tunnel was by no means empty. Daniel nodded to several of the usual patrons, signifying his desire to keep his guests safe. His wishes would most likely be respected. Just to be sure, he'd endeavor to keep the women within sight.

"What exactly is this place?" Amber eased onto a black leather chair, gawking.

"One of the more interesting establishments in town," Daniel said, settling onto the matching sofa, and motioning for Carrie to join him. "I doubt you'll find one like it in Union."

Carrie sat close, gaping.

Fanny, one of the senior bartenders, sauntered over with three tall glasses. "Hey, Daniel. How's it going tonight?"

"Quite well." He inclined his head. "My two friends are looking for excitement."

"Oh?"

Amber straightened, as though she'd suddenly remembered herself, and flashed a confident smile. "Yes, we are."

Daniel checked the contents of the three glasses and distributed them appropriately. If one of the young women accidentally sipped from his glass, the night would undoubtedly end prematurely.

Fanny snapped her fingers and three young men hurried across the room. Steady heartbeats verified that they were mortal. All were young and attractive, all wore variations on the same black leather theme, and all flexed and posed.

Daniel tried not to laugh.

Fanny crouched behind Amber's chair and studied the young men over the woman's shoulder. "Any of them interest you?"

Amber's jaw dropped for a moment, then she regained her composure and shrugged. "Yeah, sure."

"Which one looks the most luscious?"

"The one in the middle." Amber motioned with her head toward the tallest of the three, a dark man with classical good looks.

The other two frowned, turned, and retreated into the shadows as the chosen man raised one eyebrow suggestively.

"Good choice. That's Niki," Fanny said. "I tend to enjoy Russians myself now and then." The tip of her tongue flicked across her upper lip. Then she stood and glanced questioningly at Carrie, who quickly rested her hand on Daniel's forearm.

Niki extended a hand to Amber, which she took, and they faded into the growing crowd on the dance floor.

Daniel turned his full attention to Carrie, who sipped from her wineglass and glanced around furtively.

"Tell me, Carrie, what is it you wish to do with your life?"

"My *life*?" She shrugged. "I haven't gotten to the end of this week yet."

"You don't plan ahead?"

She laughed this time. "No, not really. I mean, I've tried to plan ahead, but things never work out right, you know? I'm twenty-six and stuck working behind a cash register."

"You have no dreams?"

"Sure, everyone has dreams. I want to go to college, but I don't know how I'll ever find the dough."

"What is it you wish to study?"

She grinned sheepishly. "I want to be a lawyer, work for Legal Aid."

"Ah, quite noble."

She shrugged as her face reddened.

He leaned close to let her scent invade his senses once again, considering how much he would enjoy the emotions of one so young.

But first, he must fill her with the joy he wished to share.

"And what would you like to do tonight?"

She looked at him with wide eyes. "Like, what?"

"Like anything you wish."

"Anything?"

He leaned closer, brushing his face across her hair. "Anything." He felt a shiver run through her. "Tell me your deepest, darkest fantasies."

"I . . . couldn't do that."

He slid the backs of his fingers up her arm to her shoulder, then across to the side of her slender neck. "You can. I promise to keep your secrets."

She didn't respond, but her breathing quickened to match her pulse.

"Maybe, um, we should dance again," she said.

Daniel smiled and straightened. "Lovely idea."

He led her onto the dance floor, staying near the edge of the crowd to avoid bumping into others. Holding her close, he enjoyed her warmth. She molded her body to his as they moved together, resting her head against his chest.

Empathizing with the moth, he closed his eyes to enjoy Carrie's life's flame. His own flame had once been powerful and bright, and he sometimes missed it, much as he missed the heat of sunshine on his bare shoulders, and the noises of daytime. Funny how differently the night sounded than the day.

What would it be like to have one to hold in such a manner

as he drifted off to sleep? He'd always wondered, but never dared. Existence as a night creature was solitary, as had been life as a thief.

Not that he regretted his immortal existence. Far from it. Centuries passed much faster than he would have ever guessed. How many more would he be allowed?

As the music changed, Daniel glanced down into the sparkling eyes of his dance partner. "Are you enjoying yourself?"

She nodded.

"Good."

They danced a while longer, and he traveled the length of her spine with his palm, memorizing small indentations and rises. As he approached her buttocks, he felt her thigh press against his and he groaned with delight.

Then she pushed herself away from him.

"Is something wrong?" he asked.

She looked around. "Have you seen Amber? We're supposed to stay together."

Daniel searched the crowd, then glanced at Fanny. She met his gaze and motioned toward the rear of the building with her head.

"I believe your friend is otherwise engaged."

"What do you mean?"

"I believe," he said, brushing loose hair back from her cheek, "that she has chosen to visit the back room."

"The *back room?*"

He nodded.

"Why? What's going on in the back room?"

Noting a hint of unease in her voice, Daniel squeezed her arm gently. "No need to worry. Nothing's going on that she will find displeasing."

"What the hell is that supposed to mean?"

He leaned close. "I imagine she is involved in a sexual encounter, but that's only a guess."

"*Sex*? With some guy she just met?"

"Most likely. Don't you enjoy sex in Union, Missouri? With a name like that—"

"Not with guys we don't know."

She sounded agitated, and her worldliness slipped a few notches.

"Would you be more comfortable if we checked on her?"

She nodded.

"All right. This way."

With his hand on the small of her back, Daniel led Carrie into the darkened hallway of rooms hidden behind the Tunnel. Some of these rooms served as sinister places for vampires to feed, and some held drug dealers and their clients, but most simply provided some measure of privacy or comfort for intimate encounters.

These encounters, however, often involved more than two people, and Daniel noted noises issuing from several closed doors indicating group activities.

When he picked up a whiff of Amber's scent, he stopped and listened.

"I believe you'll find her in here."

"How do you know?"

He grinned. "Educated guess."

Daniel quietly eased the door open and ushered his guest inside a dimly lit room with black walls. In the center of the room was a large, low cushioned platform, a bed of sorts, with space for at least a dozen. Against the walls were several love seats: seating for observation. This was not one of the private rooms.

Amber and Niki lay together in the center of the bed embracing, most of their outer clothing discarded. Both stopped and glanced up at the intrusion.

"Please," Daniel said, "don't let us interrupt." He led Carrie to one of the love seats and sat beside her.

After a bit of hesitation, the couple returned to their rather unimaginative foreplay, and Daniel stretched his arm across the back of the love seat. He leaned close to whisper in Carrie's ear. "Have you ever watched before?"

The young woman shook her head, and her heartbeat quickened.

"Stimulation begins in the brain," he said. "Watching will often trigger a physical response."

He turned his gaze on the couple, who had now removed all of their garments. Niki's hand hid one of Amber's ample breasts, and the dark pink nipple of the other puckered as the Russian kissed and nibbled her neck.

Daniel's fangs began to ache.

"See how she squirms with delight when he kisses her neck, and gooseflesh rises on her arms? You can almost feel his hot breath on your own skin, can't you?"

Niki rolled up partially on top of the young woman, parting her legs with one of his own, and ran his hand down her side.

"His hand is dark against her alabaster skin, his heated palms rough. She tenses with uncertainty as his hand moves lower. Ah, but his phallus is swollen with need, and quite an appealing size, don't you think?"

Carrie gulped.

Daniel's lengthening fangs pressed against his bottom lip, and his own cock began to swell.

As first he worried that his date may not be responding as hoped, until he caught a whiff of her arousal. Smiling, he nuzzled the side of her neck.

Carrie tilted her head away from him, giving him access to her pulsing life force.

For one moment, Daniel heard the moon beast calling, tugging at his soul, but he would not ruin the evening by taking the offering too soon. No, the moment had not yet arrived.

He glanced back at the bed to find Niki positioned between

Amber's thighs, guiding his shielded prick toward her, and silently cursed the man for making such a hurried mess of the whole thing. How could he possibly seduce his partner this way when the show would soon be over?

Not that their union was anything less than passionate. As Niki entered her, Amber drew her fingernails up his back, leaving red streaks in his skin, and they both groaned. She wrapped one leg around his and met his hasty thrusts, taking all of him into her each time.

To Daniel's surprise, Carrie's hand suddenly rested on his thigh, and she squeezed as a soft noise rose in her throat.

He took the hint, lifting her chin so he could press his lips to the tenderest part of her neck, tasting warm saltiness. Her vocal cords vibrated against the front of his fangs. He inhaled sharply, and the scent of her juices worked its way into his brain, leaving eddies of temptation behind.

She clung to the front of his shirt and buried her fingers in his hair.

"Perhaps we, too, should stretch out," he whispered.

"Yes."

Trying to make the move look more difficult than it was, Daniel scooped Carrie into his arms and bore her to the bed, where he placed her gently on her back. Watching excitement build in her eyes, he unbuttoned her blouse and pants, and removed them.

She quickly shed her undergarments as she watched him undress.

He had always been physically attractive to women, both a blessing and a curse throughout his existence. His looks had bought him immortality, and then torn him from the only woman who'd ever stolen his heart. Now he had no choice in his appearance; he was as he had been when he'd given up the ghost.

Daniel discarded the last of his clothing and Carrie grinned.

A few feet away, Niki grunted his release, and Amber groaned in time with his thrusts.

Turning his attention to his companion, Daniel let his fingers traipse across her fine flesh, finding indentations and rises, circling her breasts and brushing teasingly close to the patch of coarse brown hair at the crown of her thighs.

Carrie shivered under his touch and closed her eyes.

He followed the paths of his fingers with his lips and tongue, careful not to slice her brown skin with his fangs. She cooed and gulped in sharp breaths as he crossed her most tender places, and he noted their locations. He'd always been fascinated by the subtle differences in each woman's body.

"That feels great," she whispered.

"Lovely," he muttered against her soft belly.

As he stroked the tender insides of her thighs, he teased the hard buds of her breasts with his tongue.

Her back arched with pleasure and she opened her legs to his hand.

The steady beat of her heart echoed in his head, reminding him of his own need, urging him to increase his speed, and he obeyed. He penetrated the warmth of her cunt with his fingers, pleased to find her sticky and wet, then slid over her so he could settle between her legs. With the head of his stiff cock pressed to her heated cunt lips, he returned his mouth to her neck.

When he sucked gently on the flesh above her pulse, her legs clamped around his hips and sounds of desire rose in her throat. Her fingers massaged the muscles of his back.

And then more fingers brushed across his bare shoulders; he glanced up to find Amber on her hands and knees, lust glistening in her eyes.

Daniel watched as Niki rose up behind her. What the young man lacked in finesse, he made up for in stamina, for he made quick work of entering her again and soon monopolized the redhead's attention.

Carrie also watched the action, and responded by lifting her hips into him, taking his swollen rod into her in one thrust.

Daniel closed his eyes momentarily to enjoy the rush of pleasure.

Oddly enough, the face he pictured was not that of his partner, or even of Running Deer, but that of a woman he'd only seen once before, less than an hour earlier at the bar.

Blinking away the surprising vision, he focused his attention on the writhing woman beneath him, rubbing his cock against her swelling clit with carefully calculated movements as he kissed and nipped sensitive spots on her shoulders.

"Oh, God," she said. "That's so good."

"Yes." He allowed himself harder thrusts.

She neared release.

Amber screamed through gritted teeth as she came, and Niki grunted again, pounding flesh to flesh.

Daniel held Carrie near the precipice, careful not to push her over the edge until the moment was right. Her body heated as muscles tightened and strained, and she clung to him with her arms as her legs opened wider.

"Please," she whispered.

"Give yourself to me," he said.

She pressed her head back to the bed, her eyes shut tight.

He felt her need bubbling to the surface, heard her blood pounding through her veins. Opening his mouth on the side of her neck, he buried his rock-hard shaft in her hot cunt, torturing her swollen clit with the movement, pushing her past the point of return.

As she dug her fingers into his back and her tight internal muscles squeezed his cock, he pierced her flesh.

Her scream of release echoed in his head, heralding the wonder to follow, and he stilled his thoughts.

Torrents of emotion flooded his brain with bright lights and joy, setting off sounds and pictures. He knew her in that instant as no other did, felt her ecstasy, experienced her pleasure. He knew her dreams—much stronger than she'd admitted—and her fears. He understood the heartbreak left by her soulless spouse, and the excitement she'd felt this very night. He tasted her joy as she drew him to a climax with her sweet cunt, and felt her shudder as her orgasm waned.

Fighting the desire to continue, he withdrew from her neck, holding his lips to her sizzling flesh as it healed.

The last of the climax rolled through his body, but the emotions raged on, and he let them, sampling each one as a long-lost treat. As always, the variety amazed him, and the intensity left him shaken and weak.

Their movements slowed and stopped.

Daniel rolled them over and held Carrie beside him, listening to her heartbeat and breathing, enjoying and returning tender caresses.

"I don't know how you did that," she said, "but it was amazing."

"I, too, am impressed." He stroked her hair. "You have a wonderful body."

She studied his eyes intently, finding only the truth, no doubt, since it was, and she smiled. "Thank you."

3

"I can't believe the night's almost over."

Daniel glanced up at the sky, now light enough to silhouette the tops of buildings and trees. Dawn's approach gnawed at his gut. "Another three-quarters of an hour."

Carrie squeezed his arm with hers. "This has been a wild night."

"Yes, it has. I hope you don't regret it."

"No way. It was exactly what I needed. I feel *good.*" She whooped, and then laughed. "And Buddy Wittman can go to hell."

"Wonderful." He grinned down at her and patted her arm.

She glanced back to where Amber and Niki trailed them, talking about the next time they might meet. "I think Amber had fun, too."

"I believe you're right," he said, winking.

The woman grinned.

They stopped at the front door to the massive hotel. Holding her hands in his, Daniel studied Carrie's face, recalling her dreams and fears. "One thing I truly believe is that you will be a great lawyer someday."

She beamed at him and her eyes filled with tears. "Thanks."

He drew her hands to his lips and kissed each, then pressed a kiss to her warm cheek before stepping back with a flourish. "Farewell, Carrie."

The tears escaped her eyelids and she waved, then turned and hurried through the front door.

Amber, tipsy and giggling, kissed Niki once more, and then followed her roommate's trail. "See ya'."

Daniel patted Niki's back. "Until later, my friend."

The young man yawned, nodded, and turned back toward the Tunnel.

Fighting heavy limbs and a growing need to sleep, Daniel started toward his own abode as quickly as he could without attracting attention.

Trying to ignore the shadow of St. Francis Cathedral looming behind him, he detoured through the hallway of La Fonda hotel, striding past glass cases of jewelry and clothing and the empty bar, and dashing up the stairs to an open terrace room where a large crowd had celebrated a marriage ceremony. A few former revelers sprawled in chairs, snoring, and long tables held what was left of cakes, fruit, and exotic chocolates, along with a few small sandwiches, quickly growing stale.

Daniel glanced around as he filled his pockets with the food he considered most nutritious, and then added a few chocolates for good measure.

Continuing, he trotted down another flight of stairs and pushed through a fire exit to the street.

Two blocks further and around a corner, he stopped at the entrance to an alley where six young people huddled together to sleep. He'd known this group for awhile, although the members had changed somewhat with the season. The oldest, Alex, stirred and glanced up as Daniel crouched.

"Hey, man, what's up?"

Daniel shrugged. "The usual." He emptied his pockets onto a makeshift cardboard table. "Can't stand to see food go to waste."

"Cool." Alex sat up and poked his girlfriend, CC, in the ribs.

CC rubbed her eyes as she stretched, and then quickly awoke at the sight of the feast. "Wow. Thanks."

"My pleasure." Daniel rose.

Watching the small band come silently to life and huddle around the food reminded him of his own childhood on the streets of London. How could he still feel the dread and fear that had nearly overtaken him the first night after escaping the orphanage? Could it truly have been four centuries ago?

Leaving the group to their meal, he continued his trek, picking up speed. The sky took on a hint of orange somewhere behind the gray.

In spite of the growing urgency, he stopped suddenly a block from his street, feeling a stranger's stare as surely as a touch.

Someone was watching him.

Glancing around and seeing no observer, he walked on, listening for footsteps behind him. He heard none.

Shortly after turning onto his street, he ducked behind a tree and froze.

Tuned to every movement, every hint of noise, he waited.

Nothing, not even the hint of a pedestrian. A single automobile passed along the main street, a member of the police department, but that was it.

After ten minutes, with the need to be indoors becoming more immediate, he dashed across the street and slipped into his small adobe house. Wasting no time, he locked the door and secured the metal window shutters. Then he stood in the middle of the main room and worked to calm his jittery nerves.

When was the last time he'd been followed? He couldn't remember for sure. Why would someone follow him now?

Once again, for some reason he couldn't begin to identify, the memory of Meg surfaced.

Meg. Why was she pestering his thoughts? What was it about her that kept him coming back to the memory of her scent?

"Perhaps you're losing your mind."

Considering his own suggestion, he prepared for bed. What would eternity be like if accompanied by insanity? Would he forget who he was and where he'd come from?

Lying in bed and folding his hands over his stomach, he wondered when he'd picked up the habit of self-examination. It hadn't been something he'd carried with him on the filthy, cold streets of London. It wouldn't have served him well when picking pockets or swiping potatoes from market stands. And it didn't serve him much better now, did it?

He turned his head to stare at the nightstand drawer, tempted to open it and touch the relic inside. He knew the smell of the dark, stained wood, the feel of the stake in his hand. The last time he'd opened that drawer, he'd fallen into a month of depression, listening to the sound of his true love's agony echoing through his head, a sound so old that it should have been quieted long ago.

Perhaps he'd never be able to silence the scream.

He would not, however, allow himself to wallow in self-pity again. He couldn't afford it.

As the sleep of death approached, Daniel recalled the green eyes of a woman he'd only met briefly, but felt as though he'd known before. Why did she remind him so much of Running Deer? Certainly Running Deer had had a similar effect on him when he first saw her.

So many years ago . . .

* * *

"*Ch-Ch-Christ*, no." The words rose as a hoarse whisper from Daniel's parched throat.

He struggled to push himself farther under the log but managed little movement with his injuries. He listened again for the wolves' howls. How close were they? Fifty yards? Less?

Trying to silence his chattering teeth, he searched the icy darkness for movement. Pain from his wounds radiated through most of his body, missing only those places frozen beyond hope.

Clouds broke before the moon, which spread its cold light through the woods. He saw their yellow eyes and clouds of breath as they moved in, one step at a time, wary of their living prey. If he'd still had his musket, he would have justified their fears. Now he could do nothing more than surrender to them.

"Blood-d-dy bastards."

Then something amazing happened. The wolves stopped, looked around, and dashed away into the night, yelping like frightened pups.

Daniel would have laughed if he could, but he knew it didn't matter. Either to the teeth of wolves, or the teeth of the winter cold, he would surrender his life this night. He couldn't hang on much longer.

With the last of his strength, he sat up, leaning against the icy log and panting. His blood-soaked shirt had long since frozen to his skin, and he felt nothing below his knees. Closing his eyes, he searched for some way to pray, to ask forgiveness for his criminal life.

Unfortunately, he'd never learned the ways of praying men. He had no understanding of the remorse he knew he should feel. He'd done what he needed to in order to survive, and perhaps a little more at opportune moments.

When he opened his eyes, he stared at a heavenly sight. In the snow-covered clearing twenty feet away stood the most beautiful woman he'd ever seen. Her long black hair hung nearly to her waist and glistened with frosted moonbeams, and her eyes glowed against the darkness. She wore a buckskin dress unlike any he'd seen before, and her feet were bare, but she showed no sign of feeling the bitter cold.

As he watched, she walked toward him, one silent step at a time. Was she an angel? Or maybe a demon sent to escort him to the waiting flames?

How could anyone so beautiful be a demon?

Even in the dim light he could see that her skin was unmarked, smooth, evenly brown, and her hands and arms were slender. Her clothing hugged the curves of her bosom and narrow waist, and rose above her knees when she stepped, revealing wondrously enticing legs.

"Wh-who are you?"

She smiled and spoke in a voice more musical than any he'd ever heard. "My name is Running Deer."

Kneeling before him, smelling of soft leather, campfire smoke, and some ancient herb, she wrapped her arms around him and cradled his head to her breast.

Daniel closed his eyes and released his tentative hold on consciousness.

When he woke, either moments or days later, he found himself in a dark room, full of movement and strange sounds. As his senses sharpened, he realized he lay beside a fire in a massive cave, and dozens of people circled him. All wore buckskins similar to Running Deer's, and all stood just at the edge of the light, swaying in the jumping shadows and humming a tune foreign to his ear. These people looked a little like Algonquin, but they definitely weren't. They weren't from any tribe he'd seen before. Firelight glistened on gold armbands, adorned with odd lettering, and most wore feathers and beads braided into strands of hair.

The circle parted as two women approached. One he recognized as Running Deer; the other appeared to be a leader of some kind, judging by the way the onlookers bowed.

"This is Moon Dancer," Running Deer said, kneeling beside him.

Daniel tried to sit up, but couldn't. Pain shot through his body as if from a dozen spears, and he groaned.

"No, don't move." Running Deer stroked his hair tenderly and leaned close. "Fever has taken your body, but Moon Dancer can cure you. Then you'll be one of us."

He looked up into her eyes, transfixed by the strange tints. Her eyes seemed to change from brown to blue, to green in but a few seconds.

She smiled sweetly, easing his pain with her touch.

"I'd like that," he said.

Running Deer moved around to kneel behind him, lifting his head and placing it in her lap.

The humming increased in volume to some kind of chant, and the circle moved closer. Moon Dancer stood in the center, clad in a buckskin robe ornately decorated with strange symbols that could have represented the moon, and perhaps dogs, or wolves. She stood close to the fire and raised her arms out from her sides.

Two women stepped forward and reverently drew back her robe, leaving her completely naked.

Daniel tried to look away, but found himself unable to do so. She was tall and big-boned, with full curves and plump breasts, but she was by no means matronly. Firelight dancing on her skin made it glisten like new honey, and her long, black hair hung down her body in silky strands to her waist. Gold bands circled her arms and ankles.

She moved with an unreal grace, motioning two of her subjects, a man and a woman, forward. The two stood facing each other, and Moon Dancer circled them, caressing their faces and necks tenderly, urging them closer. As the couple gazed into each other's eyes, she drew off their robes to reveal well-formed bodies and circled again, touching their backs and arms.

The chanting increased in volume; the couple touched each other's face, neck, and arms.

Moon Dancer settled on a flat rock near Daniel, giving him a clear view of the encounter.

The touching grew more intimate as the man caressed the woman's breasts and her hands slid down his stomach to his hips.

In spite of his state, Daniel felt himself reacting to this unusual sight as his breeches tightened. He glanced up in shame at Running Deer, but found her also watching the couple, her lips parted and her eyes glistening with firelight. She showed no sign of shame, embarrassment, or even surprise.

The couple no longer stood alone as the crowd gathered around them, chanting and touching them. The man's phallus stiffened, and his eyes closed when the woman stroked it with both hands. She knelt and drew his cock into her mouth, taking more of him than seemed possible, and the crowd held him upright.

Daniel clenched his fists against the desire to touch his own swelling cock.

The woman moved back and forth, sliding her lips along the length of her partner's shaft, and the man's body jerked as his muscles quivered.

And then the crowd drew them apart, lifted the woman, held her legs open, and urged the man to his knees. His face disappeared between her thighs, and the woman began to tremble and groan.

Hot desire flooded Daniel's body, tightening his ruined muscles and burning his feverish skin.

The man rose and the crowd pushed him forward with a dozen hands on his back. His wet, swollen cock disappeared into his mate a little at a time, drawing from her sounds of delight Daniel barely heard above the chants.

With horror, Daniel realized he was stroking himself and looked down. But his hand was not the one sliding across the front of his breeches. Moon Dancer now knelt beside him, touching him as she watched the coupling. When he tentatively reached up and touched her breast, she smiled down at him and leaned forward to press her flesh into his palm.

The chanters now moved as a mass with the couple, pushing them together and drawing them apart, and their song took on the sounds of desire. The young woman's body, supported by six or seven, undulated with need, and the man gripped her thighs as he fucked her.

Daniel felt his own seed gathering, swelling, ready to spill inside his clothing. And then his clothing began to slip away.

He looked over to find Moon Dancer and Running Deer drawing off his tattered garments. At one point, it felt as though they were ripping away his skin and he sucked in a quick breath at the pain. They stopped until the pain passed, then continued to work.

He glanced down at his own torn flesh, disgusted by the filth and oozing gore. Algonquin knives had done their best to end his life as he'd struggled against three scouts, and they'd nearly succeeded.

Moon Dancer didn't seem to notice his condition as she touched the uninjured sections of his skin and Running Deer massaged his shoulders and chest. His pain slipped farther and farther away, and he vaguely wondered if he were dying. Perhaps all this was merely the dream of someone freezing to death in the middle of a winter storm.

Their touches felt real, however, and he responded. As his cock rose into the air, Moon Dancer ran her fingers up and down the shaft in a featherlike touch.

Daniel choked back a whimper.

Others' groans echoed through the cavern as the coupling continued. The woman's back arched and her hands clenched into fists. She must be on the verge of a climax, and Daniel felt as if he might come with her. Then the man fell forward onto her, his face buried against her neck, clutching her body to his, and she screamed her ecstasy.

Daniel closed his eyes, working to keep his cock from erupting. When he opened them again, he found Moon Dancer straddling him, muttering something in an ancient tongue as she drew lines down his stomach with her fingernails. She leaned forward and licked the base of his neck, and Daniel gulped for air as desire tightened his throat and burned in the backs of his thighs.

He looked up at Running Deer, who smiled at him, and then returned his attention to Moon Dancer. She rose high on her knees and reached between her legs to hold his cock, then eased slowly down onto the head. Her cunt felt wet and tight, but surprisingly cool, as it swallowed him one glorious inch at a time.

As he fought to hold on, she leaned forward, rocking back and forth, brushing his sensitive skin with her soft hair, her face getting closer to his with each pass. She smelled exactly as Running Deer had, of smoke, leather, and some strange herb.

Daniel touched her smooth, cool skin, wanting to know more of her, wishing he could rise up and take her in his arms. But it was all he could do to lift his hands.

His prick, however, functioned quite well, and his seed welled once again, burning for release. As her breath brushed across his face, he lost his struggle, erupting with the strength of a spring gale. Holding her with the last of his strength, he blasted his hot semen deep into her body, reaching for her soul.

She fell onto him, pressing her mouth into his neck.

And then she pierced his flesh.

His eruption continued, too intense, drawing his voice out in a scream as she sucked hard, draining what little life he had left.

He opened his eyes and looked up at Running Deer, expecting her to react, to do something, but she only smiled and stroked his face. As the ecstatic pleasure continued, Running Deer's face began to fade, first to light and then to darkness.

And then the joy subsided, and his body felt as though it were floating in a sea of cold air, all the pain gone.

"Drink," he heard whispered in his ear. "Drink and become one of us."

He did as instructed, swallowing coppery liquid as best he could, trying not to retch. All he wanted was to rest, to be warm and safe, but something deep inside him fought to wake.

He gasped as death took over, and his body turned to stone—cold, unmoving, unbreakable. He was no more.

Death's sleep.

As he lost the thread of the memory, Running Deer's words remained in his head. "Death's sleep."

Daniel woke to find himself standing in his bedroom, his hands splayed on the wall behind him.

What had wakened him so suddenly? A sound?

Real, or imagined?

He listened, but heard nothing.

Purposely loosening muscles, he stepped forward. Was the idea of someone pursuing him causing paranoia? He had good reason not to want unnecessary attention, but he had no proof that such attention existed at the moment.

Shaking off apprehension, he showered and prepared for the night.

The memory of his dream hung about him like a cobweb clinging to his hair, and he worked to brush it away. He understood the dangers of living in the past. Those few he'd known who'd tried to do so had been vanquished in one way or another, perhaps because they found no reason to exist.

He'd never had that problem. Existence was a wonderful thing, full of excitement and wonder. Tonight he would hunt for someone who shared that wonder, someone with an uplifting attitude.

Someone who wasn't drunk.

In spite of enjoying Carrie, her blood's alcohol content had left him groggy.

Donning a snappy dark outfit and his best boots, Daniel checked his appearance in the mirror on the way to the door, locked his front door behind him, and started down the sidewalk whistling an old seafaring song.

He stopped midstride.

What was that familiar scent?

Turning a slow circle, he sniffed the air.

Yes, he knew that fragrance, one that had affected him so strongly the night before. Meg the constable had been in this very spot.

What the bloody hell had she been doing in front of his house? And while he slept, no less?

4

Anger bubbled in Daniel's chest, tempered only by curiosity. Had this woman, Meg, guessed his true nature? Was she hunting him? Had she been the reason he felt someone watching on his way home?

Following her scent, he turned left at the street, and then stopped just before a corner when he lost the trail. Perhaps she'd escaped in an automobile. He studied every vehicle he could see and found none that looked out of place.

"What are you playing at?" he whispered to the night air. "Beware you don't get hurt, little vixen."

He would keep his senses tuned. If she were truly hounding him, he'd soon know it.

With his step less light, he continued toward the crowded plaza, where he'd most likely find the night's companion. No Tunnel this time; too many vampire wannabes who knew no joy in living.

No, tonight he wanted light, happiness, optimism—

"Get lost, Roberto! How many times do I have to tell you?" A very pretty woman, hands on her hips, glared at the young man standing in front of her, his dark eyes wide with hurt. "Are you *stupid*?"

When he didn't move, she waved him off with one hand. "*¡Vete!*"

Two other women, apparently waiting for her, laughed, and the young man's eyes welled with tears.

He spun around and marched away, swiping angrily at his cheeks.

The woman, also laughing, joined her waiting friends and the three headed for the closest bar, arm in arm. Her short skirt and tight blouse revealed a figure that left little doubt she'd soon have a herd of male suitors.

The wounded Roberto continued down the street, plowing through two separate crowds, leaving behind cursing tourists.

For a reason he couldn't explain, Daniel followed.

At Alameda, Roberto strode across the major street without slowing or even looking. In his dark clothes, he couldn't have been more than a vague shape to drivers of approaching vehicles.

Daniel hesitated for a moment, listening to the whine of an oversized truck engine, gauging the vehicle's speed as it bore down on the unsuspecting pedestrian. Within seconds, Roberto's heart would no longer be the only part of him broken.

In a movement too fast for human sight, Daniel dashed forward, grabbed the man by the collar, and jerked him from the path of the oncoming truck.

"Hey." Roberto stumbled several steps as he recovered his senses and his balance. "What the fuck you doin'?"

Daniel sighed. "Saving your life, I believe."

"Screw you, Jack. I didn't ask you for nothin'." The young man stepped forward as he swung.

Even in his mortal days, Daniel would have seen the punch coming and had time to duck. At this point in his existence, he could have taken a stroll, sipped tea, and returned before the punch landed. He stopped the fist in midflight with one hand.

To Roberto's credit, shock at the result didn't prevent him from swinging again, and Daniel again stopped his fist.

The young man stepped back, his body tensed. "What the hell are you, some kind of kung fu guy or something?"

"Perhaps." Daniel folded his arms and studied the figure before him. "Do you care so little for your life that you're willing to step in front of a speeding vehicle?"

Roberto huffed as he dug a smashed pack of cigarettes from his pants pocket and extracted a crooked smoke. He lit it with a plastic lighter and took a long drag, exhaling smoke with his words. "What's it to you?"

"I, more than most, *appreciate* human life. I will not stand by and watch one tossed away out of ignorance."

"*Ignorance?*"

"Yes, ignorance. If you knew what you were doing, you would be with your female companion right now instead of standing on the sidewalk talking to a stranger."

Roberto smoked and watched Daniel out of the corner of his eyes for several minutes before speaking again. "What are you talking about?"

Daniel sighed as he grabbed Roberto's sleeve and guided him along the sidewalk toward the Plaza. "What I'm talking about is that you obviously know nothing about romance, about how to seduce a woman."

"Oh, and you do?"

"Yes," Daniel said with a smile, "I do."

Roberto seemed to want to toss back a sarcastic comment, but came up with nothing.

Daniel released his sleeve and slapped the young man's back. "This is your lucky day, Roberto."

"How do you know my name?"

"I know many things."

"Yeah? So what's your name?"

"Daniel Ward, at your service." He nodded in a formal gesture, the significance of which was lost on his companion.

"Look, Dan—"

"Daniel, not Dan."

"Whatever. I don't need no help."

The human made this statement without conviction, and Daniel smiled again. "Of course, you don't. I beg your pardon." With another quick bow, he turned and started away.

"Wait."

Daniel turned back to face Roberto.

"What do you mean, it's my lucky day?"

Closing the gap between them in easy strides, Daniel spoke softly. "I have many years of experience with women. In fact, I've made it my life's work to study the fairer sex. Tonight, since I have nothing particularly better to do, I'm willing to teach you enough to win over the heart of your lady love."

"You talk weird, man."

Daniel shrugged. "It's a relative thing. I find your speech patterns a little odd, too."

Roberto frowned and glanced around. "Why you want to help me?"

"Because I'm a romantic, I suppose."

When the young man didn't respond, Daniel started walking, giving his companion a chance to match his step, which he did.

"What do I have to do?" Roberto flicked what was left of his cigarette into the gutter.

As they walked, Daniel studied the young man. Roberto wore absurdly baggy pants, a T-shirt with holes and obscene remarks, and cloth shoes he hadn't bothered to tie. He slouched. His face, however, had classic lines with high cheekbones and a strong chin, and showed little sign of acne, but his hair hadn't been well combed in ages.

"Do you have any other clothes?"

"What's wrong with my clothes?"

Daniel raised one eyebrow. "Trust me, they send an undesirable message. Do you have any pants that actually fit?"

"Sure."

"And a shirt with perhaps buttons? Or, at least, without holes?"

"Yeah."

"How long will it take you to change and return?"

"I don't know, about a half hour, *más o menos*."

"Fine. I'll meet you at Cowgirl's in one hour."

In the cool evening, a soft breeze had inspired the management to light gas heaters on Cowgirl's patio. Daniel sat in a corner, sipping red wine, observing the crowd.

There were several tables from which he could cull a partner or two for the night, if his protégé didn't appear. One group, two tables away, included a particularly fetching female who flirted with several men while keeping an eye on him.

If, however, Roberto arrived, Daniel would lower his sights just a little. Two women, slightly less attractive and a bit older, sat alone at a booth drinking wine and picking over dinner plates. They seemed to be looking for companions, and had cast furtive glances his way. To one of those glances, he raised his glass in acknowledgment, which left them with their heads together in whispered conversation.

Roberto arrived two minutes early, looking greatly improved. He wore black jeans that fit him, a new checkered silk shirt still marked with creases, and black leather shoes. With a sullen frown, he dropped into a chair at Daniel's table. His expression improved, however, when he eyed the plate of food.

"Can I have some of that?"

"You may have all of it," Daniel said, pushing the plate in his direction.

The young man spoke between bites. "What do I do now?"

"We need to work on two things: your basic understanding of what women want and your confidence in being able to provide it."

Roberto scowled. "I know how to screw. I don't need no lessons."

"Precisely my point. Women want to be seduced, not screwed."

"My first girlfriend liked screwing."

Daniel waved off the comment. "I'm not saying females don't enjoy sex. It's how you get there that's important. Do you see the two women in the booth to your left?"

"Yeah. So?"

"So, before the night is over, we will be in bed with them, and it will have been their idea."

The mortal's eyebrows rose slowly.

"First step is to choose the woman you want and assure yourself she's worthy of your attention. I assume you have done this already."

Roberto's gaze dropped to the food in his hand. "Yeah. Berna is a beautiful lady, inside and out."

Daniel smiled. "I knew there was a touch of romanticism in that heart somewhere."

Roberto's spine stiffened. "So? You want to—"

Daniel raised a hand to the angry response. "That was a compliment."

The young man slowly relaxed and returned to eating.

"The next step," Daniel continued, "is to let the woman know you are interested. In this case, we'll take care of that now." He raised a hand to the waiter—a young man in a cowboy hat and skintight jeans.

"Another drink?"

Daniel shook his head. "We'd like to refill the glasses of the two ladies in the booth and invite them to join us for dessert."

The waiter grinned conspiratorially and hurried away. When he delivered the drinks and message, the two women smiled and nodded, and the waiter returned.

"The ladies accept your invitation. They'll join you as soon as they finish their meals."

"Wonderful. Thank you." Daniel slipped the young man a folded bill.

"What do we do when they come over here?"

Daniel leaned forward. "We act like gentlemen. Do you think you can manage that?"

"Yeah, sure."

"Good. All you have to do is—"

Daniel stopped as a scent drew his head around. He froze and watched Meg hurry past.

"I'll return in a moment."

His chair screeched across stone as he jumped up and followed her into the building. He caught her by the arm at the far end of the barroom.

"Hey!" She swung around and grabbed his wrist with a surprisingly strong grip. "Get your hands off me."

"Not so fast," he said softly. "Why are you following me?"

Try as he might to be angry, the combination of her exotic scent and the memory of the feel of her in his arms left him only irritated at not having an excuse to hold her again. She stood before him glaring, her eyes the color of a turbulent sea. She wore brown pants with a tan sweater, and he found himself thinking how perfect an emerald would look at her throat.

"Why would I be following you? I don't even know you." She tried to twist her arm from his hand.

"Of course you do. You kissed me last night."

"What? Are you nuts?" Her eyes suddenly widened. "Oh, yeah. You're the guy in the bar. Look, I'm sorry I had to do that. I'd explain, but it's a long story and I really need to . . ." She gestured to the restroom sign over her shoulder.

Daniel released her and stepped back. "I'd like very much to hear your explanation. I'll wait."

One side of her luscious mouth curved up into half a smile. "Okay."

She walked off with a strong, confident stride that he both admired and enjoyed watching.

Daniel turned away from the alcove and leaned one shoulder against the wall. Something about this woman affected him in ways he hadn't been affected in ages. He felt almost human in his need to be near her.

Although the steady beat of her heart intrigued him, that wasn't what drew him to her. He wanted to kiss her, to hold her, to make love to her, and he had no idea why. He felt on the verge of madness around her.

When she returned, he would do his best to seduce her. Once he drank from her, he'd know the truth, and perhaps he'd know what it was about her that produced such longing in him.

Through the front windows, he saw Roberto looking around nervously, and he felt a twinge of guilt at abandoning his project, but not enough to keep him from doing so. Not when the choice was between helping Roberto get his wish and holding Meg.

Meg. Just the thought of touching her produced a delicious tightening in his body and a slight ache in his fangs.

As his wait continued, Daniel glanced back toward the women's restroom. The door opened and a child emerged. She ran back to her table, her shoes flopping against her feet.

Tuning his hearing, he heard nothing coming from the room. He approached the door. Was she hiding from him?

With just his fingertips, he eased the door open and listened again.

Nothing.

Shoving the door against the wall, he strode in and looked

around. Narrow doors revealed empty stalls. One door still moved, perhaps from the child inhabitant he'd watched leave.

Meg was not in the restroom. As he sampled the air, he realized she'd not entered this room at all.

Hurrying back to the alcove, he checked for other possibilities. One was the men's room, and another was a smaller hallway.

Like a bloodhound on a trail, he picked up her scent and hurried down the narrow hallway. It turned and ended in a door that he pushed open, and he stepped into a small alley.

She'd been here. Although the breeze carried away her scent, he caught a hint before it dissipated.

His hands curled into fists at his sides. She'd lied to him and escaped. She'd deceived him; she knew exactly who he was. Her acting abilities exceeded all but his own. She'd probably lied about trailing him.

He studied every shadow and found no sign of her. What was she after?

"Damn you," he whispered. "Next time you will not get away so easily."

With a sigh, he reentered the bar, working to release his anger and apprehension as he slowly crossed the room. He wanted to believe Meg posed no threat to him, but he worried that he might be wrong. Resolved to pay closer attention to his surroundings, he returned to his table.

Roberto nearly jumped up when he appeared. "What the hell happened to you?"

"I ran into an acquaintance."

"You scared the crap out of me. I thought you'd run off and left me with these ladies." The young man reddened at the admission of fear.

"Don't worry, you're doing fine."

"Yeah? So what do I do when they come over here?"

Daniel sipped his wine. "You relax. Don't appear too anxious, but let her see that you're interested in everything about her. Allow yourself to be honest. If you fake it, she'll know."

"Aw, shit." Roberto gulped from his glass of beer, and wiped his mouth with the back of his hand. "They're coming over."

Daniel rose as the women approached. After a brief moment, Roberto did the same.

"How do you do?" Daniel nodded politely. "I'm Daniel, and my friend is Roberto. I'm pleased you've agreed to join us." He pulled a chair out for the taller of the two, a woman with long golden-red hair and hazel eyes.

"Lucia," she said. "And my friend is Ellen."

Ellen, a slightly younger and smaller woman, sat between Daniel and Roberto, tucking her short blond hair behind her ears as she did. "Hi."

"Hi," Roberto answered.

Daniel noted with approval the look Roberto and Ellen exchanged. Perhaps he'd stumbled across just the right mate for his somewhat inarticulate protégé.

Lucia rested her elbows on the table and smiled at Daniel.

"May I offer you dessert?" he asked.

"Coffee for me," she said.

"Ellen? Would you like something more substantial?"

The girl blushed. "Do they have ice cream?"

"I like ice cream, too," Roberto said.

"Perfect." Daniel flagged down the waiter once again and placed their orders.

"You aren't having anything?" Lucia asked.

"I'm quite happy," he said, raising his wineglass. "Please, tell us about yourselves. Are you from Santa Fe?"

Daniel leaned back in his chair and listened as the women offered sketches of their lives. They were both teachers at a local school, enjoying the weekend, both single, and both unattached at the moment. He understood the signals; they weren't looking for serious relationships, but something more provisional, exactly as he'd hoped. It wouldn't be long before they suggested a private place to relax.

Lucia was more attractive than Daniel had first realized. She had deliciously full lips and womanly curves, and carried herself with the self-confidence of an experienced woman.

Ellen, although slightly less confident, appeared to be no less interested in an intimate evening, and slid her chair close to Roberto's to share a bowl of ice cream. They laughed when their spoons clinked together.

The evening breeze continued, carrying with it sounds of deepening night and scents of turning leaves. Daniel enjoyed listening to Lucia's throaty voice over the din of the crowd, and answered her questions as honestly as necessary. He observed Roberto watching him discreetly and imitating his actions.

In spite of enjoying the moment, however, he found his thoughts drifting back to Meg. Oddly enough, they retained none of the anger he'd felt a short time earlier. Would their paths cross again? Undoubtedly, he could find her if he worked hard enough. Why did he feel compelled to do so?

"I'm in the mood for a good soak. I don't suppose you have a hot tub?"

Daniel grinned at Lucia. "I think I can probably locate one somewhere." He drew his cell phone from his jacket, punched in a number, and made a reservation.

Rising, he dropped several folded bills on the table and offered Lucia his arm. She accepted, and they led the way to the sidewalk.

"Shall we walk, or would you rather ride?"

"Is it far?"

"A few blocks."

"Walk, by all means," Lucia said. "It's beautiful out tonight."

Daniel glanced over his shoulder to where Ellen and Roberto strolled side by side. "I agree," Ellen said.

"Then, walk it is." He stroked his partner's bare arm with his fingertips. "Tell me, Lucia, do you enjoy teaching?"

"Very much so, but it can be, well, limiting."

"Oh? In what way?"

"As a teacher, I have to be careful with my private life. Some *indulgences* aren't allowed."

He leaned down to ask softly, "Unless made discreetly?"

She grinned. "Yes."

They crossed a side street and strolled alongside a small park that bounded the meager Santa Fe River. Sounds of the city provided a pleasant background to their spurts of conversation.

"I don't have a suit with me," Ellen said.

"Don't worry," Daniel said. "We'll find one for you if you wish. But it is optional."

"Oh. In that case, I don't need one."

Daniel imagined Roberto's heart skipping a beat at the news.

Not long afterward, they climbed the steps to the massive El Dorado hotel and were met in the lobby by the night manager and two assistants.

"Señor Ward," the manager said with a formal bow. "It's always a pleasure to have you join us."

"Thank you, Max. Please send up a bottle of champagne."

"It has already been delivered. Let me know if you need anything else."

"I most certainly will."

Once in the elevator, he caught the look the women exchanged and enjoyed their excitement. He found no use for money beyond sharing it with others.

On the top floor, a bellboy waited at the door to the Presidential Suite; Daniel tipped the young man as they passed him. The door closed behind them.

He always enjoyed this suite, with its enormous living room

and tasteful Southwest motif. His three guests walked around gawking and he stepped back to let them take it all in. A bottle of champagne chilled in the middle of a copper-covered table beside a bowl of fresh fruit and a plate of cheese.

When Daniel popped the cork, Roberto jumped and the women laughed. Daniel filled glasses and handed them out.

"My favorite part is back here," he said.

"Oh?" Lucia sipped.

"Yes." He led the way into a sitting room where a fire roared in a kiva fireplace, and he shoved open the sliding door to the rooftop patio.

A hot tub gurgled to his left as he stepped out.

"Oh, my God. This is amazing," Lucia said.

"It may be a little more room than we need," Daniel said, "but I couldn't think of a more private hot tub off the top of my head."

"Holy shit," Roberto muttered.

Ellen laughed. "I agree."

The four of them leaned on the parapet wall and sipped champagne as they enjoyed the view of the city.

Below, automobile lights flickered and crowds flowed past streetlights. Daniel found himself searching the groups for a familiar form, and wondered why he did so. He felt almost melancholy, and the memory of wandering the earth after losing Running Deer swept over him.

Lucia moved closer, brushing Daniel's arm with her own. "Do you live like this all the time?"

He shook his head. "No, this is a special occasion."

"But they know your name."

He shrugged. "You reserve this suite more than once and they remember you."

"I bet. And do you reserve it often?"

He glanced down at her. "Does it matter?"

She shook her head and laughed. "Not in the least."

Daniel motioned with his glass. "The hot tub is prepared. If you want a masseuse or a masseur, I can have one sent up."

"I don't think that's necessary," she said. "We'll just go look for towels or something."

As soon as the women disappeared inside, Roberto stepped closer. "Hey, look, I appreciate all this shit, but how the hell am I supposed to do this for Berna?"

"Tonight, we are working only on form. Location is irrelevant. Think of the equivalent in your own life. What's your favorite place?"

"I don't know. There's a hot springs in the Jemez not many people know about. It's pretty up there."

"Invite Berna to your hot springs, and remember what you learn tonight."

Roberto considered the suggestion for a moment, and then grinned. "Okay."

They turned to watch their companions reappear wearing white terry-cloth robes.

At the edge of the tub, the women shed the robes, revealing the fact that they wore nothing underneath, and stepped into bubbling, steaming water.

"I think maybe we should join them," Daniel said.

"Oh, yeah." Roberto upended his glass as he started working on his shirt buttons.

Daniel laid an arm across the young man's shoulders. "Remember, patience is the key."

Although Roberto nodded, Daniel guessed by the quickness of his step that he might not be completely listening.

5

Daniel draped his arms across the edges of the tub and leaned back to enjoy its bubbling warmth.

"This is perfect," Lucia said.

He had to admit, he couldn't have planned it better. The moon rose over distant mountains into a cloudless sky, hazy through the steam, vanquishing his early memory of melancholy.

Lucia floated closer, and Daniel drew tender circles in her bare shoulder. The feel of her warm skin aroused him, and he guessed he was having the same effect on her when she brushed the back of her hand against his leg.

He raised his head and met her gaze with a look of invitation, and she accepted, turning as she floated around to straddle him. Holding his shoulders, she kissed him.

Her mouth, warm and wet, opened against his, and Daniel took the opportunity to probe, tasting champagne on her lips. As she slid her hands around to the back of his neck, she sucked on his tongue, drawing him deeper.

He wrapped his arms around her waist and drew her close,

savoring the wispy underwater meetings of skin to skin. His cock rose, brushing against her buttocks, and he groaned.

Lucia knew how to kiss. Tilting her head, she offered more and he took it, feeling the growing need in more than just his phallus. A kernel of hunger swelled in his gut, and he worked to quiet it for now. In his role as instructor, he had a long way to go before that hunger could be fed.

She tore her mouth from his and tossed back her head to expose her neck, and Daniel nearly forgot his intentions. He swallowed hard against the desire to drink.

Instead, he pressed his lips to her neck and enjoyed the steady rise and fall of her pulse as he ran his hands over her back and sides, leaving a film of water between his palms and her skin.

She shivered under his touch and raked her fingers through his hair.

He drew her down to his cock and her knees banged against the side of the plastic tub.

Raising his face, he met her gaze again. "Perhaps we should retire to where there is more room."

She nodded agreement.

Daniel stood, holding her body to his, and stepped from the tub.

Lucia locked her legs around his waist.

Before he walked into the room, he stopped and glanced at Roberto and Ellen, who watched in surprise from the tub. "You're welcome to join us."

Leaving a trail of water on the white carpet, he deposited his date on the long end of an orange sectional that faced the fireplace. She adjusted pillows behind her back and, combing her long, silky hair back with her fingers, smiled up at him.

Daniel sat on the end of the sofa and took the time to admire her body. She wasn't virginally young, but hadn't yet reached the point of having to worry about sagging flesh. Instead, her body was smooth and full and joyously tempting.

He wrapped his hands around her ankles and eased her legs apart.

She didn't resist.

Kneeling, he leaned forward and kissed the insides of her knees.

She laughed a full, rich laugh.

Touching her with only his mouth, he moved up her legs, nipping and kissing the tender insides of her thighs. He smelled her arousal overrunning the remnants of chlorinated water as he went, and the scent urged him on. Savoring the thrill of anticipation, he worked slowly, refusing to touch his swelling cock, denying the desire to plunge it into her hot cunt.

Sliding to the floor and turning her with him, he knelt where he could reach her easily and pressed his mouth to her fragrant cunt lips. She bucked under him in surprise, then groaned softly and buried her fingers in his hair.

As he ran his fingers in a feathery touch down the backs of her legs, Daniel teased her swelling clit with his tongue.

Lucia's groans grew louder and she raised her hips toward his mouth.

He focused on her reactions, sucking her clit and then thrusting into her cunt with his tongue as her movements grew more violent with need. He pushed her toward the edge, waiting to hear desperation in her voice.

"Oh, yes, that's so good," she whispered.

Behind him, he heard Roberto and Ellen tiptoe in and felt the air move as they settled on the floor near the fireplace.

Opening his mouth more, he sucked harder, tasting her juices, drawing against her tightening muscles.

She held fistfuls of his hair in shaky hands. "Oh, yeah. I'm so close."

But she wasn't yet desperate and he backed off just enough to keep her needing.

As he licked her cunt in hard strokes, she rose in time with his movements, whimpering.

He turned his head and nipped her thighs.

"Oh, God, please. Don't stop."

Daniel smiled. There it was, the desperation he'd sought. Centering himself again, he drew her in long, slow strokes to a shattering climax.

With her legs open wide and her back arched, Lucia cried out as she came, releasing thick cum against his lips. Daniel relished every drop, massaging her pulsing muscles until the orgasm slowed and stopped.

Had his focus not been on showing Roberto the meaning of restraint, he would have fucked her then, and she wouldn't have stopped him. But that wasn't what he had in mind.

Sitting back on his heels, he gazed up into her heavily lidded eyes as he caressed her trembling legs. "Nice."

"Nicer for me," she said.

Daniel turned at the sounds behind him to find Ellen and Roberto lying on the floor, kissing. Roberto had his hand between Ellen's legs and his swollen cock pressed into her hip. In two seconds, he'd be inside her.

Daniel eased closer. "Slow down," he whispered near the young man's ear.

Roberto raised his head and scowled at Daniel.

"I have an idea," Daniel said, sitting up. "Why don't we all move to the bed where we can be comfortable?"

"*All* of us?" Roberto asked.

"Sure. There's plenty of room." Daniel drew Lucia up by the hand and led the way to the king-sized brass canopied bed. She sat beside him and he kissed her soundly on the lips.

When Roberto and Ellen arrived, Daniel held a hand out to Ellen. She took his hand and let him draw her in for a quick, friendly kiss, then sat on the bed beside him, her hand on his shoulder.

Roberto frowned at the three of them, his hard-on completely lost.

Lucia reached out for him. He hesitantly took her hand and followed her onto the bed.

"I've never, uh, done this," Roberto said.

"It's okay," Lucia said. "We have." When she shoved his shoulder, Roberto submitted and rolled onto his back.

Lucia stretched out beside him and stroked his chest and stomach as she smiled at Daniel.

Daniel also stretched out where he could watch, drawing Ellen down in front of him with her back to him. He pulled her up against his body, positioning his cock between her thighs, still damp from the hot tub, and holding her close, he propped his head on his fist. Ellen reached back and caressed his buttocks with a firm hand.

Lucia's hand drifted down over Roberto's flaccid penis and it came to life, rising to meet her touch. As she wrapped her fingers around the shaft, the young man sucked in a quick breath and closed his eyes for a moment.

Encouraged by his reaction, she scooted down the bed and added her tongue to the action, running it up from the base to the head and then back down.

Roberto's cock swelled almost instantly, and he groaned. "Fuck," he whispered.

Ellen wriggled out of Daniel's grip to join the pair, kissing first Roberto and then Lucia, who returned her kiss as she slid her hand up and down Roberto's cock. The young man reached up, touching Lucia's breast and Ellen's thigh.

Daniel rested his hand on his own cock and watched, tracing his growing fangs with his tongue when he was sure no one noticed. Hunger returned, blossoming into an urgent need. Before long his eyes would start to glow with the moon's ancient light.

He moved closer, caressing the fine lines of Ellen's back, tracing her spine and enjoying the heat. She lowered to her hands and knees and returned to kissing Roberto, offering Daniel entry.

He knelt over her from behind and reached around to tease her clit with his fingers as he rubbed the head of his cock between her legs. She responded by raising her ass into him.

Kissing the back of her shoulders, Daniel eased his fingers into her, surprised by how slick she already felt. He used her juices to lubricate the nub of a clit, playing with it as it hardened and swelled.

Ellen raised her face from Roberto's as her movements quickened against Daniel's hand, and her juices began to run down his fingers. He clamped his mouth onto her shoulder and sucked, refusing to give in just yet, and she responded by backing into him.

Daniel opened his eyes and glanced across the bed to where Lucia lowered herself onto Roberto's cock, and he watched her cunt swallow more and more of the man's shaft until she had it all. With her hands splayed on Roberto's chest, she rose up and lowered herself back down, and rose again, exposing his glistening cock to view.

Ellen rubbed against Daniel, whimpering with need, and he obliged her by easing into her while he gently pulled on her clit.

She grunted and slammed back into him, her cunt biting his cock with sweet spasms of release. Daniel wrapped his arm around her waist and drew her up. Shielding his actions from the other two with her body, he pierced her shoulder.

She screamed out with ecstasy and he drank from her, letting the joy echo in his head and radiate through his body. Thrusting into her cunt, he drew hard for a moment, and then extracted his fangs and held his mouth to her to stop the flow.

In this situation, he couldn't afford to lose himself in the moment.

As her orgasm faded, Ellen collapsed under him and Daniel withdrew. Sitting back on his heels, he watched as Roberto raised his hips off the bed, releasing his seed into Lucia. She rode out his thrusts, then rose up off him and turned to Daniel.

"And now for you."

Daniel lay back and held her waist as she mounted him, then he caressed her heavy breasts, thrilling to their fullness and heat.

He fought the urge to pull her to him as she rode him mercilessly, rubbing her clit against the base of his aching shaft. Her muscles tightened, but offered no release.

Daniel glanced over to find Roberto watching the action, his cock swelling again with interest. He looked up at Lucia and smiled. "How about both of us?"

She smiled back and raised one eyebrow. "Not a bad idea." Then she moved off him. "But I want you in back. I think you have more control."

He nodded and rolled over.

Roberto began to frown his uncertainty again and Daniel sighed. "Don't worry, you'll definitely enjoy this."

As Daniel caressed her back and lovely ass, Lucia guided Roberto's cock back into her cunt, and rode it long enough to bring it back to full attention. Daniel watched the union as his fangs ached again.

When the couple stilled, he knelt between Roberto's legs and carefully eased into Lucia's tightest opening a little at a time, waiting for her to adjust to him, until he'd buried his cock in her ass. He rocked gently, and felt Roberto's cock thrusting against his own. He closed his eyes to enjoy the pleasure.

Lucia trembled against him, and then began forward to meet Roberto's thrusts, and Daniel moved with her. He held her around the waist, feeling her body heat up in his arms. Her breath came out in stuttered gasps.

"So full," she said. "Too much, too . . . much."

Her body stiffened and then writhed with release, and Roberto cried out from under her, exploding into her. All this Daniel felt, unable to resist any longer, and he sank his fangs into the side of her neck and drank as he came.

The three of them rocked together, and the intense pleasure bounced through Daniel for the second time. This pleasure felt more mature, more determined, and filled him with a joy unlike any he'd known in some time. He tasted her excruciating ecstasy and knew the exhilaration she felt at having both of them at once, fulfilling a fantasy she'd long held. He knew her sense of power at drawing Roberto to his second orgasm. And he saw himself through her eyes as a man of mystery and excitement, not unlike the man of her most secret dreams.

Before the memories could come, he stopped drinking from her and let himself ride out the rest of the climax as a mortal would. He couldn't risk exposure of his true identity.

He eased away from Lucia and she fell forward onto Roberto, and the couple panted together. When she finally rolled off and rested her head on the young man's muscular shoulder, Daniel backed off the bed. Ellen lay on her back with her eyes closed.

Reeling from the sensory input, Daniel staggered to the patio and eased down into the bubbling tub. He loved the way water swirled heat around him and gave him glimpses of the moon between clouds of steam.

As he relaxed and the emotions ebbed, he decided the time had come to leave. Roberto had learned as much as he could in one night. The next night he would approach his love and either succeed or fail.

After lounging in the tub for awhile, enjoying the New Mexico night, Daniel climbed out, dried off, and dressed.

He stopped at the bed and shook Roberto's foot.

The young man jumped and raised his head. "You're leaving?"

Daniel glanced at the two women. "I think you have this under control. Make sure they get home safely."

The young man nodded.

"I'll see you tomorrow night. Call your lady and ask her to meet you at Cowgirl's."

"What if she won't come?"

"Then it will be her loss."

Roberto grinned and dropped his head back to the bed.

Daniel stuffed fruit from the table into his pockets on the way out and slipped down the back stairs.

Meg slumped further into the seat of her car. With her dark clothes and shadowed parking space, she felt sure he couldn't see her.

Across the street, Daniel hurried along the sidewalk, the pockets of his dark jacket bulging, his black hair lifting from his shoulders with each step.

Each time she saw him, the initial shock took her breath away. He had to be the best-looking man she'd ever seen. At just under six feet, he had wide shoulders, long legs, and sharply chiseled features. Even set against his relatively pale skin for New Mexico, sky-blue eyes made his looks all the more striking.

He walked with a confidence rarely seen—that of a man sure of himself, but unpretentious. He seemed to be aware of everything around him, but not wary as a criminal would be.

He was, however, a criminal. Of that she was certain. She'd witnessed him picking a pocket.

Sort of. She'd at least been at the scene. She'd watched Bedford shove his wallet in his pocket moments before it disappeared.

The big question now was, just how guilty was he?

He turned the corner and stopped, and she sat up a little straighter to see.

Speaking to Alex Trahan and CC White, he crouched and

emptied his pockets. At first she thought he was delivering stolen goods and her pulse quickened with excitement, but the goods turned out to be apples and oranges that the group distributed and quickly worked on devouring. They waved to Daniel as he rose and left.

Strange thing for a criminal to do.

Checking for traffic, he trotted across San Francisco and strode down Washington until he'd disappeared from Meg's line of sight.

After waiting a little while, she jumped out, locked her car, and ran across San Francisco. Spotting him nearly a block ahead, she matched his pace.

At the next corner, he turned right.

She slowed as if looking for an address, then hurried forward when she no longer saw him.

At the corner, she stopped.

He hadn't been far ahead of her, but he'd disappeared. She searched the shadows and doorways, and found nothing. Where the hell had he gone?

Had he realized she was tailing him and lost her on purpose? Or had she just missed something?

Continuing slowly, she listened for the echo of boots on sidewalk, or the screech of a door's hinge.

Nothing. Not a damn thing.

"Shit."

She stopped under the shelter of a small tree and waited.

How would she find him now? Maybe she should return to the street she'd followed him to the night before, but she had no idea which of the many houses he'd gone into. And it wouldn't be easy to hang out there without being spotted.

Her only other choice was to wait until the next evening and troll the Plaza area again. Downtown certainly wasn't very big, and Daniel whatever-his-name-was stood out in a crowd.

She should have introduced herself with a last name so

maybe he'd have done the same. If he drove, she could have tracked him down long ago. So far, she hadn't seen him climb into a vehicle.

Sighing, she started back toward her car, wishing for a cigarette. Two months and she still craved a smoke when frustrated.

If only she knew for sure that Daniel had something to do with Elena, she'd feel better about working so hard to track him down. She could be wasting precious time.

Was it purely coincidence that he knew Alex Trahan, and had apparently picked the pocket of Gordon Bedford? And she'd seen him with Elena two weeks before the woman had disappeared. He'd caught her off guard at Cowgirl's. How was it he kept turning up in the right places if he had nothing to do with Bedford's operation?

Gritting her teeth and balling her hands into fists, she silently screamed. *Someone* had to lead her to Elena.

Assuming she was still alive.

Daniel crouched on the roof of the library and watched Meg march down the sidewalk, anger echoing from the blows of her shoes on pavement.

She had, indeed, been following him.

Why?

He considered hopping down in front of her and asking, but doubted he'd get an honest answer.

He could learn the truth quite easily. With one bite, he'd know everything there was to know.

Somehow, though, the thought of attacking this woman appalled him even more than it should.

He must find out more about her. At least now he had the opportunity to do so.

Glancing up at the nearly full moon, he opted for a traditional method of travel, leapt to the ground, and trotted back to San Francisco, where he flagged down a taxicab.

"Follow that automobile," he said, pointing to the maroon vehicle Meg steered away from a curb. "But not too closely." Then he passed two hundreds forward.

The overweight, gray-haired driver grinned at him in the rearview mirror as he tucked the bills in his shirt pocket. "You got it. She'll never know we're back here."

"Excellent."

They wound out of the downtown area and followed Cerrillos Road to where it widened south of town, then turned off into a quiet neighborhood of small houses constructed close together.

Meg pulled up in front of one of the dwellings, and the taxicab stopped a block away around a corner. Daniel thanked the driver.

"Most fun I've had all week," the man said, grinning. "Want me to wait for you?"

"No need."

"Call anytime and ask for Jack."

As the vehicle eased away, Daniel strolled quietly back around the corner and stopped across the wide street from where Meg had parked.

Inside the house, she turned on lights and her silhouette passed in front of a large window. Houses on each side lay dark as if empty or filled with sleeping occupants. Considering the early morning hour, the latter seemed reasonable.

Seeing no signs of a housemate, Daniel crossed the street and stopped near the front window of Meg's house. He heard her moving around—kicking off her shoes, taking a beverage from the refrigerator and opening it, flipping through television channels. She murmured complaints until she turned off the television and left the room.

She padded through the house and he crept to a side window, where he heard her brushing her teeth and preparing for bed. She either had a pet of some kind or spoke to herself as she undressed. The only words he made out plainly were "women" and "bastards." At one point, she stood still for a minute, and then said, "Who the hell is he?"

Was she wondering about him?

The question made him smile.

Mattress springs squeaked as she dropped onto her bed, muttering, "Shit."

Daniel leaned to peek through the window and noticed soft light emanating from the ceiling. He stepped back and glanced around, then jumped up to the roof. Balancing on the parapet wall, he spotted three windows in the roof, and moved silently to the one most likely to be over her bed. On his hands and knees, he eased to the edge, where he could peer down at her.

Meg lay sprawled in bed on top of a wrinkled comforter, wearing only a short gray undershirt and low-cut panties. Folding one arm behind her head, she ran her hand over her stomach and breasts, then down between her legs, where it stayed. Her eyes were closed, but her lips parted as he watched, and then her hips hinted at movement.

Daniel moved closer to get a better look, unable to turn away. Meg's hair fanned out on her pillow like rays from the sun, framing her simple looks with a suggestion of beauty, and her nipples poked up against cotton fabric as she stroked herself.

His fangs elongated in response, as did his prick. He wanted nothing more than to drop through the skylight and take her as both man and beast.

No, that wasn't quite true. He wanted to carry her to a moonlit forest and make love to her under an open sky. Or maybe transport her to a foreign beach where they could watch the moon rise and couple with abandon in the waves.

He froze when she opened her eyes, but she didn't see him. Instead, she rolled over, opened a night table drawer, and withdrew something he couldn't make out at first. But when he heard a soft buzz and watched her rub the object between her legs, he realized she had a vibrating dildo.

Lifting her shirt and caressing a breast with one hand, she slid the dildo under her panties and moved it back and forth over her clit.

Daniel's fangs began to ache with a dull, throbbing pain, and his cock swelled to generous proportions. He rearranged his pants to relieve the pressure and stretched out beside the window to watch.

She drew her bottom lip in between her teeth as she dipped the end of the phallus into her cunt, then eased it back out. Moonlight glistened on the wet plastic, and Daniel bit back a groan. He could practically smell her scent, and longed to taste her thick juices.

She dipped the dildo in a little deeper, and then more, until most of the plastic cock lay buried inside her.

How he wished it were him instead.

He heard soft noises as she slid the vibrator in and out, raising her hips to the slow, easy rhythm. She pinched one nipple between forefinger and thumb, and then the other.

Daniel massaged the shafts of his fangs with his tongue, barely able to keep from growling with need. He stroked the bulge of his cock.

Her head went back as her rhythm increased, and the dildo moved faster, deeper. He imagined the way her heart pounded, and closed his eyes to picture the pulse at the side of her neck rising in rapid, steady beats.

She groaned, and he opened his eyes to watch her come. Her body stiffened and her hips rose higher, then he saw the orgasm break in her expression of pained relief.

Riding the waves, she jerked against the vibrating phallus and stroked it with her cunt.

If he'd had a mortal neck within reach, he would have been unable to resist the drive to feed. And if he hadn't had the window between himself and Meg at that moment, he would have been filling her as he drank of her life force.

He longed to taste her dreams and uncover her secrets, to feel her arms around him. Would she be as different as the strange effect of her presence suggested?

Would she be as unique as Running Deer had been?

Her body stilled and relaxed and her eyes fluttered open.

She stared up at him.

6

Daniel rolled away from the roof window, but he knew he was too late.

"Son of a bitch! Who's up there? I'm calling the cops!"

He heard a drawer slide open, and then the click of a revolver's hammer drawing back. Before Meg started shooting holes in her roof, he jumped up, vaulted over the parapet, and hit the ground running.

Moving at speeds too fast for human sight, he returned to downtown Santa Fe and stopped in the small park near the river. He leaned against the dark side of a tree, standing still to calm his body and mind.

He hadn't truly meant to spy on Meg, at least not at first, and felt a nip of guilt. But she had been the one following him, after all. She could just as easily have caught him in the middle of a similarly compromising act if she'd followed him into the hotel.

Perhaps she had been at the hotel. Focused on his companions, it hadn't occurred to him to look for her in the lobby.

Why did this situation bother him so? He wasn't even alive anymore by mortal standards, and certainly felt no need to abide by their social mores.

Yet he experienced a degree of self-loathing because of breaching the walls of Meg's privacy.

Odd.

Wondering once again about his mental state, Daniel followed the sidewalks to the Plaza, where he sat in darkness watching other night creatures on the move. Bats winged overhead, alley cats scaled fences, and one or two other moon-worshippers passed by with a nod.

When the heaviness of dawn began to weigh in his arms and legs, he started and checked his watch. How could he have been sitting there for two hours without taking notice of the time?

Damn this mortal witch. Whether she meant to or not, she just might be the reason for his demise.

He hurried home, bolted his door, and fell into bed still dressed. The nourishment he'd taken earlier had already begun to wear off. Giving up his grip on consciousness, he drifted off.

Running Deer came to him then, as beautiful as ever, standing in a circle of sacred moonlight.

He crouched at the edge of the woods and watched as she shed her clothes, knelt in damp grass, and raised her arms to the moon. Her soft chants floated over an open field of flowers and caressed his skin as only a night breeze could.

She spoke a language that tore at his heart although he understood not a word. Instinctively, he knew the meaning.

In the moonlight, her skin glistened like waxed mahogany and her hair glowed like ravens' feathers. Every movement of her hands defined grace as she splashed symbolic waves of cleansing night air onto her face.

Unable to help himself, he approached her in silence.

Somehow, she knew he was there. As she placed her palms on her thighs, she closed her eyes and lowered her head for a long moment, and then she rose to her feet.

"You shouldn't be here." She turned to face him.

He stopped within reach of her, but managed not to do so. Not right away, at least.

He'd wanted to touch her for two years, since the first night Moon Dancer had brought him into the clan. He could still feel Running Deer's soothing strokes to his forehead and face as his life drained away. He remembered looking up into her calm, welcoming smile.

"I love you."

She shook her head. "No. We can't love. We can only want."

"How do you know? Just because Moon Dancer says—"

She stopped him with her hand over his mouth. "Everything she says is true."

He held her wrist and kissed her fingers, then drew her hand down to cover his cold heart. "Are you so certain?"

She nodded, but he saw a spark of doubt in her dark eyes.

"Then," he said, stroking her silky hair, "I have wanted you since I first saw you."

She broke eye contact long enough to glance around. "I, too, have felt the longing, the hunger."

Hunger. That was exactly what he felt for her, but it was a hunger like no other. He hungered to touch her, to kiss her, to lie with her, to become part of her. This hunger filled every waking moment and every dream. He'd found no pleasure in feeding, or anything else, unless it resulted in being close to her.

At first, he'd worried that Moon Dancer would notice. Once he drank from his killer-savior, he knew the rules. He could drink from no other in the clan without her approval, and, concerned that jealousy would tear the clan apart, she rarely gave such approval. She may be right to worry, but he didn't care. If he had to forfeit the clan to be with Running

Deer, he'd do it. One moment of touching her would be worth decades alone.

"I don't care what happens to me," he said. "But I won't put you in jeopardy unless you agree."

Hell's flames, he hoped she'd agree.

"Do you understand what will happen?"

He studied the moonlight sparkling in her eyes and shrugged, not knowing what to expect.

"We will be connected for the rest of time. If one of us feels joy, we both feel joy. If one of us suffers, we both suffer." She stepped closer until he felt her words on his face. "If one of us leaves this world, we may leave together. Is that what you want?"

He stroked her soft cheek and ran his fingertips across her lips. "Yes."

She closed her eyes and leaned toward his touch.

Before he formed a second thought, he drew her into his embrace and his breath caught in his throat as if he were mortal. He wrapped his arms around her bare body, spreading his fingers across her skin to feel all of her.

She didn't resist. Her palms rose to his sides.

He took her mouth in greedy need, stumbling and steadying himself as she stretched up against him. He felt her breasts pressing against his flesh and groaned with joy.

Suddenly, cruelly, she pushed him away.

He stared at her, terrified that she would now deny him.

Instead, she stepped toward him and began to remove his clothes in ritual fashion, folding each piece and placing it on the ground at her feet.

When they stood together naked, he froze, unsure what to do, unsure how to express his raw emotions in touch.

Running Deer smiled and raised her head, offering her most vulnerable spot to him.

Daniel's fangs dropped to their full length in a sudden rush, just as his cock swelled with need. Gently holding her shoulders, he pressed his mouth to her neck.

A shiver ran through her body and caused the same reaction in him as he kissed her cool flesh and inhaled her perfect scent.

He straightened and looked at her for a moment, closed his eyes, and raised his head.

Running Deer's slender hands slid down the front of his body as she kissed his neck, tasting his flesh with her tongue, teasing him by pressing the tips of her fangs to his skin.

His knees threatened to buckle, but he managed to remain on his feet.

Her fingers skidded down the length of his swollen cock and a strange strength surged through his torso. Not the strength of lust, or even immortality, as he'd felt upon waking from his first sleep of death, but something more feral, more dangerous. He felt the strength of a monster shaking off sleep, ready to rule, intent on taking over the one who sheltered it.

With a grunt, he clutched her shoulders and took her mouth again, this time thrusting his tongue between her lips, circling her mouth in a greedy duel. The monster expanded, threatening to displace whatever there was of goodness and purity.

Had he actually thought he loved her?

The truth shone in his heart now. He hungered for her in a base, primeval way.

Wasting no tenderness, he drew her down to the ground with him and pushed her to her back.

She stared up at him with red glowing eyes, her mouth open to reveal glistening ivory fangs.

Then he stopped, entranced by the beauty of the woman-beast bathed in hallowed moonlight. She smiled and welcomed him with open arms.

Love rushed back into the void of his soul, and he lowered himself to her waiting body, parting her legs with his own.

"I've dreamt of this," he whispered.

"I, too," she whispered back, running her open hands over his back.

He wanted nothing more than to penetrate her with his cock and his fangs, but he knew the value of waiting and he lowered his mouth to her neck.

She touched him with all of her. Her hands slid over his back, her legs closed around his hips, and her lips locked on the skin of his shoulder.

The line between them blurred as he wrapped himself around her. He felt no heat from her cool flesh, but sensed a warmth deep inside as if light returned to his heart. He remembered the sensation of sunlight on skin, and the warmth of soft bedcovers on a chilly morn. He recalled the taste of ripe plums, warm from the tree, and hot cider from a steaming cup. Every good thing he'd experienced in life rushed back to him then, memories growing stale with passing years.

She lifted her hips into him.

Unable to wait, he entered her, thrusting with the strength of denied desire, burying his cock in the tight depths of her wonderful cunt. He sighed at the amazing feeling of finding true joy.

She matched his sigh with a stuttered breath of desire.

He ran his lips slowly over the side of her silky neck, relishing the scent of her. His human needs intensified, driving him to withdraw and thrust again. She moved under him, meeting each new entry with legs spread wider.

As his cock grew, she took it deeper. He needed more, and she gave it as she dug her nails into his back.

Her growl sparked a rebirth of the beast in his soul, and he felt himself shoved aside until he served only as observer, experiencing the joy and fear of what was to come.

He pressed the tips of his fangs to her skin and held them

there until she penetrated his shoulder. Waves of erotic pleasure rolled over him, strengthening the creature. Snarling, he bit into her flesh.

Joined this way, both as man and woman and as immortal beasts, they rose from earthly bindings into bliss. He drew from her the taste of her joy, the feel of it, the knowledge, the experience, and offered back his own.

Yellow and red lights sparkled behind his eyes. He felt release, too intense to be real as he filled her. Nothing could be more perfect, more powerful.

And then his world split apart.

When his own joy ripped into him through their connection, it was heightened, sweetened, strengthened tenfold.

He clung to her, trembling, needing every drop.

Time stopped.

Every memory, every thought, every happiness and misery in her life came to him, blended with his own, until they were the moments of one life, not two. He knew happiness as a daughter, the thrill of motherhood, and love as a wife. He knew pain and suffering, and pure pleasure.

They were truly joined, fused.

Perfect connection of souls.

Finally, the beast eased away, sated.

Daniel withdrew his receding fangs and felt her do the same. The burning brand from her teeth faded, but the light of her heart did not.

Perhaps it never would.

He held her tighter, more enraptured than ever. "My love," he whispered.

She answered him in a strange language he shouldn't have understood, but did.

"Always to be mine," she said.

They lay together in cool, damp grass, and sounds of night rose around them, completing the peace. An owl screeched from a great distance, and frogs sang in echoed harmony. Moonlight warmed his back and buttocks.

A twig snapped at the edge of the clearing and Daniel lifted his head.

"Son of a whore! You will pay!"

Against the darkness, he saw the silhouette of Wolf, his feet wide, his hands in fists at his sides.

And he knew at that moment that the man had loved Running Deer many years longer than he had.

Daniel felt her regret and fear of the future as he withdrew from Running Deer and rose to his feet. Even as he prepared for attack, he knew it wouldn't come. That, too, was against the rules.

Would it be sunlight, burning his flesh from his bones? Or a cold steel blade pushed slowly through his neck? Or perhaps, even more hideous, wet salted leather tightening across his throat as it dried, squeezing his head from his shoulders as he stood in a shrinking circle of shadow? The risk was clear to him now. He would not be simply banned from the clan.

He jumped when Running Deer's hand came to rest on his shoulder. Glancing back, he found a tall, slender woman standing in her place, clad in jeans and a white shirt, short brown hair replacing long black. Glistening green eyes stared back at him.

"What in the hell—?"

Meg? How could she be here?

Daniel opened his eyes to a shapeless, empty ceiling.

The vision of Meg faded, along with the sounds of a long-ago night.

He lay for a time trying to refresh the memory of Running Deer, but gave up as he ascended to true consciousness.

Purposely pushing the past away, he rolled from his bed. He had work to do this night, and focused on the future. The past held too many threats to his happiness.

Perhaps the future held some, too, especially with this green-eyed female in it, but he refused to worry. Not yet, at least.

Wearing black pants, high boots, and a black jacket over blood-red silk, Daniel lounged in his favorite chair at Cowgirl's waiting for the showdown.

Roberto arrived as nervous as a treed cat but dressed better than he had been before. He dropped into the chair closest to Daniel.

"What the hell am I supposed to do when she gets here?"

Daniel grabbed his shoulder. "Relax. Breathe. Remember, you know how to please a woman. And you have a romantic's heart. What more could any woman ask?"

The young man took several deep, slow breaths.

Daniel sat back. "When she arrives, don't rush. Order drinks and then tell her how much she means to you. Be truthful. Whatever you do, don't beg, and don't sound desperate."

Roberto frowned. "Shit. I am desperate."

"You needn't be." Daniel considered the resources he had available and decided to risk one. Without it, Roberto might not be able to maintain his self-confidence. Perhaps, if they had a week together, he wouldn't need to resort to this, but Daniel found that thought unbearable. He had other things to do—a green-eyed nymph to figure out.

"If you hear a voice in your head," he said, "listen to it."

"A *voice*? You mean, like the voice of God or something?"

"Not quite." He smiled. "Trust me."

"Shit."

Daniel motioned to a nearby table. "Sit over there and wait."

Roberto did as ordered and sat facing the patio entrance. One leg twitched, and his hands opened and closed against the metal chair's arms.

Daniel stilled his senses, closed his eyes, focused his energies to one spot in front of him, and moved that spot across the space between them. He entered Roberto's mind, letting his awareness and senses merge with that of the mortal man's. He felt a chill against heated skin, heard with the muffled ability of a human, and tasted bile.

Relax. You have nothing to fear.

Roberto started with surprise at hearing his voice. Then he heard Roberto's retort. *Relax? Shit.*

Berna stepped onto the patio and stopped.

Roberto stood and stared at her. When their gazes met, heat rose in the young man's chest and neck, and he swallowed hard.

You have much to offer her. Pull out a chair and wait.

Roberto drew back a chair and held it.

After a moment's hesitation, Berna sighed, strode forward, and took the chair. "I told you, I'm not interested."

"Would you like some wine? Or something else?"

She glared for a full minute, the shrugged. "Fine. One glass of wine. White. Then I'm leaving."

Roberto waved to get a waiter's attention and ordered two glasses. Then he leaned back in his chair and smiled at her. "You are the most beautiful woman I've ever met."

She glared at him, huffed, and looked around as if scoping out possible dates.

Anger swelled in his chest.

Calm down. Talk to her. Truth and confidence.

"I know I've been a . . . a—"

"Pendejo?"

He winced. "I guess so."

"You guess so? You show up at my job, you wait outside my house, you bug me every day for a month and you *guess so*?"

I won't bother you any longer.

"Look, I won't follow you around anymore. I just want to tell you how I feel. Then I'll leave you alone."

"Promise?"

The waiter delivered wine and they both sipped. Warm confidence slid down Roberto's throat and into his system.

"Yes," he said, "I promise."

"Okay. You get three minutes. I'm listening."

He hesitated, waiting for the voice, but Daniel remained silent. This, the mortal had to do on his own. It was his story.

"I see the way men treat you, especially Varela."

She stiffened. "José's all right. He's got money, and he buys me things."

"He pushes you around and looks at other women when he's with you. He's the *pendejo*. You're too good for him, Berna."

"But not for you?"

Roberto dropped his gaze to the table for a moment. "Yes, you're too good for me, too, but at least I know it." He looked up and found her studying him. "I would never treat you like he does. I would spend every second I'm with you trying to make you happy. If that makes me stupid, then I'm stupid. If it makes me a *pendejo*, then that's what I am."

Her eyes widened and began to glisten with tears.

"I know about *tu hija*, and I'd make her a good *papá* if you wanted me to. All I want is a chance."

Tears overflowed her lids and ran down her cheeks.

Roberto reached forward and gently wiped both cheeks with his fingers, then he caressed her face for a moment. His body reacted to touching her, and Daniel enjoyed the tingling sensations in his crotch.

Movement and screeching chairs drew Roberto's attention in time to see José Varela charging toward the table. The man, at least ten years Roberto's senior and several inches taller, grabbed Berna's arm and jerked her from her chair.

Roberto jumped up, shoved the man away, and stepped between them.

Varela sneered. "You think you can take me?"

Fear merged with anger, souring in Roberto's gut, but he stood his ground.

Daniel pressed his thoughts forward again, letting the monster rise to just below the surface. Determination in Roberto's eyes hardened to murderous rage and he leaned close. "I *know* I can."

Varela saw it. He knew the truth instantly, and he swallowed hard.

"You should leave while you're still able," Roberto said through clenched teeth.

Varela stepped back and glanced around. People watched, waiting.

The older man huffed. "You think the bitch is worth it, you can have her."

Roberto jumped forward, ready to swing, but Varela backed out of range, then spun around and marched away.

Daniel leashed the monster and retreated, and Roberto returned to Berna. "Are you all right?"

She nodded and wiped fresh tears from her cheeks.

He waited until she sat down and retook his seat.

She studied him again, and her expression softened. "You stood up for me. No one's ever done that before."

"They should have." Struggling with a growing knot of emotion, Roberto glanced down at the menu. "You want some ribs?"

She shrugged. "I'll get barbeque sauce all over me."

He leaned close and licked his lips. "I can take care of that."

She laughed.

Daniel withdrew, leaving Roberto marveling at the wonderful sound of Berna's laughter.

He returned to the cold emptiness of his own shell and the moment of regret he always felt. Struggling against heavy limbs and hunger, he retuned himself to his preternatural senses and waited. Dozens of heartbeats rose around him, drowned by voices, clinking silverware, and blaring car horns. After a moment of excruciating racket, the sounds dulled to bearable and Daniel opened his eyes.

Roberto glanced over and raised one eyebrow, and Daniel winked. He took one more sip of wine, rose, and straightened his jacket. With his mission complete, he'd earned a good drink. Perhaps he'd spend the rest of the night at the Tunnel, mingling with his own kind. No doubt there'd be a crowd.

Meg leaned around the corner and watched Daniel cross the patio. At the gate, he stopped and turned so that she saw his profile. He frowned as if confused.

She pulled back, hiding behind the wall.

Dear God, the man was magnificent. Every movement oozed sex appeal. Her belly tingled.

She took a sip of cold water and bit back ridiculous thoughts.

Once again he'd appeared at Bedford's favorite place while Bedford was there. Yet, Daniel hadn't made contact that she could see. In fact, he hadn't moved from his chair.

The man she'd seen with him before sat at his table for a minute, then moved to another where a woman joined him. Was this Bedford's contact? She'd keep an eye on the pair to see what they did.

The weirdest thing was the way Daniel seemed to meditate or something right in the middle of the restaurant. In fact, it looked like he slept through the whole near-fight thing with his friend and the cowboy. And then, once it was all over, he just got up and left.

Strange.

Meg drank from her water glass, and then glanced out to find the couple still at the table, ordering food.

What worried her more was why she'd imagined Daniel on her roof the night before. Just after she'd finished jacking off, fantasizing about him the whole time, she'd opened her eyes and seen him above her, watching.

It had to have been her imagination. No one could have climbed off her roof and disappeared by the time she got out there. He couldn't possibly have jumped to the ground without making any noise.

No, she must have still been in fantasy mode. The man's eyes hadn't even looked human when she'd pictured him. For some reason, his eyes had glowed a strange gold color.

He'd looked hungry.

Good Lord, this was crazy. Why was she fantasizing about a man she didn't even know?

Bedford passed her table on the way to the restroom and she raised the menu to hide her face. She smiled at the waiter, shaking her head as he started toward her. He glared and moved to another table.

She hated tailing Bedford, especially when he seemed intent on doing nothing more than feeding his face and guzzling beer.

She glanced out around the wall again to where Daniel's chair remained empty. Maybe she'd run across him again tonight. If so, he wouldn't shake her so easily next time.

7

Daniel woke to another vision of Meg, this time standing in the doorway to his bedroom. She wore jeans and a blue blazer over a tan sweater that hugged her slender body. He smiled and rubbed his eyes.

His vision remained.

As he sat up, he noticed the glimmering black handgun she pointed at his chest.

Perhaps she wasn't a vision after all.

"How did you manage to get in?" he asked.

Keeping him in her sights, she entered his room one step at a time. "It sure as hell wasn't easy." She stopped and felt the wall. "Don't you have any lights in here?"

Daniel reached over and switched on a lamp.

Meg squinted against the sudden illumination, then widened her eyes and looked him over from head to toe.

Glancing down and realizing he'd slept in only pajama bottoms, he stood. "Please pardon my appearance."

"Hold it right there."

He shrugged. "If you insist."

She swallowed hard as she stared at his bare chest, then she motioned with the weapon. "You can get dressed. Just don't try anything. I don't want to shoot you, but I will."

With a nod, Daniel stepped into the closet, shed his pajamas, and pulled on fresh clothes. He stepped out again, clad in black pants, a pale blue shirt, and boots.

"Jeez, how'd you get dressed so fast?"

He shrugged. "I didn't wish to keep you waiting."

She narrowed her eyes. "You haven't even asked me why I'm here."

"No, I haven't. Tea?"

"Huh?"

"Would you like some tea?" He motioned toward the living room.

"After you."

He led the way to the kitchen where he located a kettle, filled it with water, and placed it on the stove. As he packed an infuser with tea leaves, he took advantage of the work to shed the remnants of death's sleep and gather his thoughts.

He assumed Meg chased him because she knew what he was. That's why most people chased him eventually. However, if she did know the truth, she should realize that her weapon offered no defense against him.

Could there be some other reason for her appearance?

Perhaps she felt the same attraction he felt for her.

That wouldn't provide a reason for her breaking into his home. She could simply have stayed at Cowgirl's with him instead of escaping out the back door.

He found himself sincerely hoping she had some other reason to be in his house. If she'd discovered his secret and was intent on exposing him, he'd have to eliminate her.

The very thought sickened him. How could he harm this woman when all he really wanted to do was hold her?

He carried the cup of fragrant, steeping tea to the kitchen

table, sat, and motioned for her to join him. Passing the cup under his face, he inhaled and smiled at the memory of his once favorite drink. "Why *are* you here?"

She stood across the table from him with her handgun raised, looking confused. "I'm here for information."

"Please," he said, motioning with upturned hand, "enjoy your tea. I won't harm you."

"I know you won't harm me. I've got the gun."

She must not know the truth.

Good. There was still hope of getting close to her and leaving her alive.

He sat very still for a long moment while Meg decided what to do. She settled in front of the tea, placed her weapon on the table to her right, and lifted the infuser out of the cup. He presumed she held the cup with her left hand so she could shoot him if she needed to.

She sipped and raised her eyebrows. "This is good."

"My own special blend, just for guests."

She sipped again, then deliberately placed the cup on the table.

"I'd offer you scones or biscuits, but I'm afraid I have none."

She didn't seem to notice his comment. "Tell me about Bedford."

"Bedford? Massachusetts?"

"Why would I want to know about some town in Massachusetts?"

"I don't know. You asked."

She shook her head. "No. *Gordon* Bedford."

"Who?"

"The man whose pocket you picked the other night."

He smiled at the memory. "Ah. The night you kissed me. I remember it well."

Color flashed in her cheeks and she sipped more tea. "How do you know Bedford?"

"Apparently, I picked his pocket. Beyond that, I don't."

She stiffened and rested her hand on her weapon. "Right. And you just happen to appear every time he's around."

"Do I?"

She glared at him and he studied her face. She had somewhat Nordic features with a hint of Irish ancestry. Her green eyes seemed to take in every detail and flashed more emotion than she probably wished. A hint of freckles darkened her nose and cheeks, and her lips approached full.

Focusing on her lips made his pants tighten.

She bore no signs of makeup, and wore her hair in a simple cut, long and straight with bangs at the front. Her slender neck led to shoulders on the broad side for a woman, and he knew by the way he'd seen her run that she could boast athletic abilities.

Focusing on her neck and the hint of a pulse rising and falling there made his fangs tingle.

"You expect me to believe you don't know him?"

His gaze snapped to hers. "Who, Bedford?"

"Of course, Bedford."

"No, I don't know the boisterous fool beyond challenging him to a game the night you and I *met*."

Again the flash of color. Very nice.

Daniel felt a sudden need to touch this woman again, to kiss her mouth, to experience the magic of her presence.

The monster growled and rattled his chains, seconding the desire.

Not since Running Deer had the beast felt so strong. That realization frightened him. Running Deer had had the ability to meet the monster head-on. This woman didn't stand a chance.

"What about Alex Trahan?"

"Who?"

"Alex Trahan, lives on the street. His current girlfriend is CC White."

He nodded. "Yes, I know Alex and CC. I bring them food when I can."

"Why?"

He shrugged. "Because they must eat. Isn't that a sufficient reason?"

"Dammit." Grabbing her handgun, Meg rose and strode from the room.

Daniel hesitated for a moment, then jumped up and headed her off, stepping between her outstretched hand and the front door. He couldn't let her leave under these circumstances, not until he knew for certain her intentions.

"Jesus Christ," she said, startled. "How the hell do you do that?"

"Do what?"

"Move so fast."

Standing only inches from her, he suddenly recalled the effect she'd had on him when he kissed her, and he leaned closer to inhale her unusual scent. A black fog descended over his brain, something laced with need.

She pressed the barrel of her handgun to his belly. "Back off."

In too quick a move to register in her mortal brain, he snatched the weapon from her.

She stared at her empty hand, astonished, and then backed slowly away from him.

He watched her, glad she moved out of reach before the monster made him do something he didn't want to do.

"Who the hell are you?" She backed into a wall.

Daniel left the weapon on the hall table and strolled across the room, hands clasped behind his back, keeping himself in her escape route. "You broke into my home. I should be the one asking questions. I think that's fair, don't you?"

He stood a good head taller than she did, and he used that fact to his advantage as he approached.

To her credit, she didn't shrink away, in spite of her obvious fear, but stood straight and stared him in the eye.

"Let's start with why you broke in." He stopped an arm's length away.

"I told you why. I thought you knew Bedford."

"And now you don't think I do?"

She shrugged. "I'm not sure."

"Hmm." He leaned forward and placed one hand on the wall beside her head. Her fragrance wafted into his brain again, making him a little light-headed. "And you had no other reason?"

She shook her head.

He leaned closer still, catching a whiff of citrus soap mixed with tea, fear, and a hint of excitement.

His entire body tingled now, anticipating her touch.

"Too bad." He ran his index finger gently over her warm, soft cheek and down the side of her neck.

She trembled and swallowed hard.

"I can think of other reasons for you to be here," he whispered, thrilling to the caress of her heated breath on his throat.

If his senses had not been heightened by her presence, he might not have felt the air move in front of her knee. He stopped it with his thigh before it contacted his balls. Had he been human, he would have been cowering on the floor in pain at the moment. She knew how to disable an opponent.

Smiling, he backed up enough to see her expression of terrified surprise. "There's no need for violence. I don't intend to hurt you."

Yet.

No, first he must determine just how much of a threat this vixen posed.

He walked away from her, convinced she understood now that she had no hope of escape unless he allowed it. Even with his back turned, he knew exactly where she stood and could picture her watching him.

"Why do you care if I know this Bedford fellow?"

When she didn't answer, he turned and looked at her.

She frowned as if working out how much to tell him.

"Has he done something to you?"

"Yes. Well, not to me personally, but to someone I know."

"What?"

"He's responsible for kidnapping women and selling them."

"*Selling* them?"

She nodded. "Overseas. Most of them go to houses of prostitution in Asia, where they're chained and beaten. Some are sent to Africa. Some don't make it anywhere."

A familiar rage bubbled up inside him at the thought of someone enslaved, lonely and hurt, struggling to survive. He remembered stealing food from carts as a child, running from angry shopkeepers, reaching into other's pockets for coins, wondering if he'd go to sleep hungry. He recalled waking with rats crawling across his hands, and the sting of the whip on his back, and he seethed. "Bastard," he muttered.

He took a moment to rein in his anger before he spoke again. "That loudmouthed parasite Bedford does this?"

"Yes."

"Why hasn't he been taken into custody?"

"Mostly he takes women from the street, the ones nobody misses. His latest victim is Elena Montano. She used to hang out with Alex Trahan sometimes. Besides, no one has ever proven anything."

Elena. He recalled encountering a woman named Elena on

the streets the day he emerged from his monthlong fast. Could it be the same woman?

"And you're out to prove it?"

"Yes."

He moved to the leather sofa and sat. "How?"

Meg stepped forward, her fear apparently forgotten. "I've got to figure out where he hides them."

"How many women has he kidnapped?"

"Two that I know of, this time. Probably more." She perched on the edge of a chair facing the sofa. "I don't think they've left the area yet. My guess is he'll be moving them in the next few days. He holds them somewhere for a week or so, either scaring or starving them into submission. Then he moves them to California, and from there smuggles them out."

"He has done this before?"

"At least twice. The Feds almost caught him last time, but he got away."

Daniel considered the speed with which Meg had nearly incapacitated him, and the self-confidence with which she brandished a firearm. She had claimed before to be some kind of law enforcer, but without specifics. "How is it you're qualified to search for these women?"

"I used to be a cop. I'm a private investigator now."

"I see." He crossed one leg over the other. "I've paid quite a bit to secure my house. How were you able to break in? Do they teach you that in the police academy?"

Her cheeks reddened. "My father was a professional burglar. He taught me everything he knew about locks and security systems." Turning in the chair, she eyed the metal shutters on the living room windows. "I'll admit this place took some work. Why such heavy defenses?"

He nearly answered her question, wondering how she'd react. No doubt she'd be on his trail again if she knew the truth, and that would be her downfall.

"Perhaps I can help you find the kidnapped women."

Her gaze jumped to his. "Why would you want to do that?"

He smiled. "I sympathize with their plight."

She studied him as she tried to work out the meaning behind his statement, then she seemed to come to a conclusion. "How can you help?"

"I have certain abilities you might find useful."

"No doubt," she muttered.

"What do you have planned, beyond breaking into my home?"

Meg rose and paced the living room.

Daniel watched her, appreciating her graceful movements and long legs. If these attributes translated into her performance in bed, she would make quite a partner.

His traitorous cock began to harden, and he labored to change his line of thought.

"I've searched everywhere," she said, "except his house. It's the one place I can't get into."

Daniel smirked. "You're able to break into my home and not his?"

"He has live guards. They're harder to get past."

"How did you know I didn't?"

"I rang your doorbell earlier today."

"Ah." The sound of a doorbell would have done nothing to wake him during daylight hours. "And you need help getting into his home?"

"Actually, I have a plan already."

"What is your plan?"

"He's having a party tomorrow night. I'm going to crash it."

"I see." Daniel rose. "Perhaps it would be easier to crash this party if you had an escort. You'll find I can be quite handy getting around guards."

"Somehow that wouldn't surprise me." She rubbed the back of her neck and frowned. "But you might turn me over to Bedford once I get there. For all I know, you two could be best friends. Why should I trust you?"

Daniel crossed the room to stand close to Meg once again, this time allowing her an escape route. She stood her ground, but he heard her heart rate quicken.

Yes, this was a woman he needed to become much better acquainted with. She drew him to her in ways he could neither understand nor deny.

"If I told you why you should trust me, you wouldn't."

She frowned.

"Where should we meet?"

She shook her head as if to clear it. "I'll pick you up here."

Daniel followed her to the door and held it open. "Good night, Meg."

She picked up her firearm and shoved it into a holster under her jacket. "Good night."

As she passed him, he sampled her scent once more before allowing her to leave.

Meg tried three times to get the key in the ignition of her car. Her hands shook violently.

Once the engine cranked, she held the steering wheel, took calming breaths, and stared at the front door of the house through the windshield.

Just who the hell was this man?

He seemed able to move at superhuman speeds, but part of that may have been because of the strange effect he had on her. She always felt like she was about to lose her balance around him. No one had ever made her feel that way before.

The other thing no one had ever done was disarm her so easily. She knew better than to be within reach of a suspect at gunpoint, but even then her reflexes were generally faster than most.

Pulling away from the curb, she reviewed events of the past twenty-four hours.

After Daniel had left Cowgirl's, Bedford met with two men she couldn't identify, but one looked like he was Chinese. When the meeting ended, Bedford continued to drink and try, unsuccessfully, to pick up women at the bar. Then he'd gone back to the restroom. As she'd watched the door, Daniel's friend had also gone in.

They came out of the restroom almost simultaneously, and Daniel's buddy had immediately left the restaurant with his date. Had the two men exchanged information? Bedford hurried away ten minutes later.

She'd wondered if this meant Daniel was the one holding the women, and found herself sincerely hoping not.

Bedford had gone straight home.

She'd started home, too, but thought better of it. Parked at the far end of Daniel's block, she watched him return shortly before dawn and wrote down his address.

After a quick nap, she'd taken the address to her contact at the department, assuming he'd hand her a name, driver's license, the usual stuff. Instead, he'd told her the house was owned by a company, the Moon Group, and he had no info on them.

Her own research had turned up nothing on the Moon Group. She'd decided it could be a front for Bedford's activities.

Without a car in the driveway, it wasn't easy determining if Daniel was home or not. About six that evening, she rang his doorbell. She didn't know what she'd say if he answered, but it hadn't mattered. The doorbell had echoed through what she assumed was an empty house. A quick circuit of the property convinced her that her assumption was right, and that she needed real tools to get in.

Oddly enough, Daniel had never even threatened to call the cops on her for breaking and entering.

Who the hell had steel doors and metal shutters over their windows? He had to be up to something. But what?

Now she'd agreed to let him "help" her. Had she lost her mind?

Somehow, though, she knew he wasn't responsible for the missing women. His sudden anger had felt sincere, and she'd become pretty good at judging when someone was lying. She'd actually seen him giving food to Alex and his friends.

Man, she'd love to know more about this Daniel character. Maybe she'd pick up some information at the party.

Why did he have to be so incredibly good-looking?

Meg sighed. At least she would be driving the next night and should be in control of the situation.

Hopefully.

Daniel waited in deep shadows at the side of his house. He'd stood in the same spot for over an hour, wondering if perhaps Meg had escaped his grasp once again. Perhaps she had no intention of following through on her invitation. The thought filled him with both rage and a strange loneliness—a dangerous combination.

When she finally eased her vehicle into the driveway, he waited and watched.

She looked around, but didn't see him, then stared at the front door, emotions running across her face in a series of unreadable expressions. After a long while, she rose from the driver's seat.

He'd never seen her in anything but jeans. The black dress she wore accentuated her long legs and made her look even more tempting than usual. Daniel's fangs tingled.

Just one little taste would no doubt be a wondrous thing.

Wrestling back the hunger and desire, he stepped from the shadows.

She jumped and then struck a purposely relaxed pose. "There you are. Ready?"

He watched her green-eyed gaze run down to his toes and back up, and enjoyed the look of approval she momentarily forgot to hide.

"Quite." He slid into the passenger's side of her automobile.

She wore an artificial fragrance that mimicked gardenias. Unnecessary, but not unpleasant. Daniel inhaled deeply and smiled.

She stared at him.

"Yes?"

She motioned with her head. "Seat belt."

"Ah." He fumbled with the contraption, finally managing to connect the ends.

"You don't travel by car much."

"No."

"Okay," she said softly, backing the vehicle out onto the street.

Her driving abilities seemed to be quite good, and they wound through the narrow, crowded streets of downtown Santa Fe without incident. Street noises and smells assaulted his senses when, focused on her, he forgot to filter them out.

Spending an evening with Meg could prove even more difficult than he expected it to be.

"Is there an occasion for this party?" he asked, trying to focus on the future.

"Don't know. Bedford hired a dozen security guards from a local company, one of the best chefs in town, and a valet service. Whatever it is, it's big."

"Ah, so we should be able to blend in."

She glanced over at him and raised her eyebrows. "At least one of us will."

He scowled. "Am I not appropriately dressed?"

She laughed. "It's not your clothes, although the boots are, uh, different."

"What is it, then?"

"Nothing, don't worry about it."

They rode in silence past Bishop's Lodge. Meg eased the vehicle onto a crowded, narrow lane and wove through expensive automobiles until she found a place to stop within sight of the front door to a mansion.

A limousine passed and drew up in front. One of the valets opened a door with a polite bow.

"Oh, crap. I think we might be in trouble."

Daniel followed her gaze to the couple emerging from the limousine.

The man rose first, dressed completely in black and wearing sunglasses, in spite of the darkness. He stood at least six feet tall and sported black hair silvered at the sides.

When he moved to one side and Daniel saw the man's date, he understood Meg's concern. The woman wore a bizarre leather outfit that barely covered the essentials, and six-inch spike heels. Her bleached-blond hair was piled high on her head, and her makeup gave her the look of someone to be both feared and desired. She was greeted by a woman in a black spandex body suit wearing a spiked collar around her neck.

"I don't think we're in Kansas anymore," Meg muttered.

8

"This should prove interesting." Daniel grinned, considering how attractive Meg might look in a leather outfit. He glanced over at her in time to see a splash of color brightening her cheeks.

"I don't need interesting," she said. "I just need to get in and look around. How the hell can we get past all these guards?"

He took advantage of the situation to study her more closely, enjoying the bronze of her sun-kissed skin and the wild glint of frustration in her green eyes as he buttoned the top button of his shirt.

"If you remove your undergarments, raise your skirt an inch or two, and darken your lipstick, I'm quite sure you'll have no problem getting inside."

"What am I going to do about my twenty-five?"

"Your what?"

"My pistol."

"Where is it?"

She raised her skirt on one side just enough to reveal a strap around her thigh, apparently holding the weapon in place.

"I don't think you'll want to carry it there."

"Well, where am I going to carry it?"

"I don't believe you'll need it. If we find the women, you don't want them in the middle of a firefight anyway, do you?"

She stared at him for a long moment, and then sighed deeply. "Fine. I'll take off the bra and twenty-five, but I'm keeping the panties."

Daniel shrugged.

"Do you mind?"

She motioned for him to avert his eyes and he did. When he looked back, she was applying dark red lipstick.

"Okay?" She turned to face him.

"Nearly." He raked his fingers through her silky hair, lifting it and giving it a bit of flair. Sitting back to assess his work, he nodded. "Perfect."

She sighed again.

Once out of the vehicle, Daniel offered Meg his arm and she took it. He noticed that she wasn't terribly adept at walking in heels, and patted the hand resting on his forearm. "Feel free to use me for balance," he said softly. "Or anything else you wish."

"Don't get lost in your role again."

"I'll try not to."

At the door, a man at least as tall as Daniel and twice as large stepped in front of them. "Invitation?"

Invading the guard's mind would leave Daniel temporarily weak, and swiping an invitation from another guest might cause an unwelcome scene. He opted for a more traditional means of entry.

"Of course." He made a show of checking his pockets. "Except that I seem to have misplaced it. Perhaps you can check your list."

The man lifted the clipboard he'd held by his side. "Name?"

"Ben Franklin."

The guard's eyebrows arched in disbelief.

"Truly. See? I'm right there." Pointing to the list, Daniel deposited a half-dozen folded bills on the page, an old sleight of hand he'd perfected over the centuries. Each bill sported Ben Franklin's face.

The guard hesitated several moments, perhaps calculating how long it would take him to earn the equivalent in wages, then slipped the bills into his pocket with a nod. "Enjoy the party, Mr. Franklin."

Inside, lights were low and mostly strange colors. People sat and stood in small groups, all clad in various degrees of revealing garb suggesting a variety of sexual tastes. To his right, a large woman wearing a red velvet bustier and black leather pants held leashes attached to collars around the necks of two young men, each wearing almost nothing. The man and woman they'd seen emerge from the limousine earlier had found a nearly matching couple and were exchanging prolonged greetings. Two well-formed shirtless men stood with their arms around each other's waists as they conversed with another man.

"What the hell is this?" Meg whispered.

Daniel leaned close to answer. "It appears to me to be a celebration of freedom."

"I suppose. Looks a little freaky to me."

"Quite so."

He had to admit, he liked freaky. These people tended to be less apt to notice his behavior when he addressed his hunger.

"We should look for locked doors," Meg said. "Maybe a basement."

When she started to pull him across the room, he drew her back. "I suggest not being quite so obvious. There are cameras all over the place."

He felt her tense at his side. "There are? I don't see any."

"Trust me, I can sense such things." In truth he heard the

electronic buzz of each hidden contraption within seconds of stepping inside.

Daniel stopped a passing waiter, handed Meg a glass of white wine from the tray, and took a red for himself. "I suggest we mingle a bit."

"You have got to be kidding."

As he directed them toward two couples, she took a hearty drink from the glass. He allowed himself to enjoy the feel of her warm touch on his arm and the heat from her body against his side. Had they been alone, he might have attempted something more intimate at that moment.

Daniel nodded politely to the small group. "How do you do?"

"How? Or what?" A large-breasted redhead laughed at her own joke, and the other three joined in.

The second woman, a dark-haired beauty, ran a hand down Daniel's arm. "You two interested in hooking up?"

He grinned at her. "Perhaps later."

"Of course." She squeezed his arm before releasing it. "You have to taste the hors d'oeuvres before they're gone. The oysters on the half shell are magnificent."

The man standing closest to the dark-haired woman wrapped an arm around her waist and slid his hand slowly across her stomach. "And they work, too."

The group laughed again.

"If you'll excuse us, then, we'll go in search of oysters." Daniel motioned to Meg, who nodded in response.

As they worked their way across the room, she leaned into him and spoke softly. "Hooking up? Did she mean what I think she meant?"

"Most likely."

"Holy crap."

"You never know. You might enjoy it."

She drained her glass and deposited it on a coffee table they passed. "I'm not here to enjoy myself."

Too bad. The longer they walked side by side, the more interested Daniel became in *enjoying* Meg.

"Come on," she said, "let's check down here."

Leaving his own glass behind, he followed her out of the main room and down a narrow hall, watching their flank as she opened a door and peered inside.

"Laundry room."

They continued past a man who ignored them. She found the second doorway locked.

"Maybe this is it," she whispered.

Daniel tuned his hearing to penetrate the door, and listened to the rhythmic slurping.

"Of, fuck . . . that's it." The man's voice preceded muffled grunts and groans of release.

Daniel stepped back. "I don't think this is the room you're looking for."

"How do you know?" She jumped when the door swung open.

Two young men hurried out of the bathroom, one zipping his pants.

Meg blushed. "Oh."

They continued down the hall.

The third doorway opened to a stairway leading down, and they descended quietly.

At the bottom, a guard stepped out from behind a post. "Looking for something?"

"Indeed," Daniel said. "We're looking for a little *privacy*."

The man motioned toward doorways behind him. "Try the second one to the left."

"Thank you, sir." Daniel directed Meg toward the door with a hand on her lower back.

He followed her into a small room that held only a bed and

a wooden chair, and he closed the door behind them. Fixtures hidden behind casements high on the walls provided dim light that bounced off the ceiling.

Alone with Meg, hints of desire and hunger welled in his gut and chest, and he marveled at the strange urges to both fall at this woman's feet and to drain her life.

What was it about her that needled the primeval monster to life?

Fighting wobbly heels, Meg circled the room, looking for doors or secret passages, but found only a small half bath. As she backed out of it, she bumped into Daniel and turned.

Instead of moving out of her way, he stood before her looking down, his playful smile from earlier gone.

In that instant, all the oxygen seemed to disappear from the room.

Something about this man suggested timelessness. Dark waves of hair reaching his shoulders could just as well be resting on the metal of knight's armor as the thin wool of his black Armani jacket.

Dizziness swept over her again and she reached out to steady herself. Her open palms landed in the middle of his wide chest.

He held her arm with one hand and stroked her hair with the other. "You are indeed a beautiful woman," he whispered.

His mysteriously accented words wormed through her brain, leaving behind glittering trails of heat, and she closed her eyes.

He pressed his lips to the side of her head.

At that moment, she would gladly have fallen into his arms and stayed there as long as he allowed her to.

Somehow, a small measure of sanity crept into her thoughts and she stepped away, opening her eyes to gaze up into his face. His eyes reflected the dim light in the room in the strangest way she'd ever seen, as if his irises were a million tiny mirrors.

And then the effect faded.

"We've got work to do," she said.

But he didn't release her, in spite of her attempt to step away from him. Instead, he held her by both arms and drew her back to him.

The man was stronger than he appeared. She couldn't begin to break his grip, and she knew better than to try to bring him down with her knee. She tried to shove him away, but could just as well have been pushing against a granite boulder. "Hey."

His whispered words in her ear stopped her struggle. "We are probably being watched. You should pretend to be interested."

A wave of heat washed over her, something between horror and terror. "Cameras?"

"Most likely."

"Dammit. What do we do now?"

"I have an idea." He leaned back just enough to raise her face to his.

His mouth against hers took her by surprise.

Suddenly, her traitorous body remembered the encounter in the bar, and it weakened as her insides began to quiver.

He tasted of cool wine and something she couldn't identify, something delicious in a foreign way. His hand caressed her face as he opened her mouth with his, and his tongue swirled around her own. He seemed to be tasting her more than kissing her, and longing blossomed in her belly in response.

She slid her arms under his jacket and around him as he drew her close, and she encircled a torso of steel. Not just muscular, but unyielding. And cool like steel, not hot like her body suddenly felt.

He tilted his head to reach deeper.

She clung to his shirt, drawing on his tongue, desperately needing more of him.

A soft growl vibrated up through his chest, tingling against her breasts. Her nipples hardened to points, aching for his touch.

As if reading her thoughts, he slid his right hand down her neck and circled her breast with a feathery touch, teasing the nipple. She gasped against his mouth at the pleasure.

She eased her knee between his, and he allowed her access this time. Her thigh and hip, pressed into his crotch, met with a hard bulge straining against fabric.

He reached down and caressed her butt, squeezing, massaging.

Longing burst into flames, creeping up the backs of her legs. Her vaginal lips seemed to swell and thicken, and spasms of need rippled up toward her trembling belly.

She pushed harder against him, wanting him, needing him.

In a sudden rush of movement, he lifted her from the floor, carried her to the bed, and placed her on her back.

Gasping for air, she stared up at the man leaning over her on his hands and knees, studying her face like someone memorizing a cherished photograph. His eyes had that mirrored look again, this time reflecting blue and red lights without source, and his expression both terrified and aroused her more. He looked desperate, almost frantic.

He looked hungry.

Her emotions spun around in her like a tornado, confusing and disorienting her. She wanted more of him.

Unable to fight it, she reached for him and held his waist as he rose up to shed his jacket. His dark red silk shirt looked like pooling blood in the dim light, but the thought didn't repulse her as it should have. She couldn't imagine anything about Daniel repulsing her.

As he studied her again, she loosed the top few buttons of his shirt to expose pale flesh over collarbones, and a hint of soft, dark hair. More buttons freed from their holes, and she exposed the chest she'd practically panted over the first time she saw it.

Dark hair softened his flesh, thickening in the center and across the tops of his pecs.

Dear God, the man was gorgeous. She ran her open palms over his chest, and his eyes closed in response.

He eased down slowly, covering her body with his, and she slid her arms around him again as she raised her face to meet him.

He kissed her, and she felt his restraint as if it were her own. She opened her mouth, fisted her hand in his hair at the back of his head, and drew him close.

His luscious tongue circled her mouth, and his hard, solid body pinned hers to the bed. As his hand slid down the length of her to her butt again, she spread her legs, aching to feel the sharp angles of his hips bruising her thighs.

Instead, he slid to her side, and she groaned.

His hand moved around from her butt to the heat between her legs, and she jumped at his unexpected touch.

He deepened the kiss, matching the movement of his fingers stroking the crotch of her panties with his tongue. Her body responded with undulations she couldn't control, and she silently cursed her decision to keep her panties on.

She tried to stop him as he tore his mouth from hers, but then he pressed his lips to the side of her neck.

Flames of heated desire threatened to engulf her. She turned her head to give him access.

His lips parted against her flesh and he sucked gently, and the flames melted every muscle in her body at once.

She cried out with need.

His fingers breeched her panties, easily parting her slick lips and finding her swollen clit.

She squeezed her eyes shut and clenched her jaw against the need to scream.

Carefully, cruelly, he stroked her clit as he sucked on her neck.

She'd never felt such intense need burning through her before.

"More," she breathed. "Deeper."

His wet fingers penetrated her with each stroke.

She rose up to meet him. Her body tightened, trembling, needing still more.

Hard, cold points pressed against the side of her neck, blades pushing into her skin. She turned her head farther, ready to open a vein to relieve the threatening inferno.

And then the flames exploded inside her, catapulting her to another dimension. Every nerve ending fired at once.

He reached deeper, piercing the center of her. Her pulsing muscles swallowed his fingers. She clung to him.

More. She needed more.

He drew on her soul.

She wanted all.

Cruelly, he stroked her throbbing pussy, drawing her blazing orgasm out until her flesh sizzled.

As the flames cooled and flickered, she collapsed.

Panting for air, she lay still as he withdrew his fingers. His mouth moved up the length of her neck, chasing the last crackling trace of desire.

He kissed her lips tenderly, then her cheeks and nose and forehead.

With her heart pounding and her senses still reeling, Meg suddenly remembered where she was. Not only was she lying on a bed with a man she didn't know, but she might also be performing for a camera.

Humiliation replaced desire and she tugged her skirt down as low as it would go.

Daniel relaxed beside her, burying his face in her hair. "Wonderful," he whispered.

In spite of the embarrassment, that single word sent a shiver up her spine.

What power was it he wielded with such ease? One stupid word and she was ready to give herself to him again.

Christ. Maybe she shouldn't have stayed single so long.

The worst part was that she'd momentarily forgotten her mission. She wasn't here to give herself to the handsome stranger she'd been fantasizing about for days. She was here to find a group of terrified, possibly injured young women.

The door flying open made her jump, and she sat up.

A couple rushed into the room, then stopped. The man, an older blond, wore a shirt already unbuttoned over pants unsnapped. His partner, a woman who couldn't be over twenty, stumbled and tugged at the front of her strapless dress to cover her too-perfect breasts.

"Sorry," the man said, grinning. "Hope we're not ruining a beautiful moment."

Meg expected Daniel to answer, but he said nothing.

"Don't worry," she said, "we were just leaving."

The couple continued forward and the woman dropped to her knees, her elbows on the bed.

The man stood behind her, caressing her ass with one hand as he pushed his pants down. "Don't leave on our account," he said. "We don't mind."

The woman smiled and nodded, then reached back and drew up her skirt. *She* hadn't bothered with panties.

Before Meg could even look away, the man pulled his cock from his pants, crouched, and began to work it into the young woman from behind. His partner responded with appreciative noises as she raised her buttocks higher.

Meg gulped and turned to scoot off the bed. When she got to her feet, she found Daniel standing beside her slipping into his jacket, one eyebrow arched.

"If you want to stay, I don't mind," he said.

"Uh, gee, I don't think so." Straightening her dress, she hurried to the door.

Just before stepping from the room, she glanced back to find the intruders screwing with abandon, the man's cock glistening in dim light as it emerged.

It wasn't like she had any right to say anything. Moments earlier, she'd probably been caught on candid camera reaching a screaming climax.

Great.

"Come on," she said softly. "There have got to be more rooms to search."

"As you wish," Daniel answered, also softly, his voice deeper than it had been before.

She wondered if their encounter had affected him at all. Had he been turned on? Or maybe turned off?

With a deep breath, she struggled to focus on work. She couldn't let Elena die because she was getting sidetracked by some unusual stranger.

Daniel followed Meg down the dark hallway, listening to her heartbeat. It raced still, and he wondered if the speed resulted from their encounter or from fear. Perhaps both.

Whatever the reason, he found its musical rhythm deeply distracting.

Mentally shaking himself, he fanned out his attention to include sounds from the rooms they passed. In one, he heard leather whipping through air and slapping flesh. In another, at least four people engaged in an encounter. The third they passed he thought empty, until he heard a woman moan softly.

He pictured Meg under him, her long legs spread, waiting for him to enter her.

Focus on matters at hand.

The basement gave way to an underground labyrinth that seemed twice as large as the house above, and reminded him of the back rooms at the Tunnel. Ideal for someone with things to hide. Perhaps Meg was correct about the women being held here.

Footsteps approached, and Daniel drew Meg back to him, shielding her with his body.

The guard who rounded the corner stopped when he saw them. "Lost?"

"Perhaps," Daniel said, smiling as if in on a secret.

The man nodded. "I'll show you where it is."

Wondering what *it* was, Daniel took Meg's hand and followed the guard into the bowels of the underground maze. They stopped at a massive metal door, which the guard pushed open before he stepped aside.

With warning gnawing at the back of his neck, Daniel entered a spacious room filled with people, most naked. He recognized many from the initial crowd upstairs. Low beds and divans lay scattered around, all graced with at least two people. Waiters worked the crowd, filling glasses of wine and offering trays of food.

"You two, over here." The dark-haired beauty from earlier motioned for Daniel and Meg to join her, her partner, and another couple. She sat on the edge of a bed wearing nothing at all, which didn't appear to bother her. She was, indeed, quite attractive.

"I'm glad you made it," she said.

"As am I," Daniel said, sitting beside her. He offered her a hand. "Daniel."

"Raven," she said, accepting the handshake. "And this is Van, and Rita and Gene."

Van, the oldest of the four, shook Daniel's hand and nodded. The other two just smiled.

"My partner is Meg," Daniel said.

They greeted Meg and she settled to Daniel's left.

"You're a little overdressed, don't you think?" Raven asked.

Daniel shed his jacket and unbuttoned his shirt. He glanced at Meg, and she narrowed her eyes in warning.

Van rose from the bed. "I'm off to find the men's room. Save my place." He disappeared, leaving Raven at Daniel's side.

She moved closer, propositioning him with a sultry look.

For some peculiar reason, Daniel hadn't the slightest interest in Raven. He'd never experienced such a lack of sensation in the presence of a beautiful woman, but managed to smile anyway.

All of his senses were tuned to Meg instead, and he battled the desire to draw her back into his arms. He knew she had no interest in physical contact at the moment; she scanned the crowd with tense watchfulness.

The whole room seemed unusually quiet, as if people waited for something. Some engaged in heavy petting, and a few went farther, but mostly they lounged, sipping wine and eating hors d'oeuvres.

"Have you met our host?"

Daniel glanced at Gene. "Only in passing."

"He's quite amazing," Raven said. "I've seen him perform twice, and both times just blew me away. I don't know how he does it."

Meg whispered, "Perform?"

Daniel shrugged. He couldn't imagine Bedford performing anything he'd care to watch.

As he scrutinized the room, he noticed that a large bed in the center, covered in red velvet, stood empty. Could this really be some kind of sexual performance? By a big-mouthed, pot-bellied, middle-aged oaf?

It couldn't be. Why would people want to—?

The door to the room burst open and four young men strode in, all dressed in buckskin loincloths. Behind them, four very attractive young women entered, wearing little more. All had long black hair and bore familiar adornments of beads, feathers, and gold armbands.

Daniel froze. His mind struggled to take in the scene before him. How could this be? After four hundred years, had some of the clan survived?

One of the young men motioned toward the door with upraised palm and said, "Our master, El Lobo."

The room exploded with applause.

Daniel's body stiffened as he remembered the silhouette standing at the clearing's edge and heard a voice from the past. "You will pay!"

The man who strode into the room wearing a ceremonial buckskin robe was none other than Wolf.

9

Meg watched the surreal scene, entranced. One of the women played some kind of Native American flute and a man, sitting cross-legged on the floor, played a drum. She'd never heard a tune quite like the one they produced.

The leader, El Lobo, stood in the center of the room, looking over the audience as if studying his subjects. He was a tall man, Native American, with hair to his waist, a handsome face that could have come from Greek mythology, and intense black eyes.

People all over the room whispered.

When he raised his arms, two of the women removed his cloak, and he stood in only a loincloth.

His physique was magnificent. Smooth skin covered the tight, lean muscles of a warrior's body. Around his upper arms he wore gold bands that glittered in the lights.

In graceful movements, he performed an ancient dance, his arms defining wings one moment and wind the next, and his bare feet keeping rhythm without sound.

In all her years of visiting local pueblos, she'd never seen a dance like this.

His movements changed as the music grew louder, taking on a distinctively sexual flavor. His body swayed, and his hands caressed an imaginary lover.

Meg swallowed hard and glanced over at Daniel to find him equally entranced, but wearing an expression that suggested terror. What about this unusual performance could possibly cause him fear?

The dancer began to chant in a foreign language, softly as if calling a partner to bed. The three couples not playing music approached in matching dance steps, encircling him, and he moved around them, touching each tenderly on the cheek.

He circled one young man, the tallest of the three, touching his shoulders and arms. The young man smiled, nodded assent to a silent question or command, and removed his loincloth. Naked, he continued to dance, his flaccid prick dangling in front of him.

Several women in the audience applauded and laughed.

El Lobo then turned his attention to those seated about the room. He danced his way around beds and groups of people, studying each. Some reached out as he passed, but he evaded their touches.

Meg watched, unable to look away, as he approached. His gaze washed over her from head to toe, then moved to Daniel.

He stopped and his eyes widened.

Beside her, Daniel rose suddenly to his feet.

The two men stared at each other, both braced as if about to be attacked.

This must be someone Daniel knew, and Meg wanted to ask him what the hell was going on, but she couldn't move. She felt almost drugged.

El Lobo's mouth curved into a vicious smile and he spoke in a foreign language.

"No," Daniel said.

Had he understood?

El Lobo began to move again as he studied the group on the bed behind Daniel.

Meg felt his gaze this time like icy fingers traipsing down her spine, but he seemed to dismiss her quickly. His gaze rested on Raven, and Daniel stepped in front of the woman.

El Lobo hissed something, moved past him, and reached out to Raven. Grinning, she placed her hand in his, stood, and followed him back to the center of the room.

Daniel moved to protest, but El Lobo shot a fierce glare over his shoulder that could have wilted a healthy tree.

Daniel eased back down to the edge of the bed.

Meg leaned toward him. "What was that?"

"Stay away from me," he whispered. "When you get a chance, get out of here, get to your automobile, and leave."

"What—"

"Don't come back."

His voice held the threat of a loaded weapon, and Meg shrank away from him, her heart beating wildly at the unknown danger he seemed to fear.

For the first time, she noticed two armed guards blocking the doorway. Did they intend to prevent the audience from leaving? If so, why?

If only she had her twenty-five. Screw Daniel for talking her out of wearing it.

Trembling, she sat and watched as the performance continued.

El Lobo placed Raven before the young male dancer and moved around her, stroking her arms and breasts as if trying to entice the man in front of her.

The young dancer's cock responded by swelling and rising as he watched. The other dancers approached him, their hands on his back, and they urged him toward Raven.

He touched her then, swaying to the music as he caressed her breasts and slid his hands appreciatively over her body.

The dancers moved behind her, chanting, touching, caressing. Sexual tension crackled through the air.

Raven stood still, her body visibly shaking.

The dancers supported her, pulled her back until her feet left the ground. They held her horizontal, drawing her legs apart, and the naked man danced between her thighs.

El Lobo circled the action, touching here and there, chanting louder as the music rose in volume and tempo.

Meg found her own body reacting to the dance, in spite of her concern. She rubbed her hands back and forth along the tops of her legs.

The dancer began to undulate as he got closer, as if answering some ancient call to mate.

El Lobo touched Raven's forehead and her head dropped back, but her body didn't relax.

Around the room, couples began to copulate.

The dancer must have penetrated Raven then, because her body responded to each of his movements. Her nipples tightened and her buttocks quivered. The dancer held her waist as muscles in his back and arms bulged, but he didn't come. Instead, the dance went on, building in intensity.

El Lobo moved the other dancers away one by one and took their place at Raven's head, until just he and the male dancer held her up. Then he lifted her body so that she rose to meet her partner with her legs locked around his thrusting hips. Raven locked her arms around the dancer's shoulders.

Her eyes were closed, but she was definitely conscious. Her fingers dented the muscles of her partner's back.

With El Lobo standing behind her, he circled, leading the pair to follow. Meg watched them turn, viewing their coupling from all angles, amazed at the ease with which the young man held Raven as he withdrew and thrust again.

By the second rotation, Raven's body glistened with sweat, and her head went back, this time to mark the start of her orgasm.

The young dancer leaned forward, pressing his face to her breast. It looking almost like he was biting her. Raven shrieked with pleasure and spasms racked her body.

But that wasn't the end. The young man continued to fuck her and turn, and El Lobo continued to circle.

The young man's feet left the floor.

Meg stared, open-mouthed, as the couple rose into the air.

There had to be wires, but she sure as hell couldn't see them.

El Lobo's hands directed the pair's movements with slow, deliberate signals.

The couple stopped rotating and turned in the vertical until the man lay on top of Raven at least six feet off the floor, now pounding his massive cock into her. Her reactions seemed to be slowing.

Then El Lobo turned his hands palms down and the couple descended to the empty bed. Just as they reached the surface, the young man's body stiffened and stilled.

Raven's hands fell limply from his shoulders.

The music stopped and the audience applauded.

The young man rose, wiping the back of his hand across his mouth.

Raven lay still.

El Lobo bowed. As he straightened, he glared a challenge at Daniel, who didn't move a muscle. After a long moment, El Lobo turned to bow in the other direction.

The music started again as the group of dancers lifted Raven from the bed and carried her above their heads from the room by way of a back door.

Daniel rose and stalked around the edge of the room toward that door, staring at El Lobo as he went.

Meg felt like she'd walked into the middle of a mixed-up play. She hated the confusion as she recalled the fear she'd heard in Daniel's voice when he'd told her to leave.

The guards had moved away from the door to talk to several women who appeared to be trying to entice them into bed. Meg took the opportunity to walk calmly to the door, open it, and step out into the darkened hallway, easing the door closed behind her.

She shook against the desire to run as fast as she could toward the stairs, although she wasn't really sure where the stairs were. All the noise in the basement came from the room behind her as she hurried down a hallway with one hand on a wall.

The passageway curved and turned several corners, feeling as if it circled back on itself, and she expected to return to the door she'd just passed through, but she didn't. Instead, lights grew dimmer until she could barely see, and she had to slow to one step at a time.

"Shit." She stopped and looked back over her shoulder. This couldn't be the way out. She'd have to retrace her steps and hope no one stopped her as she passed the main room.

Just as she started back, she heard a muffled noise that sounded like someone calling out through a gag.

She stopped and listened, and heard it again.

"Elena?"

The noise grew decidedly louder, and Meg moved her head left and right to locate it. "Elena?"

Another voice joined the first, both coming from behind a

door she'd just passed. She returned to it and tried the knob, but it was locked.

Meg patted herself down, frustrated that she hadn't found a way to hide even a credit card on her body. She tested the door with a good shake and decided she might be able to break the wooden frame.

"Stand back," she said. "I'm coming through the door."

Then she backed up, slipped off her shoes, hiked her skirt, and charged forward, delivering her best kick.

The impact shivered back up her leg and hip, but also produced a loud crack, so she kicked again.

This time, the door flew open into darkness.

"Elena?"

Egged on by excited responses, she felt her way along the wall inside the room until she located a light switch and flipped it up. A bare bulb glared, revealing a small room where four women lay bound and gagged on dirty mattresses on the floor. They all wore ragged street clothes.

Cringing against the stench of rotting food and filth, Meg quickly untied the women, accepting hugs from Elena.

"I can't believe you found us," Elena said.

Meg helped her to her feet. "No time for talk. We need to get out of here."

She searched the small room and found a short piece of metal pipe that she tried in her hand. It might not be lethal against one of the guards, but she'd leave a mark on anyone trying to stop them that they wouldn't soon forget.

She motioned to the women. "Come on." Outside, she snatched up her shoes and carried them by the heel straps.

The five women trotted down the hall in silence, hugging one wall.

Meg's heart pounded as she thought about the crowded

room ahead. What would she do if someone opened the door as they passed? What if they ran into one of the guards between here and there?

At a sharp corner, she stopped and the women stopped behind her.

"What's going on?" Elena whispered.

Meg pressed a finger to her lips, then turned and eased forward to check the passageway.

The face that met hers drew a scream from her throat. She fell back against Elena.

"Well, now, what's this?" El Lobo, wearing his buckskin cloak, stepped around the corner and stood facing the group, his arms folded and his stance wide. "A rescue party?"

She hadn't realized just how tall he was in the crowded room, but looked up into his black eyes as she raised the piece of pipe and backed away. "Stay back."

He laughed something cruel and threatening.

Her skin crawled at the sound.

"Or what," he said, following her progress. "You'll attack?"

"Damn straight, you crazy bastard."

He laughed again. "You really think you can hurt me?"

"*I* can."

The man spun to face the voice behind him, and Meg stretched to see around him.

Daniel stood in the middle of the hallway with his hands in fists at his sides. He wore his jacket over his open shirt, and muscles in his stomach bunched as he tensed. She'd never been so happy to see anyone in her life.

"Perhaps I chose the wrong female for my performance," El Lobo said.

Daniel didn't respond, but stalked forward. He faltered when his opponent drew a knife from the inside of his cloak.

Dropping her shoes and gripping the pipe in both hands, Meg took her best swing at the maniac's head. The pipe rang as it contacted his skull, then bounced back as if it had hit steel and flew from her hands.

A normal man would have dropped from such an impact, and possibly died.

El Lobo turned, sneering. He raised his knife, and then suddenly disappeared from sight.

He reappeared when he crashed against the far wall and fell onto the floor on his back, and Daniel spun around to face her. "Get them out of here." Then he turned back and charged his rising adversary.

Meg grabbed Elena's sleeve and took off running with the woman in tow, hoping the others followed. Behind them, bangs and thuds accompanied the continuing fight.

They passed the closed door to the main room, as well as several other doors. Amazingly, no one appeared in their path.

At the stairs, Meg stopped long enough to be sure all four women followed, then trotted up and eased open the door. She peered out and found this hallway also empty.

They tiptoed down the hall, but stopped just before the bathroom. Meg could hear two men talking.

"I guess everyone's still downstairs."

"How long will they stay down there?"

"Probably another half hour or so."

She motioned with her head and led the escapees in the opposite direction. They found an empty library, which they hurried across. Meg pushed open French doors, and they all rushed out.

Trying to ignore the sting of goat-head burrs, Meg ran around the massive house and wound between parked cars, crouching in order not to be seen. At her own car, she opened the door, dug the keys out from under the seat, and started the engine as soon as the back doors closed. Fortunately, no one had parked behind her, and she eased the car out to the road.

Her passengers began to sob as she sped down Bishop's Lodge Road, headed for the police station.

She glanced in her rearview mirror at the house shrinking into the distance behind her, hoping Daniel had won the fight, or at least survived it.

Meg limped from her car, cursing the goat heads she hadn't yet completely dug out of her feet. At the door to Daniel's house, she rang the bell, waited, then knocked.

She gulped at the knot of fear rising in her throat when he didn't answer.

Glancing around to be sure no one watched from a neighboring house, she dug the picks out of her bag and unlocked the door. The second time didn't take a tenth of the time the first had taken. Now she knew the mechanism.

Stepping inside, she closed the door and stood in the dark. "Daniel?" When he didn't answer, she drew out a flashlight and started forward. "Anyone home?"

At the table, she stopped, shone the fading beam around the room, and then switched on an overhead light.

This had to be the strangest night she'd ever lived through. After the weird party where she'd let Daniel ravish her and she'd found the kidnapped women, she'd reported the whole thing to the police and waited while they raided the house. She'd hoped they'd make it in time to save Daniel from the madman, but they'd returned without news of either Daniel or El Lobo. The two men seemed to have disappeared, along with the rest of the Native American dancers. Cops had escorted a number of wealthy people from Santa Fe and Albuquerque to jail on charges of drug possession, lewd behavior, and a variety of misdemeanors. All had posted bail and left by the time she'd headed home.

Elena had been checked into the hospital along with the other women for observation, but none seemed to sport more than a few bruises. Elena had promised to move into one of the local shelters once she was released instead of returning to the street. Meg planned to help her find a job. She'd been a valuable informant, and was a truly kindhearted person when she wasn't plastered.

Now, however, Meg worried about Daniel.

Something about the guy terrified her, although he'd never truly threatened her in any way. And his touch instantly turned her into a jellyfish. She'd never reacted this way to any man, even the one she'd thought she loved.

Maybe that's what frightened her.

What if he was dead? She'd never seen such violence in a fight, and El Lobo had been armed.

That thought started her hands shaking and nearly sent her over the edge. Now that she'd found Daniel, she didn't want to lose him.

Something clanged in another room, like someone bumping into furniture.

Meg turned her head and waited, but didn't hear anything else. She drew her thirty-eight from the holster and held it at her side.

"Hello?"

She made her way slowly to Daniel's bedroom where she'd found him before, the last time she thought his house was empty. This time, her flashlight beam fell across a vacant bed.

A snake's hiss issued from the far wall, and she swung the light in that direction.

What she saw made no sense at first. Had she cornered an animal of some kind?

Eyes reflected her light like those of a cat, but the face looked relatively human, although covered with blood. And the clothes . . .

"Daniel?"

"Stay back." He slid along the wall, shading his eyes with one arm.

She lowered the light to his feet and found a trail of blood. "Oh, shit, you're really hurt. I'll call an ambulance." After holstering her weapon, Meg reached into her pocket for her cell phone.

"No!"

She stopped, and then ran the light up to several obvious stab wounds in his chest. "You'll bleed to death if I don't get you to a hospital."

An inhuman growl vibrated through the air. "Get out of here," he said, his voice low and dangerous.

Even as adrenaline coursed through her system, she stood her ground. "No way. I'm not leaving you like this."

When he suddenly appeared an inch from her face, she gasped, stumbled backward, and fell. The flashlight rolled across the floor, casting an eerie light on the wall.

Daniel towered over her like Death. "You can't help me."

He was wrong, though, and she knew it. She'd had years of first aid, and even carried an EMT certification. If anyone could help, short of a surgeon, she could.

Biting back fear, she turned to push herself to her feet. "I can help. You just—"

She rose to face empty darkness.

He'd disappeared.

"Daniel? Where are you?"

Fighting a wave of dizziness and nausea, she grabbed the flashlight and quickly scanned the room, and then the bathroom. Returning to the front area, she found it also empty.

"Daniel?"

She hadn't been down the hall to her left, and had no idea what waited at the end. Opting for the known first, she pushed open the door to the kitchen and flipped a wall switch.

Daniel leaned against a counter, drinking from a large blue glass and squinting against the light.

Leaving the flashlight behind, she hurried to him. "Don't drink. It won't—"

As she reached for the glass, he snatched her wrist and jerked it away.

"Ow," she said, trying to pry his fingers loose.

Watching her with his strange, mirrored eyes, he continued drinking until he'd emptied the glass, which he deposited on the counter with a thud.

His look, almost feral, made her question her decision to stay. At the same time, it held her in place like some kind of sci-fi stun gun.

Leaning toward her, he sniffed. "You smell good."

His quiet, ragged voice sent a chill up her spine, and she had trouble getting a breath.

"Too good," he whispered.

Meg gulped and shook her head. "How the hell can you think about *that* at a time like this?"

"Quite easily," he said, stepping forward, walking her backward. He reached out with a bloody, filthy hand and cupped her jaw. "You are all I can think about right now."

She closed her eyes.

He leaned forward, almost touching the side of her face with his mouth. "Perhaps you *can* help me."

His cool lips brushing the side of her neck made her tremble. She grabbed the counter behind her to keep from falling.

"Look," she said, trying to retake control of the situation, or at least her senses, "let me examine your wounds. You probably need stitches. Maybe surgery. We can—"

He licked a slow line up from her collarbone to just below her ear.

Her breath came out in a stutter.

How insane was this? Suddenly, all she could think about was how wonderful his arms had felt earlier, and how deliciously he'd brought her to a climax. If she hadn't just lost the power of speech, she might have asked him to hold her.

His lips locked onto the side of her neck, and she heard the growl again. This time, it vibrated through his mouth to her flesh, awakening nerve endings she didn't even know she had.

She whimpered as her knees collapsed.

He released her wrist, wrapped an arm around her waist before she fell, and drew her up close. She could smell the blood that covered him, but it only registered as an afterthought.

God, she wanted him to take her, to rip her clothes off and make love to her.

His hand slid down to the base of her lower back and he drew her hips into his.

No, it wasn't love she wanted.

She wanted sex.

She wanted him to fuck her, *needed* for him to fuck her, there on the counter, or the floor.

Gripping his sticky shirt with one hand, she rubbed her crotch against the bulge in front of his pants.

He grunted an animalistic sound and pushed against her, pinning her to the counter. Her breasts swelled and ached for his touch.

She felt the sharp points of his teeth against her skin, just as she had before, and she turned her head to give him better access.

If only she could breathe, she'd beg him to take her. "Daniel." It was all she could get out.

He froze, as if turned to stone, for a long moment, and then he let out a pathetic sound—a soft, mournful wail—and released her.

Meg caught herself on the counter.

Daniel backed across the room until he reached the far counter, then he stood there and stared at her.

"Daniel," she managed, "your wounds . . . the hospital."

He shook his head slowly, and grinned. With his face as grimy as it was, the grin looked more terrifying than jovial. "Your hospital can't help me. And it may not be able to help you, either, if you don't leave soon."

Was he threatening her?

"I don't understand. What do you mean?"

He glanced toward the shuttered window. "It's nearly dawn," he said, more to himself than to her. Then he focused on her again. "What I mean is that if you find out my secret, you may die. Are you ready to take that chance?"

She gulped. What secret could he possibly have that might mean her life? Was he some kind of spy?

But that didn't make sense.

Maybe he was just delusional.

The crazy part was that now she needed to know, no matter what the threat. Besides, she'd faced death more times than she could count on one hand. She knew how to take care of herself.

"I'm ready," she said.

He studied her for a long time, until she was about to protest, then he nodded. "All right."

Moving with some difficulty, he shrugged off his shirt to reveal a torso covered in drying blood. Then he grabbed a towel from the counter, ran water over it, and wiped a spot clean on the left side of his chest, just over his heart.

In the middle of the clean spot was a pink line of pinched skin.

He pointed. "I was stabbed right here less than five hours ago with a six-inch blade."

She stared. "That's not possible. You should be dead."

He grinned again. "I am."

10

Daniel studied Meg's face, waiting for her emotions to slow.

The few times in the past four hundred years he'd shared his secret with humans, he'd watched them go from disbelief, to skepticism, to amazement, and finally to horror.

Meg's expression stopped first on skepticism. "What do you mean, you *are* dead?"

"I mean, I am not alive."

She narrowed her eyes. "You're telling me you're a ghost or something?"

"Something."

"Right." She huffed. "What, a werewolf, or a vampire? Something like that?"

He nodded.

"Shit. You really had me going for a minute there. What is that, an old scar?"

"No." He stepped forward, startling her, grabbed her hand, and flattened her palm to the left side of his chest.

Once confusion registered in her green eyes, he released her hand.

She reached up and touched the side of his neck, then the other side, then pressed her ear to his chest.

He tried not to enjoy the feel of her face against his skin.

"Son of a bitch." She tried to back away, but had nowhere to go. "That isn't possible."

He slipped his shirt back on, shrugged, and crossed the room to the refrigerator, where he withdrew another bag of O-positive from the freezer and dropped it onto the counter. The frozen block produced a hollow thud. He'd have to wait a half hour before he could consume this part of his emergency supply, as unappealing as it was. It would complete the healing process, however, and perhaps take the edge off his desire for the woman standing behind him.

Desire really wasn't a strong enough word. He yearned for her, craved the scent and feel of her. If he'd given in to the hunger moments earlier, he probably would not have been able to stop until he'd drained her.

As it was, the thought of tasting her sweet nectar made him shake.

"How?" She followed him to the sitting room. "How can you exist?"

Daniel sighed as he dropped onto the sofa. "I gave up trying to understand long ago."

"How long ago?"

He smiled at her curiosity. Few ever made it to that phase. "You want to know how old I am."

She nodded and perched on the edge of the chair across from him.

"I was born near the end of the sixteenth century."

Her eyes widened and she fell back into the chair. "The *sixteenth* century, as in the fifteen hundreds?"

"Yes."

She simply stared for a long time, and he couldn't tell if she'd accepted the truth yet or not. "Do you plan to kill me?"

"You sound amazingly calm for one asking such an important question."

She leaned forward again. "Would it do any good to get hysterical?"

He shook his head, amused by her logic.

"And I guess my thirty-eight won't do me much good either, right?"

"Correct, although it wouldn't be an enjoyable experience for me."

He met her gaze and the yearning bubbled up again.

She swallowed hard. "What now?"

Daniel sighed. "I think I'll shower."

"How do you know I won't leave?"

He shrugged. "I don't."

"But, you said I might die if you told me your secret."

Daniel pushed himself to his feet. "Regrettably, that possibility remains." He started toward his room, but turned to face Meg when he heard her following.

"Why? How?"

The stench of his blood-crusted body did nothing to help him ignore his hunger. If he didn't remove himself from temptation, he wouldn't be able to resist her much longer. The approach of dawn did not help, either, as it brought with it a heaviness he must also fight.

"If you wish to stay here, I'll explain all after I shower. If you leave, you may be in grave danger."

She took a deep breath and blew it out. "I guess I'll stick around."

He decided not to mention the fact that staying involved an element of risk, too.

"Help yourself to tea, if you wish. Or anything else you find in the kitchen."

She nodded.

He felt her watching him as he made his way to his room.

Perhaps by the time he'd finished cleaning up, his icicle dinner would be thawed.

If not, he may find it necessary to lock his guest in the storage room to keep her safe.

Meg sat at the table, sipping from a steaming mug. The tea really was the best she'd ever tasted.

What she wouldn't give for a cigarette.

Water had quit running awhile ago, but Daniel had not yet returned.

Staring into the mug, she wondered if she might be dreaming.

But everything felt too real. Although she dreamed in color, she rarely noticed if things were hot or cold. The mug definitely felt hot.

Maybe Daniel had extremely low blood pressure, or some unique medical condition that made it difficult to hear his heartbeat. If so, he was using the situation to deceive her for some reason.

Another possibility occurred to her. Perhaps he was some kind of hypnotist. She'd never been hypnotized before, even when she'd volunteered at a Vegas show, so how did she know she wasn't hypnotized now? Maybe the guy was a delusional hypnotist, drawing her into his fantasy.

"But, why?"

What did he have to gain by all this? It wouldn't do him any good to try to get money from her; she had none to give. If it was sex he was after . . . well, he knew he didn't have to go to all this trouble. She'd been pretty obvious about her attraction to him when they'd been *acting* for the camera, hadn't she?

Was he doing all this to throw her off Bedford's trail?

She'd found the kidnapped women and freed them, but Bedford hadn't been among those taken into custody.

Who would go to all this trouble just to keep her from looking for a two-bit hoodlum for a few hours, or even days?

The only thing that made any sense, in a crazy sort of way, was that it was all true. Daniel was a four-hundred-year-old vampire that she just happened to run into in a bar in Santa Fe.

Yeah, *right*.

Why the hell hadn't he come back from his shower?

Angry at the whole impossible situation, Meg jumped up and marched into Daniel's room. She stopped just inside the doorway.

Through the open door to the bathroom, she saw Daniel sitting on the side of the bathtub, holding his head in his hands, and wearing only a black silk bathrobe barely closed by a belt at the waist. Water from his hair dripped down the front of his robe.

He raised his head and stared at her through eyes glowing red and gold. Glistening fangs protruding from his open mouth dented his lower lip.

She couldn't move.

Never had she seen anything so frightening and beautiful at the same time. He rose slowly, gracefully, and moved toward her as if floating.

Her heart pounded in her chest, and she couldn't find any air for her lungs.

He didn't speak, but a strange vibration swirled through the room, emanating from him. His fangs visibly lengthened as he approached until he resembled a lion ready to pounce.

As the top half of his robe fell open, she saw a dozen marks like the one he'd revealed earlier, all looking like ancient scars.

She knew now for sure that it was all true, no matter how absurd.

He stopped just inches from her, wearing the most seductive, sexy, deadly smile she'd ever seen.

That's when she realized she was probably about to die, and there wasn't a damn thing she could do about it.

Oddly enough, she wasn't afraid. At least, not like she should have been.

She was aroused.

Every nerve in her body seemed to be humming with desire. If she could have raised her hands, she would have grabbed the front of his robe and pulled him to her.

All she could do was raise her head, exposing her neck to him. Instinctively, she knew that's what he wanted, and had no idea why she wanted it, too.

The same sad sound he'd made before rose from his chest again, this time reminding her of the last breath of an animal critically wounded. Whatever the strange hold he had on her was snapped, and she staggered forward, reaching for him.

But he wasn't there.

At the wall, she turned and found him watching her from his bedroom door.

"Wait here," he said.

When he left, Meg slid down the wall and sat on the floor, gasping for air.

Daniel stood in the kitchen, empty glass in his hand, as his body processed the nourishment, which did nothing to slake his thirst for Meg.

Just a taste.

Even as he thought it, he knew it to be a lie. He wanted so much more than a taste. He wanted all of her—body, heart, and soul.

The craziest part was his desire to keep her close, in spite of the risk to both of them. He'd learned the danger of allowing himself to love with Running Deer, and at least she'd been as immortal as he. He had no hope of a lengthy future with Meg.

Not that his time with Running Deer had been more than a moment, in the grand scheme of things.

If only he knew where Wolf now hid.

Once he was sure Meg and the women had escaped, he'd focused on surviving the fight. Wolf had the strength of vengeance on his side.

Daniel's only advantage was speed. His ability during life to steal a loaf of bread without being apprehended had translated into amazing agility, which he'd nurtured for centuries. Before Wolf was able to rip Daniel's head from his shoulders, he'd used the man's knife against him several dozen times and made good his escape.

No doubt he hadn't seen the last of Wolf.

Daniel rinsed his glass and left it in the sink. He removed two more pint bags from the freezer and slid them into the refrigerator, just in case he needed reinforcement, then straightened his bathrobe as he returned to his bedroom. At least the drink had taken the edge off his vicious hunger.

Meg had no idea how close she'd come to death, or something near it.

God, he would have loathed himself if he'd harmed her.

He found her sitting on the floor, legs outstretched.

She'd changed into jeans since the party, and wore a pale green pullover that accentuated her eyes beautifully.

The scent of her fear and arousal filled the room, and would have dropped Daniel to his knees if he'd not been standing beside the bed. He sat quickly and studied her.

Meg scrambled to her feet, frowning. "How do you do that?"

"Do what, exactly?"

"Zap me, or whatever you call it. I'm standing there like a statue. I couldn't even move my pinkie."

Daniel shrugged. "I'm the hunter and you're the prey."

"Prey?" She swallowed hard. "You've been wandering around killing people for four hundred years and no one has publicized the fact you even exist?"

"I've killed fewer people as a night creature than I did as a man."

"You mean you don't have to kill them to, you know, drink their blood?"

She certainly was one for details.

He shook his head. "No. Most humans don't even know they've offered up a pint or two."

Her fingers rose to the side of her neck. "Have I?"

He shook his head again, careful not to reveal the hunger her question sparked.

"Okay, so what's the zapping thing?"

"Something akin to the hypnotic control of a snake charmer, I imagine. I hold you with the power of my will."

"Willpower, huh?" She brushed off the back of her pants. "I wish you'd keep it holstered."

He nodded. "I'll try my best."

"You promised me an explanation."

"Indeed I did. What precisely would you like to know?"

"What happened at Bedford's after I left?"

Daniel stretched out, resting on one elbow. "I don't know all the details. Once I was able to escape, I did."

"What about El Lobo?"

He shrugged.

"You knew him." It wasn't a question.

"Yes. We met many years ago."

Meg sat on the edge of the bed near his feet and drew one knee up between them. "And?"

"And we both loved the same woman." Daniel sighed, trying not to remember the past too clearly. "Because of me, she ceased to exist."

She looked at him for a long moment. "Is that why I'm in danger?"

"Yes. Wolf vowed revenge a long time ago, and I'm quite sure he intends to fulfill that vow. He'll look for a way to make me pay."

"One thing I don't understand." She rubbed the back of her neck. "Raven said that El Lobo, or Wolf, or whatever, was the host of the party, but that house belongs to Bedford."

"Obviously he's Wolf's lackey. Makes life easier to have a human on the payroll, someone who can make daylight appearances, sign papers."

"You don't."

He laughed. "No. I've never needed a payroll."

"Ah. So you're a loner."

"I suppose."

She hopped up and paced the room. "How do we keep you safe?"

"*We?*" He sat up.

"Yes, we." She stopped before him, her hands on her hips. "You shared your secret with me. You don't expect me to just forget it, do you?"

He stood and stared down at her, this strange woman who didn't know when to be afraid. "He is like me, a vampire."

She raised one eyebrow. "I guessed that much."

"He could kill you as easily as swatting a fly."

"Yeah, I got that. But you said it, there are times when it helps to have a human around. Maybe there's something I can do—"

"No." With panic rising in his chest, he grabbed her by the shoulders. "You must concentrate on your own safety."

She stared up into his eyes, and he saw something in her expression that truly terrified him.

She trusted him.

He traced a line down her warm, soft cheek with one finger.

"One of us is insane," he whispered. Then he leaned forward and took her mouth.

She resisted for only a moment, and then she slid her arms around him and opened her mouth under his.

He felt wildly human in his lust as he explored her willing mouth and her body. She trembled at his touch, and her reaction awakened both monster and man.

She drew hard on his tongue, demanding more, her hands curling into fists against his back.

In his mind's eye, he saw them together in a sunny field of yellow flowers.

With one hand caressing her sweet ass, he lifted her and she wrapped her legs around him. He savored her kiss, lost in her warmth and wonderful flavor.

She suddenly pulled away from him. "Ow." With one arm wrapped around his shoulders, she touched the fingers of her other hand to her tongue. "What the hell?"

He smelled the blood before he realized he'd cut her with his incisors, which had now extended far enough to be dangerous.

With a gulp, he eased her down until her feet touched the floor, and backed away. He sat once again on the edge of the bed.

His entire body shook as he realized what could too easily happen.

"I'm sorry," he said. "You really must go."

She checked her fingertips, then dropped her hand and looked at him. "Go where? Home? Where I'd be alone against some immortal maniac? And leave you here alone? That doesn't make sense. If we're both in danger, we should stick together."

Anger stemming from frustration roughed his voice. "You don't understand. If you stay here, you'll need protection from *me*."

Her eyes widened a bit, but she quickly hid her reaction. "Why?"

"Because I want you."

She swallowed hard as her heartbeat rose, echoing through the room like the sweetest music. "What if the feeling's mutual?"

"The feeling is *not* mutual." He leaned forward, gripping his knees. "I don't just want to fuck you, I want to drink your blood. I want to puncture that beautiful vein in your neck and drain your life force. I want to experience your dreams and fears and joys, and know more about you than anyone else ever will. I want to make you a part of me."

She drew her bottom lip in between her teeth in a perfectly innocent gesture, as if considering an offer.

"I could kill you," he said. "Do you understand? You might not survive."

She frowned. "You've said you don't have to kill people to drink their blood."

He gritted his teeth and growled.

Her eyebrows rose.

Damn her. Why didn't she just run away?

Somehow, he knew she wouldn't. Perhaps that was part of why he'd trusted her.

"The desire to feed is tied to my desire for the rest of you, my dear, and I'm in a rather weakened state."

"But you *can* control it." She walked toward him slowly, her steps sure. "And my blood would help you heal?"

With her hands on his shoulders, she straddled his legs, crawled up, and settled onto his lap.

Unable to resist, he held her, groaning at the wonder of her heat against his raging erection. How could he be so hard already?

She kissed his face softly, combing her fingers through his hair, then drew his face up to kiss his lips.

Her tenderness broke what there was of his heart, but it also nudged the ancient monster forward. He pushed her pullover up with his open palms against her sides, enjoying the warm indentations between her ribs, and the coolness of her shoulders.

She raised her arms and let him remove her top. Then, meeting his gaze with her own, she unsnapped her bra and dropped it to the floor.

Her breasts were more beautiful than he would have imagined. Not large, but full and warm.

He kissed them carefully, not wanting to mark her pale skin, and terrified of what would happen if he drew blood again. He licked circles around her nipples and flicked the puckered buds with his tongue.

She sucked in breaths between her teeth, gripped his shoulders, and pressed herself against his cock.

Daniel closed his eyes to enjoy the unbelievable pleasure. Even through thick fabric, her heat would have melted an iceberg.

When he opened his eyes again, he found her studying his face. Then she slowly, deliberately raised her chin and turned her head.

He stared at the steady rise and fall of the pulse in her neck, and the beast within roared with joy.

Holding her warm body, he pressed his lips to her flesh and felt her blood whoosh by.

"Sweet Meg," he whispered against her skin. "*You* are the dangerous one."

11

Goose bumps rose over Meg's entire body as she waited.

Daniel's hands trembled against her back, but held her close as he pressed his lips to her neck.

Would it hurt? She clenched her jaw in preparation.

He grabbed her shoulders and pushed her back, just enough to look up at her.

Again she saw the amazing creature she'd found when she'd entered his room. His eyes glowed indefinable colors, a jungle cat's night eyes mixed with the kaleidoscope she'd had as a kid.

When he opened his mouth, fangs glistened.

"Not yet," he said.

"Why not? I'm ready."

He flashed that wicked smile again and a shiver tickled up her spine.

"No, you're not quite ready." Without effort, he lifted her as he rose and placed her on her feet in front of him. Then he shed his bathrobe. "But you soon will be."

The shiver grew to more, settling as a tremor in her belly as she studied the man before her.

He was perfect.

All male, with tight, rippling muscles, he stood before her tensed. Soft hair darkened the center and top of his chest, and trailed down the middle of his stomach.

She'd never seen a dick swollen to quite such proportions, and the tremor grew to engulf her entire body. Muscles tying her vagina to her womb quivered with anticipation.

He turned her and eased her onto the bed, then crawled forward, urging her back. Satin cloth felt cool under her hands, and then her bare back as he maneuvered her down. She looked up into a face framed by shoulder-length black hair, still smiling, still predatory.

She'd never wanted anyone or anything as much as she wanted him.

When he lowered his mouth to her neck, she closed her eyes, again ready.

He didn't bite her.

Oddly, she found herself disappointed.

Until he started kissing and licking and nibbling his way down her body.

Each time she felt a sharp fang press against her skin, she understood his restraint, and it excited her even more.

He knew exactly what he was doing as he slowed over the most sensitive spots—the undersides of her breasts, base of her ribs, sides of her stomach, insides of her hips. He drew her pants and panties off as he went, leaving her bare, exposed to his gaze and touch.

Her heart beat wildly. He kissed the tops of her thighs and worked his way around to the insides, easing her legs apart.

She'd never been exactly thrilled with her appearance, and had always hated stripping in front of a new lover—the few times she had—but this was different. Her bare skin felt alive, receptive, tingly, waiting for his touch.

When he rose up to look at her, she saw approval in his expression and felt beautiful.

Dropping her head back to the bed, she closed her eyes. Slick satin caressed her skin, setting her adrift in a cool, dark, erotic sea.

Raising her knees and touching the backs of her thighs, he lay between her legs and brushed his lips up the inside of one thigh.

The room tilted, sending ripples across the surface of her sea as his mouth came to rest between her legs.

Slowly, cruelly, he licked up the length of her, parting her vaginal lips with his tongue.

Her buttocks quivered and her hips rose from the bed in response.

He licked again and again, sliding deeper each time, hinting at pleasures to come.

Her juices welled, threatening, as she melted into the dark sea, becoming part of it, floating.

He found her clit and caressed, sucked, teased.

Pleasure tugged at the depths of her soul, drawing her down. She bit her lip and whimpered.

He turned his head and pressed his mouth to her thigh, and a deep vibration tickled the skin under his lips.

Meg's sea calmed into long, slow swells.

After allowing her a moment's rest, he moved up her body, touching and kissing here and there, lingering on her breasts only long enough to make them ache with need. She squirmed under his attention and the inky depths darkened beneath her.

Then his mouth was near her ear. "The sweetest flower," he whispered. "Give yourself to me."

His body covered hers with cool, taut, strength, and he spread her legs wider with his own. She trembled, unable to stop, sinking.

She felt his cock between her legs, lying across her wet cunt, then rising, poised to enter.

"Surrender," he hissed. "You are mine."

She lifted herself into him, offering all.

He took it, filling her, stretching her, lifting her into the air.

As he withdrew and thrust deeper, the sea beneath her began to roil. She felt his need, matching her own, growing more desperate.

He thrust deeper still, until she knew she could take no more.

Aloft, every muscle singing with the approach of release, she clung to him, savoring the way he filled her completely as he stayed buried, waiting.

Her buttocks and belly burned and the air heated, drawing all breath from her, hardening her limbs to rock.

He held her above the threatening depths, cruelly keeping her poised, and she cried out in protest.

"Mine," he said, his voice a deep growl.

And he pushed deeper, claiming her, plunging her into the sea, shoving her under the surface.

Waves crashed into her, over her, liquefying every nerve, pounding against her body from the inside, drowning the hollows of her need. Spasms shot through her, gripping his cock.

Amazing, blessed release.

Then she felt the burning penetration at her throat, and her dark sea exploded into white light.

Blinding, hot, pure.

She saw them together as if watching strangers, their bodies joined in white-hot union, thrusting together. Ecstasy pulsed through her with new strength, ripping desire from her chest in a scream.

Suddenly she knew his bliss, his anguish, the extent of his longing for her.

Bordering on pain, her body tightened and exploded again as the joy of his orgasm swept through her.

She wrapped herself around him, taking all of him, giving everything.

The erotic sucking at her neck sizzled down to her cunt and back up.

Then she saw the beast.

Bloody teeth gnashing, gore dripping, blind hunger, claws shredding the air. The chain, attached to Daniel's soul, snapped with each lunge.

Terror peeled the joy from her body.

And the beast faded.

Light melted to darkness, heavy.

Her arms fell to her sides and her body stilled.

A scream like that of a cat sliced through her brain as he withdrew, abandoning her.

She lay alone, shivering, lost.

Darkness swallowed her.

Daniel woke slowly, savoring Meg's scent. He knew her now, and the knowledge only reinforced his desires. She was solitary, like himself, and she had an inner strength born partly of disappointment, mostly in her felonious father.

The oddest thing was the way one taste of her had banished his past, wiped clean his slate. How could that be? He'd had so much for which to atone before Meg. His green-eyed vixen had turned into his savior. His cold heart warmed with love.

When he opened his eyes and discovered her lying with her back to him, he panicked for a moment.

Why had she remained beside him? Had he taken her life after all?

A hint of warmth radiating from her body assured him that she lived, and he felt a rush of joy.

Turning, he draped an arm over her and drew her into him, bathing in her heat.

She wriggled back against him, and he kissed her bare shoulder.

How wonderful it was to wake to her. He mourned all the evenings he'd returned to consciousness alone. And all those yet to come.

"Hmm." She stretched and turned to look at him through sleepy eyes. "What time is it?"

He brushed her soft hair back from her face. "The sun has just set."

She sat up. "I slept the whole day?"

He decided not to mention how thrilled he was she wouldn't be sleeping through eternity.

Instead, he rolled out of bed, found his bathrobe and slipped it on, and walked to where Meg still sat.

He extended a hand, and she accepted assistance getting to her feet. When he released her, her knees buckled, and he caught her with an arm around her waist.

"Whoa," she said. "I don't know why I'm so light-headed."

He winced. "Because of me, I fear."

She looked at him and her eyebrows rose. "Oh, yeah, I guess I can see that." She reached up and touched his cheek. "But I'm still here."

He nodded.

After recovering her balance, she stood on tiptoe to kiss his lips, and then padded off to the bathroom.

Watching her stroll naked from his room aroused him and he frowned. The only woman he'd wanted so desperately just after he'd had her had been Running Deer.

Until now.

Wondering why the comparison kept returning to him, he walked to the closet in search of clean clothes.

The encounter with Meg came back to him in a rush and he caught himself on the door frame. He'd nearly been overtaken by the beast, but had managed to battle it into submission in time to save her.

Her life force was strong. In another time, another body, she would have been a warrior.

The strangest thing was the realization that he'd given her what she truly wanted when he'd told her his secret. He'd given her something to protect, someone to fight for.

Him.

He smiled at the thought.

Leaving a fresh shirt and pants on the bed, he wandered into the bathroom.

Meg hummed an unfamiliar tune from behind the glass shower door. Daniel listened and watched her fuzzy outline as she lathered shampoo into her hair and rinsed it out.

She squealed when he opened the shower door, but quickly recovered. "Shouldn't you ask before barging into the shower?"

He closed the door behind him, grinning. "It's my shower."

"Oh."

She ran her soapy hands down the front of his body and he nearly swooned.

Stepping into the steaming spray, he wrapped her in his arms and kissed her. Her wet, naked body against his felt wonderful.

She turned her head to catch her breath, still clinging to his neck, and he whispered in her ear. "I know your fantasies."

Her head snapped around and she stared up at him. "What?"

"I told you I'd know you better than anyone ever would."

She wiped water from one eye. "Yeah, but I didn't realize—"

Before she could finish, he spun her around and pinned her to the marble wall.

"Hey." She pushed against the wall, but he held her, one arm wrapped tightly around her waist. He understood her darkest desires, and found both joy and pleasure in fulfilling them.

"Don't fight me," he said softly, his voice nearly drowned out by the water. "I want you *now*."

Her resistance faded and she stood with her back to him, panting.

He smelled her excitement, and felt it in the air as surely as the water beating against his skin.

Licking a line across the back of her shoulder, he rubbed his hard cock against her buttocks and they quivered. He locked his mouth over the nerve bundle between her spine and shoulder blade. She squirmed in his arms. Then he lifted her hips and entered her with swift strokes, burying his cock in her wonderfully wet heat.

She cried out as her cunt tightened around him.

He growled at the pleasure, barely resisting the urge to taste her again.

Reaching around her, he found her swollen clit and pinched it with careful cruelty.

Her cries grew in volume and urgency. She reached back and grabbed his ass.

In rapid movements, he thrust into her again and again until he felt the start of her pulsing release, and then he slowed, matching the spasms of her body, drawing out her pounding orgasm.

When it ended, he held her, his forehead against her shoulder, reining in the monster as he inhaled her wondrous aroma and felt her juices sliding down the base of his cock.

Warm water slithered between them, washing away the remnants too quickly.

He withdrew from her and reluctantly released her heated body.

She turned and collapsed back against the shower wall, panting.

He kissed her mouth. Then he straightened and stood under the shower spray. Once he'd rinsed off, he opened his eyes to check on her.

She stared at him, her expression unreadable.

"What is it?" he asked.

She shrugged and straightened. "I'm just trying to figure out what the downside is to this relationship."

He grinned.

Then he felt it, that nagging at the base of his skull.

"You may be about to find out." He turned off the water.

"Hey, I'm not—"

He grabbed her arm and urged her from the shower. "Someone else is here."

"*Someone?*"

He nodded, tossing her a towel. "Wolf, perhaps. Or one of his group."

"Oh, shit."

He hurried to the bedroom and dressed, then returned to find her pulling on her sweater.

"We need to hide you. Follow me."

"Wait." She fought his grip. "I don't want to hide. Besides, it's you he's after. I can help."

"Don't you see?" He stopped and stared into her glistening green eyes. "He wants to punish me, not kill me." He brushed hair back from her face. "Taking your life would be my punishment."

Her eyes widened, and she nodded. "Okay. But I'm taking my thirty-eight." She grabbed her holster from the bedside table as they passed it.

"You can't kill him with that."

"I know, but you said it wouldn't be pleasant. At least I can make him pay."

Daniel hurried to the back bedroom and ushered her into the closet. "If he finds you here, aim for his heart." Then he held her face in his hands. "No matter what you hear, don't come out."

She swallowed hard, and he quickly kissed her lips.

When he turned to leave, she grabbed his sleeve. "Daniel."

He looked back.

"Be careful."

He winked at her and hurried out, closing all the doors he could between them. If he kept Wolf busy, perhaps the bastard wouldn't hear her thundering heartbeat.

The nagging pinch grew stronger. Whoever it was must be just outside the door.

Daniel dug the bloodstained wooden stake from his night-stand and stared at it. He'd carried it around for four centuries, wondering if perhaps he'd need it again.

He remembered clearly the way he'd wept as he'd driven the stake through Running Deer's heart. He'd hoped that her promise of their connection was true, and that he'd cease to exist when she did.

How ironic it would be to drive this stake—the one he'd used to end the suffering of the woman he'd loved—into Wolf's cold heart.

Shaking himself from his reverie, he carried the stake to the sitting room and hid it under a sofa cushion.

With the sound of popping steel and splintering wood, his front door flew open.

Wolf filled the doorway, dressed in his traditional loincloth, his knife sheathed at his waist. He glared with eyes burning red. Not a sign of the wounds Daniel had inflicted the night before remained.

"You did not think you could hide from me behind this flimsy door."

Daniel shrugged. "I'd hoped. But I see you've regained your strength."

"Doubled it," Wolf said, sneering. "I know now the dark-haired one was not yours, but she was quite filling anyway. As was my assistant."

"Bedford?" Daniel stared, amazed the man would take the life of his own lackey.

Wolf laughed. "I don't need him anymore. I've found the one I sought." Withdrawing his knife, he stepped forward. "I plan to bleed you slowly, perhaps for a week or more. I want you to scream in agony as she did, scorching in the sunlight because of you. I want you to feel the centuries of pain I've carried."

Daniel stepped back, moving toward the sofa. "I couldn't help how I felt about her. If I'd known—"

Before he finished the thought, Wolf appeared in front of him, holding him by the collar with his knife at Daniel's throat.

He truly had doubled his abilities. Daniel would be unable to outmaneuver him this time. His only hope was that Wolf was so focused on revenge, he wouldn't consider the existence of another woman who truly mattered.

He regretted that he wouldn't get a chance to hold Meg again.

He also regretted the pending loss of his existence. In spite of all the years, he wasn't ready to go. And he sure as hell didn't want to contemplate just where he might be headed.

Wolf drew his knife down the front of Daniel's chest in a long, slow, searing line.

Daniel bit back a howl, clenching his jaw against the unbelievable pain. "This won't . . . bring her back."

Wolf flashed a sadistic grin, and Daniel wondered if he'd lost his mind. Four hundred years of seeking revenge would likely warp the strongest among them.

As the man drew the blood-soaked knife blade across his tongue, Daniel decided that in this case, it had.

Halfway through cleaning the blade, Wolf stopped and

frowned at the knife. Then he stared at Daniel and his eyes lit up with delight.

"There is another. How marvelous." He cocked his head as if reading the wind. "And she's here!"

Terror fired Daniel with strength and he lunged for the knife, but Wolf spun it out of his grip, drove it into Daniel's chest three times, and let him fall to the floor.

Wolf turned toward the back room.

The air exploded with the sound of gunfire. Five shots, each slowing Wolf's progress.

Before the echo from the fifth shot faded, Daniel had the stake in his hand and was charging forward.

Wolf spun around, staring at the holes in his chest, all within less than an inch of each other, and all directly over his heart.

With every bit of his remaining strength, Daniel drove the stake through Wolf's chest and held it until he felt the madman falling. Then he stepped back and let him drop.

Wolf collapsed and rolled onto his back with the stake protruding from his chest. He grabbed ineffectively at it as he snarled. Then, finally, he lay still.

Daniel stared as four centuries passed in moments, turning the massive body to bones, and then dust. The stake thudded to the floor and rolled away.

When he looked up, he found Meg gripping her smoking weapon in both hands, pointing it at the floor. They stared at each other for a long while.

"I told you to stay in there no matter what you heard," he said, shrugging off his shirt as he swayed against a wave of weakness. He wadded the shirt and used it to stop the blood flow from the slice and holes left by Wolf's knife.

Meg holstered her handgun and hurried forward, grabbing the shirt from him. "You obviously needed help. Here, let me do that." She directed him toward the sofa.

He stretched out and let her check his new wounds.

"These look bad. How long will they take to heal?"

"Not long if you'll pour me a drink."

She cringed. "A *drink*?"

He nodded. "Just empty one of the bags from the refrigerator into a glass."

She swallowed hard as she straightened. "All right, I guess I can do that."

When she returned, she carried the glass farther out in front of her than was necessary, but then she knelt beside him and helped him drink.

He knew his eyes changed and his fangs lengthened as the monster picked up the scent of blood. Meg, however, didn't flinch.

When he finished the nourishment, she placed the empty glass on the coffee table and used his shirt to mop blood from around his closing wounds.

He watched her work, concentration wrinkling her forehead, and realized how much he truly cared for her. Although the realization terrified him, it also warmed him like a cook fire on a cold night.

She glanced up at him and smiled. "We make a good team."

"Indeed."

She dabbed some more and then lifted the shirt away. "This really is amazing."

He glanced down at the healing wounds, already little more than scars. Once again, drying blood covered his chest and arms.

"I'm afraid you need another shower," she said.

He grinned.

She shot him a playful glare. "Alone this time."

"Ah," he said, struggling to rise, "you have a cruel streak."

* * *

"What is that wretched smell?"

Meg glanced up from her bowl of tuna fish. "You said I could help myself to whatever I found in the kitchen."

"Yes." He wrinkled his nose as he passed her.

When he returned, he sat across the table from her, sipping from a dark glass.

She tried not to consider what the glass held.

He'd finished his shower this time, and even combed out his hair. He wore a black shirt and black pants, and his clothing, along with his wavy black hair, set off his blue eyes nicely. As man or beast, he was incredibly attractive.

He watched her eat.

"What about the rest of Wolf's troupe?"

He shrugged. "I'm sure they've dispersed. No one wants to risk breaking the rules for someone else's vengeance."

"Rules?"

"Thou shalt not kill?"

She huffed. "You use that one, too?"

"More or less. The community frowns upon a night creature destroying its own kind."

"Community?" She straightened. "How many of you are there?"

"A few."

She shook her head and returned to the last of her dinner, as meager as it was. Perhaps she should bring over a bag of non-perishables.

Assuming she returned.

"Daniel."

"Yes?"

She looked up and met his steady gaze, honesty tightening her throat. "I don't have many friends."

"I know."

She wasn't sure how she felt about him knowing her so damn well.

"Nor do I," he added, rising. "Perhaps we should team up."

As he walked past her, he leaned over and kissed the top of her head.

When he returned from leaving his glass in the kitchen, he didn't sit at the table. Instead, he lounged in the doorway to the bedroom. "Tomorrow night, you must let me take you out to dinner. You need more than canned fish."

She shrugged. "It doesn't matter much to me."

"Oh," he said, strolling toward her, hands clasped behind his back, "it matters to me. We must keep up your strength."

She gulped at the gleam in his eye.

12

"Daniel?"

"In here." He clicked off the television and tossed the remote control aside.

Meg sauntered in, depositing plastic bags on the table as she passed it.

"What's all this?"

She motioned toward the bags with a wave. "Just a few things, coffee filters, peanut butter and jelly. You know, essentials for us mere mortals." She plopped down beside him.

Daniel reached out and grabbed her, dragging her over to his lap. "I find nothing *mere* about you, my dear," he said.

"Hey." She slapped his shoulder. When he released his grip, she straightened, straddled him, and looped her arms around his neck. "Where are you taking me tonight?"

He studied the line of her jaw he already knew so well, and enjoyed her sweet familiar scent. "I thought maybe we should stay in tonight."

"Oh? And why is that?"

She ground down on his lap as she spoke, and he knew she understood exactly what he suggested.

"Because, my dear," he said, raising her blouse to expose bare skin to his fingers, "it has been a week since we've stayed in. I think you're properly *restored*."

She kissed him, flooding his taste buds with the flavor he craved when she was gone, inviting him in. He accepted the invitation, taking her willing mouth.

A mild throbbing ache started in his teeth as he considered how wonderful it would be to make love to her again, to taste her life force. Each time was more amazing than the last. And the week he insisted on waiting between rounds always felt like a decade in passing.

Suddenly she broke free of him, backing off his lap. She settled onto the overstuffed chair across from the sofa with one leg over the chair's arm, teasing him by draping her hand in front of the crotch of her jeans. "Don't you want to know where I was last night?"

He nodded, unwilling to open his mouth and reveal his level of interest in not talking.

"You remember Elena, the woman we rescued from Bedford's place?"

He nodded again.

"Last night was her first night at dispatch. She's now working for the Santa Fe Police Department."

He smiled at her delight. "Wonderful."

"Yep." She looked away, distracted. "We never found Bedford's body."

He doubted they ever would. A body was an easy thing to lose, especially when one needed to hide the cause of death.

In a flurry of movement, Meg stripped off her clothes, and then returned to her position in the chair. As she spoke, she lazily ran her fingers over her wonderful cunt.

He couldn't take his eyes off her fingers.

"Did I tell you I started working on my family's genealogy last week? It's amazing what you can find on the Internet."

The tip of her middle finger disappeared, and emerged glistening.

Daniel licked his lips.

"I traced the line all the way back to my Irish ancestor, one of the earliest here. Maybe you even knew him. According to the records, he lived in Jamestown for a year."

Her finger dipped in again, farther this time.

His pants tightened and his fangs dropped into place. He gripped the arm of the sofa as the sound of her heartbeat echoed through his head.

"Of course, you never know how accurate the records from that time are. There were plenty of stories, and I'm not sure I even have his name right."

She slid two fingers in and left them there for a long minute before sliding them back out, wet. He inhaled her scent from across the room.

Daniel ripped off his shirt as he kicked the coffee table aside. By the time he reached her, he'd shed his clothes.

She laughed.

He grabbed her ankles, opened her legs, and released them behind his hips. Then he wrapped his arms around her waist and knelt in front of her, barely resisting the urge to simply mount her like an animal.

She massaged his shoulders and grinned at him. "Took you long enough."

He licked a circle around one breast and raised his gaze to hers. "I do believe you enjoy playing with fire."

"Maybe."

Nipping her shoulder, he drew her down onto his waiting cock, and she didn't resist. She locked her legs around his waist, relinquishing total control.

As her heat swallowed him a little at a time, he sighed and

kissed her neck, tuning in to her soft sounds of pleasure as he lowered her farther.

Once he had sheathed himself in her, he kissed her mouth.

She'd learned how to avoid his razor-sharp fangs, and drove him wild by sucking hard on his tongue.

She started a slow, mind-blowing rhythm with her hips then, sliding back and forth on his slick cock, and he groaned at the intense pleasure as he tore his mouth away from hers.

"Meg, please stop."

"Why, Daniel?" She continued the rocking.

The beast snarled and lashed out at him, urging him on.

"Because you feel too good," he said, staring into her eyes.

He felt her tightening around his cock.

"I want all of you." His voice deepened as his grip on the beast faltered. "Surrender to me, Meg."

She turned her head, offering him what he wanted, and he sank his fangs into her neck.

His world exploded with her essence, filling with sunshine. He tasted her orgasm as his own, seeing himself through her eyes as he loaded her sweet cunt.

He moved deeper into her soul, savoring each new joy and sorrow, allowing each new experience to sink into his brain.

He smelled the night air as she ran from her car to his door, felt her excitement as she slid her key into the lock.

Deeper still, he enjoyed her elation at discovering new stories of her ancestors, trying out her latest hobby. He traveled with her as she pictured centuries past, wondering about his life.

He saw the burly redhead, Liam McDougal, swinging an ax in the sunshine, surrounded by wood chips. He heard the man's grunt as the ax head stuck in the sweet gum.

Withdrawing from her, Daniel pumped the last of his cum as he enjoyed her slowing spasms biting his cock. He lowered his head to her shoulder.

Moving her from what had to be an uncomfortable position, he eased her onto the floor and stretched out beside her, drawing lazy lines across the soft skin of her stomach as he watched the pink marks on the side of her neck fade.

She lay on her back with her eyes closed, smiling and taking deep breaths, and she ran the back of her hand across his chest. He loved the feel of her, both against his body and in his head.

"Damn," she said. "Does it ever get less intense?"

He laughed. "I hope not."

"Yeah, me, too."

They lay in silence for a long time.

"I knew him."

She opened her eyes and looked at him. "McDougal?"

"Yes. When I met him, he had a child, an infant."

"Jonathan. Liam's wife died just after their son was born. He later remarried and had four or five more children. I'm descended from Jonathan, though, who married a Swedish girl. I'm still working on information about her."

Daniel pictured McDougal again and remembered him holding the boy, who had black hair and honey-colored eyes. The two looked nothing alike.

"The story is that Jonathan's mother was Native American. Did you know her?"

"No."

"Her name was something like Running Bear, or Running Deer, but that was never recorded officially."

Daniel stared at Meg, stunned.

Could she really be descended from the woman he'd loved? Was that the reason he'd originally been drawn to her? Had it been her connection that allowed her to cleanse his barren soul?

After all this time, had he finally paid his penance for destroying Running Deer?

Meg studied him with her sea-green eyes. "What?"

He shook his head. "Nothing, my dear. Just history playing tricks on me."

"Oh?" She raised herself up on her elbows.

Daniel kissed her shoulder and then nipped it.

"Hey, you already did that. My turn for a bite." She scrambled to her feet. "Good thing I brought peanut butter."